continued . . .

URGENT CARE

CJ Lyons

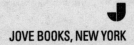
JOVE BOOKS, NEW YORK

THE BERKLEY PUBLISHING GROUP
Published by the Penguin Group
Penguin Group (USA) Inc.
375 Hudson Street, New York, New York 10014, USA
Penguin Group (Canada), 90 Eglinton Avenue East, Suite 700, Toronto, Ontario M4P 2Y3, Canada
(a division of Pearson Penguin Canada Inc.)
Penguin Books Ltd., 80 Strand, London WC2R 0RL, England
Penguin Group Ireland, 25 St. Stephen's Green, Dublin 2, Ireland (a division of Penguin Books Ltd.)
Penguin Group (Australia), 250 Camberwell Road, Camberwell, Victoria 3124, Australia
(a division of Pearson Australia Group Pty. Ltd.)
Penguin Books India Pvt. Ltd., 11 Community Centre, Panchsheel Park, New Delhi—110 017, India
Penguin Group (NZ), 67 Apollo Drive, Rosedale, North Shore 0632, New Zealand
(a division of Pearson New Zealand Ltd.)
Penguin Books (South Africa) (Pty.) Ltd., 24 Sturdee Avenue, Rosebank, Johannesburg 2196,
South Africa

Penguin Books Ltd., Registered Offices: 80 Strand, London WC2R 0RL, England

This is a work of fiction. Names, characters, places, and incidents either are the product of the author's imagination or are used fictitiously, and any resemblance to actual persons, living or dead, business establishments, events, or locales is entirely coincidental. The publisher does not have any control over and does not assume any responsibility for author or third-party websites or their content.

URGENT CARE

A Jove Book / published by arrangement with the author

PRINTING HISTORY
Jove mass-market edition / November 2009

Copyright © 2009 by CJ Lyons.
Cover image of "Nora" by Claudio Marinesco; cover image of "Doctor" by CURAphotography.
Cover design by Rita Frangie.
Text design by Kristin del Rosario.

ISBN: 978-0-515-14705-6

JOVE®
Jove Books are published by The Berkley Publishing Group,
a division of Penguin Group (USA) Inc.,
375 Hudson Street, New York, New York 10014.
JOVE® is a registered trademark of Penguin Group (USA) Inc.
The "J" design is a trademark of Penguin Group (USA) Inc.

PRINTED IN THE UNITED STATES OF AMERICA

10 9 8 7 6 5 4 3 2 1

This book is dedicated to all the nurses I have been privileged to work with during my seventeen years of practicing pediatrics.

You all have taught me more about the true art of medicine than any school could. You have inspired me, grieved with me, and made me laugh.

Thanks for all the lives you save!

ONE

Thursday, 6:42 A.M.

NORA HALLORAN HURRIED THROUGH THE HOSPItal's parking garage, shoulders back, pepper spray clenched in shaking hands. She struggled to control her fear, lock it away, but the more she denied it, the worse it got.

Every morning for two years, she'd fought her panic, battling fear to work her shift as a charge nurse in the ER. It was her daily, dreaded ritual. A battle she never lost.

She couldn't lose. Her patients depended on her—and she needed them as much as they needed her.

On high alert, Nora scanned the shadows. No one. Not many cars in the employee garage this early. Fewer places someone could hide.

She entered the stairwell, heart stuttering in time with her steps. Twelve down, three steps around the landing, twelve more. She counted the familiar cadence, holding her breath as long as possible as she sprinted for the door.

One of the lights on the final landing was burned out. *Can't stop.* She raced through the darkness. Slamming through the exit, gulping in the frigid December air, she propelled herself outside.

Her feet hit the sidewalk. Inhaling deeply, she straightened her posture, mastering her stride and with it, her emotions.

Tomorrow she'd do better. Tomorrow would be different.

The sun streaking the eastern horizon surprised her, a slit of gold-rimmed crimson, blinding in intensity as it reflected from the pavement slick with melted frost. She'd sat in her car, psyching herself up for the walk, long enough for the morning light to edge through the indigo darkness.

Despite the fact that it meant she was running late, Nora welcomed the light. As she walked beside the wrought-iron fence surrounding the cemetery across from Angels of Mercy Medical Center, a splash of unnatural color caught her eye.

It was inside the cemetery fence, filtered through a snaggle of barren forsythia. Too large to be trash blown in through the fence, too gaudy to be a memorial. Nora stopped, grabbed the fence post, and stepped up onto the lowest rung, trying to make sense of the bright splashes crowding the shadows.

Pushing aside the forsythia branches, she could finally see where the color originated. The marble statue of a weeping angel had been defiled by vile, hateful curses streaked across it in neon spray paint.

Face down in the frost-speckled grass below the angel lay a naked woman, more graffiti scrawled across her body.

Primal instincts screamed at Nora to run. To hide. Save herself.

Shoving her fear aside, she grabbed her cell phone and sprinted toward the cemetery entrance, wishing for longer legs as she ran. She didn't bother calling 911, not with Pittsburgh's busiest trauma center right across the street.

"Angels of Mercy, Emergency Department," came the clerk's chipper voice.

"Jason, it's Nora. There's a woman down in the cemetery. Get me a trauma team over here, fast."

"Hang on, here's Dr. Fiore."

Nora raced into the cemetery, crossing over graves, the slick grass threatening to send her sprawling. Her bag smacked against her hip as she dodged headstones. Her breath came in short bursts, fogging the air.

No other sounds disturbed the cemetery's peace. Long shadows stretched across the grass, but they couldn't obscure the freshly painted graffiti that stood out sharply from the somber grays and whites surrounding the woman's body.

Nora reached her just as Lydia Fiore, the ER attending, came on the line. "What's up?"

"There's a woman down. In the cemetery. Unconscious." Nora's voice sounded surprisingly normal, but after all, she was a charge nurse and this was what she did best—taking control of chaos, including the chaos of her own emotions.

She knelt in the grass, snow melting into her jeans. Yanking her gloves off, she felt the woman's pulse. Not all of the color came from spray paint, she realized. "Bleeding—looks like she was stabbed. She's breathing on her own, but her pulse is fast, poor capillary refill."

"Hang on. Help's coming."

Through the fence, Nora saw the ER's doors open across the street, releasing two figures pushing a gurney laden with equipment. A man dressed in surgical scrubs sprinted past them, a blue blur as he bolted across Mathilda Street, almost getting hit by a car. Seth Cochran. *Lord, couldn't it have been anyone else?*

"You'd better call the police," Nora told Lydia, wrapping her free hand around the woman's wrist—the only comfort she could offer until help arrived.

"Already on it. We'll have Trauma One ready and waiting for you."

Nora squeezed her cell phone so hard it almost slipped away. Before hanging up, she added, "Lydia. She's going to need a rape kit."

"Nora!" Seth called from five graves away, startling a

solitary bird from the holly bushes. He was too loud for this place. That was Seth, always somehow larger than life—too alive, too vibrant, too . . . much. "Are you all right?"

Of course she was all right. She was always all right. Even as she knelt in wet grass, hands covered in sticky neon paint and another woman's blood, her insides churning, bile clawing its way up her throat, Nora was all right. She had to be. It was her job.

"Multiple stab wounds, she's shocky, blunt trauma." Nora reported as she concentrated on the woman's pulse fluttering beneath her fingertips.

"What the hell?" He skidded to a stop beside her, kneeling at the woman's head. "Help me turn her over. Watch her c-spine."

Elise Avery, one of the flight nurses, ran to join them, bringing with her a paramedic, a stretcher, and a backboard. Seth cradled the woman's head in his large hands, supporting her cervical spine as they rolled her onto the backboard. The woman now lay face up, the extent of her injuries revealed.

"My God," Elise said as she fastened the c-collar. "It's Karen Chisholm."

Seth's face blanched the same chalky white as the tombstone beside him. Karen was a nurse anesthetist at Angels. She was also the reason Nora and Seth had split up five months ago, after Nora discovered Karen and Seth naked together in a hospital call room.

But she couldn't think of any of that now. Now Karen was a patient. Her patient. Nora's fists tightened with the effort as she clamped down on her emotions.

"Get the O₂ on her," she ordered.

Seth listened with his stethoscope. His hands shook. Anyone except Nora would think it was from the cold.

"Left lung is down, heart sounds distant," Seth pronounced, his voice grim as he palpated Karen's naked torso, ignoring the graffiti and blood. "I need to crack her chest."

They maneuvered the backboard onto the stretcher. "I lost her pulse," Nora announced, starting CPR. Elise grabbed a bag to force oxygen into Karen's lungs.

"Call the ER," Seth ordered the EMT as they pushed the gurney over the grave sites and bounced back onto the pavement. "We're going to flash and crash. Tell them to get the OR ready."

"Room thirteen?" Elise asked, now jogging beside the gurney as traffic stopped to let them cross the street. "Not upstairs?"

Seth was shaking his head. "She won't make it upstairs alive. Room thirteen is our only choice."

"Not much of a choice," Nora replied. The small but well-stocked operating room behind the ER was used only for patients too unstable to survive the short elevator ride upstairs to the main operating rooms on the fourth floor. Most OR 13 patients died.

They pushed past the ER's doors and raced down the hallway. Ahead of them two night-shift nurses were scrambling, getting the lights on in Room 13 and unpacking sterile instrument trays.

"Anesthesia and the trauma team are paged," Lydia Fiore, the ER attending on duty, said when they banged through the operating room's doors.

Nora continued CPR. Elise prepped the patient, throwing some drapes over Nora's hands and splashing her with Betadine, while Lydia intubated and hooked up a ventilator and monitor.

"C'mon, people, let's hustle." Seth snapped on gloves, not bothering with a gown or mask as he grabbed a ten blade and sliced open the left side of Karen's chest. Dark maroon blood splashed him, puddling at his feet.

Golden-brown Betadine soap swirled around the neon glare of the spray paint, not hiding the hateful words so much as highlighting them. Nora threw on gloves, their bright purple color clashing with the graffiti punctuated by dozens of stab wounds across Karen's chest and abdomen. Nora slid into position beside Seth, grabbing a sponge and a Satinsky clamp.

"IV's in, blood on the rapid infuser," Elise announced.

"Clamp," Seth said, holding his hand out blindly. Nora slapped the Satinsky into his palm as she reached in to clear the field with the sponge. "Aorta cross clamped. Someone mark the time."

"Five hundred cc's out of the chest tube already," Lydia told him. "And her belly's distended."

"One thing at a time," Seth muttered as he delicately snipped a hole in the bulging membrane surrounding the heart. A gush of blood poured out.

"I've got a pulse."

"Good." Seth straightened, a smile of satisfaction flickering across his face. Two surgical nurses rushed in, gowned and scrubbed and looking askance at Nora in her civilian clothing. She stepped aside as Seth dumped more Betadine over Karen's abdomen. "Okay, let's get to work on that belly. Knife."

The flash of a camera blinded Nora for a moment. Elise lowered the camera. "Sorry."

"No, good thinking," Lydia said as an anesthesia resident took her place at the head of the bed. "Document as much as possible. I have to get back to the ER. Nora, can you do the rape kit?"

"While you're at it, I need a Foley," Seth said, starting a vertical incision that extended from Karen's chest down to her pubic bone.

Nora grabbed a sterile gown and wrapped it around her body, then changed her gloves. Elise held Karen's legs apart to help Nora insert the bladder catheter.

Seth glanced up, scalpel poised. "Any time now, ladies."

"Give her a break," Elise snapped at him. "He used a knife on her. Everything's messed up down here."

Nora ignored them, instead focusing on the small, intimate space before her. "Foley's in. Elise, take photos while I start the rape kit."

She turned away, shaking her head until the room stopped blurring before her. Small, tiny shakes, casting away her feelings so that she could focus.

The sounds of machinery and the murmur of voices faded into the distance. Blocking out everything around her, Nora carefully collected as much evidence as possible. She swabbed and combed and plucked and dried and labeled and sealed everything into the shoebox-sized evidence kit.

It was easier to move around the blood and paint and people if she simply denied their existence. A roaring noise commandeered her brain, but her hands continued to function, to do their job of caring for her patient.

Seth's hand fell onto her shoulder just as she finished clipping Karen's fingernails, dropping them into a white envelope and sealing it, scrawling her name across the seal. "Nora, did you hear me?"

She glanced at his bloody hand on her shoulder. Blinking, she realized the room had gone silent; she and Seth were the only ones remaining. There was no *whoosh* of the ventilator or beeping of the cardiac monitor. Only the sound of her gown rustling as she straightened.

"She's gone," he said, his voice cracking. He swallowed hard, his gaze darting toward Karen, then ricocheting back to Nora. "I tried everything, but the bastard trashed the vena cava. I couldn't get her back."

He turned his back to her, stripping the gloves from his hands, snapping them into the garbage. His shoulders hunched together as he gripped the edge of the biohazard container for a long moment before facing her again.

The neon graffiti desecrating Karen's body sparked in Nora's vision. Seth's scrubs, neck, and face were speckled with blood. His brown hair was long and shaggier than she remembered it—they saw each other every day, but she'd forced herself not to notice these things that were the purview of a girlfriend, telling herself that he had someone else to take care of him.

That he didn't need her. That he had Karen—sexy, skinny Karen with her extensive knowledge of the Kama Sutra. Karen who smiled and laughed all the time and who Nora bet never cried when Seth made love to her, who never freaked out and refused to leave the house without his checking the shadows and holding her hand.

Karen who lay cold and dead on the table before her.

God, how Seth must feel, to be the one who lost her, who couldn't save her . . . Pushing aside her own emotions, Nora looked at him, wanting to help but too numb to know what she could do. She stared at the evidence envelope gripped between her fingers. She still had work to do. For Karen.

"Nora? Are you all right?" He tilted his head, a heart-breakingly familiar little-boy expression that could mean anything from guilt to concern wrinkling his eyes. "Why don't you leave that for the police and medical examiner?"

She dropped her envelope into the evidence kit and reached for the oral swabs. "I need to finish."

"No. You don't. C'mon, leave it."

She turned her back on him and walked around the table to the head of the bed. The drape had been dropped, covering Karen's once-perfect body. Her once-perfect face was marred by scarlet paint, sprayed across her closed eyes and forehead with the word *whore*. One eye was swollen and bruised, as were both cheeks. Red marks circled Karen's neck along with more bruises.

Nora slipped her fingers between Karen's jaw and the endotracheal tube, felt the jaw slide sideways, and knew it was broken in at least two places. Seth made a choking noise and turned away.

Nora collected the swab, resting the fingers of her free hand against Karen's eyes. Shiny material crusted the lashes, sealing them shut. Superglue. Nora remembered the pain, eyelashes ripping free, corneas abraded.

Just as she knew the pain of the swollen throat. It was days before her voice had returned to normal; to her colleagues she'd blamed the winter flu bug. She remembered countless showers and baths and hours scrubbing at spray paint with turpentine and mineral spirits, leaving behind red, raw, burning skin.

And the pain. Not just the bruises and aches and scrapes, but the pain inside, deep inside. The same pain that sometimes returned to haunt her even now, almost three years later.

"I'm sorry," she whispered to the dead woman. "I'm so sorry."

She stroked Karen's hair, the once long, shining tresses now hacked haphazardly as if by a scissors-wielding toddler throwing a tantrum.

No, not scissors. A knife. Long, wide, one edge serrated, the other razor sharp.

"We're all sorry." Seth caught her arm, pulling her away from the corpse. "You're shivering. Come with me; I'm getting you out of here. Lydia never should have asked you to do that rape kit."

Nora wrenched away from him. "She didn't know. I'm the sexual assault examiner on duty. It's my job."

"Not today. Leave it."

She glared at him, then spun on her heel, sealing her evidence kit. Her handwriting was shaky as she finished signing her name. "It's all my fault."

"No. It's not. There was nothing more you could have done for her." His voice sounded distant even though his hands held hers tight, pulling her away from the sexual assault kit. The neon graffiti blared through her vision; she couldn't look away.

Seth was the only person alive who knew Nora's secret: that on New Year's Eve two years ago, long before she'd ever met Seth, she'd been raped. But she hadn't told Seth everything. Not about what had happened to her, not about what she had done. She'd thought she had left it all behind, had created a new life, one where the rape was a secret buried forever.

"Who could have done this?" he said, his voice shredded. "A gang—high on crack or meth?"

Slowly she raised her glance to meet his. "It wasn't a gang."

She glanced at the corpse beside her, sucked in her breath until her chest was tight and there was no room for anything else. She needed to tell him the truth.

"It was the same man, Seth." Her voice rang hollow, echoed from the tile walls of the empty OR.

"What?" He squinted at her as if that would help him hear more clearly. "You mean—" He shook his head violently. "No. It couldn't—"

"It was. It is. The same man."

Seth stared at Karen's ravaged body, his face morphing into a mask of horror and confusion. "You— Karen—"

With his hand clamped to his mouth, he rushed past her, his face splotched with crimson. He raced down the hallway and slammed open the door to the clean holding room.

Snapping her gloves off and tossing them into the red biohazard bag, Nora started to follow him, but she stopped outside the OR's doors. She couldn't leave Karen's body unattended.

Miguel from housekeeping turned the corner, whistling as he pushed his cart.

"Miguel, could you do me a favor? Watch that door, okay?" She barely waited for his nod before she followed Seth's path to the clean holding room.

She knocked on the door, opening it without waiting for his response. He was bent over the sink in the corner, heaving up his breakfast. His body shook violently even after he stopped vomiting.

Nora grabbed a towel from the shelves, ran cool water over it, and wiped his face clean. She let the water run, rinsing the acrid smell away. She didn't look him in the eyes, but gave him some semblance of privacy as she kept one hand always on his body, ready, waiting.

Finally he inhaled, straightening as the air filled his body. He pressed his hand against his eyes for a long moment. Then he exhaled, a plaintive *whoosh* that echoed above the sound of running water. He opened his eyes, met her gaze.

"Are you all right?" She gave his arm a quick squeeze.

She immediately let him go, realizing the familiarity was no longer her prerogative. An awkward silence passed between them. She'd never felt awkward around Seth before—furious, sad, irritated, yes, but never this blind, stumbling, knowing-too-much feeling.

"I'm so sorry," she tried again, but her words sounded hollow and meaningless.

She wanted to comfort him, to help, but she didn't know how. All she could do was stand there, staring, hanging on to a dirty, wet towel instead of reaching for him. He wasn't tall, only five-ten, but compared to her five-three he'd always felt tall enough. Just right for tiptoe kisses or for him to lift her in his arms. Once upon a time.

Nora focused all her attention on wringing out the towel. Suddenly the room felt too small for the two of them and everything that lay between them.

His hand reached out for her, then dropped back to his side, empty. "You said you'd been drinking that night," he started, then faltered to a stop. "New Year's. Two years ago."

She nodded, concentrating on hanging the towel from the sink's edge. She turned the water off. Silence fell. She tugged on the hem of the towel, making it line up, perfectly even. "I had a few drinks."

"I thought you meant you were both drunk, things went too far—"

"That I said no, and he heard yes? Just another date rape, nothing too disturbing, right?" Fury colored her words. "And so you didn't ask any more questions, didn't need the details since they'd put the blame on me, too drunk to keep a guy's filthy hands off me. I made it easy for you, didn't I, Seth? Maybe too easy."

He backed away, banging into a metal shelving unit, sending a stack of suture trays to the floor. "I didn't—I couldn't—" His Adam's apple bobbed as if something sharp and painful were caught in his throat. "Tell me. Tell me what really happened."

She was tempted to. But even after everything that had happened between them, she couldn't. It was bad enough he'd seen Karen's body, seen the outward evidence. No way would she burden him with more details. Or the fact that Karen had obviously suffered even more than Nora had. The rapist had terrorized Nora with his knife but had never cut her, not like he had Karen.

"You don't really need to know all that. What you really need to know is that it's my fault Karen was killed." She licked her lips, but it didn't help; her tongue grated against them like sandpaper. "It's my fault. Because I never told anyone. Not until I told you."

"The police?"

"No, Seth. I never went to the police. And now I have to face the consequences." Her vision wavered, but she didn't sway or fall. She stayed in control, finished her confession.

"Karen is dead because of me."

TWO

Thursday, 7:32 A.M.

THE SAVORY AROMA OF COFFEE DRIFTED FROM THE front of the ambulance, inviting Dr. Gina Freeman to abandon the oppressive gray of the Pittsburgh winter and fly away to exotic lands populated by wandering bands of baristas toting portable espresso machines. She turned sideways in her seat in the rear of the ambulance, the better to keep an eye on the two paramedics up front—and the coffee they'd just picked up from Eat 'n' Park.

Trey Garrison, the EMS district chief, was riding with Gina and paramedic Scott "Gecko" Dellano. The two men couldn't appear more different from the outside—Trey was a little over six feet, dark skinned and intense, while Gecko was wiry, tattooed, laid back and never without his signature Oakley shades—but when they worked together it was like watching a symphony in action.

A symphony so well rehearsed that Gina sometimes felt like a kazoo player thrown into the mix. Working with the medics was part of her duties as a third-year emergency medicine resident, but she'd missed some shifts and was now making up for lost time.

Trey always seemed to arrange things so that he worked with Gina when she did her EMS ride-alongs. Gina wasn't sure if it was because Trey felt protective of her after she'd almost died in a drive-by shooting during her first ride-along last summer or if he was keeping tabs on her and reporting back to her boss in the ER, Lydia Fiore. Whom he also happened to be living with.

After Trey pulled a cup of heavenly brewed caffeine from the cup holder and handed it to her, Gina decided she honestly didn't care.

She gulped her first sip. It was still hot enough to scald, but too good to resist. "Thanks, Trey. You're a life-saver."

Gina was exhausted. Squeezing in the ride-alongs in addition to her regularly scheduled shifts in the ER had put a definite crimp in her free time—including time to sleep. And personal grooming time. She patted her mass of braids, which she'd pulled back with a scrunchie. Antonio, her stylist, was going to shriek when he saw her.

She prayed the jolt of caffeine would keep her eyes open through her shift. Her medical student roommate, Amanda, hadn't helped—flouncing around the house at an ungodly hour as if a stint in the pediatric ICU were more fun than sex (something Gina had about given up on these last two weeks) and grinning like the twenty-five-year-old in love she was. Amanda was engaged and looked the part.

Gina was engaged and looked like a hag.

Jerry, her fiancé—just thinking the word made her panic—was being patient with her request to keep their engagement a secret. But even his patience had an end. He wanted her to announce their engagement at the big Angels of Mercy gala on Saturday night, where Gina was receiving a Carnegie Medal for heroism.

That plan had a few problems. First, Gina was no hero—she felt like a fraud accepting the medal. It was actually another doctor, Ken Rosen, who had been the real hero back in July, during the riots. Unfortunately a reporter had caught *her* on film. The media and public—not to mention her father's lobbying with his influential friends—had done the rest. And despite Gina's urging, Ken refused to step up and take the credit that was rightfully his.

Second, her parents were expecting her to announce that she was leaving her emergency medicine residency to join her mother at the Freeman Foundation, raising money for causes deemed worthy and spending a lot of time in designer gowns associating with the "right" kind of people—a group that most definitely did not include Jerry Boyle, a detective with the Major Crimes squad.

Suddenly working double shifts to avoid thinking about the mess she'd got herself into felt like a blessing.

"Heard you were late in the ER last night." Trey's tone had a faint ring of disapproval, but she ignored it.

"Was supposed to get off at twelve, but a drug OD kept me there until two." Which meant home and to bed around three and back up again to ride in the ambulance by seven.

"You okay to work? I'd rather have you take a day off than compromise patient care."

"I'm fine." She took another sip of coffee, mainly to hide her yawn. She craved a smoke, but Jerry had finally persuaded her to quit, so instead she jammed a piece of nicotine gum into her mouth.

A call came through, interrupting Trey's interrogation. Gecko, who was driving, glanced back at her in the rearview mirror. "How come no bulletproof vest today? You must have a good feeling about riding with us."

Gina glanced down at the navy polo she'd tucked into her cargo pants. "I forgot it," she admitted. As long as they didn't run into Jerry, who was overprotective even for a cop, it wouldn't matter.

"Surprised you're talking to us peons, what with being given the key to the city on Saturday. You know Ollie and I have to be there, full dress uniform and everything."

"I didn't ask for it."

"Well, least you can do is introduce me to a few cute nurses when the dancing starts."

Gina wasn't sure she'd even make it through to the dancing—half the time she found herself fantasizing ways to escape Saturday's gala all together. "No problem."

Trey hung up the radio. "Make a U-turn, we're heading to Heinz Prep," he instructed Gecko. "Code Two."

"What's up?"

"School nurse thinks a kid might have meningococcemia. He came in with a fever, and she sees a rash. Kid's acting fine otherwise."

"Shit." Meningococcemia was a highly contagious bacterial disease that could quickly go from no symptoms to near death. "Any other kids with the same symptoms?"

"They're going to check. Might be nothing—you never know with school nurses—but she got verbal permission from the mom for us to transport him for a full eval. In fact, the mother insisted on it, has her personal physician on his way to meet us at Angels' ER."

"Personal physician? Who are these folks, the Rockefellers?" Gecko asked.

"Could be," Gina said as a stately white-brick mansion surrounded by several other large buildings came into sight. A wrought-iron gate announced their arrival at Heinz Prep, her alma mater. "Rockefellers, Kennedys, Carnegies, they've all attended."

"Are those dormitories?" Trey asked as they parked between two colonial-style brick houses.

"Yes. Students come from all over the world."

"If it is meningococcemia—" Trey began.

"Then we might have a disaster on our hands," Gina finished for him.

DR. LYDIA FIORE TOOK ADVANTAGE OF A FEW moments of calm and sat at the ER nurses' station, completing Karen Chisholm's death certificate.

She filled in the tiny spaces on the crowded form, writing as neatly as possible, worrying the fingers of her free hand through the uneven layers of her dark hair. She hated paperwork. Especially the way it diminished a person to a few sterile facts. She hadn't known Karen, but that didn't matter. Karen had been one of their own. She deserved more than meaningless words on a smudged form destined for a dusty drawer in some bureaucrat's office.

To Lydia, every patient she lost deserved more. But she didn't have the luxury of investing in that emotion. She had to focus on her other patients, give them the best she could.

"Hell of a way to start a shift," she muttered, scanning the nurses' notes for the exact time of death.

"How do you think she ended up in the cemetery?" a nurse asked as she pretended to straighten the stacks of paperwork at the desk.

"Did you see the stuff they spray-painted on her?" another said with a shudder. "Like a horror movie."

Lydia watched, on alert. She'd called in a crisis counselor, but he hadn't arrived yet. A few of the staff had broken down, sobbing after Karen's failed resuscitation. Most swallowed their emotions, their movements now stiff, angry, guarded. And then there were the ones whose curiosity outweighed their grief. As if arming themselves with details about Karen's death would keep them safe.

"We need more security around here," one of the older

nurses put in, banging a chart down on to the shelf beside Jason, the desk clerk.

"What do you want?" Jason asked. "Armed guards patrolling the hallways? This isn't Baghdad."

"You're not a woman. You don't understand. I'm afraid to walk to my car. They make us park so far away, and that parking garage is always dark and deserted."

Lydia turned to Jason. "Speaking of security, did you send the guys across the street to guard the place where Nora found Karen?"

"Yeah, they're waiting for the cops to take over. Here comes Glen now," Jason said.

"Morning." Glen Bakker, the head of security, was a man whose posture screamed military. His shoulders were squared, jaw jutting forward, as he extended his hand and shook Lydia's. He insisted on shaking hands every time they met— she wasn't sure if it was a measure of respect or if Glen used the handshake the same way Lydia's mother had taught her to use it: as a way to get close enough to gauge a person's real intentions, to get inside their guard. "Rough day all around, isn't it?"

"Did the police find anything at the cemetery?"

"Didn't look like it. They're combing the place now, will probably be there for hours." Glen looked around the ER, his eyes moving back and forth. Cop's eyes, Lydia recognized. "Is Nora okay? I heard she was the one who found the victim."

"She's fine," Lydia said, even though she wasn't sure if that was the truth. She made a mental note to check on Nora as soon as she could. "What about security cameras? Did they show anything?"

Glen was shaking his head. "The only outside cameras are at the hospital's main entrance, the ER"—he jerked his chin toward the ambulance bay doors—"the clinics, and the parking garage exits. None of them would have been aimed in the right direction."

"Maybe you should think of getting some more," one of the nurses said.

"They've been in my capital budget for two years, but keep getting the ax. As it is, Tillman and the administration are going to balk about paying for the extra manpower I'll be asking for."

"Even if they approve the money, it will take weeks for you to hire anyone," Lydia said.

"Yes'm. I'll be pulling some overtime myself, hang around down here, keep an eye on things. If anyone feels uncomfortable walking to their car, you make sure they call us. We'll get them an escort as fast as we can."

"I'm sure everyone will appreciate that," Lydia said, wondering if Glen would make good on his promise. The nurses huffed and walked away. They'd heard it all before.

"Well, let me go rearrange my men's schedules. They're going to love me for this. Especially with everyone wanting time off for the holidays." He flashed her a salute and sauntered off.

"What about the Critical Incident Team?" Lydia asked Jason, whose own escape from the emotions the morning had brought seemed to be his video game and iPod. "Did you call them?"

"Yes. Tommy Z is on call for them today."

"Tommy Z?" Great. Lydia and the condescending social worker didn't get along under the best of circumstances, and these certainly weren't those. "He's trained in crisis counseling?"

Jason grinned, his video game beeping triumphantly. His grin faded as one of the nurses glared at the raucous music. "Don't worry. The Z-man is cool."

Lydia's previous run-ins with Tommy Zwyczaje had convinced her otherwise, but if he had the training, she had no choice but to let him do his job. Not that she wouldn't be keeping an eye on him—last thing she needed was a know-it-all social worker messing with her people's heads.

"He knows what he's doing," Jason added, sensing her skepticism.

"I wouldn't count on that," she muttered.

"Lydia," came a voice smooth as whiskey from behind her. "So good to work with you again."

Lydia didn't flinch, even though she hated anyone sneaking up on her. Instead she slowly swiveled in her chair. She was the one caught badmouthing the man, but Tommy Z was the one who appeared to be blushing as he held a hand out for her as if a peace offering. He had dark, wavy hair and rugged Eastern European good looks, though marred by a bad case of rosacea. His wide mouth was stretched into the "aw shucks" grin of a snake oil salesman.

"Have you run a critical-incident debriefing before?" Lydia cut to the chase, ignoring his hand.

"Too many, I'm afraid. I'm on the countywide team, have worked incidents at all the major hospitals and a few in the field, like the Ebenezer Church fire where those firefighters died." He glanced around, then drew closer to her. "What can you tell me about what happened today?"

"One of my nurses found a woman, stabbed, beaten, sexually assaulted, left for dead in the cemetery." She kept to the facts. It was the safest way. She had to set an example, couldn't risk revealing her own emotions. Not here in the ER, not with patients to care for and her staff needing her.

He winced at her harsh summary of the facts. "The cemetery? So close to the hospital. How's the victim?"

"She died. She also worked here as a nurse anesthetist. Karen Chisholm."

"Oh my God, but I know Karen! I mean . . . knew. Such a sweet person, I can't believe . . ." He stared beyond her toward the trauma rooms as if expecting to see Karen's body there. He cleared his throat and coughed, his face now completely suffused, almost the color of wine. "Has anyone spoken with her family? Do you need me to call them?"

"The police will take care of that. But I'd like you to talk

with Nora—Nora Halloran. She's the one who found Karen.
And Seth Cochran, he's a fourth-year surgery resident who
tried to save her. As well as the others involved in her resuscitation."

"A case like this, one of our own, it's going to traumatize
everyone." He nodded slowly as if accepting a burden. "How's
Nora holding up?"

"Good enough to do the rape kit."

"Still, it's going to be hard on her. Just because she's a
sexual assault forensic examiner doesn't make her immune.
Especially when it hits so close to home. I think I should
start with her."

"Why don't you set up in the family room for now?"
Lydia countered as she spotted a pair of familiar faces coming through the ER doors. "I need to see who the police want
to interview first."

"Of course, I understand. I'll be there, waiting to help
anyone who needs my services." He took two steps down the
hall leading to the small family room before turning back to
look at her over his shoulder. "And I'll be saying a prayer for
Karen's soul."

Lydia ignored him, grabbing Karen's chart before walking
over to greet Detective Jerry Boyle and his partner, Janet
Kwon. As cops went, Kwon and Boyle were better than most.
Which, coming from Lydia, was pretty high praise.

"Hi, Lydia," Jerry Boyle greeted her. He shook her hand
as he looked around the ER, taking in the number of people
hovering nearby, all pretending not to listen. "You the physician of record?"

"Afraid so."

He slanted a glance at his partner. "Janet, why don't you
secure the body? I'll be down shortly."

Kwon, a thin thirty-something who would have been
pretty if not for her perpetual scowl, nodded and left for OR
13. Boyle motioned to Lydia to join him in an empty exam
room.

"So, how's Gina? She tell her parents about you two yet?" Lydia was one of the few who knew about Jerry Boyle and Gina Freeman's engagement. Boyle had sworn her to secrecy— Gina didn't even know that Lydia knew.

Boyle hadn't wanted privacy to chat about Gina. But Lydia wasn't quite ready to go over everything that had happened to Karen. A moment of normal conversation, a quick reminder that there was life outside of the ER. That was all she needed.

His smile dimmed. "No. Not yet. She's fine with my family—even came for Thanksgiving. But her folks and this whole Carnegie Medal thing have her freaked, big time."

Lydia sighed. Oliver Tillman, the hospital CEO, was presenting Gina with the award at the annual Angels gala on Saturday. More pressure the emergency medicine resident didn't need. "I'll talk with her."

"I appreciate it." Boyle pushed away from the gurney, nodding his thanks. "Before we get into what happened here this morning, I need to talk to you about something else."

Lydia wondered what had Boyle suddenly nervous, not meeting her gaze.

He reached into his pocket and handed her a flash drive. "I asked a friend in L.A. to send me a copy of your mother's homicide investigation. Here's everything LAPD had."

She stared at the utilitarian black plastic rectangle. So small, it was the size of her finger. Yet it held everything known about her mother's murder eighteen years ago, when Lydia was twelve.

Well, almost everything—she hadn't told the L.A. cops that she had actually witnessed her mother's brutal killing. Boyle was the only person who knew that. A momentary weakness, confiding her deepest secret to him—and this was how he repaid her? By prying into her life?

Anger prickled the hair on the back of her neck. "How dare you? You had no right!" Her voice emerged tight, high pitched like a young girl's. Like a twelve-year-old kid's.

The emotions she'd corralled all morning, since Karen's death, stampeded through her. It wasn't anger flooding her veins; it was fear. Fear that had remained bottled up inside her until it had aged into stark, naked terror.

Boyle seemed to understand. He didn't back away at her outburst. Instead, he touched her lightly on the arm. "Hey. Are you okay?"

She flinched at his touch. "I'm fine."

"I know you have a sore spot when it comes to trusting cops—"

"Only because it was a cop who killed my mother!"

"Someone wearing a uniform and carrying a gun, but that doesn't necessarily make him a police officer. Anyway, you should know, LAPD did work it as hard as they could. Hit a wall, though, when she became a Jane Doe."

"What are you talking about?" Lydia and her mother, Maria, might have occasionally lived on the streets and lied to others about who they were, but her mother was no Jane Doe.

"You didn't know? Lydia, there is no record of a Maria Fiore. No official records of her at all. You didn't have any, either, not until you went into the foster care system and children's services documented you."

"But that's impossible—" Her stomach did a slow dive. The one truth she'd always held on to—even after Maria had died and she had lost everything else—was the Fiore name. That somewhere there was a family she belonged to.

"Sorry, but it's true. The only trace of Lydia or Maria Fiore came from your statements to children's services. They did find a newspaper photo published a few weeks before your mother was killed that identified both of you as Lydia and Marie Ferraro."

One of their aliases. "When I won that stupid essay contest." The annual American Legion contest on your greatest hero of history. Lydia had chosen Thomas Paine. "Maria—" No, *not* Maria. Not Jane Doe, either. Damn it, Maria had been *someone*. She was Lydia's mother. "My mother didn't realize the picture had been taken. She was so furious about it; I never knew why."

"They had her fingerprints, but they led nowhere. There's DNA, but with no family besides you to compare it to . . ."

"It's like she was never even real." Lydia's throat tightened. Her whole life was a lie. As fictional as the fairy tales Maria used to spin for clients when she told them their fortune. Maria had lied to her, had fooled Lydia as easily as she had the people she'd conned for a living.

"I'd say more like she was on the run from someone. Someone who finally found her." Boyle stared at her, his gaze filled with compassion and worry. They both knew one thing the L.A. cops didn't: the man who killed Lydia's mother hadn't been searching only for Maria.

He'd wanted Lydia.

Janet Kwon came barreling through the door before Lydia could think of an answer—or even the right question to ask.

"Don't you people know anything about documenting evidence?" she demanded, glaring at Lydia.

"What's the problem?" Boyle asked.

"See for yourself. We've lost this case before we've even started."

THREE

Thursday, 7:48 A.M.

AMANDA HELD THE BOY'S HAND AS SHE DOUBLE-checked the settings on the ECMO machine. "The flow rate is holding?" she asked the tech manning the heart-lung bypass machine.

"Yes, *Doctor* Mason," the tech said, addressing her as if she were his superior instead of a mere fourth-year medical student. Amanda opened her mouth to protest, but he flashed her a grin to let her know he was only kidding. "Last gas looked good; we're fine here."

"Okay, thanks, Michael. I just want to be sure before the family comes in."

He nodded his understanding. "I know. It's a long haul. They understand he might not make it, if we can't wean him off the bypass?"

Amanda blew her breath out, rustling her bangs, her gaze focused on the three-year-old boy lying in the bed below her. "They know."

She squeezed Zachary's hand. The little boy had never said a word to her—she'd never even seen him awake—but he had touched her heart, he and his family. She and the rest of the PICU team had worked so hard to save him, though despite everything they'd tried, he was still as likely to die as to live.

Two days ago, Zachary had wandered into his grandpa's garage. Thirsty, he'd taken a sip from a glass soda bottle, not realizing it contained kerosene instead of cola. By the time he'd been Lifeflighted to Angels he was already in respiratory failure, his lungs sloughing, poisoned from the mouthful he'd aspirated.

The whole thing was so senseless and tragic—and touched Amanda even more because the exact same thing could have easily happened at her family's marina back home in South Carolina. Her father was constantly storing things in smaller containers after he bought in bulk. Not anymore, not after Amanda had called him that first night, reminding him that even though her brother's baby was only crawling, he was a grandfather now. She'd woken him at four in the morning with that call, but he hadn't been angry.

Instead, he'd listened to her rant and cry and vent, had told her he'd take care of everything that very day and promised her everything would be okay. The phone call had almost been as good as a long-distance hug and had given her the strength to walk back into the PICU to face Zachary's family.

Amanda and the PICU fellow had worked over Zachary all day, through the night, and until Amanda had finally been forced to go home yesterday afternoon. They'd intubated Zachary, switching to the hummingbird—the high-frequency-jet ventilator—when conventional ventilators didn't work, inserted chest tubes on both sides of his tiny body as his lungs collapsed, then placed him on the lung bypass machine known as ECMO in a last-ditch effort to keep oxygen flowing to his brain and other vital organs. She'd been relieved to see that he was still alive this morning when she'd gotten back to the PICU.

Her attending and the PICU fellow had both realized that Amanda had a good rapport with Zachary's family, and they allowed her to lead the difficult discussions regarding Zachary's chances of living: what they should do if his heart stopped, how far they should go, when they should stop.

The PICU staff all complimented her on how well she handled the family and such a complicated case—her attending had pretty much said she'd be getting an A for the rotation—but that didn't make the meetings any easier. Each time she left the Millers she felt more exhausted than she did after a night on call. She'd go to the restroom, lock herself in for a precious five minutes of solitude, and cry.

Then she'd come back to Zachary's bedside and hold his hand. At this point, there was little more she could do to help him. Modern medicine was forced to take a backseat to the age-old tincture of time.

"Amanda, got a consult for you," Terry Wyshkoff, the PICU fellow working with Amanda, said. "Lydia Fiore called from the ER, thinks this kid might need to come up here."

Amanda pulled away from Zachary, throwing him a mental kiss, and scrubbed her hands with the bedside antibacterial foam. "That doesn't sound like Lydia—"

"You're telling me. Usually she calls up with a diagnosis and treatment plan and tells me what to order." A hint of resentment crept into Terry's tone. Lydia had that effect on a lot of other doctors, not only because of her brusque manner or that she was fairly new to Angels, but mostly because she was usually right. "Guess this kid is a diagnostic dilemma. Sounds like there might be more going on as well; Lydia was a bit vague about the whole thing. Why don't you check it out, let me know?"

It wasn't a request, but still it was nice that Terry phrased it that way. Amanda nodded. "No problem at all. I'll head right down there."

NORA WANTED TO RUN AND HIDE, SLIP AWAY AND find a dark corner empty of memories. Instead, she straightened her shoulders and turned to walk away. She had to get back to work. To her patients.

Seth stopped her. "Nora. You didn't kill Karen. It's not your fault."

She didn't want to lash out at him, but her anger and frustration had no other target. "You can't say that. You don't know anything."

"I want to. I want to know everything." He reached for her with both hands, but she pulled away, shaking her head.

"No. No, you don't." She clawed at the neck of the surgical gown she still wore, fighting for air. Her pulse rushed through her, drowning out all sound with its thundering.

Seth didn't try to argue or use logic. Instead he stepped forward, wrapping his arms tight around her. He said nothing, merely held her, filling her with his presence. Slowly, one heartbeat at a time, she relaxed, now able to hear the rustle of his breathing, feeling the comforting rhythm of his heart as she pressed her face against his chest. The familiar tang of his sweat—God how she loved that smell, the taste of him—competed against the memory of the sharp, sweet scent of fresh paint, the odor of fear, the taste of her own blood.

She pushed him away. She was the one who should be comforting him, not the other way around. Besides, she didn't need him, didn't need anyone.

"Nora—" Seth reached for her.

"No." The word emerged in a brittle waver. "No," she repeated, stronger this time. She couldn't risk it; Seth knew her weaknesses all too well.

The door banged open, harsh light crashing in on them.

"What do you want, Lazarov?" Seth asked over her shoulder, addressing the intruder.

"The cops are looking for you two," Jim Lazarov, one of the emergency medicine interns, said, with no hint of apology for disturbing them. "They're pretty mad."

Nora clamped down on the emotions the morning had

unleashed and turned to face Jim. She vaguely remembered Jim hovering on the periphery of Karen's resuscitation. "Mad? About what?"

"Something about chain of evidence—"

"Chain of custody." Nora rushed past him, Seth close on her heels as she jogged down the hallway toward OR 13.

"Nora, what is it?"

"Oh God, this can't be happening," she muttered, her mind spinning with recriminations. She pushed through the door to the OR. Jerry Boyle and his partner were arguing with Miguel.

"All I do is clean the floor," Miguel was saying, his face clouded with distrust. "That's my job. I never touched anything, just mopped the floor."

"Who told you to clean in here?" Jerry's partner, Janet, demanded.

Miguel pointed at Nora. "She did. She said to wash the floor. I wash the floor."

Nora groaned. She turned to the detectives. "I asked him to *watch the door*." How could she have been so stupid? "It wasn't his fault. Miguel was just doing his job." A job that didn't normally include standing guard in front of an OR.

She glanced around and saw that the floor was smeared with soapy water. The only blood came from her own footsteps, her street shoes still carrying traces of it. Karen's body lay where they had left it, looking untouched—but who could know for sure?

"Thanks to you, even if we catch this creep, he'll walk." Janet Kwon paced the room, agitation bouncing off her.

"Why?" Seth asked. Jim Lazarov stood behind him, eyes gleaming as he watched.

"Because there was no chain of custody," Nora answered him, her voice tight. "We left her alone, Seth. They won't be able to use any evidence they get from her body."

"The autopsy doesn't do us any good when a defense

attorney can argue that someone may have tampered with the body before the medical examiner got to it," Jerry explained. "But you did a rape kit, right?"

"Nora did one," Seth answered.

"Where is it?" Nora asked, turning to the steel table where she had left the rape kit. "Miguel, did you see a small white box, size of a shoebox? Big yellow sticker on it?"

He shook his head. "No, ma'am. I didn't touch anything. All I do is the floor, that's my job."

Nora searched the debris surrounding Karen's body. Nothing. "It's gone."

THE SCHOOL NURSE, MRS. PRITCHARD, WHO MET them in the hallway outside the Heinz Prep infirmary was different from the one Gina had known when she'd been a student here more than a decade ago, but otherwise, nothing had changed. This nurse wore the same starched white uniform and white stockings, even a nurse's cap. She looked more like Hollywood's idea of a nurse than any of the real nurses Gina worked with every day.

Mrs. Pritchard obviously also felt she knew more than a hospital nurse—or a pair of seasoned paramedics, not to mention a third-year emergency medicine resident. "I gave him a dose of ceftriaxone so as to not waste time," she reported. "Here's a complete copy of his chart. He has an IV in his left antecubital vein, and we'll be starting the rest of the school on rifampin immediately."

Trey and Gina exchanged glances as Gecko made a grinding noise with his jaw and turned away to organize their equipment. "Under whose orders did you administer the ceftriaxone?" Trey asked in a nonjudgmental tone, as if he needed the information for his documentation.

Gina was less diplomatic. "Who's the idiot who decided to push a broad-spectrum antibiotic before we can document anything? You do realize all of our cultures will be useless now; we'll have no way of verifying if the kid actually has meningococcemia."

Mrs. Pritchard gave a sniff, squared her shoulders, and ignored Gina. To Trey she said condescendingly, "Dr. Frantz is Harold's private physician, and he gave me verbal orders. He also decided to prescribe the prophylactic antibiotic to protect the rest of the student population."

"Did he assess the patient first? Has anyone done anything to confirm your nursing diagnosis?" Gina asked.

This time the nurse turned to stare at her with an appraising gaze that started at Gina's cornrows and worked its way down to her black work boots. Then she pivoted on one foot, almost military style, to address Trey once more. "Dr. Frantz will examine Harold at Angels as soon as he's free. He's already arranging for an ICU bed to be made available."

Obviously, as far as the nurse was concerned, Gina didn't exist. It was clear she didn't realize Gina was a doctor. Probably thought her a medic—a junior one at that. Gina opened her mouth, ready to protest, to instruct the woman in the fine art of taking orders from a physician standing right before her rather than a distant voice on the phone, to inform Nurse Pritchard that Gina was once a student here and happened to be the daughter of the world-famous attorney and major Heinz Prep alumni fund contributor, Moses Freeman.

Then she caught Trey's warning gaze. He had obviously figured out what was going on three steps ahead of Gina and was, as usual, playing the role of diplomat. "Gina, why don't you start the patient assessment?"

She gave Mrs. Pritchard a final glare, pushed past her, and opened the door to the infirmary, Gecko behind her with the gurney. There, sitting up in bed, bouncing as he played a video game, was a skinny redheaded teenager. He punched the buttons and a triumphant cheer erupted from the game's speakers.

"Hoo-rah!" the kid cheered, slapping the mattress in victory. "Take that, mo'fuckers!"

Gina glanced around. Besides them, the infirmary was empty.

"This is our critically ill patient?" Gecko asked.

"Like I said, be prepared for a disaster."

"LYDIA, CT SENT THE GIRL IN TWO BACK BECAUSE she keeps vomiting. You want to check her again?"

"I'll be right there; let me grab her chart," Lydia said, trying to sound nonchalant. As if a nurse, one of their own, hadn't died. As if Nora hadn't lost a rape kit and potentially damaged evidence in a homicide—how the hell had that happened?

As if Jerry Boyle hadn't told Lydia that in the eyes of the law, her own mother had never even existed. She rubbed her eyes, holding them shut for a long moment, long enough to breathe in, breathe out. "Did my ACS patient get up to the cath lab?"

"Ten minutes ago. Some school nurse has called twice, said she's sending in a kid with meningococcemia. Vitals normal except for a temp, and he has a rash she says is petechial."

"Is he coming by car?"

"No. Med Seven is bringing him."

"Go ahead and set up the isolation room just in case. And let me know when they call in to report." Lydia found Narolie Maxeke's chart. The thirteen-year-old girl had been bequeathed to her by the night attending, who had spoken with the clinic doc and agreed it was all psych. But Lydia wasn't so sure. Which was why she was going ahead with the brain CT and having the PICU look at her.

She brushed back the curtain and joined Narolie and her aunt. They shared an ebony complexion darker than any Lydia had seen before, along with musical, softly lilting speech patterns. Although the aunt didn't seem comfortable speaking English, she appeared to understand without difficulty.

"Dr. Fiore," Narolie said, shyly brushing back her hair and trying to shield the emesis basin's noxious contents. As if Lydia were the one who needed taking care of instead of this too-thin girl who had already seen more horrors than most adult Americans could ever imagine. According to the social history in the clinic chart, the girl's family was originally from Somalia and Narolie had been born in a refugee camp. In her young life, she'd already seen two siblings killed and another die of starvation. "I'm sorry, I tried—"

"It's okay, Narolie," Lydia tried to reassure her. "Let me check you again and then we'll get you more medicine to quiet your stomach. I think you'll also feel better if we put a tube down your nose, to empty your stomach."

"Of course, anything you say." The aunt, Mrs. Darbane, broke in with a long stream of Somali. "My aunt wants to know when I can go home. She has to get to work and doesn't want to leave me alone." Another exchange between the two. "But she can't leave the boys with the neighbor much longer. They need to go to school."

"Who usually cares for the boys when your aunt is at work?"

Narolie seemed surprised. "I do, of course. I'm the oldest. I take care of the house, watch the boys." Her aunt must have gotten the gist of what Narolie was saying because she beamed at her niece with pride in her eyes, softly stroking her hair. "Back home I'd be married already, raising a family of my own. So this is good practice."

"We do things a little differently over here," Lydia said with a smile. "Still, it must be hard, juggling school and everything at home." She didn't want to buy into the clinic doc's theory that Narolie's weight loss, vomiting, and mood swings were from an eating disorder and stress, but it was worth exploring the home situation.

"Not hard at all—until I got sick. That's why it's so important that you find out what's wrong with me. I want to go back to school. I miss my friends, my teachers. I just"—she hesitated, looking down and speaking softly—"I just want my life back."

The girl's heartfelt whisper made Lydia wish she could promise that everything would be all right. "I understand. I hope this CAT scan will give us the answer. But I don't think it's wise for you to go home today no matter what it shows. I'd like for you to stay here in the hospital. Let us check everything out."

Narolie translated for her aunt, who looked both relieved and anxious. After a long moment the aunt nodded her head. She grabbed Lydia's hand. "You make her better. All better."

"Yes, ma'am, I'm trying my best."

THE ER WAS ITS USUAL MIX OF CHAOS AND EFFI-ciency. But Amanda sensed an unusual undercurrent of anxiety. Two nurses huddled in a corner, heads bowed together as if the dropped suture tray on the floor between them were a disaster. Everyone moved slower than normal, half-oblivious to the calls from patients. Even Jason, the usually ebullient desk clerk, was strangely subdued.

"Who died?" she asked him jokingly as she grabbed her patient's chart.

He pivoted on his stool to glare at her. Everyone at the nurses' station stopped talking, and the sudden silence felt heavy. "You didn't hear?"

"Hear what?" she asked, distracted by the strange name on the chart. Narolie Maxeke. *How do you pronounce that?*

"Karen Chisholm died. Was killed."

Karen? Amanda knew her—hadn't liked her— Wait, she'd been killed? Surely she'd heard wrong. "Karen was *killed*?"

"Stabbed and raped," a nursing assistant put in. "Left for dead in the cemetery."

A cold finger skittered down Amanda's spine. She walked past the cemetery every day. Often alone and in the dark. "Did they catch the guy?"

"No," said a nurse. "When they do, I hope he resists and the cops bring him here. Let him see the real meaning of suffering." Despite her words, the nurse, who didn't look much older than Amanda's own twenty-five, seemed more frightened than angry.

"They say she was grabbed while she was walking to her car in the parking garage last night," one of the others said. "Amanda, you park in that garage. We're starting a petition demanding better workplace security. Our union rep will take it to administration, but med students and residents are welcome to sign it as well."

Amanda scrawled her name on the form without really thinking as Lydia strode down the hall, scattering the staff with a glance. But even Lydia's stride seemed less assured than usual.

"You down for my possible PICU admission?" she asked Amanda, pulling her aside to a dictation cubicle where they'd have some privacy. "It's a touchy case. Thirteen-year-old, moved here eight months ago from a Somali refugee camp with her aunt's family and her two younger siblings. Father missing, mother stayed behind with the rest of the family. She's a straight-A student until the last three months when she began missing school for recurrent vomiting. Also, occasional headache and her aunt says she's been very moody—irritable and depressed."

Amanda scribbled notes on an index card. It was unlike Lydia to go into such detail about a patient's social history, so she assumed it was all relevant. "Has she seen a doctor?"

"That's the problem. She's a clinic patient. Been seen there twelve times in the last ten weeks. Workup was all negative, except for a small calcification near her right ovary they found on her upper GI. Incidental finding—probably a fecolith; the rest of her labs have all been normal. They think she has depression, PTSD, and an eating disorder. In fact, she was scheduled to see a psychiatrist today but came in here because of severe vomiting and the worst headache of her life."

Amanda looked up at that. A headache that bad could mean lots of serious things, including a brain tumor or leaking aneurysm. Or it could be the exaggeration of a teenage girl with underlying psychiatric problems. "Is her neuro exam normal?"

"Yes. And she's still dry-heaving after three hours of fluids; her electrolytes revealed a bicarb of only twelve, so the vomiting was definitely for real; and her amylase and lipase are slightly elevated."

"You're thinking pancreatitis?"

Lydia hesitated—so unlike her. "Maybe a mild pancreatitis, but I don't think that's the underlying problem. I called the clinic doc to admit her. I want to get a head CT and if that's normal, a scan of her belly, but he refused. Won't even admit her, doesn't want me to do anything but order a psych consult. Said he'd follow her up in the clinic."

Now Amanda understood the problem. If the patient's attending physician refused to admit her, the only way Lydia could keep the girl in the hospital would be to get another attending to admit her—highly unlikely for a clinic patient—or to send the girl to the PICU.

"She sounds sick," Amanda agreed. Mainly because she trusted Lydia's judgment. "Question is: is she sick enough for the ICU? It's gonna be a hard sell since we only have one open bed."

"Even if it's only overnight, at least you could make sure she has a proper workup—more than I can do for her down here in the ER. I just have a feeling that there's something going on. Something bad."

FOUR

Thursday, 8:21 A.M.

GINA KNEW SOMETHING WAS WRONG AS SOON AS they hit the ER. No nurses waiting for them—hell, knowing Lydia was on today, she'd expected the attending there herself. Instead, Jason, the desk clerk, simply waved them into the isolation room.

The kid's name was Harold Trenton III, but he'd told them to call him Tank—even though he was a skinny-assed, pimply, pale-faced fourteen-year-old. As they transferred him from the gurney to the hospital bed, Gina glanced through the glass walls. The ER was too quiet. There was no one laughing at the nurses' station, no one hanging out in the hall, razzing lost interns or med students. Just an irritating quiet that made her palms itch.

Amanda and Lydia stood across the hall, neither looking very happy. She rapped on the window, getting their attention and beckoning Lydia into the isolation room. Lydia nodded, said something to Amanda, then sent the med student into another patient's room.

"What's up?" Lydia asked. "This isn't the mening kid, is it?"

"Yeah, didn't you get our report?"

Lydia grimaced. "Sorry, things have been a bit crazy around here this morning."

Trey looked up at that, but Lydia didn't elaborate. He finished his run sheet as Gina gave the case summary. "Fourteen-year-old from Heinz Prep, previously healthy until this morning he developed body aches, dizziness, and a fever of one-oh-two. School nurse spotted petechiae on his arm, and we found more on his trunk and back."

Lydia was already examining Tank as she listened to Gina. She lifted his shirt, scrutinized the few lesions he had, looking for petechiae or broken blood vessels under the skin that form a reddish-purple pinpoint. "They don't blanch, but they're not classic. No purpura? If these are petechiae, there aren't very many." She turned to Tank and smiled. "That's good news; it means we caught this early. How long have you had these red spots?"

Tank shrugged. "Don't know."

"Were they there yesterday?"

He looked blank. Lydia tried again. "When you took a shower yesterday, did you see them? Or these on your shoulder; did you notice them when you looked in the mirror?"

"Don't remember." He started his Game Boy again, the volume loud enough to set the IV pole shaking.

Lydia grabbed the game and turned it off, staring him full in the face. "Harold. This is very important."

"Tank. My name is Tank."

"Tank. I need you to think hard. When did you first see the rash? Has it been coming and going? Do you remember the first spot? Is it itchy or painful at all?"

"I don't know, I don't know, I don't remember, no, and no." He held out his hand for his video game. Lydia didn't relent.

"Any vomiting, diarrhea?" she asked.

Tank gave up talking, his face set in a sullen stare, responding to her questions with a mere nod or shake of his head. Lydia ran through a litany of questions, trying her best to get an accurate history—she got further than Gina had, but in the end Tank's symptoms were still irritatingly vague, other than the documented fever and the rash. Finally Lydia returned the game to him.

She joined Gina and Trey in the corner. "We'll get blood, do a spinal tap, but I don't know, it doesn't feel like meningococcemia to me. Although with the rash, I can see why the school wanted him checked out."

"Oh, they want more than that," Gina said.

"Didn't Dr. Frantz call you?" Trey asked.

"No. Who's Dr. Frantz?"

"Kid's private physician. Ordered the school nurse to give him a slug of ceftriaxone—"

"He already got antibiotics?" Lydia yanked the chart from Trey, scanning through his notes. "That changes everything—we'll never be able to culture any bacteria. What was that bozo thinking?"

"It gets worse," Gina said. "He's also reserving a PICU bed for our 'critical' patient."

"Amanda said they only have one bed left, and I have another patient who needs it."

"Hate to say it, but I have a feeling Mr. Memory here is gonna trump whatever patient you have—unless he or she's related to the governor."

"Why don't we get some labs back, by that time one of the parents might get here and we can get a better picture of things. In the meantime, I'm going to check on my other PICU patient."

"Translation: you're going to try to grab the PICU bed before Tank here takes it."

Lydia gave her the barest hint of a smile.

"You okay here, Gina? I'll be right back," Trey said, moving to follow Lydia out of the room.

Gina watched him intercept Lydia. The way he brushed against her and suddenly the two of them were in perfect sync, strolling down a public corridor yet obviously in a world of their own. Gina touched the simple gold chain that hid Jerry's ring beneath her shirt. Why was it that when she saw couples like Lydia and Trey, or even Amanda and Lucas, she felt empty inside? Like maybe she just wasn't meant for that kind of love.

Tank's video game let out a bone-crunching shriek. "Aw shit!" he shouted, flopping back against the pillow. "Son of a bitch!"

"Hey." Gina whirled on him, tired of his wannabe-punk attitude. "This is a hospital. You will play quietly or not at all."

At first she thought he was going to call her bluff and stick out his tongue at her, but something in her body language must have given him second thoughts because all she did was take one step toward the bed and he sat up straight, silenced the machine, and nodded his head. "Yes, ma'am."

Ma'am? Hmmm . . . she liked that. "Okay, then." Still no nurses—where was everyone today? It wasn't her job, but as Lydia was constantly reminding her, in the ER every patient was everyone's job, so she hooked him up to the monitor. "Let's get a set of vitals on you."

"Am I going to be okay?" He didn't sound scared, but he didn't sound too cocky about his chances, either.

Before Gina could answer, the door was flung open by a high-heeled, high-polished woman wearing a power suit. Armani. *High-class wannabe*, Gina's mother would have categorized her.

"Harold!" She clattered across the room, heels clicking like a metronome on overdrive. "What happened? Are you okay?"

Tank hid his face in his game, brushing her embrace aside. "I'm fine, Mom."

"No, you're not. Oh, my poor baby!" Mrs. Trenton stood, clutching the bedrail but not touching her son. She did an about-face to address Gina. "Are you his nurse? Where's Dr. Frantz? Why isn't he up in the ICU yet?"

"I'm Dr. Gina Freeman. I helped transport Harold"—Tank winced at her use of his real name—"from Heinz Prep. If you're his mother, we have a few questions."

"Of course I'm his mother!" Mrs. Trenton seemed unable to avoid exclamations, her chin bobbing with every sentence, adding emphasis—and threatening to make Gina dizzy. "I know you! You're LaRose and Moses Freeman's daughter! We've met before, at your parents' club. They'd said you'd gone off and done something crazy like joining the Peace Corps—I never dreamed they meant you'd be working here! If Angels didn't have the best pediatric specialists, we'd never come—"

Gina's glare interrupted her. Great, friends of her parents. Just what she didn't need. "Mrs. Trenton, the school nurse, wasn't able to give us any information about Harold's vaccination status. Did he receive the meningococcemia vaccine?"

"Of course not! Harold has never had any vaccines! His grandfather is Harold Trenton, you know, the chiropractor? So we know all about the dangers of vaccines! I'd never allow any of my children to risk their lives to satisfy a government bureaucracy. Do you have any idea how much harm vaccines cause each year?"

As opposed to the millions of lives saved? Gina kept her face neutral—she'd had tons of practice holding her tongue around her father and his cohorts. Why was it rich people thought they knew everything without ever actually bothering to learn anything? "When did you notice your son's fever and rash?"

"Rash? What rash?" She laid her hand against Tank's forehead. "Oh my God, he has a fever! He's burning up! Why haven't you people done anything for him?"

Gina gave up. Let the ER sort it out. Luckily she could escape with Trey and Gecko on the ambulance. "Later, Tank," she said, opening the door.

"Wait! You can't leave us. Dr. Frantz isn't here yet. Who's going to take care of Harold?"

"The ER staff will take good care of him. I have to go."

"Gina, please. You can't. I'm sure your parents would want you to stay and help us out. In fact, we're sitting at their table on Saturday. They invited us to watch you get that award. I'm sure someone brave enough to save all those children can bend a few rules and help out a friend."

"I'm so sorry, Mrs. Trenton. But I have to go save lives. I'm sure everything will work out just fine for you and Tank— in fact, I'll send in Dr. Fiore."

"Dr. Fiore? I heard about her! She almost killed a man!"

"Really? Well, I'm sure he deserved it. Good luck." Waiting until the door was closed behind her, Gina chuckled. The rich were so easy to mess with—one of life's simple joys.

"YOU OKAY?" TREY ASKED AS HE AND LYDIA walked down the hall. They stopped inside the ambulance bay where the cold wind whipped at the doors, some of it sneaking past, but it was otherwise quiet. "You look upset."

Lydia turned her face to the outside doors, searching for any hint of sunlight. The day had turned an impenetrable gray; she couldn't even tell if it was still morning or close to sundown. So typical of this town. "We lost a patient this morning. It was bad."

Trey took her hand in his, gave her time. He was good at that.

"It was a nurse," Lydia continued. Her emotions leached into her words. She couldn't afford to break down, not with almost an entire shift left. She clamped down on the memory of Karen's body—somehow it was mixed up with the memory of her mother's. "She was attacked in the cemetery. Raped, stabbed, beaten. And then they sprayed graffiti over her—like she was a piece of garbage, worthless."

She stopped. She couldn't go on, not without letting loose all the emotions roiling inside her. Clenching a fist so tightly that her fingernails cut into her palms, she tried to squeeze all her sharp and dangerous feelings into a ball, roll them out of the way so she could focus on her job.

Trey pulled her into a tight hug. She couldn't return it at first, afraid that if she relaxed her guard she wouldn't be able to stem the tidal wave of emotions, but Lord, how she needed it. After a long moment, she was able to squeeze him back and actually take a deep breath again.

Someone called her name from the ER. "Thanks," she told Trey, reluctantly pushing away from his embrace. She squared her shoulders and trudged back to the nurses' station.

Despite her best efforts, she still couldn't banish the vision of Karen's body.

GINA, TREY, AND GECKO LEFT THE ER AND WERE walking back to the ambulance when Gina stopped short. The ER entrance and ambulance bay were on a slope, elevated enough that she could spy yellow ribbons of crime-scene tape fluttering around the statue of a weeping angel across the street in the cemetery. The angel was covered with neon-colored graffiti. Jerry crouched among the tombstones, measuring off distances and checking sight lines.

"What the hell?" She was half-tempted to shout out to Jerry, get the inside scoop from him, but knew how he hated to be disturbed at work. Besides, if he saw her dressed like she was, she'd have to lie about her bulletproof vest.

"They found a nurse over there." Trey opened the rear doors to allow Gina and Gecko to slide the gurney back inside. "Raped and stabbed. She died."

"Did they catch the guy?"

"Lydia didn't say, so I'm guessing not."

Gina shivered and wrapped her arms around herself, wishing she'd grabbed her jacket for the short run into the ER. "Who was it?" Then she saw Jerry jogging across the street, coming toward them. "Oh shit."

"Hey guys," Jerry said by way of greeting. He had that wide-eyed flushed look he always got in the early stages of a case—before the exhaustion of working nonstop ground it out of him. "Trey, I need a favor—"

Gina tried to edge behind the side of the ambulance, but it was too late. Jerry turned to her, his head cocked to one side in worry and confusion. "Where's your vest?"

"Don't worry," Gecko said. "She's riding with the A-team."

"Don't tell me when to worry." Jerry's voice snapped like an elastic band stretched too far. "Riding with you didn't stop her from being shot last summer."

"Jerry, calm down," Gina said.

But he ignored her, aiming his glare at Trey. "I asked you to look after her."

Gina stomped a booted foot to get their attention. She'd have loved to aim it a bit higher at a certain someone's ass. *Jerry* was the reason why Trey kept hovering? She'd been blaming Lydia for assigning her the district chief as watchdog.

"Hey," she said, stepping between Trey and Jerry. "Stop talking about me like I'm not here."

Jerry didn't even have the good grace to look chagrined. "You promised you'd wear your vest."

"I forgot it. Sue me. I'm only human. But I'm not a child, I don't need looking after."

"But Gina, I only—"

"Forget it, Jerry. We're not having this discussion again. Call off your babysitters and get back to work." She climbed into the ambulance and slammed the door shut.

Through the door, she heard Jerry ask Trey to spread the

word among the medics to let him know if they'd seen anything in the cemetery that morning. And then, fueling her anger further, Jerry apologized to Trey for Gina's surliness.

She added a fresh piece of nicotine gum to the wad she was already chewing, chomping down hard, wishing she had a cigarette. Why was Jerry always trying to protect her? She knew he loved her, but sometimes . . .

Her ear popped as her jaws worked the gum harder. But she couldn't avoid the truth. That sometimes Jerry reminded her of her father.

And that was never a compliment.

NORA STOOD OUTSIDE THE OR DOORS, WATCHING in silence as the crime-scene investigators searched and cataloged every scrap of cloth and paper surrounding Karen's body. Still no sign of the rape kit.

Behind her, less than forty feet down the hall, the noise from the ER sounded small and tinny as if it came from a mistuned television. She was supposed to be in charge, but it sounded like they were doing just fine without her.

Jerry Boyle's partner, Janet Kwon, had taken her statement, treating Nora as if she were a suspect herself. Nora had showered and changed into scrubs, but she still felt unclean. Maybe because she hadn't yet been able to find the words—or the strength—to tell anyone about what happened to her two years ago.

She'd gone over every step of her walk from the parking garage, showing Janet where she'd found Karen and explaining about the rape kit. Without ever mentioning that she knew this rapist's work, up close and personal. Of course, Janet's resentment over the lost evidence, implying that Nora was at best incompetent and at worst an accomplice to murder, hadn't helped.

She'd wait and talk to Jerry, Nora promised herself. A few hours wouldn't make a difference. Wouldn't change anything.

It wasn't like she had any concrete evidence to offer—she hadn't seen her attacker and his voice had been disguised.

All the same excuses she'd been using for two years, trying to rationalize her silence.

The medical examiner's team had taken a sterile sheet and used it to wrap the body before bundling Karen into a body bag and onto their stretcher. Nora stood silent as they wheeled the body past her. It seemed as if the entire ER quieted to a hush.

A hand touched her arm, and the noise rushed back. Nora shook her head against the barrage. She glanced up, expecting the hand to belong to Seth. Instead it was Jim Lazarov, the snotty intern was the last person she was in the mood to see.

"What?"

"I need a nurse to observe while I examine a teenager, and you're the only one not doing anything." Without waiting for her answer, he strode off in the direction of the OB-GYN room.

Nora rolled her eyes but followed. Unfortunately, Jim was probably right. With the police pulling her away from her duties, the other nurses had been busy picking up the slack. Jim pushed open the door without knocking. The clash of metal against metal sounded just as Nora arrived.

"I told you to get the hell out of here!" the girl shouted. She was maybe seventeen, dressed all in black with multiple facial piercings marring her otherwise flawless porcelain complexion. "I changed my mind!"

Nora entered and closed the door behind her. The girl had backed herself into the corner near the instrument cart, her eyes wide, the skin around them dark—and not just from the Goth makeup she wore.

"You need to let me examine you," Jim said, yanking on a pair of gloves.

"No, I don't! Leave me alone!"

"You came here for help, Glory. Now let me help you."

"Jim, why don't you let me talk to her?" Nora asked, edging toward the girl.

"I can handle it." Jim threw her a glare. Then he turned his focus back onto Glory. "The guy beat you up. Why are you protecting him?"

"You don't know what you're talking about. He *loves* me. Why won't you leave me alone?" The girl was crying now, tears streaking black and blue down her cheeks.

"Sorry, no can do," Jim said, gesturing imperatively at the exam table. "Now sit down and let me examine you."

Glory had other ideas. She grabbed a pair of surgical scissors from the instrument tray. They weren't blunted like bandage scissors, but sharp and deadly. She brandished them at Jim, then turned them on herself, holding them to her neck right over her carotid artery.

"Stay away or I'll kill myself," she warned.

FIVE

Thursday, 11:02 A.M.

"OH SHIT," JIM SAID. HE BACKPEDALED AS IF HE were the one in danger.

Not trusting Jim to do anything but aggravate the situation, Nora centered her attention on Glory. Grabbing a box of tissues from the counter, she stepped forward to hand it to the girl. The door slammed open and shut again as Jim plowed through it.

Glory started at the movement, gesturing with the scissors, but Nora simply held the tissues out, her hand remarkably steady.

"Looks painful," she said, nodding at an ugly burn on Glory's wrist about the size of a cigarette.

Glory grabbed a handful of tissues and rubbed them across her nose and cheeks. "Yeah. That's why I came. Until he"— she jerked her head at the door Jim had escaped through—"got all up in my face, asking questions."

"How old is it?" Nora kept her voice level. "I'm worried it might be infected."

The teen still held the scissors but hesitated, her gaze

going to the burn. "Couple of days. He didn't mean anything by it, honest. It was all my fault. I was in the toilet, didn't answer his text fast enough."

"He texts you a lot, I'll bet. Likes to keep tabs on you—even in the middle of the night, right?"

Glory looked surprised. "Yeah, how'd you know? That way my folks don't know. But"—her voice betrayed her fatigue—"sometimes I wish . . ." She trailed off. "I don't want to get him in trouble. He loves me."

Nora had heard it all too often. Women mistaking manipulation and coercion for love. It was a common pattern—especially in this era of instant communication when it was impossible to hide from an obsessed partner.

"Do you love him?" she asked softly.

"Of course I do." Glory looked wistful. "Sometimes he can be so sweet. Treats me like a princess."

"Have you ever hurt him?" Glory shook her head. "Ever give him a black eye? Burned him with a cigarette?"

"Never! How could I? I love him—" She broke off, looking confused. The hand with the scissors drifted downward.

Before Nora could reach out and take them from Glory, the door crashed open and the head of security, Glen Bakker, ran inside. In one swift movement, he shoved Nora aside and rammed Glory, smashing her wrist against the wall. The scissors fell to the floor with a clatter.

"I got her," he shouted triumphantly.

Glory struggled futilely, cursing, but then slumped down to the floor, weeping in surrender.

"Nora, are you okay?" Glen asked in a breathless voice.

"I'm fine. She's harmless, a victim. Get off her." Nora yanked on Glen's shoulder with all her weight. He resisted her for a moment, then stood, leaving Glory crumpled on the floor.

Nora sat down on the floor beside the teen and grabbed a handful of tissues to mop Glory's face clean.

"It will be okay," she told the dazed teen. "I promise, it will be okay."

Footsteps sounded behind her. Nora turned, expecting to see Jim. Instead, it was Tommy Zwyczaje from social services hovering by her side. He'd brought reinforcements—a nurse and the psychiatric social worker. Nora helped Glory to her feet.

"They're going to take good care of you, Glory. Okay?"

Glory nodded and released Nora's hand. Glen shifted his weight, his bulk appearing ludicrous beside the slightly built teenager.

"I'm sorry," he said to Nora. "Lazarov said—"

"Jim's an idiot," Nora snapped. "But thanks anyway, Glen." She nodded to Tommy, who was gesturing for her to join him in the hallway outside the room.

"Good work. Let's take a walk," he said in that rich voice that always reminded her of Christmas Eve midnight mass. She let him lead her down the hall and past her colleagues at the nurses' station, turning the corner and entering the family room.

"Coffee? Doughnuts?" Tommy offered.

Her stomach rumbled even though she knew she couldn't possibly face food, not with this knot twisting her gut. She lowered herself into a vinyl chair, placing her hands on both of its arms, and perched on the edge, her back straight, head upright. To her left stood a wastebasket three-quarters filled with used tissues and crumpled foam coffee cups.

Tommy eased into the chair beside her, his posture almost as stiff as hers. His left hand was close enough to brush hers, the overhead light winking from his wedding band. He didn't try to make eye contact.

She knew the drill. Defuse the situation, encourage talk, mirror the emotional distress, and slowly bring it back to normal. Kind of like dealing with a crackhead or a wailing toddler trapped in a tantrum. She choked back the hysteria bubbling up inside her, fearing that if she let it escape it would leave behind a vacuum she'd never be able to fill up again.

"Tell me about Karen." Tommy finally broke the silence. "Whatever comes to mind."

Nora swallowed hard, shaking her head, flashes of neon graffiti sparking through her vision.

"Okay, then." Tommy eased back in his seat. "We can talk about anything."

There was a long silence. Nora fidgeted, her fingers worrying a torn piece of vinyl on the chair cushion.

"How's Seth doing? When I saw you last, it seemed like things were getting serious."

She pulled her knees up, her entire body embraced by the chair, her focus on the torn cushion. "We broke up a few months ago."

Another silence. "Oh. I'm sorry to hear that. You seemed happy."

"I was." The words were out before she could stop them. Even worse, tears tumbled out with them. "We were. At least I thought we were."

Damn, she needed to stop. Tommy didn't need or want to hear all this. She wiped her mouth with the back of her hand, blinking hard, but the tears kept on coming. "Until I found him in bed with Karen."

"Karen Chisholm? The victim?"

Overwhelmed by sobs, Nora could only nod. She reached blindly for the box of tissues on the table beside her, wiped her eyes, and blew her nose.

"Nora." Tommy's voice dropped, low and serious. "Have you told the police about Seth and Karen?"

She shook her head. Seth had always denied his affair with Karen, continuously insisting that there was nothing between him and the nurse anesthetist. But she'd seen them together. And Karen had made a point of filling her in on intimate details whenever Nora saw her. Still, she was certain Seth had nothing to do with Karen's attack. "He was on call, here at the hospital. He couldn't have had anything to do with this."

"Don't you think the police should know?"

Nora shrank away from Tommy, burying her fingers deep in the hole in the cushion, wishing she could crawl in after and hide from the world.

Of course the police should know. Just as they needed to know that there had been a prior victim, that this wasn't the rapist's first time.

Somehow she had to find the courage to face her past. The truth was supposed to set you free. But to Nora, it felt as if the truth were a dark labyrinth, a monster's lair, one that she might lose herself in. Maybe forever.

Slowly she uncurled herself from her fetal position. She pushed out of the chair and stood. "I need to get back to work."

"But, Nora, we've just begun."

"No. I can't—" She backed toward the door, edging past the chair, putting it between her and Tommy. "I can't do this now."

"We'll talk later," he called out as she went through the door. She swiped at her face, sucked in a breath, and strode over to the nurses' station. There she found Lydia on the phone, her face flushed as she paced in a circle, tethered by the phone's cord.

"What's going on?" Nora asked Jason.

"Some attending is trying to steal the last PICU bed from Lydia's patient." He lowered his voice to a whisper. "First fight I've seen her on the losing side of."

"Have you seen Jerry Boyle? Is he still here?" Nora was almost afraid to ask, but if Jerry was still here, she'd tell him everything. Now, while she still had the courage.

Jason shook his head. "Sorry, they already left. Do you want me to call him?"

"Yes, please." She wrung her hands together, realized what she was doing, and instead pressed them flat against the counter as she waited. Jerry must have answered immediately because Jason handed her the phone a few moments later.

"Nora," Jerry said, his words undercut by the sound of traffic. "What can I do for you?"

"I was wondering if we could talk." She looked around; too many people here at the nurses' station. "About this morning."

"Was there something you needed to add to your statement? Want me to send Janet back?"

"No, no, don't bother Janet." She laid her forehead against her palm. Last thing she needed was another interrogation from Janet. "I know you're busy—"

A man's voice shouted to Jerry in the distance. "I'm coming," he called back. "Sorry, Nora. It's a bit crazy. Listen, I'm meeting Lydia tomorrow morning around seven—want to ask her about coming along? Unless it's urgent; I can try to get free—" His words were crowded out by the sound of other voices.

Nora sighed. "No, it's not urgent. Tomorrow's fine."

"You sure?"

"I'm sure." She hung up, sapped. It had taken all of her energy to build up the courage to talk to Jerry.

Lydia hung up the phone with a bang. "Idiots!"

A middle-aged man wearing a wool overcoat came barreling into the ER from the ambulance bay. "Where is Dr. Fiore and what the hell is she doing interfering with my patient?"

"Uh-oh," Jason muttered. "Better run for cover."

Lydia turned to the man with a wide smile. A smile so fake that Nora could see Lydia's jaw muscles spasm with the effort. "Dr. Frantz, I presume?"

LYDIA'S TEMPER SNAKED THROUGH HER—IT HAD been a bad day, a frustrating day, a day that seemed to churn up all the anger, fear, and anxieties of her youth. Usually she could compartmentalize, shove aside outside worries, but not today.

Damn it, she wasn't going to abandon Narolie to the idiots in the clinic or assholes like the one who stood before her.

"Your patient is in our isolation room, waiting for you," she told Frantz, biting back the adjectives she wanted to use. "His mother is with him. He's fine—although his rash has a petechial appearance, it's not classic for meningococcemia."

"Labs?" Frantz demanded, handing his scarf and coat to Jason as if the ER had a coat check.

"Normal except for a slightly low white count."

He yanked the paper from her hand. "I'm sure you're aware that a low white count is a sign of sepsis."

"It's also consistent with a virus—look at the lymphocyte predominance."

"Then why does he have bands, if it's only a virus?" He raised his gaze to sneer at her. "I know you ER docs consider yourselves masters of all aspects of medicine, but I think the subtleties of early sepsis are beyond you. Good thing I acted fast to treat him."

"Yes, giving that preemptive high dose of ceftriaxone was very helpful." Her sarcasm was lost on Frantz. "It destroyed any chance of our culturing his blood and proving that he has meningococcemia. And the mother refused a lumbar puncture. Getting spinal fluid could be our last chance to confirm the diagnosis. But if we're going to do it, we need to move fast."

"Hmpf." Frantz ignored her, leafing through his patient's chart. "Call in an infectious-disease consult and get neurology down here to do the spinal tap. I'll get the mom's consent. By that time his bed in the PICU should be ready."

"Don't you want to examine the patient before calling in consults?" Asking a neurologist to come down to the ER to do a simple LP was like calling a plastic surgeon to trim a hangnail.

"No. Like you said, time is of the essence. Make the calls. I'm going to talk with my patient and his family." Without a glance, he left the nursing station.

"Gee, Lydia, didn't know you were aiming for my job working the phones," Jason said with a grin. "It's harder than it looks, you know. I'm not sure if you're qualified."

"Hah. Very funny. You call in the ID consult—I think Ken Rosen is on for them. I'll call neuro and try to explain why they're being asked to drop everything to do a simple spinal tap." No sense in Jason getting chewed out on Frantz's behalf.

Lydia slid into a chair—it felt like the first time she'd sat down all day. As she waited for the neurologist to return her page, she watched Nora. The charge nurse was flipping through the triage notes of patients waiting to be seen, prioritizing them, making notes on patients who would need follow-up in the waiting room if they weren't seen soon, and creating a list of orders—obvious labs, X rays, and the like—to help facilitate the process.

Yet Nora seemed to be moving at half speed, reading a chart, then moving on, checking herself, and going back. Distracted. Lydia fingered the small flash drive Boyle had given her, rubbing it like a worry bead before slipping it back into the pocket of her scrubs. She understood the feeling. But the ER was no place to be working when you were distracted. Good thing it wasn't too busy.

The phone rang. "Lucas Stone here," came a man's voice. "Someone page neurology?"

Thank goodness it was Lucas—he wouldn't mind doing the LP; he loved procedures, even simple lumbar punctures. Plus, ever since he and Amanda had announced their engagement after Thanksgiving, he'd been incredibly easygoing about everything. Lydia couldn't remember the last time they'd gotten into one of their usual good-natured debates. Or that she'd been able to get him started on a rant. Although he was still as germophobic as always—but she hated to tease him about that. Not with more important things like the wedding on his mind.

At least she didn't have to worry about Trey ever getting googly-eyed like Lucas. What she and Trey had was good, was great, but it definitely wasn't headed anywhere near an altar. Not anytime soon. Thank God. It was hard enough handling living with someone, much less 'til death do us part.

"Lucas, it's Lydia. I'm going to apologize up front, but it's not my call. I have a private patient down here; his attending is certain he has meningococcemia, although I don't buy it. Anyway, the attending, a Dr. Frantz, wants you to do the LP."

There was a pause and she almost hoped that Lucas would snap at her—or at least vent a little at Frantz's stupidity. But no, instead he merely said, "When do you need me?"

"Well, to complicate things, the kid got a slug of antibiotics before he even hit the ER. So the clock's ticking."

"No problem, I'll be right down. Oh, and I have those bridesmaid dresses for you to look at." He hung up before he could hear Lydia groan.

To prevent any perception of a conflict of interest because Lucas was an attending physician, Amanda and Lucas wanted to be married before Amanda began her internship in July. But as a medical student, Amanda was too busy to plan a wedding, so Lucas—being more than a little obsessive-compulsive—had taken over the plans. And was surprising everyone by apparently enjoying the process.

Nora joined her at the desk, shuffling the triage charts. Lydia flipped through them, signing orders for the labs and X rays.

"When Lucas comes down, tell him the spinal tap kid is in the isolation room."

"Where are you going?" Nora asked.

"To check on my patient in bed two. But don't tell him that—he has more bridesmaid dresses for us to look at."

"I haven't even found a dress to wear to the gala on Saturday and he expects me to pick out something for a wedding that's not until May?"

"I thought you were working Saturday."

"I am, but only seven to three. I promised admin that I'd be at the gala by four—they asked all the charge nurses to act as hostesses."

"You don't sound too happy about it. Want to trade places? Trey has me signed up for a cookie-baking marathon with his mother."

"It'd be different if I had a date. And"—Nora shook her head, a frown creasing her eyes—"getting all dressed up seems so frivolous after what happened today."

Lydia watched the expressions flit across Nora's face. Something beyond Karen's death was troubling her. Lydia wasn't sure whether to push the issue or let it be.

Nora solved the problem by standing up. "I'm going to look for that rape kit. It has to be around here somewhere."

AMANDA PULLED THE CURTAIN ASIDE AND WAS immediately struck by the delicate beauty of the girl sleeping in the bed beyond it. High cheekbones that would put even Gina's to shame; an ebony complexion so dark it was almost blue; small, delicate hands with long fingers. Wow. And Narolie was only thirteen—wait until she came into her own as an adult.

The girl was alone. She looked so peaceful that Amanda hated to wake her. But as Amanda approached, a spasm of pain contorted the girl's face and she clutched her belly, arching up as if about to vomit. Amanda rushed to grab the emesis basin from the girl's bedside, holding it at the ready.

Sweat coated Narolie's face as the pain racked her body. Then she relaxed and pushed the basin aside. "I'm okay," she said in a strangled whisper, eyes still closed. "I'll be okay."

"Narolie? I'm Amanda Mason. I'm here to see about getting you a bed upstairs so we can find out what's wrong with you."

Narolie opened her eyes fully and turned her gaze to Amanda. "And heal me, yes? Please, I need to be healed. I have prayed and prayed and now you are here, the answer to my prayers."

Another wave of pain brought tears to the girl's eyes as she clutched Amanda's hand with crushing strength. "Please," she repeated.

"I'll do the best I can," Amanda vowed. After the spasm passed, she kept hold of Narolie's hand. The girl was so young, so alone. "When did the pain begin?" she asked, settling in to take Narolie's history.

They'd barely begun when the curtain parted and a man in a dark blue suit entered. "I was told we have a mystery patient here," he said, extending a hand for Narolie's chart.

Amanda held on to the chart and stood up. Before she could ask, he said, "I'm Dr. Frantz, and you, I believe, are Amanda Mason?"

"Yes." She stood up straighter. Dr. Frantz was one of the private pediatricians with attending privileges at Angels. He never let medical students or residents near his patients. And he never, ever saw clinic patients—his patients were the elite of Pittsburgh. "Can I help you?"

"Actually, I think I can help you. The nurses said you were having a hard time getting an attending for your case." He nodded at Narolie as if she were a lab specimen. "I'm here seeing one of my patients and while I'm waiting for a few consults, I thought I'd see if I could help out."

"Uh—sure, that would be great." This wasn't the Dr. Frantz she'd heard about—the man who called medical students "scut-monkeys" and residents "gorillas." She handed him the chart. "This is Narolie. She began to experience dizziness, headaches, and vomiting—"

"No need for the full history, I have it all right here." He gestured with the chart, motioning for her to join him outside in the hall. "What's your plan?"

"Admit her for pain control, IV fluids, and further testing. CT should be ready for her shortly. If that's negative, I'd like to also do an MRI, rule out any mass—"

"Evidence of increased intracranial pressure on exam?"

"Well, no, but—"

"Then a brain tumor that wouldn't be seen on CT is highly unlikely. I see she's from Africa—stool studies?"

"The clinic has already done them four times. No evidence of parasites. And she's never had any diarrhea."

"Still, those can be pesky buggers to track down. Since the ER already has it set up, I guess we can go ahead with the CT. Write up the orders for her IV and some Zofran, and I'll take it from there."

"Don't you want to exam her?"

He beamed down at her. "I'm on the match committee for the pediatrics residency program, Ms. Mason. I've seen your application to match here in pediatrics. Excellent recommendations. You've garnered some high praise from the attendings you've worked under. I think I can trust your exam. Dictate the history and physical and the admission note and I'll sign them."

Lucas appeared from the direction of the nurses' station. "Dr. Frantz?"

Amanda was surprised at the deferential tone in Lucas's voice. Lucas was the youngest attending in neurology, but usually that didn't stop him from being a stubborn and sometimes loudly intense patient advocate—one of the reasons she'd fallen in love with him.

Dr. Frantz turned his attention to Lucas as if he were granting Lucas a royal audience. "Stone. Good to see you again. How'd the LP on my little guy look?"

"Normal opening pressure, fluid was clear. I'm waiting for labs, but I didn't find any signs of meningitis on exam."

"Good, good. Harold's mother will be pleased to hear that."

"I'll dictate a note, page you if anything shows up on the gram stain."

"You'll go look yourself?" Dr. Frantz made it sound like a statement rather than a question.

Lucas glanced at his watch. "Sure, no problem."

"Very good." Dr. Frantz turned to leave, then stopped, including both of them in his beaming gaze. "By the way, I understand congratulations are in order. I wish you the best of luck and hope Ms. Mason is able to continue working here at Angels. It would be such a pity if things went awry and she didn't match here, had to leave us."

Amanda watched him walk away, then turned to Lucas. "Why do I feel like I've just been threatened?"

SIX

Thursday, 12:17 P.M.

NORA ABANDONED HER PAPER SHUFFLING AND walked down to OR 13. The police had placed a large X of crime-scene tape across the double doors, like on TV. The yellow tape looked bizarre, surrealistic. But what had happened behind those doors was all too real.

She shook herself and looked down the hall. OR 13 was in the back of the ER, at the end of a short corridor. The only other rooms down here were the locker rooms and clean holding. Then was the intersection with one of the main ER corridors: turn left and there was security, the trauma rooms, nursing station, and at the end, the ambulance bay. Turn right and you'd hit the corridor leading to administration, the conference rooms, cafeteria, atrium, and auditorium. Or you could loop back around into the ER.

The place was a maze. Whoever had stolen the rape kit had to have been someone who knew the ER, could move around without anyone noticing. She sighed, tugging her fingers through her hair, using the pain to focus. If Karen had been in one of the ER's resuscitation rooms, everything would have been caught on tape—they all had cameras, for teaching purposes. But there was no camera in Room 13.

She and Seth had only been gone maybe ten minutes at most. And Miguel had been there the whole time. Or had he? She stared at her reflection in the dark glass of the OR doors, trying to visualize the frenzied moments after Karen's death.

Miguel had had his trash cart with him when she'd run into him. He would have needed to go back down the hall and around the corner to the janitor's closet in order to get his mop and bucket. Trying to walk at the same pace as Miguel pushing his cart, Nora went down the hall and turned the corner. It took less than a minute.

The door to the janitor's closet was open, cleaning supplies scattered on the hallway floor. The police obviously had had the same thought and searched here already. No crime-scene tape, so she was guessing they didn't find anything.

Okay. But if Miguel was down here while the rape kit was stolen, could it have been hidden somewhere in the ER? It would be a gutsy move. Whoever took it could have easily been seen by Miguel or anyone once they turned out of the OR hallway.

"Nora, what are you doing?" Seth's voice interrupted her reverie.

"Trying to find that rape kit." She didn't have energy for Seth right now. It was easier to focus on solving the problem of the missing evidence than dealing with their problems.

"I wanted to see if you were okay."

"I'm fine." She shoved the cleaning supplies back into the closet and shut the door. Miguel wouldn't appreciate the mess, but patient safety came first.

"Hey, look at me." Seth touched her elbow. "Are you sure?"

She could feel his gaze on her, but she didn't look up to meet it. "I told you, I'm fine."

"That's what you always say." He tipped her chin up so that their eyes met. "This is me, remember? You can't lie to me. It's your freckles, they give it away."

She shook her head at his attempt at levity. Leave it to Seth to make a joke at a time like this. Life was one long beer commercial to him.

"Did you tell them, um, about before?" he asked. "That it was the same guy?"

"No." The single syllable fell like a lead weight between them. "No," she repeated. "I didn't tell them. But I will."

Seth shifted his weight, fiddling with the hemostat clipped to his waistband. "Anything I can do to help?"

"I didn't tell the police about you and Karen, either. But it came up when I was talking to Tommy Z. The police are going to find out."

"What makes you think I didn't already tell them?"

"Did you?"

He looked down at the floor, worrying at a seam in the linoleum with the toe of his shoe. "No. I didn't think it mattered. Karen and I weren't together. I keep trying to explain that to you, but you won't talk to me unless it's about a patient."

"Yeah, right." She turned her head, refusing to look at him. He'd tried to get her to believe that same old malarkey back in October, had even come close to stalking her, leaving her favorite flowers for her day after day. "Whatever."

He surprised her by touching her arm. Startled, she jerked away so hard she hit the wall behind her.

Seth stepped back, giving her room. "No. It's not all right. I'm sick and tired of you not listening—I didn't push things before because it seemed to only hurt you more, but I can't let you keep thinking—"

"Thinking?" Nora straightened, staring at him head on. "How about seeing? I saw you, Seth. Naked. In Karen's bed." She spun on her heel, walking away. "Leave me alone."

He followed her. "Damn it, I did not sleep with Karen."

His voice was loud enough that a passing X ray tech turned to stare at them as he walked past. Nora felt herself blush—more fodder for the rumor mill. The anger that had been building in her all day seeped past her restraint. She whirled on him. "Shut up. I don't want to hear your excuses."

"It's not an excuse. It's the truth." He grimaced. "I was sleepwalking."

She stopped, frowning at him. Then laughed. "Sleepwalking? That's the best you can come up with? We lived together for three months and you never walked in your sleep."

He flushed. "I haven't done it since I was a kid."

"Yeah. Right. Why even bother denying it? I saw you and Karen together, Seth. Naked."

"You saw me in her bed. You did not see us having sex. I swear to God, nothing happened. I guess I stripped naked while I was on call and started wandering the halls. Karen took me to her room, tried to make me think we had had sex. She wanted to break us up, so when you came along . . ."

Nora shook her head, trying to make sense of all of this. "C'mon, Seth, do you really expect me to believe any of that?"

"That's why I didn't tell you before. I knew you'd never believe me. Ask Lucas if you want."

"Right, like your best friend isn't going to lie for you."

He clenched his fists, his face flushing with frustration. "But now I can prove it."

"Don't bother. It's too late for us, Seth."

"No. It's not." Seth's trauma pager blared through the air between them. "Shit. I have to go."

He didn't move, waiting until she finally met his gaze. Dark brown eyes that warmed her despite the distance between them. "I have never lied to you, Nora. Never have, never will."

"Right. Like my own eyes lied instead." Nora wasn't sure what she felt—anger, disbelief, or betrayal that he'd continue to argue the facts. How could he? She'd *seen* Seth and Karen together. It wasn't rumor or gossip or innuendo. It was the truth.

Seth merely shook his head as the trauma alert sounded once more. "Someday you'll believe me."

He turned and sped down the hallway toward the resuscitation rooms.

"ROLLOVER MVA, RESTRAINED DRIVER, TWENTY-seven years old, no LOC, complaining of substernal chest pain and right shoulder pain." Trey called the bullet to Lydia as he and Gina wheeled a man strapped to a stretcher into the trauma bay. "Two large-bore IVs in, one and a half liters LR, O_2 by mask, pulse ox ninety-eight, pulse one twenty-eight, resps twenty-two, BP one twelve over seventy-two."

"Move on three," Lydia directed her team as Seth Cochran rushed in. They transferred the patient to the ER's bed and she allowed Seth to take command, following along behind him to make sure he didn't miss anything. The nurses kept looking to her for confirmation of his orders as he ran the resuscitation. She remained silent, reinforcing Seth's authority.

He did a good job. Thorough, efficient, not distracted by the chest pain or seemingly normal vitals, quickly making a diagnosis of a subcapsular splenic bleed.

"Nice work," she told Seth as they stepped outside while the nurses packaged the patient for transfer up to the OR.

He leaned against the wall, one hand twirling his trauma shears, looking down at the floor. "Wish I could have done as well with Karen."

"You did everything you could. We all did. We just got to her too late."

He shook his head, glancing over to the nurses' station, where several nurses stood, arms crossed over their chests, glaring at him. "Too late for a lot of things."

Glen Bakker strolled past them, making yet another highly visible circuit of the ER. Lydia understood that he was trying to reassure the staff, but it was getting damned annoying bumping into him every ten minutes. Seth stepped forward into the security head's path.

"When the hell are you going to tighten security in the garage?" he demanded. "My car got keyed again."

Glen stopped, hooked his thumbs in his belt loops, and rocked back, angling his gaze down at Seth, who was shorter by several inches. "Dr. Cochran, right?"

"Right. Remember me from last month when someone bashed out my taillight? I keep filing reports, but nothing is ever done and my insurance premiums are going through the roof."

"Well now, doc, you could always park on the street if you don't like the hospital parking accommodations." Glen's mouth twisted. "I'm sure you understand that I need to place the safety of the people who work here over a few dings and scratches to your car."

A small round of applause broke out at the nurses' station with that pronouncement. Seth reddened, then stepped forward into Glen's space.

"I'm not worried about my car, you idiot," he said, not backing down despite the fact that Glen had several inches and about twenty pounds on him. "I'm worried about the people who work here. Like Karen. And Nora Halloran, the nurse who found her this morning. What are you doing to protect them?"

Glen glowered at Seth, who responded by taking another step closer to the head of security. Lydia put her hand on his arm, stopping him before things could escalate into an all-out war—one the surgical resident was sure to lose. "They're ready for you up in the OR, Seth."

He did a double take and backed down. With a parting glare at Glen, he followed the stretcher with his patient down the hall to the elevators.

"That boy needs an attitude adjustment," Glen said in a conspiratorial tone.

"He's had a rough day. And he has a point. Better security in the garages might have prevented what happened to Karen."

"So I keep hearing. Don't you think I want to do my job the best I can? But I also have to answer to Tillman and the board," Glen said as Tommy Z emerged from the family room. His demeanor changed instantly from defensive to amicable. "You talk with Tommy yet, Dr. Fiore? He's real good."

Lydia remembered the crushed expression Nora had worn after her chat with the crisis counselor. "I'll pass, thanks."

Tommy joined them and exchanged a glance with Glen. "I have time now, Dr. Fiore," he said, gesturing to the family room with a sweep of his arm. "No waiting."

"Crisis counseling is voluntary. I'll take care of things on my own," she said, wondering at the way the two men had teamed up. Then she realized who had to be pulling their strings. Oliver Tillman, the hospital CEO, had a habit of barreling into situations with his swayback gorilla tactics. "Tillman told you two to keep an eye on me, didn't he? What, does he think that I can't keep control of things down here in my department?"

Glen frowned and cleared his throat. "Uh, you might want to go ahead and talk with Tommy, doc. Would be a good example for the staff, good for morale and all."

Lydia wasn't sure of Tillman's angle—and she didn't really care.

"Mr. Tillman was—er—concerned," Tommy said. "Especially after what happened two months ago when you refused counseling then."

"Excuse me? Tillman blames *me* for some lunatic breaking into my house and trying to kill me?"

"It reflected poorly on the hospital when you nearly killed the man. I think he was hoping you'd be more of a team player this time around," Glen said, having the good grace to at least look embarrassed at having to do Tillman's dirty work. "The staff is a bit nervous. Mr. Tillman doesn't want anything to cause further—"

"Consternation," Tommy Z finished for him.

"He asked us to—er—help you see the light," Glen added.

"I'm sure you understand. We can talk about anything, really," Tommy Z said, placing his hand on her arm as if leading a blind woman.

"Tell you what, boys," Lydia said, shaking off Tommy's hand. "I'll attend counseling as soon as Mr. Tillman does."

Both men watched her with mouths gaping open as she strolled back to the nurses' station and picked up another patient's chart.

Jason gave her a thumbs-up and handed her the phone. "Line two is for you."

Lydia answered the phone, expecting it to be an update on one of her patients. "Dr. Fiore."

"Lydia! It's Pete Sandusky. How the heck are you?"

She barely avoided a groan. Sandusky was Pittsburgh's answer to the Drudge Report—a blogger who occasionally grabbed headlines in other media as well. "I'm busy, Sandusky."

"Wait, don't hang up. I heard on the scanner this morning that the cops were responding to a sexual assault case over there." His voice sped through the line with the force of a freight train. If she hadn't met him in person and known that was his usual breakneck pace, she'd wonder if he was on drugs.

"Didn't think much of it, but happened to be driving by and saw crime-scene tape in the cemetery, and lo and behold there was our favorite homicide detective, Jerry Boyle, digging in the mud. So"—he paused for effect—"what kind of assault was it? Some kind of warped vampire cult? Maybe a voodoo ceremony gone awry? None of the papers or TV channels have squat yet. C'mon, Lydia, give. You owe me."

"I don't owe you anything, Sandusky. Good-bye." She

hung up, his sputtering protestations still echoing from the receiver.

Lydia leaned back in her chair and closed her eyes for a brief moment. When was this day going to end?

SEVEN

Thursday, 12:34 P.M.

WHILE GINA WAITED FOR TREY AND GECKO TO
finish restocking after their MVA patient, she glanced through
Tank's chart. He was still in the ER, waiting to go upstairs—
from the orders, it looked like Dr. Frantz had won the battle
over the PICU admission.

"Reading anything interesting?" A familiar voice made
her smile despite herself. Ken Rosen, an immunologist and
infectious-disease specialist. And the real Hero of Angels.
Ken had saved a bunch of kids during the riots last July, even
though it was Gina who had gotten the public credit.

Ken smiled back—he was almost always smiling, this
small *I-know-something-you-don't-know*, infuriatingly Zen-
like smile that drove Gina nuts.

When Gina had once tried to explain the way Ken made her
feel, Amanda had said it sounded like chiggers: an itch just under your skin that you could never scratch and irritating as hell.

"I see Dr. Frantz called in the big guns, consulting neuro
and ID. You tell him your thoughts about pretreating with
broad-spectrum antibiotics?" she asked Ken.

"Didn't have the chance. He was too busy schmoozing the mom." He took the chart from her but didn't open it, instead holding it between them like a shield. "So, Gina. How are you?"

"I'm fine." Now she had to force her smile. "Got a great dress for Saturday night. You'll be there, right?"

A swift frown shadowed his face, gone before she was even sure it was there. "No. Sorry." Now he opened the chart and seemed intent on studying it, drifting away from the nurses' station as he headed toward the isolation room.

Gina watched him go, annoyed that she even cared. But damn it, she wanted to try to get things right—this time. Ken was the real hero. He was the one who deserved a medal, not her. She rushed after him. "Are you certain you won't reconsider and come to the gala?"

"Do I really look like the gala type?" He gestured to his rumpled lab jacket, jeans, and polo shirt. "Why is this so important to you?"

"I want to give the award to you. You and the guys from Med Seven. You guys were the real heroes that day."

"No thanks. I'd rather skip the medal and the gala. Besides, I doubt Moses would want to see me there."

"So what if my father sued you for malpractice? That will be true of half the doctors who'll be there. He won't notice—he's going to be pretty upset when I make my announcement."

"What announcement?"

"That I'm marrying Jerry Boyle." Gina had no idea why she said it—she hadn't even told Amanda about her engagement yet, and here she was, blurting it out to Ken Rosen of all people.

She tugged the engagement ring free from under her shirt to show him. "Moses doesn't exactly approve."

Ken's smile vanished. He started to turn away, then turned back. He cleared his throat. "I see. Well then, I guess I have an early wedding present for you. It's up in my office."

"What?"

"Your Kevlar vest. The one with the bullet in it."

Gina's hand automatically went to the back of her neck where the bullet would have hit if not for the bulletproof vest. "The one I was wearing that day? I thought it went missing from the ER. You have it?"

He was already three steps away from her, speeding up. Then he skidded to a halt. "Don't marry Jerry. It's a mistake."

Gina did a double take. "Are you kidding? Jerry's a wonderful guy. He cares about me. He loves me."

"That's the problem. Jerry *is* a wonderful guy. He does love you. But you don't love him."

Gina stared at him, stunned. Fury and confusion battled as she felt her cheeks heat up. "What the hell would you know about it?"

He looked over his shoulder as if searching for an escape, but then turned back to her. "Jerry's got you swaddled in bubble wrap and Kevlar. But that's not what you need, Gina."

"Go to hell." She straightened to her full five-ten, meeting him head-on. "Jerry's not like that—I can damn well take care of myself."

"No. You can't. But you need to learn how to." He met her stare without flinching or backing down. "You need someone who believes in you enough to let you stumble and fall, someone who will watch your back while you pick yourself up, someone there, ready to offer a hand when you ask for it. Someone more than a caretaker."

The slap surprised her—it just happened, as if her hand had a mind of its own. And damn, it hurt her more than it hurt him. He merely rocked back, didn't even touch his cheek where her palm print burned red.

"You have no idea what I need."

"Neither do you."

NORA RETRACED HER STEPS, HEADING TO THE security office. There she found Glen Bakker working at the front desk, a schedule spread out in front of him.

"Just call me the Grinch," he said, making a notation beside one of his men's names. "Stealing Christmas from everyone." He laid down his pen and leaned back in his chair, appraising her. "How's the girl? I didn't hurt her, did I?"

"She'll be fine. Psych is admitting her for observation, and I tipped the social worker to what's going on with the boyfriend."

"The way some men treat women." He shook his head, scowling. "So, what can I do for you, Nora? Are you headed home? Need an escort to the garage?"

"No. I was wondering if the police found the rape kit yet."

He stood and came around to join her on the other side of the desk. "Not that I know. Why?"

"I want to find it. We were only gone a few minutes. How could anyone have known where to find it or when to grab it?"

He nodded slowly, appraising her as if trying to decide if she was trustworthy. "I've been wondering the same thing. What if the perp came from here, inside the hospital?"

She held her breath for a moment, hating to acknowledge the truth in his words. "Did your cameras pick up anything?"

"Let me show you something." He led her back to his private office. It was a spartan room with bare walls and an institutional metal desk. His chair had stuffing poking through cracks in the vinyl and the only personal memento was a framed photo of Glen with his reserve unit in Iraq. A large-screen monitor sat on his desk, the picture divided into four separate video feeds.

"I gave the police copies of everything from last night and this morning, but I've been reviewing all the footage myself as well." He pulled out a chair for her, positioning it beside his own, then sat down, a captain taking command of his ship. His fingers danced across the keyboard, and four new images popped up onto the screen. "Can you narrow the time frame?"

Nora had been through all of this with Janet Kwon, but

obviously the detective hadn't confided in Glen. Why should she? Nora doubted that the prickly detective confided in anyone. "I left the garage around six forty."

"Okay, that helps. I can only do four feeds at a time, but I'll pull the ones from that side of the medical center, slow them down, and start at six twenty or so." He punched in some keys and the screen blinked for a moment, and then four images began to flow across each quadrant. They moved in a painfully slow, almost stuttering type of movement; it was hard to watch without becoming seasick.

And there wasn't a lot on them. A few workers arriving early for their shift, entering the main lobby. No one coming in through the ambulance bay or the clinic entrance, where the third camera was. Two women arriving together through the ER entrance.

"Wait," Nora said, pointing to a dark blur of motion at the edge of the frame. "What's that?"

"I'm not sure." Glen selected the ER camera's feed, and it filled the screen. He zoomed in on the area she pointed to. "A man. I think I got a piece of his back and his arm. Here."

As he zoomed in further, the image blurred even more. The back of a man from the shoulders down was visible. He wore a long black trench coat over black slacks. His gloved hand was extended as if reaching out to someone.

"What is he doing?" Nora pulled her chair closer, leaning forward so her face was mere inches from the screen.

Glen manipulated the image and it slowly, frame by frame, went backward. The man seemed to grow shorter, then taller again as he moved through the shot, his hand arching out from his side then falling back into place before he vanished.

"He threw something," she said after Glen rewound it and played it for the second time. "Is there a trash can near that camera?"

"Let's go see." Glen vaulted from his chair, his face aglow with the prospect of playing supercop. Nora had to admit, she was pretty excited as well. If they found something that would lead to the killer, she could jettison the load of guilt that had been weighing her down for two long years.

Glen grabbed his bomber jacket and handed her a windbreaker from the collection hanging on the coat rack. It was much too large for Nora's small frame, but as soon as they stepped out into the cold air of the ambulance bay, she was glad for the protection. Glen had a BlackBerry-type device in his hand, ungloved fingers punching the tiny keyboard as he squinted into the small screen.

"I can control all the cameras and security from this, but I have to admit my eyes are getting old. It's a lot easier from my computer. Okay"—he strode to the far right of the ambulance bay, halfway between it and the main ER doors—"this is it."

"It" was a small piece of wall that jutted out at an angle, demarcating the ambulance bay and employee entrance from the main ER entrance. It was also the place where smokers gathered, sheltered from the wind and out of sight of the public. A nursing assistant, arms crossed over her chest, no jacket, saw them coming, quickly snuffed out her cigarette, and hustled inside before they reached her.

Nora went straight to the trash can. Inside it she found fast-food debris, a few surgical caps and booties, tons of cigarette butts, and a paper bag half-split open, revealing its colorful contents: blaze orange, neon green, and scarlet spray paint cans, all smeared with fresh paint.

"Bingo," she said.

"He was probably too smart to leave prints," Glen said, now using his PDA to make a phone call, "but this should give the police a time frame so they can check alibis."

"What was the time stamp on the video when we saw him?"

"Six thirty-eight. He would have dumped the body right before."

Nora turned and stared across the drive. She could see over the fence into the cemetery and the weeping angel where she'd found Karen. And she had a clear view of the parking garage exit. The one she used every day.

He had watched—he'd seen her find Karen.

Despite the windbreaker, she began shivering uncontrollably. Hugging her arms around her chest didn't help.

He'd been watching her.

EIGHT

Thursday, 12:41 P.M.

THE TECHS CAME TO TAKE NAROLIE TO HER CT scan. Amanda followed Lucas out to the nursing station. He walked beside her without touching her—he was always so hyperaware of decorum. Especially once they'd realized that if she was going to be a resident at the same hospital where he was attending physician, then they needed to get married first. He had even flown home to South Carolina with her over Thanksgiving to meet her family and ask her parents' permission to marry her.

"How's your little boy in the ICU?" he asked.

"Not so good." She glanced at her beeper to make sure she hadn't missed any pages. "I hope we can buy him enough time with the ECMO for his lungs to heal."

"Too long on bypass and you risk brain injury." He held a chair out for her at the dictation area.

"I know." Then she brightened. "At least I was able to help Narolie. I can't believe Dr. Frantz gave up his PICU bed for her."

"He didn't. The kid I did the spinal tap on is getting it."

Amanda wheeled around, the chair rattling. "But—you heard him. He told me to write up her admission orders."

Lucas pulled up the admission screen on the computer. "There, see. Harold Trenton, PICU. Narolie Maxeke, regular pediatric bed, twenty-three-hour observation."

"Observation? So basically he's going to sit on her tonight, do nothing, and send her home in the morning?"

"Basically." Lucas typed his note on the lumbar puncture while Amanda fumed over Dr. Frantz's manipulation. "Cheer up. Maybe the CT will give you the diagnosis."

"There's something wrong with that girl—it's not all in her head, despite what the clinic doctors say."

He turned to smile at her, his blue-gray eyes crinkling in delight. He reached across to squeeze her hand, surprising her with the almost-public display of affection. "You never give up on anyone."

"It's so unfair. She came to this country to build a new life. She shouldn't be treated this way just because she doesn't have insurance."

"Anything I can do to help?"

"I don't know. I need to find time to get a complete history from her—every time she's seen a clinic doctor, it's been a different one and the doctors have only done short, complaint-focused histories. I'm sure there's a missing link to everything."

He scanned Narolie's chart. "Have you thought about abdominal migraines?"

"Maybe. But there's no good test for them other than a trial of medication. I guess if I only have twenty-three hours to work with, I'd better rule out anything that needs special testing first."

"How are you going to get Frantz to sign off on that testing? You're only a medical student."

She flipped to the order page on the chart. "He already did. Look at how the lazy son of a gun signed the admission order: 'further orders per Amanda Mason, MS4.' All I need to do is get a resident to cosign what I order. They won't know or care; she's not their patient."

"Amanda—"

She recognized the warning in his tone but didn't care, already thinking of the differential diagnosis and what tests she could order in the next twenty-three hours. "If the CT is negative, can you pull some strings, help me get her in for an MRI of her head?"

"You could lose your residency slot over this—Frantz is very powerful."

"If so, it'd be worth it." She scooted her chair closer to his, rubbing her leg alongside his. "Look on the bright side— we wouldn't have to rush the wedding."

"Yeah, because we might *both* be on the unemployment line."

"HAVE YOU SEEN GINA?" TREY ASKED, LEANING over the counter at the nurses' station so that his face was close to Lydia's. "We're ready to roll anytime she is."

"Would you be okay with her skipping the rest of her shift?" Lydia asked. Nora was listlessly rearranging patient charts and seemed oblivious to the rest of the ER.

"Maybe. Why?"

She gestured for him to join her down the hallway across from the trauma bay. "I'm worried about Nora."

"Finding a murdered colleague has a tendency to screw up your day."

She hadn't told him about the missing rape kit or that Karen, the victim, had also once been involved with Seth Cochran. Or her suspicions that there was more going on, distracting Nora. "I don't want her to be alone. Was thinking about sending Gina home with her."

Trey glanced at the clock. "Sure, that's fine with me. Not like Gina is skipping out on her own. She's made up most of her shift; that's what counts." He threaded his fingers through hers. "You going to fill me in on all the details later?" He didn't wait for her answer, but instead shifted his weight as if off-balance. "My mom wants to know your schedule over Christmas."

"I'm working."

"Right, like you were working Thanksgiving." ·

"I *was* working Thanksgiving."

"Lydia. I know you traded shifts with Mark Cohen to work Thanksgiving."

"Is that a crime? The man deserves to have time with his family."

Trey's stare hardened. "Look, I know this is hard for you. Family stuff. But they really want to celebrate the holidays with you. We've been together five months; you can't avoid them forever."

Five months? Before Trey, the longest she'd let any man stick around was five weeks. Operative word being *let*—as in she was in control of the situation.

Not with Trey. Anything but in control. It was as if she'd somehow allowed her life to gallop away, a horse without a rider.

"It's just one day. What can happen in one day?"

A lot. People lived their whole lives and died in one day— as a street medic, he knew that as well as she did.

It wasn't that Trey's family wasn't nice—they were. Too nice. And loving. All those questions, concerns, trying to get to know her, watching out for Trey, judging her . . . not to mention the noise, the laughter, old jokes, old memories, things she could never share. Weekly dinners were bad enough. A full day with Trey's loud and loving family scared the crap out of her.

As usual, Trey picked up on her vibes better than she did herself. "There's no reason to be scared. It's only Christmas."

"You make me sound like some kind of freak, an alien from outer space."

"Doesn't matter. They'll still love you. That's what family is all about." The radio on his belt sounded an alert. He kissed the top of her head, his hand lingering as if reluctant to pull away from the contact. "Gotta go. I'll see you at home."

Lydia stared after him as the ambulance bay doors swished open and shut again. Home. She had a home—her home, his home, their home. When would those simple facts become real to her?

NORA LEANED AGAINST THE NURSES' STATION, feeling numb. Worse than numb—numb would be a blessing. Instead, she had tons of feelings reeling around, colliding inside her gut, ricocheting down her nerve endings.

A stream of lab techs, nurses, and finally Ken Rosen wandered into the isolation room. She knew the patient in there was some kind of VIP, yet she couldn't find the energy to do more than direct traffic.

She'd thought that she'd outrun her past; she'd accepted the lies she told herself and everyone else, had re-created herself after the rape. She'd left her apartment and found a new one, left her old friends behind, abandoned all her old routines. She'd survived the attack—put it all behind her—had even tried her best to give something back by becoming a sexual assault nurse examiner. It had been a year before she dared to trust a man, date again. Seth. Look how that worked out.

And now her carefully crafted wall of denial was crumbling.

She sat down and began to mindlessly organize the lab results spewing forth from the printer. Jim Lazarov jogged out from the isolation room, his mask hanging jauntily from the neck of his Tyvek gown.

"Aren't my labs back yet?" he demanded.

Nora reached for the last of the papers and handed the stack to Jim.

"Why didn't you bring them in? Dr. Frantz was waiting."

"They just came up," Nora responded before she could stop herself. She didn't owe an explanation to anyone, much less a snotty intern. "Everything is normal except for the white count."

"We already knew that from the earlier CBC," he said, dismissing her with a wave of his hand and marching back to the room, holding the papers aloft as if they were hard-won trophies.

Nora watched him go, her vision blurring as she forgot to blink, allowing herself to be transfixed by the fluorescent lights overhead. Footsteps pounded the linoleum to her left, but she didn't focus until a large shadow blocked out the light.

"Is it true?" Oliver Tillman, the medical center's CEO, towered over her, leaning across the counter and bracing his elbows on it.

Nora blinked hard, twice, before meeting his gaze. His eyes were narrowed, his lips compressed into a tight line, but other than that his face was devoid of expression. His Donald Trump mop was in dire need of a comb.

"How could you?" His voice thundered through her. Jason, the desk clerk, jerked his head up and spun out of his chair to stand beside Nora as if she needed protection. Tillman's face flushed scarlet, and he spoke as if Nora had injured him personally. "What is wrong with you that you could be so incompetent, so careless? Answer me!"

Nora had no answers. No matter how much logic told her otherwise, she couldn't help but feel that her lies and secrets were as much the cause of Karen's death as the killer's blade. Worse, she felt powerless—like she had two years ago, waking up in the freezing cold.

Lydia emerged from a patient's room. "Mr. Tillman," she

said, chiseling herself between Nora and the administrator. "Can I help you?"

"I had to come down and see in person the woman who—"

"The woman who fought to save another nurse's life? Nora did a commendable job. I wonder how many others walked past that cemetery and chose not to get involved?" Lydia wasn't much taller than Nora's own five-three, yet she seemed larger as she stood up to Tillman's fury.

"A nurse who is dead. She lost the damn rape kit." Tillman's voice dropped to a dangerous rumble, surprising Nora with the force of his emotion. Tillman was a jerk, but usually a slick, back-stabbing jerk. Last time she'd seen him this upset was when he was trying to get Lydia fired. "Then she left the body unattended."

"I'm sure your concerns focus on the safety of the staff." Lydia's tone had an edge to it. "You're not accusing my nurse of any involvement in this vicious crime, are you, Mr. Tillman?"

"I'm accusing your nurse of incompetence. That's enough to warrant an investigation."

"I'm certain your investigation will find no evidence of incompetence or wrongdoing. Nora is one of the best nurses I've had the pleasure to work with."

Nora barely heard the war of words being fought over her head. She was drowning, being dragged down, with no energy to fight her way back up to the surface.

"We'll see about that," Tillman snapped, firing his parting salvo. His footsteps echoed down the hallway as Lydia crossed around to Nora's side of the counter.

"Come on," she said, taking Nora's elbow. Nora was surprised to find herself standing under her own power. Lydia escorted her away from the many staring eyes at the nurses' station and down the empty hallway behind the trauma rooms.

"Gina's here," Lydia said. "She's going to take you home, stay with you."

Nora somehow found the strength to shake herself free. "I'm fine. Really. I can finish my shift."

"No, you can't. You can either sit here and let everyone stare at you, feeling sorry for yourself, or you can go with Gina."

"Lydia, I said I was fine. I can rest tomorrow on my day off, but today I need to work."

"This isn't about what you need, it's about what's best for the patients. Think about it, Nora; you'll see I'm right."

Nora opened her mouth to protest, then reconsidered. Lydia stood, arms akimbo, as unyielding as granite. "Fine. Whatever," Nora conceded. "But don't bother Gina. I'm going to head on home."

"Then Gina can drive you there."

Normally, Nora would have rebelled against anyone taking control of her life like Lydia had. Normally, she was the one in charge, the one giving the orders. But today she felt anything but normal.

Jim Lazarov sauntered around the corner, interrupting them. "Did they ever find that rape kit, Nora?" he asked with a too-innocent expression.

Lydia dismissed him with a wave of her hand, her gaze never leaving Nora's face. "Not now, Jim."

"What the hell?" he asked. "*She's* only a nurse, but she's allowed to jump all over me when I make the slightest slipup. You know what your problem is?" he said to Nora, who was trying her best to ignore his sneer. "You're obsessed by these sexual assault cases. Seeing abuse everywhere you look."

"I don't care," Lydia said, now bringing the weight of her glare onto the intern. "This is not the time or place. Go see a patient."

"Yeah, right. At least you won't have to worry about *my* killing them," Jim said, his tone triumphant.

Nora felt the blood rush away from her body, her cheeks suddenly burning with cold.

"No wonder Tillman says she's incompetent," Jim continued. "I heard her tell Seth Cochran that she killed Karen."

Nora lashed out without thinking. She shoved Jim against the wall, cracking his head against the tile. "That's not what I meant, and you know it, you eavesdropping little—"

Amanda and Gina turned the corner and came to an abrupt halt as Lydia pulled Nora off Jim, who stood looking at her with wild eyes.

"You all are witnesses," he said. "She assaulted me. Without provocation. I'm calling a lawyer."

Nora stumbled back, alarmed by what she had done.

"I didn't see anything," Lydia said.

"Neither did I," Amanda said.

"Don't look at me," Gina chimed in. "But if you want a lawyer, my dad's one of the best in the country. Uh-oh, sorry, he'll probably be the one suing *your* ass."

Gina and Amanda closed ranks on either side of Nora.

Jim glowered at them, then speared Nora with a glare. "You're going to regret this."

"No one is going to regret anything," Lydia said, stepping between Jim and Nora. "This has been a bad day for everyone. Jim, you go see your next patient. And Nora, let's get you out of here." Hands on her hips, she stared at Jim until the intern grudgingly left them and moved on to his next patient.

"I can't wait until I have to give him an evaluation," Gina said.

Amanda pursed her lips, watching the intern turn the corner. "Think he could have taken the rape kit? He's had it in for Nora ever since he started."

Nora shook her head. "Why? What good would it do him?"

"It would make you look bad. Especially if he got word to the right people, like Tillman," Lydia replied.

"What rape kit?" Gina piped up, obviously peeved at missing a good scandal. "And what does the hospital CEO have to do with anything?"

NINE

Thursday, 1:22 P.M.

"SO, WHAT'D I MISS?" GINA ASKED AS SHE WALKED Nora over to the employee parking garage. Seemed a long way to go. Gina usually managed to snare a spot in the closer patient garage, even though it was against the rules.

Unlike the patient garage, the employee one was fully automated, accessible only via employee IDs. The atmosphere was dark and stifling once they passed beyond the outside walls. Their footsteps echoed eerily as they trudged up the concrete staircase illuminated only by a flickering, low-wattage bulb at the top of each flight.

Nora looked even paler than normal in the dim light, her freckles pronounced, her eyes red-rimmed, with sagging circles beneath them. Gina wondered if maybe she needed a spa day more than a shoulder to cry on. Actually a spa day wasn't a bad idea all around—Gina was past due for a pedicure, and her hair was crying out for Antonio's magic touch. God, she was going to look awful at that damn ceremony Saturday night. . . .

They arrived at Nora's Accord, and still Nora remained silent as she grudgingly handed Gina her keys.

"You don't have to tell me," Gina said, starting the car and revving the engine before backing it out of the slot. "I can ask Jim Lazarov. He seemed to know everything."

Nora straightened and sent her a glare that Gina deflected with a grin as she slid on her sunglasses. The Accord jetted out the exit, barely missing the barrier gate as it swung open, and then turned out onto the street.

"I found Karen Chisholm in the cemetery this morning," Nora finally answered, her voice a monotone that struggled to reach Gina over the sounds of traffic. "She'd been raped and stabbed. She died in room thirteen."

"No shit. You're the one who found her? You're okay, aren't you?"

Nora didn't answer. Gina turned to give her a quick once-over. She looked numb. Lifeless. Sign-her-up-for-the-next-zombie-movie-casting-call dazed. "Karen, the nurse anesthetist? The same chick who was screwing Seth?"

Nora opened her mouth, then closed it again, merely nodding.

"What's the deal about a lost rape kit?" Gina pressed as the light turned green and the Accord surged forward. Not bad for an economy car. Still, she'd rather be behind the wheel of her BMW.

"Seth and I left the body unattended . . . I should have seen, known better."

"Right, of course. I forgot, you're a charge nurse, you see all, know all."

Nora didn't rise to the bait like she usually would have. Instead she curled farther back into the passenger seat. "The police can't use any evidence found on the body. And the rape kit I did went missing."

"Lazarov was there?"

"Lots of people were there; that's the problem. Tillman even came down to the ER, implying that I'd lost the kit on purpose."

"Tillman's an idiot." If anyone in the ER had stolen that kit, it had to be Jim Lazarov. He and Nora had been waging a war of wills ever since he'd started at Angels. For some reason, the intern couldn't seem to understand that the charge nurses didn't just run the ER, they owned it. Even the attendings bowed to their authority.

Gina glanced once more in Nora's direction and made an executive decision, deciding on a detour to Antonio's. Nothing like a little pampering to purge your mind of a bad day. And it sounded like Nora had had a hell of a bad day already.

Her decision was reaffirmed as she drove. Nora jumped every time they stopped, looking around her as if expecting the killer to spring out from every alley they passed. When Gina finally arrived at Antonio's, Nora didn't get out of the car until after Gina handed the keys to the valet and came around to open her door.

Even then Nora hesitated, craning her head to look over her shoulder, down Walnut Street. "I think that black SUV followed us here."

Gina restrained herself from rolling her eyes. "It's Walnut Street, the week before Christmas. Everyone and their mother is down here. Relax, Nora. It's not like this guy is after you."

AMANDA RETURNED TO THE PICU IN TIME TO help the respiratory therapist suction Zachary's lungs. It was a tricky procedure, threading the catheter down his tiny endotracheal tube, taking care not to dislodge it, instilling a small amount of hypertonic saline to irrigate his damaged bronchi, and then suctioning the resulting sloughed-off debris back out. Zachary needed the procedure done every few hours so that the dead tissue wouldn't accumulate and cause further damage. As more and more of the lining of his lungs was removed, Amanda could only hope that new, healthy lung tissue was left behind.

Afterward, she went and told his family how the procedure had gone, leaving the gory details out, and escorted his parents back to his bedside to continue their vigil.

"Do you need anything?" she asked them, wishing there were something she could do to give them the answers they desired. Mr. Miller didn't appear to hear her. His wife answered with a weary shake of her head.

"Hey. *I* need something. Hey!"

Amanda whipped around to spot a teenage boy pushing an IV pole as he left the glass-walled isolation room.

"Get back inside," she ordered, keeping her voice low. He looked very healthy for a PICU patient. The other patients' parents noticed, looking up at the unruly intruder.

"Where are your parents?" She escorted him back inside the room and closed the door. According to the sign, he was under respiratory precautions. She grabbed a mask.

"Dad's out of town; Mom went to track down that other doctor. The foxy black chick who came with the ambulance."

Gina. So this was the patient who had stolen Narolie's ICU bed. "Dr. Freeman."

"Yeah, whatever." He plopped down on the bed. "I'm a prisoner. But even a prisoner has rights."

"You need to stay inside here. You're contagious and the other patients have compromised immune systems; you don't want to risk getting them sick."

"What do I care?" he said sullenly. "They all look like they're going to kick anyway."

His words had to be born of fear and frustration—no one could be that callous, not at such a young age and not here, surrounded by all these critically ill children sustained by medical miracles and hope.

"Stop that," she snapped. "Every one of those patients and their families and their doctors and nurses are fighting for their lives. You do not get to sit here, able to walk and talk, and say things like that."

"So my life's not worth fighting for?" He slumped back, challenging her with his insolent gaze.

"You wouldn't be here if that were true and you know it." She sat on his bed and paid him her full attention. "What's your name?"

"Tank." He glared at her in defiance.

"Tank. I'm Amanda. So what are you in for?"

"Don't know. No one tells me anything. They keep asking me about some rash"—he rolled his eyes—"like having a few spots was the end of the world or something."

"Can I see it?"

"Sure, I guess." He held out his arm and pulled up the sleeve of the too-large patient gown to show her a scattering of dark red and purple dots. Amanda pressed on them; they were slightly raised and didn't blanch, but a few looked like they had a fine scale, as if irritated.

"When did they start?" she asked, getting up to wash her hands.

"How am I supposed to know? Jeezit, you're just like them. Look, all I want is my freaking Game Boy. The Nazi nurses out there took it away. Are you going to help me or not?"

"You can't use it here. It interferes with the equipment, and someone could get hurt."

He flounced back on the bed as if she'd given him a death sentence. "C'mon. One little Game Boy isn't gonna hurt anyone."

"I'm sorry. But the child life department has some video game consoles that are safe to use. Want me to see if I can get you one of those?"

He closed his eyes, but his fists were clenching the sheet tight. "Whatever."

From his tone, it was clear that the audience was over. Amanda left, the isolation doors swishing closed behind her. She stopped at the desk and put in a request for child life to come by and see Tank.

"Don't know if they can," the clerk said with an exasperated tone. "His mother left strict orders that no one other than medical personnel is allowed to see him. Not sure if that includes child life or not; I'll have to check with Dr. Frantz." She didn't look too happy at the prospect. "You'd think that boy was some Hollywood star hiding out from the paparazzi or something, the way he acts."

Amanda glanced across the ICU to Tank's glassed-in cubicle. "No. He's just a lonely teenager. Needs someone to talk to."

"Well, according to his mother, he's not supposed to talk to anyone. Got the feeling it wasn't about protecting him, though—more about protecting her reputation or something. She seems embarrassed he's here, like it's some kind of secret."

Amanda sighed, glancing at the clock. Narolie should be back from CT. This running to and from pediatrics to take care of her was going to get old real fast. But if she didn't do it, who would? Certainly not Dr. Frantz. "Just see what you can do, please?"

"Sure thing, Amanda. But you owe me one," the clerk said with a smile as she grabbed the phone.

"Thanks."

"LYDIA, CAN WE TALK?" SETH COCHRAN WAS WAITing for Lydia as she emerged from a patient's room, looking more weary and distraught than she'd ever seen him before.

"Sure, let's use Mark's office." She told Jason where she was going and led Seth down the hall to the emergency department chief's office. Once inside, she closed the door for privacy and turned to Seth. "Does it have something to do with Nora?"

"How'd you know?"

"The only time you look that miserable is when it has something to do with Nora."

"Oh." He began twirling a pair of hemostats around his index finger, thinking hard. "How well do you know Tommy Z?"

"I don't *know* him at all." Lydia tried to keep her disdain from her voice.

"So you don't trust him?"

No, but she didn't say so out loud. Tommy Z and Glen Bakker were both on her radar—stooges for Tillman. And whatever the CEO had in mind, it had nothing to do with patient care or the welfare of her staff. "Why?"

"Tillman sent him up to the OR to talk to me, pulled me out of a case. 'Stress debriefing,' he called it, said it was mandatory. But I'm thinking Tillman wanted something else—knew something, something I'd told Tommy Z a while ago."

"You lost me."

He stared at her, assessing her. Lydia met his gaze without difficulty—she knew him well enough to know he'd talk if she just kept her silence. Most people did, especially people with something weighing heavily on them.

"You need to keep this in confidence," he started. "But I don't know who else to trust and I don't know what to do—"

Lydia said nothing, still waiting, then he blurted out, "Tillman was sleeping with Karen."

She blinked. Just like the megalomaniac Tillman to chase after a nurse. "How do you know?"

"Karen told me herself. Wanted to make me jealous or something. But I think it's worse; I think Tillman made Tommy Z tell him something—something I told him in confidence, something that might be bad for Nora."

"Why are you telling me?"

"Nora won't let me help her—hell, she won't even let me talk to her. I was hoping that maybe you could." He sank back against the desk, shoulders hunched. "Nora was attacked two years ago. Today she told me it was by the same man who killed Karen."

Lydia froze, processing the information. It explained so much—Nora's need to protect those close to her, her work with sexual assault patients, her rigid need for structure, control. Damn, she should have seen it.

If Tillman went public—he could ruin Nora's career. Not just through the public humiliation, but also by jeopardizing all the cases she'd worked on as a sexual assault examiner. Knowing that the nurse collecting the evidence was once a victim herself was the kind of fodder defense attorneys salivated over, claiming bias.

"Nora told you this?" she asked.

He nodded. "In June she told me she was raped on New Year's Eve, two years ago. That was the first she said anything. I kinda already knew maybe something was wrong. But it's not something you really can talk about, you know? Anyway, she said she was over it. Acted like it had been some kind of drunken mistake. She never told me any of the details, not until today." His hands clamped onto the edge of the desk. "Not until after I saw what that butcher did to Karen."

"Is that why you left Nora? Because she was raped?"

"God, no. Is that what she told you? What she thinks?" He scrubbed his palms over his face. "I wanted to marry her. I even went to a support group for families of rape victims, talked to Tommy Z. I couldn't stand the thought that I might hurt her—that anyone could ever hurt her again. And I was so angry, frustrated, felt so powerless . . ." His expression grew sorrowful, and he blinked slowly. "God, I never wanted to hurt her. But somehow that's all I seem able to do. Anyway, I screwed it all up."

Lydia scrutinized him. She liked Seth—but that didn't mean she was about to let him get near Nora again, maybe hurt her. "You screwed it up? Yeah, sleeping with Karen and letting the whole hospital see you might just do that."

He was shaking his head before she finished. "No one understands. I didn't sleep with Karen. I was so tied up in knots about asking Nora to marry me, about what I should do to protect her, make her happy, about doing all the right things so we could have a future together, that I started sleepwalking."

"Sleepwalking? Right."

"It's true. I haven't done it since I was a kid. Lucas can tell you—he even tested me in the sleep lab. Last month."

She pursed her lips, still not quite believing him. After all, Nora had seen him with Karen. Could someone really sleepwalk his way into a sexual encounter?

"You told Tommy Z about Nora, about the rape?" she asked.

"I wanted to know how to help her—it was supposed to be confidential. I thought I was helping."

"But you think Tommy Z told Tillman?"

"After what happened to Karen, Tillman is out for blood—he could fire Nora, ruin her career, or worse, tell the world about what happened to her."

No one could fake the pain that filled his face.

"No matter what we do, that might still happen. Did she tell Jerry Boyle about all this?"

"I don't think so. Not yet. Nora didn't report the assault when it happened. She's blaming herself for Karen."

"More than two-thirds of rapes go unreported. Nora shouldn't feel guilty—"

"Of course she shouldn't." He jerked his head up, ready to defend Nora. Lydia took that as a good sign. "I tried to tell her that, but, she won't listen to me. Lydia, you have to help me help her. It's not fair; she's been through so much."

"I think you already know what to do, Seth. Go to her, tell her the truth about you and Karen."

"I tried. She won't listen. And what if I make things worse? Screw up again?"

"Just be there for her."

He sucked in his breath and nodded slowly. "You're right."

"Leave Tillman and Tommy Z to me. I'll think of something."

"I DIDN'T KNOW YOUR FATHER WAS A LAWYER," Nora said, finally relaxing enough after a massage and facial to put her feet up on her chaise lounge as they waited for Gina's hair to process. Antonio and his staff had fed them a light lunch, and they now both sipped pomegranate mimosas. Well, Gina sipped. Nora held hers, staring at the beads of water sliding down the glass as if they held the secrets of the universe. Maybe not so relaxed, after all.

Gina took another drink to hide her discomfort at the mention of her father. Her family was a well-kept secret from almost everyone at Angels. Even her roommate, Amanda, had met Gina's parents, Moses and LaRose Freeman, only twice in passing. Gina had been mortified when LaRose had asked Amanda prying questions about her family in South Carolina. Amanda had lit up, describing the way her grandparents had run shrimp boats, but her father, foreseeing the demise of the family-run fishing business, had converted the family docks to an engine shop and now offered "house calls" to rich boat owners from Hilton Head to Isle of Palms.

Gina's mother had sniffed the air as if scenting diesel fuel, and when her father, the great and mighty Moses Freeman—one adjective was never enough to describe Moses—had shaken Amanda's hand, he'd scrutinized it as if she still had grease under her fingernails. And the way they treated Jerry . . . Gina's shoulders hunched in anger.

"My dad doesn't take many local cases," she said lamely, hoping Nora would drop it.

"Oh. Does he work for the government or something?"

Nora was only trying to distract herself from the events of the day, but Gina wished she'd picked another subject.

She blew out her breath and set her glass down with a bang. The attendant checking her hair jumped, then scurried from the room.

"No," she said as Nora looked at her expectantly. "My father is Moses Freeman."

Gina waited for the double take. Nora's eyes grew wide, then immediately narrowed. "You're kidding me. I thought Moses Freeman was—"

"A short, balding, fat Jewish guy. Yeah that's what everyone thinks when they hear the name. Something my father uses against them mercilessly." Actually, Moses Freeman did *everything* without mercy.

"So your dad's the personal-injury lawyer who single-handedly started Pennsylvania's malpractice crisis." Nora's lips quirked in an almost-smile.

Time for a change of topic. "You should see the dress I have for Saturday. This Vera Wang red silk. It's too bad Jerry won't be there."

"What do you mean? Of course Jerry will be there."

"I'm telling him not to come. He'll make me too nervous." The lies flew from her like sparks from a fire. What would Nora think if she told her that in reality she'd decided to tell Jerry to stay home because with her father in the audience, there was no way she could announce their engagement? She felt like enough of a fraud accepting this award as it was.

Worse, she couldn't get Ken Rosen's words out of her mind—that she was wrong for Jerry. It was as if Ken could speak a truth no one else, not even Gina except in her darkest moments, could acknowledge.

If she could figure out a way to skip the gala, she would.

Her hand trembled. A drop of pomegranate juice sparked bloodred as it splashed into her palm. She lifted her glass and drained it, imagining the expression on her father's face. Standing ovation, clapping, waiting for her to appear on stage . . . and she never did. Oh my, wouldn't that be a treat?

In her fantasy, Moses Freeman would be struck speechless for the first time ever.

NORA EDGED HER BUTT FORWARD IN THE DRIVER'S seat of her Honda. After dropping Gina off at EMS headquarters, she still hadn't gotten the seat to the right adjustment from where Gina, who was five-ten, had pushed it back.

It had felt strange, being driven by someone else in her own car. Not like this whole day hadn't been strange. Going from the ER to being massaged and painted and perfumed at Antonio's had been surreal. But at least she'd escaped the hospital rumor mill, and Gina's chatter had crowded aside thoughts of Karen.

Nora's house came into view, and she pulled into her parking space. The house's owner, Michelle "Mickey" Cohen, was a lawyer who worked for the ACLU and gave Nora free room and board in the second-floor apartment in exchange for light nursing duties. Nora had the feeling she was going to have to leave soon—Mickey had MS, but was on a new drug protocol that had worked wonders; she hadn't needed a wheelchair in weeks, and really there was nothing Nora was doing for her except providing dinner conversation.

Nora climbed out of the car, shivering in the chill evening air. The sun was already long faded from sight. She always hated how early the days ended during the winter. She walked up the brick path leading to the front steps. Mickey's law offices were on the first floor, so the front door was left unlocked during business hours. Nora entered and then stopped short.

Sitting on the reception couch, reading an out-of-date copy of *Sports Illustrated*, was Seth Cochran.

TEN

Thursday, 6:42 P.M.

AMANDA BEGAN HER EVENING IN RADIOLOGY, grabbing a resident to review Narolie's CT films with her. *Normal* was the disappointing diagnosis. Not that she wanted something to be wrong, but it would be nice to give Narolie a reason for her misery—something Amanda could help fix.

She trudged back upstairs to pediatrics and found Narolie in her room, alone. "How are you feeling?"

The girl sat up and turned to Amanda. "Better. Just a headache now, no more vomiting."

"Your test, the CAT scan, it was normal."

Narolie stared at Amanda for a long minute. "You, too—you think it is all inside my mind." A tear slipped from her eye. "What if you are right? How do I stop it? Make it go away?"

"Let's not jump to conclusions. I want to talk with you; I want to hear the whole story—when you began to get sick, what happened, everything." Amanda's pager chirped. She glanced at the display. The PICU.

"Talk, all they do is talk. They ask about school, if I think

I'm too fat, if my uncle touches me, all everyone wants is to talk."

Amanda's pager sounded again. Damn. "Narolie. I know this is hard on you. I'll be back. Sometime tonight. And I want to do more than talk. I want to listen."

The girl stared at her with suspicion. Then she nodded. "Okay. Tonight, I tell you anything."

"Okay." Amanda turned to the door. "Tell the nurses to call me if you need anything. I'll be back as soon as I can get free."

She left pediatrics and dashed up the steps to the PICU. "Someone paged?" she asked the clerk, her gaze immediately darting over to Zachary's bedside, expecting to find that he'd crashed. But all seemed quiet there.

The clerk pursed her lips. "Oh, yeah. Dr. Frantz wasn't too happy about your suggestion for a child life consult. Said you were now to officially oversee his patient's case and do whatever the parents ask you to."

"That's crazy; I've got other patients to take care of."

"Not according to Dr. Frantz. He said to consider his patient your only patient or, I quote, 'to reconsider your career options.' Sorry, Amanda. The guy's a real a-hole."

"That's okay. I can handle him. He's just a big ol' bully, and I learned how to deal with them back when I was in pigtails." Starting with her brother Andy, who was five years her senior and loved to torment her.

The clerk grinned at Amanda's Southern twang, made stronger by her irritation. "Leave me out of it from now on, okay? I need my job."

"Some things are more important than a job." Amanda turned to survey the PICU. "Like patient care." She went to check on Tank.

A tall blond woman in a red suit was pacing beside Tank's bed. "Oh, thank God," she said when Amanda entered, her words gushing out. "I keep calling and calling and nobody comes. Don't you people understand how sick he is?"

"What's wrong, Tank?" Amanda asked. Tank didn't look up, seemingly mesmerized by the video he was watching on his iPod.

"His fever is back and you people won't do anything about it!" the woman said. His mother, Amanda presumed.

Amanda glanced at the bedside chart. "They gave him acetaminophen less than twenty minutes ago."

"I know. And it's obviously not working. Feel him, he's burning up!"

Tank wasn't even sweating, although his skin did feel a little on the warm side.

"And these sheets," the woman continued, yanking up the corner of the hospital bedsheet. "I told them Harold is extremely sensitive. Organic cotton or silk only. We need to have these sheets changed immediately. Preferably silk."

Silk sheets in a hospital? "Ma'am, I don't think—"

"Don't think, do. Where's Dr. Freeman? She understands. I asked them to page her. Why isn't she answering?"

Because Gina was smart enough to stay far away from this crazy lady, Amanda thought. "Dr. Freeman doesn't work up here, Mrs. Trenton."

Mrs. Trenton stopped and wheeled on her heel. "I'm starting to think *no one* works around here." She patted Tank's shoulder dramatically. He didn't even look up. "Don't you worry, sweetheart, I'll get you everything you need." She pushed the bedside table with a covered tray of food toward Amanda. "You can take this away. It's inedible. Tank says he doesn't have much of an appetite, but could maybe eat some pierogies and a chocolate milkshake."

"Pierogies and a milkshake?" Did the lady mistake her for the dietitian?

"From the Bloomfield Bridge Tavern. I've already called in the order; they're waiting for you to pick it up."

There was a tap on the glass as the respiratory tech beckoned to Amanda to help him with Zachary's treatment. Thank God.

"I've got to go," Amanda muttered as she made her escape. "Another patient needs me."

"*I* need you." Mrs. Trenton's plaintive wail was cut off by the doors sliding shut.

"WHAT ARE YOU DOING HERE?" NORA ASKED SETH, loud enough to bring Mickey out from her office. She lowered her voice, hoping Mickey didn't have a client in there. "I told you to leave me alone."

"I asked him to stay and wait for you," Mickey said, handing Seth a DVD in a jewel case. The lawyer wasn't wearing a suit, but rather her off-duty attire: yoga pants and a wool cardigan. "You should listen to him, Nora. He convinced me, and I'm a born skeptic."

Nora looked from Mickey to Seth. "I have no idea what you're talking about, and I'm in no mood for puzzles. Do you need anything, Mickey?"

"No. In fact, why don't you take a few days off?"

"But—"

"No *but*s. You two go up and have a nice long chat. Watch Seth's home movies." She grinned mischievously at Seth. "Natalie's picking me up for bingo. I might be late; don't wait up." She gave Nora a jovial wave, gave Seth a thumbs-up and wink, and was gone.

Nora stared after her. She was glad to see Mickey feeling so good, but damn it, it was the worst timing. She spied a bouquet of lavender daylilies sitting on the reception desk—Seth's trademark. At least this time he'd brought only a single bouquet. A few months ago when he'd wanted to reconcile, he'd drowned her in flowers. Her shoulders slumped. She didn't have the energy to deal with Seth. Not tonight.

Seth climbed to his feet from the low-slung couch, working as if pushing a boulder up a hill, reminding her that his day had been as bad as hers. He held the DVD out to her, some kind of offering. She shoved it back into his hands without looking at it.

"I'm not in the mood for movies," Nora snapped, turning and starting up the steps to her apartment.

Seth followed her. Of course. It was too much to ask that he take a hint. "You shouldn't be alone. Not tonight."

"I told you, I'm fine." She unlocked the door to her apartment and let him inside. The space boasted high ceilings, wide windows, and hardwood floors. Spare Shaker-style furniture highlighted the clean angles, creating a welcoming yet uncluttered look.

"You could have come home to the town house," Seth said, following Nora's example as she kicked her shoes off at the door. "DeBakey would have loved to see you." DeBakey was the yellow lab they had shared while they lived together.

"It's your home now, not mine," she told him. His face tightened with a wince that echoed inside her. Damn it, she did *not* want to feel anything for this man. Why couldn't she stop feeling? Make herself numb like she had two years ago, after the attack?

He stepped closer to her, almost close enough to touch her, but kept his hands at his side, one thumb rubbing the seam of his jeans, the other hooked in his waistband. "Is there anything you need? Anything I can do?"

She sank onto the couch, too weary to stand and face him. "No, Seth. Go home. Just go home."

"I needed to see that you were all right." He stood silent for several seconds. "I remember the first time I saw you," he said, one hand opening and closing against his thigh as if he were trying to hold on to something. "Someone was out sick and they sent you up to the SICU to cover. You were so young. Everyone was thinking you'd fall apart. How could doling out Band-Aids for boo-boos compare to critical surgical patients?"

Despite herself, Nora smiled. The surgical ICU had

complex and critical patients, but it was a well-behaved, dainty lace doily compared to the ER's twisted skein of chaos. "Guess I showed them."

"Yeah, when that fresh coarct repair blew and there you were, helping me open his chest. Standing side by side, it was like you were in my head, handing me instruments without my saying anything; you knew exactly what I was going to do next before I did myself. Like we were two bodies with one mind."

He sank down beside her on the couch, closing his eyes. "I miss that feeling."

Nora watched him for a long moment while he couldn't see her. His eyes were hollowed with fatigue, new creases etched at the corners, his mouth also lined with worry. "So do I."

Without opening his eyes, he stretched his legs out and crossed his arms behind his head. "Good thing this couch is comfortable."

"Oh, no. You're not staying."

His eyes popped open and he sat up straight, serious once more. "Did you call Jerry Boyle yet? Tell him this nut job might be after you next?"

"You don't know that." The rasp of a knife, the stench of spray paint flitted through her mind. What if he did come after her again? Did to her what he had to Karen? Her chest tightened, lips tingling as the fear she'd held back all day flooded through her. She was hyperventilating, close to a full-blown panic attack.

Seth sensed it as well. He took both her hands in his and squeezed them tight. "Nora, you're smarter than that. C'mon, we'll go talk to Jerry right now. Then you can come home with me."

She didn't have any information that would help Jerry, nothing worth bothering him tonight. And now that she was home, surrounded by familiar things—including Seth's com-

forting presence, damn it—she couldn't stand the thought of
leaving, of facing her past. Of reliving it. "No. Not tonight.
But I will. He's meeting Lydia first thing in the morning. I'll
go over to her place, tell him then."

He stared at her, uncertain. "I have clinic tomorrow, but I
can cancel it. Go with you."

Panic fluttered through her again. She turned away. "No.
Don't do that."

"You still don't trust me."

All she could do was shrug, still not facing him, not wanting him to see the tears she was fighting.

He jumped up and snatched the DVD case from the table.
He strode across the room and slid it into the DVD player.

"I told you, I'm not in the mood for a movie."

He said nothing, but simply hit the play button and stepped
back. Static filled the screen, followed by a black-and-white
image of a patient monitor revealing heart rate, breathing,
oxygen levels, and an EEG tracing. Then she saw the name
on the monitor: SETH COCHRAN.

"I told you I had proof," he said, still facing away from
her, watching as the screen split, revealing a patient lying in
bed. Seth. "Lucas couldn't get me into the sleep lab until last
month, but if you watch, you'll see."

He fast-forwarded and suddenly there was Seth, crawling out of bed, stripping his clothes off. Naked, his hands
went through the motions of shaving, of dressing in invisible
clothing—all while the EEG recording on the monitor
showed him to be asleep.

Nora's vision blurred. No way Seth could fake *this*. Not
even with Lucas's help. Seth had been telling the truth.

But even if he had an explanation for what she'd seen in
that call room when she'd walked in on him and Karen, it
didn't solve all the problems they'd had.

"I wasn't lying." He finally turned to look over his shoulder. His gaze was filled with pleading.

"I see that." She stood, joining him in the middle of the floor. He surprised her by simply pulling her into a hug, letting her bury her face in his chest, not asking for anything more. Like he had earlier, after Karen died.

God, this was so hard—harder than she'd thought it would be. She couldn't change what had happened between them, but she could offer something more valuable: her trust.

Blinded by tears, her energy eroded by fear, craving the familiarity, the strength he offered, she said, "Stay. Just for tonight."

LUCAS ARRIVED AT THE PICU JUST AS AMANDA and the respiratory tech finished Zachary's treatment. She rushed over to him, feeling less tired at the sight of him.

"Hey, stranger," she said, stopping short of giving him the hug she wanted to give him. Instead she led him into the tiny dictation area behind the nurses' station and closed the door for privacy. "How was your day?"

"Finally over. Did you want to try to grab dinner before I go home? I have more floral arrangements and bridesmaid dresses we can go over."

"I wish, but I have a few things to finish before I can get free." Like talking to Zachary's parents, doing a complete history on Narolie, double-checking Tank's lab results . . . her mind drifted off, snagged by her to-do list. Lucas brought her back by waving an Almond Joy beneath her nose.

She snagged the candy bar, popping one morsel into her mouth and one into his. "Yum . . . now I know why I love you." She curled her arm through his and leaned her head on his shoulder as they chewed, side by side.

"Sorry I couldn't get that MRI scheduled for you," Lucas said. "I think I can get her in tomorrow afternoon. Maybe."

"Don't worry about it. There are only two things I want or need."

"Tell me, they're yours." His voice dropped into a lullaby-soft whisper, so unlike his usual neutral, public tone. This voice was for Amanda only, and it gave her shivers every time he used it.

"I want to match here for my residency with no worries about either of our jobs."

"With your grades and recommendations, that's an easy one. No matter what Frantz says. The pediatrics program here would be crazy not to rank you number one in the residency match." He tilted his head, a lock of hair falling into his eyes as he glanced down at her shyly. "What's the second thing?"

She grabbed hold of the lapels of his lab coat and stood on tiptoe so that she was level with his gaze. "I want to live the rest of my life with you happily ever after for ever and ever, amen."

She kissed him. He responded, leaning forward and coming perilously close to bracing himself against the wall before pulling back and wrapping his arms around her, holding her tight.

She laughed as he rebalanced. When they found a place to live, it was going to have to have walls of stainless steel so he wouldn't have to worry about germs. As crazy as that sounded, she didn't care.

"Amen," he whispered when they parted. "What's so funny?"

"Nothing. I'm just the luckiest girl in the world, that's all."

"Guess that makes me the luckiest guy."

"Seriously, though. You don't have to do any of this wedding stuff. My mom can do it all and we can relax, just show up."

"No. That would be the wedding she always dreamed of. I want to give you the wedding you always dreamed of."

That was definitely worth another kiss.

Too bad the pounding on the door interrupted them. "Dr. Mason?" Mrs. Trenton's voice barreled through the thin door. "Harold needs his dinner. Now, Dr. Mason. Or do I need to call Dr. Frantz?"

LYDIA LET HERSELF INTO HER BOSS'S OFFICE AND turned on the computer. A twinge of guilt ran through her as she examined the flash drive Jerry Boyle had given her. Trey would already be home by now, getting dinner for them.

Trey had lived in the Craftsman-style bungalow on the other side of the cemetery before she had, fixing it up for his mother's real estate company. Then she'd bought it, and now they lived there together. Maria would have said it was meant to be. That they were meant to be.

At first Lydia had been overwhelmed by all the space—not to mention the freedom and privacy. Fourteen hundred square feet all to herself. But now that Trey was there with her, it felt like sometimes there was no place to go. Not that she wanted or needed to hide anything from Trey, just that he somehow filled the house. His presence, even when he was gone, was everywhere.

She toyed with the flash drive. She could go home, use the computer there, but she didn't want Trey to be a part of this. Not yet. Not until she knew more of the truth herself.

Stop stalling, she told herself, inserting the drive into the USB port. She forced herself to go through the numerous files in order, so as to not miss anything, instead of randomly clicking on files with names that sounded promising. A lot of it was boring bureaucratic record keeping written in the dry language common to law enforcement, blurry scanned copies of poorly typed reports.

Was Maria even her mother? The thought kept pounding at her, and she was tempted to skip to the medical examiner's report. She'd been twelve when Maria was killed. They'd had DNA testing back then, rudimentary compared with today's technology, but they could still have easily proven parentage.

She refused to give in to the temptation to click to the autopsy protocol—too painful if the truth was bad news. All her life she'd learned not to form attachments, but here she was, attached to something she'd never realized could be taken away. Her own identity.

Living with Maria, she'd never known how long they'd be at any one place. Lydia could never count on going to the same school from one week or month to the next, much less having the same teacher, seeing the same kids—forget about friends.

If Maria got one of her urges to run, they ran. No questions asked—or as Maria liked to say, "No regrets." Later, in foster care, Lydia had learned very fast to protect what was hers or it would be taken from her. All she'd managed to hang on to were two photos of her and Maria together, as well as Maria's only legacy: a charm bracelet Lydia had worn around her ankle, under her sock, hidden from covetous eyes. Now that Lydia was an adult she no longer wore the bracelet, but she'd placed it in a small red and purple paisley silk bag that Maria would have liked.

As she read, memories flitted through her mind like pages turning in a photo album. The LAPD had done a thorough job—as thorough as they could with no victim identification. Lydia began to make a list of possible questions. It seemed likely that the photo of her and Maria, which had appeared in a local L.A. weekly, was connected to Maria's death somehow. Maybe if Lydia had never won that damn contest, then whatever Maria had been running from would have never caught up with her.

Smeared copies of Maria's three fake driver's licenses flashed onto the screen. Marie Ferraro, the name she'd been using when she was killed; Mary Fuentes; Maria Fiore. Maria always used birthdates in February—the fourth, fourteenth, and twenty-fourth—although she varied the year. She let Lydia keep her real birthday, March 25. At least Lydia hoped it was real—and not another lie.

Could Maria have been born in February on one of those three dates? Was she really thirty when she died? The same age Lydia was now. Strange to think she would live longer than her mother had.

The list of questions grew as Lydia questioned everything she knew as a "fact" about her mother and compared it with the LAPD file. Then finally, the medical file appeared. Lydia pulled away as the screen filled with a diagram of a naked woman revealing a multitude of wounds. Images of the real attack, in Technicolor slow motion undimmed by memory, ricocheted through her vision.

She quickly clicked to the next page and the next, skipping over the recitation of Maria's injuries. Then she found the ancillary tests. Maria's blood alcohol had been only 0.07—practically sober for her. No other drugs in her system except marijuana. Her blood type was the same as Lydia's, AB positive, pretty rare. And yes, there was a genetic comparison test as requested by the Department of Child Welfare for one "Jane Doe #17, aka Lydia Fiore."

Lydia's finger shook as she clicked to the results. A sob choked her vision. She blinked and focused on the words. Maria was her mother. Was really her mother.

Emotion overwhelmed her. Lydia cursed her weakness, cursed Jerry Boyle for making her doubt, cursed Maria for living the kind of life where her only child could take nothing for granted.

She laid her head on the desk and let herself cry. Might as well get it all out before she faced Trey. Her shoulders shuddered as reawakened grief tore through her.

For someone who had fought all her life against forming any attachments, she was suddenly tied down by responsibilities: a house, friends, co-workers, Trey . . . not to mention his large and loving but meddlesome family.

And now one more: finding out who her mother really was. Not just a name, who the person was.

No more lies. Lydia wouldn't stop until she found the truth.

She rubbed her palms against her arms, fighting a sudden chill. What had Maria been running from? What had been worth risking her and Lydia's lives?

ELEVEN

Thursday, 7:37 P.M.

GINA PICKED UP HER BMW FROM EMS HEAD-quarters and debated where to go next. Amanda was on call and Jerry would be working all night, but Gina didn't want to eat alone—too much temptation to binge. She'd been doing so well these past two months. Deciding to play Good Samaritan, she drove over to Diggers, the restaurant across Penn Avenue from Angels, ordered some comfort food to go, and took it over to the medical center.

She drove past the cemetery, where a crowd of hospital workers coming off shift were gawking through the fence. Instead of parking in the employee garage, she drove around to the other side of the medical center where the patient garage sat, closer to the main entrance.

Gina was walking from her car, her hand shoved inside one of the bags, rummaging for a curly fry when a man called her name. She jerked, dropping the bag, her heart leaping to her throat.

"Sorry," Glen Bakker said as he jogged over to scoop up

the grease-stained bag. He inhaled its contents. "Mmm. Smells good."

"Damn it, Glen! Don't sneak up on people like that!" Gina's heart took a moment to settle back to its normal resting place and rhythm.

"Didn't mean to startle you. I was just on patrol and thought it might be best if I walked with you. Not a good time for women to be walking alone, you know?"

"You're right. Thanks." She took the bag from him, opened it, and offered him some fries. "I heard about Karen. Do they have any idea who did it?"

"The cops?" Glen shook his head. "They have no idea."

"Sounds like you might."

He was silent for a moment. "Maybe. I don't know. But once when I was covering a night shift I came across Karen and Mr. Tillman alone in his office. After midnight and she wasn't dressed for work, if you get my drift."

"Karen and Tillman?" An image of the pompous CEO and Karen together filled Gina's mind. It wasn't an image she wanted to dwell on. "Ew, gross."

They reached the hospital's main entrance. Glen touched his forehead in a salute as he held the door open for her. "Call me or one of my men when you're ready to leave. Or partner up with someone else—we don't need any more excitement around here."

"Yes, sir." Gina left him, still trying to digest the idea of Tillman and Karen together. Talk about sleeping your way to the top—but Tillman? She shuddered and stepped into the elevator, heading to the PICU.

Amanda scowled at Gina's comfort-food offering, putting a definite damper on the warmhearted glow Gina had been indulging. "Your patient is a jerk, and his mother is a witch."

"My patient?" Gina asked, pulling up a chair, smiling at Amanda's vehemence. Nice to see that the Southern belle was learning how to call it like it was. They were in the PICU

break room, a tiny glass-walled cubicle with microwave, refrigerator, table, and four chairs. Amanda drew the curtains,
concealing them from sight of everyone in the PICU, then
joined Gina.

"Yeah. Harold Trenton."

"Tank." Gina took a piece of fried chicken, leaving the
drumstick because she knew that was Amanda's favorite. "The
parents are friends of my parents—I think I met them once at
some shindig at the club. Wait 'til you meet the grandfather;
he's a pompous SOB. A chiropractor; he'll no doubt lecture
you on the harm your modern medicine is doing to innocent
patients. I'm surprised he didn't insist Tank register under an
assumed name so that none of his patients learn that he let
his grandson be treated by anyone else."

"I don't understand how anyone puts up with their attitude."

"Hey, they want what's best for Tank." Gina wasn't sure
why she felt compelled to defend the Trentons. Except she
had liked Tank. "And I think there was some kind of scandal,
something to do with the dad, I don't know."

"Haven't met the father yet." Amanda didn't sound too
excited by the prospect. "But don't they understand that
they're obstructing their son's care? Not to mention the well-
being of other patients—"

"You mean the other patient you and Lydia wanted to get
that bed. Could have told you Frantz would win."

"He friends with your folks as well?"

"Who knows? Probably. Doesn't matter. It's all about attitude and getting what you want."

"You'd think they'd be more concerned about getting
what their kid needs. Instead of wasting time arguing about
the kind of sheets he gets and his food—do you know she
actually wanted me to leave my patients and go over to the
Bloomfield Bridge Tavern to get him some pierogies? Who
does she think I am?"

Gina didn't answer—the truth was that the Trentons and people like them never saw people like Amanda as anything but objects, instruments of their instant gratification. Once upon a time the realization would have made Gina feel angry, but now she just felt ashamed.

Amanda surprised her by reaching across the table to grab Gina's hand. "Hey. You got a manicure." She squinted at Gina's face. "And a facial. And your hair done."

"I didn't have a choice. I took Nora to Antonio's for a spa day, and she wouldn't get anything done unless I did as well." Gina smirked. There was a definite upside to playing nursemaid for a day.

Amanda frowned, looking chagrined. "I almost forgot about Karen. I heard it was bad—"

"Had to be to shake up Nora like that. I've never seen her lose it like she did today."

"I wish there were something we could do to help."

"What's to help with? Not like the guy is going to come after her."

"Do you think Seth could be involved? He was seeing Karen, wasn't he?"

"Seth? No way." Gina munched on an onion ring. "Besides, I heard a rumor that Karen was sleeping with Tillman."

"Mr. Tillman, the hospital CEO?" Amanda leaned forward—gossip was one of her weaknesses. "Do you think he could have killed Karen?"

LYDIA LEFT THE ER AND BEGAN WALKING HOME. As she passed the cemetery, she had to dodge the growing pile of flowers, stuffed animals, and votives left on the sidewalk in Karen's memory. The cemetery's gates were chained shut, and a uniformed police officer stood guard outside them.

Lydia shivered as she passed him, her steps quickening, restraining herself from running the two blocks to her house on the other side of the cemetery. She tried to shrug away the sudden fear, thankful for the nine-millimeter she carried in her parka pocket.

After being attacked in her own home a few months ago, she'd gotten a gun permit, learned how to shoot, and now carried the Para Carry-9 with her whenever she was out alone. At first she'd felt conflicted—after all, she'd seen and treated enough gunshot wounds to know the danger a handgun posed. But somehow it all seemed different when it was her own life on the line.

Lydia turned the corner from Penn onto Merton Street, gripping the nine-millimeter. Instantly the noise of the city traffic was muted by the thick growth of evergreens. There were two houses here at the corner, then her house, which sat alone down a long tree-lined drive at the end of the cul-de-sac. As she passed from the last glow of light from the houses and headed toward her drive, a dark form stepped out of the bushes in front of her. A flashlight clicked on, blinding her for a moment.

Lydia's grip on her gun tightened. She brought her free hand up to shield her vision from the light. Adrenaline raced through her, finding her fear and replacing it with a calm certainty that reminded her of how she felt when a fresh trauma came in. Her senses sharpened as she identified the sound of a man breathing, the fact that he held nothing in his hands except the flashlight, and the stench of his cologne: coconut, rum, and Iron City beer.

"Pete Sandusky, put that light down," she ordered. She kept her hand on her weapon, but as her fear and adrenaline fled, it was more about having something to hang on to than being prepared to use it. Pete was harmless, physically at least.

"Hey, Lydia! About time." The light flicked off. "I'm freezing my balls off out here."

"Glad to see you're doing your part to protect the future survival of the species."

"Ha, ha. Very funny. Listen, you need to fill me in on what's going on. What can you tell me about Karen Chisholm's death? The police haven't officially released her name, are just saying that a woman was assaulted and then died at Angels, but my sources tell me it was Karen and she was murdered."

"What sources?"

He smiled, moonlight reflecting off his brilliant white teeth. Too bad they were a bit crooked, marring the image. "I'm in negotiations with someone who can get me photos of her body. Said it was a real freak show. But I need confirmation before I invest that heavily. Know what I mean?"

"Pictures?" Lydia would have ignored Pete, told him to go to hell, but she remembered the photos Nora had taken as part of the rape kit.

"I saw the cop on duty back there." He jerked his head toward Angels and the cemetery. "So the assault actually took place on top of a grave?" He seemed excited as he pulled out his digital recorder. "And this graffiti? Was it gang related? Or maybe a satanic cult? Were there multiple attackers?"

"No comment. Put that recorder away. I'm not giving you anything for the record."

He shrugged and repocketed the recorder. It was still running, Lydia was certain. Pete wasn't one to worry about little things like off-the-record.

"Who's selling the photos?" she demanded.

"Lydia, you know me better than that. I never reveal my sources."

"Fine. I'll tell the police that you have stolen crime-scene evidence."

"I don't have anything. Yet." They stared at each other for a long moment. Then Pete surrendered. "Guess I'm barking up the wrong tree here. I'll hunt down Nora Halloran."

"Nora?" Lydia tried to play it cool, like she didn't know Nora was intimately involved.

"Nora. My source says that after Karen died, she said words to the effect that she had somehow caused Karen's death. Did something go wrong in that OR?"

TWELVE

Thursday, 8:13 P.M.

AMANDA FINALLY FOUND TIME TO MAKE IT BACK downstairs to the pediatric floor. She had just begun obtaining Narolie's history when she saw a familiar shadow lurking at the door. "Tank, what are you doing here? You could be contagious!"

"The nurse said I could take my monitor off when I go use the john—I just decided to find one down here." Tank sounded defensive but didn't meet her gaze. He scuffed his slippers. Somehow, despite all the people parading in and out of his room, he seemed lonelier than Narolie.

"Hello there," Narolie said, sounding like the perfect hostess. "Please come in. I'm Narolie Maxeke."

"I'm Tank." He looked around the room. "Wow, you get this place all to yourself? Way cool. What are you in for?"

Narolie frowned. "That is what Dr. Amanda is working to discover. She is the best doctor I have met."

"I know." Tank seemed aware that he'd said too much and

quickly covered with, "She's okay for a doctor, I guess."

"Tank, you need to be back in your room," Amanda said, although it was hard to be annoyed with him, even if he had broken all the rules. Poor kid seemed so lonely. "You shouldn't be wandering the halls without a mask on—you don't want to make anyone else sick, do you?"

"Shit. I forgot. But I feel fine, really."

"Still, we can't take a chance." Tank was standing at the end of Narolie's bed, far enough that contagion shouldn't be a worry. But Amanda wasn't going to risk it. "Sit over there, across the room in that chair, and you two can talk while I go find you a mask."

To her surprise, Tank obeyed her without question. "Is this okay?"

Now a good eight feet separated the two—and three was all that was required per CDC protocols. "That's fine. I'll be right back."

Amanda left as the two teens from different planets began chatting. No surprise that by the time she returned it was obvious Tank had fallen under Narolie's spell. She let them talk a few more minutes, gratified by the relaxed expressions on their faces as they compared the merits of *The Scarlet Letter*, which they were both studying. Finally she handed Tank his mask. "Time to go."

He started to plead for more time, and then his shoulders slumped in defeat. "It was nice to meet you, Narolie."

"Please come visit me again, Tank. I enjoy your company," Narolie said, her eyes downcast as if embarrassed by her admission.

Amanda ushered Tank out into the hall. For the first time since she'd met him, Tank smiled. "I can see her again, can't I? She's cool, for a girl, I mean. Smart, too."

Amanda couldn't stop her grin of delight as she accompanied Tank back up to his PICU bed. Wouldn't Mrs. Trenton love *this* budding scenario?

Tank seemed to read her thoughts. "You won't tell my mom, will you? She has enough on her mind."

Like driving Amanda crazy. Silk sheets!

"No, of course not." They reached the threshold to the PICU. Tank hesitated.

"Can I hang with you?" he asked. "Just for a while. I don't like this place, it's creepy."

"Are your parents coming back tonight?"

He looked away, his shoulders trembling as if he were holding something back. "Everyone keeps lying, saying my dad's at work. He's not."

His voice was so low that Amanda could barely hear him. She moved them away from the doors, down the hall where they'd have more privacy. "What happened, Tank?"

"I'm not supposed to tell." He fought to bring his gaze up to her face. "You know that rich guy in New York, the one that took like fifty billion dollars from people? My dad worked with him. Guess he was going to be in trouble or something, because he left. No one knows where he went."

Amanda took Tank's hand. "Tank. I'm so sorry."

He focused on a crack on the wall, tracing it with his finger. "Mom's kind of lost it—she can't tell anyone, but there's like no money left. We even had to move in with my grandfather."

His lips narrowed into a pale, single line. "I hate him. But now he and my mom are fighting. Over me. He says she's not a fit mother. Says she's why my dad left. Wants a judge to take me away from her. So she has to watch every move she makes. And that turns her into this wicked witch I don't even know anymore."

"It's okay, Tank. What's important is getting you better." Amanda didn't know what else she could offer him.

He tugged his hand free from Amanda's to swipe it across his eyes. "Don't even know why I told you all that. Nothing anyone can do."

His sigh echoed from the wall and died as they turned back to the PICU.

"NOTHING HAPPENED, PETE." LYDIA STARED THE reporter down. "Nora didn't do anything wrong. No one did."

He merely grinned and shrugged his surrender. "Guess we'll see about that. See you around, Lydia."

She watched him walk down to the corner and disappear into the darkness, then finished the short walk to her house. The winter night held the small Craftsman cottage in a tight embrace. In the distance, a few twinkles of light from the upper floors of the medical center could be seen, and the only other light came from the flickering glow of the TV in the front room.

Fighting a tinge of irritation—Trey couldn't have turned the porch light on?—Lydia drew close enough to see him lying on the couch watching TV. Not ready to go inside yet, she circled around through the dark carport where her vintage Triumph motorcycle was parked. She'd inherited the bike from one of the first people she'd met in Pittsburgh—Mickey Cohen's legal assistant. Now the Triumph represented freedom, escape.

She could see well enough in the dark to make out the sleek silhouette of the classic motorcycle. Unable to resist, she swung her leg over the seat and sat there. How easy it would be to speed off into the night, anonymous, unfettered, leaving everything behind.

Was this how Maria had felt when she fled her old life? This gut-pitching feeling of terror and excitement? Anticipation of new places, new choices, new challenges—like when Lydia left L.A. to come here to Pittsburgh. Or had it been more like a chance to erase the past, start over, nothing weighing her down?

Except for a child. A child Maria had never abandoned. That had to count for something. But sitting in the dark, straddling the Triumph, Lydia couldn't deny the anger she felt toward her mother. If she'd meant so much to Maria, why had Maria lied to her?

The door into the house opened and Trey stood there, framed in the warm light spilling out from the kitchen. "Why are you sitting in the dark like that?" he asked, his mellow baritone shaded with annoyance. He was wearing sharply creased slacks, a pale blue dress shirt, and his good wool overcoat. "We're late. Are you ready to go or do you need to change?"

Shit. "It's Thursday." Lydia dismounted the motorcycle, the flash drive jammed into her jeans pocket digging into her hip.

"Of course it's Thursday. The kids were hungry so Mom had to serve dinner, but she said she'd hold dessert for us." He stepped to her, bundling her in his arms and giving her a quick kiss. Then he snagged her hands in his. "You're freezing. Why didn't you wear your gloves?"

All the better to hold her gun in case the man who killed Karen came after her. Or was waiting to ambush her when she got home. Or broke into her house and tried to kill her like that maniac a few months ago.

But she couldn't say any of that—Trey didn't know she'd bought the gun, much less had begun carrying it with her when she left the house. He thought that his moving in with her was protection enough. Like a peace-loving, huggable teddy bear of a man could stop a killer.

"I forgot them," she lied.

He rubbed her hands between his, sharing his warmth as he led her out to his truck. "I don't wonder, day you guys had over there. Is Nora okay?"

There was no answer to that. Who knew? Instead Lydia climbed into the truck as Trey held the door for her—despite the fact that he knew perfectly well that she could open it herself. That was just the kind of guy he was.

"The porch light burned out," he said as he drove them to

Regent Square and his parents' house. "But we're out of lightbulbs."

"Top shelf of the pantry."

"Oh. Guess I didn't look hard enough. I was checking the basement and carport."

It was still awkward, the give-and-take of sharing a living space. Or maybe it was Lydia who made it that way—she wanted Trey there, loved having him there, but sometimes it felt like a lot of work.

"I wasn't sure if they'd crack out in the cold, so I put them in the pantry."

"Right. Surfer girl isn't used to our winters."

"I just want to see the sun again." She stared out her window at the colorful Christmas lights that adorned most of the houses, trees, and yards that they passed. "When does the sun come back?"

"Wait until your first good snow. You'll love it." They pulled up to his parents' two-story colonial, parking behind a Dodge Caravan and an Explorer with a PROUD PARENTS OF A BEECHWOOD HONOR STUDENT bumper sticker in the back window.

Lydia jumped out before Trey could walk around to get the door for her. Damn, she'd forgotten the kids would be here. She couldn't walk in with a loaded gun in her pocket. She pulled the Para Carry-9 out, released the magazine, and removed it. Trey arrived in time to see her yank the slide back to clear the bullet from the chamber.

"What the hell is that?" he asked.

"It's safe now," she answered, securing the ammunition in the glove compartment and zipping the now-empty compact nine-millimeter into her inside parka pocket.

"That's not an answer. What the hell are you doing carrying a handgun?"

Trey's obvious horror surprised her. After all, he'd grown up around guns, in a family of cops. Before she could answer, Ruby, Trey's mother, opened the door, releasing several squealing kids into the night. They ranged from four to ten and raced down the walk to be the first to greet their uncle, whom they leaped on like he was a human jungle gym. A few shyly hugged Lydia as well.

Trey laughed and made fake groaning noises like Frankenstein's monster as he hauled two hanging on his legs and one on his back across the porch. "Hiya, Mom," he said, almost losing the girl on his back as he leaned over to kiss Ruby.

"Kids, let Trey and Lydia get their coats off and some food in them before you ambush them," Ruby commanded, and the children scattered. "Lydia, how are you?" she asked, giving Lydia a warm hug. "I heard on the news there was trouble over at Angels today."

"Good evening, Ruby," Lydia said. The last thing she wanted to talk about was Karen's murder. "Sorry we're late."

"Denny had his ear glued to that darn scanner, so we knew Trey would be home on time." Trey's father, Denny, was a retired Allegheny County deputy, and Trey's two brothers and one of his sisters had followed their father into law enforcement. "But I guess there's never any accounting when the ER's going to get backed up, is there?"

Ruby's voice was tinged with disapproval. Of course she'd immediately picked up the tension between Lydia and Trey—the woman was a walking radar.

Lydia and Ruby had an uncertain relationship. Ruby had made it clear that she liked Lydia, but she also seemed to realize that Lydia had some hard edges—sharper than anyone, especially Trey, appreciated.

They shed their coats and joined the rest of the family around the large dining room table. Patrice, Trey's other sister, began serving apple dumplings, complete with hot caramel sauce and ice cream. The men talked about the holes in the Steelers' offensive line, while Ruby refilled coffee cups for the adults and milk for the kids. "Trey, Lydia, do you want me to heat up the London broil?"

"Maybe after, Mom," Trey said, digging into his dumpling. "You know what they say: life's too short, eat your dessert first!"

The kids laughed at that. Lydia took a bite of her dumpling. Much better than any roast. "Did you make these?"

"I did," Patrice said. "Enrollment is pretty low at the dance studio, so I have plenty of time on my hands."

That rolled into a discussion of the economy, but Lydia couldn't help but notice that Ruby's glance kept returning to her. And Ruby didn't look happy.

"So, Lydia," she finally said, setting her cup down onto her saucer with a clink. "I'm so glad you're going to join us on Saturday for our annual cookie bake."

Lydia held back her groan. She'd totally forgotten that Trey had volunteered her to help the "girls" bake the Christmas goodies.

"I'm looking forward to it," she lied.

"We were sorry you missed Thanksgiving. Can we expect you for Christmas dinner?"

There was a sudden hush as all eyes turned on Lydia. All except Trey. He seemed fascinated by the remnants of his dumpling, leaving Lydia to fend for herself.

She glanced at him, saw the hunch in his shoulders, the way he gripped his spoon, and realized how much her answer meant to him.

"Yes, ma'am. I'm working Christmas Eve but have Christmas Day off, so we should be here." As soon as the words were out, Lydia's nerves twanged with anxiety. Now she was committed to a full day of smiling small talk, exposing herself to their questions—Patrice, in particular, always took every opportunity to probe Lydia's "mysterious" past—and enduring their patience when she made the inevitable faux pas. Like almost bringing a loaded gun into a house filled with kids.

Trey reached for her hand under the table and gave it a gentle squeeze. His shoulders were relaxed, his smile now wide and genuine, so she guessed it was worth it. She didn't have to force her smile as she met his gaze.

"Trey, did you get your tree put up yet?" Patrice asked.

"We're not getting a Christmas tree," Trey answered.

"Why not?" Ruby asked, her tone slicing through the dinner table chatter surrounding them.

Lydia jumped in—better that she take the hit than Trey. After all, it was her decision. "It's silly to kill a beautiful living thing and bring it into the house to watch it die."

Another thud of silence. The children looked at her, eyes wide, mouths open. "How's Santa going to know where to put your presents?" one asked.

"Mommy, our tree's not *dead*, is it?" another wailed.

Ruby arched an eyebrow at Lydia. "I'm sure that's not what Lydia meant. Is it, Lydia?"

Lydia swallowed. Her cheeks flushed with a warmth that spread down her neck and chest. She met Ruby's gaze and realized she'd been less nervous about walking past Angels' dark cemetery with a killer on the loose than she was facing Trey's mother.

Family. Maybe she was better off without one.

THERE WERE MUDDY FOOTPRINTS ALL OVER NORA'S floor. In her sleep, she flailed about, trying to wipe them clean. But they turned to a sticky, smelly goo, flashing bright neon colors. The scent made her throat close tight. Sweet and sharp.

"Do you know me?" A man's voice, soft and insidious, kept time with her movements as she knelt on the floor, trying to clean. She couldn't see the man, couldn't tell where he was; his voice sounded all around her, crept inside her head. *"You know me, don't you?"*

"No, no, I don't. I don't know you. I don't know you!" She repeated the words, whispering, crying, shouting them.

The sticky mess covered the floor, covered her hands; she

couldn't scrub it off her naked body. Now a new color was added: red, bloodred, it flowed over her hands. With it came a new smell, not sweet at all. Salty, coppery.

Death was in that smell, was inside her as she breathed it in. She began to choke and gag, tearing at her flesh.

"Get it off! Get it off!" she cried out, her voice startling her awake.

Her eyes were open; she was in her room, in her bed. Clawing at the sheets, tears streaming down her face, mingling with the sweat that poured from her as terror stampeded her pulse. Then a man's form appeared in the doorway.

Instead of fueling her fear, she felt calmed. Seth rushed to her side, pulling her tight into his arms, rocking her, cooing soft nonsense words until she could breathe again.

"I'm okay," she whispered, her voice still hoarse from her panic.

"You're okay." Seth soothed her hair with his fingers. "You're okay."

Her lips and fingers tingled from hyperventilating. Her head pounded as adrenaline and fear subsided. She held a hand out before her. No paint, no blood.

"I'm okay." This time it was a statement of fact. She slid free of Seth's embrace and threw back the covers. Her nightgown was soaked through with sweat, reeking of fear.

She went into the bathroom, stripped naked, and showered the stench away. By the time she emerged, dressed in clean pajamas, wrapped in a comforting flannel robe, Seth was waiting for her in the kitchen, a pot of milk heating on the stove.

"Half cocoa, half cinnamon tea, just the way you like it," he said, mixing the concoction he had created for her night terrors when they'd lived together.

She took the mug from him and withdrew to the living room to avoid the mess he'd left behind in her kitchen. She'd deal with it in the morning.

Curling up on the chair, she sipped the soothing drink. "I wish DeBakey were here."

Seth walked in, carrying his own mug, and sat on the side of the couch nearest to her. "You can come home. Anytime. Or he can come here. Anytime. You know that."

She shrugged one shoulder. She did know that. But she didn't have the heart to confuse the dog. Not to mention breaking her heart fresh every time she'd have to see Seth to exchange custody. Hard enough to see him at work where she could divorce her feelings from her job.

"Who's taking care of him tonight?"

"Bradley." The kid who lived next door and whose mother was deathly allergic to dogs. Or so she said. She didn't seem to have any problem with Bradley watching DeBakey before and after school and on nights when Seth was on call. "He's having a hard time with his dad again, so I think he sees our place as a refuge. Kid's practically been living there since I came back on the trauma service."

Nora nodded. Bradley's dad was in the National Guard and was a strict disciplinarian when he was home, which wasn't often.

A comfortable silence settled between them. She finished her drink but pretended to keep sipping, not wanting to leave Seth's company. Things had been so good—she and Seth, what they had had was good. Until she made the mistake of telling him about her rape.

Then things had changed. Seth had changed. Watching her constantly—she'd seen the questions in his eyes, but he never asked them aloud. He was solicitous, but after that night when she'd told him, he hadn't tried to make love to her again. Barely touched her. Like she would break—or was already broken.

Not that their love life had ever been stellar. She'd always wondered why a guy as handsome as Seth, a guy who could have any woman he wanted, had put up with her. She tried her best to act normal during sex, but it was always an act, he had to know that. And then there were her night terrors, her fear of the dark, her panic attacks.

No wonder it had been so easy to believe that he'd turned to a woman like Karen. Karen could meet his needs—all of them. Fun, sexy, beautiful Karen. Perfect for Seth, the answers to his prayers.

Anger burned through her. That she'd been so stupid— that he had let her go. Even if she believed his sleepwalking excuse, that didn't explain everything. He must have wanted to let her go, and his subconscious had sent him into Karen's arms. Made it possible for them to break up without him telling her the real reason: she was damaged goods.

She stood up and set the mug on the table, resisting the urge to take it to the kitchen and wash it. "I'm going back to bed."

He sat on the couch, elbows on his thighs, looking up at her, holding his mug with two hands. "Are you sure you're okay?"

"I'm fine."

He gave her a sharp look. "Right."

"Okay, maybe I'm not. But I'm alive. That's got to count for something." Her anger spilled over into her words, giving them an edge. It felt good.

"Of course it does." He got up, leaving his mug beside hers on the coffee table. He stepped around the table to her side. "Nora—"

"No, Seth. Don't." She grabbed the mugs and fled to the kitchen. He followed, watching from a safe distance as she gave in to the urge to clean up, finding solace in the repetitive movements.

"Don't what?" he finally asked as her movements grew less frenzied. "Try to help?"

"Just don't. It's hard enough taking care of myself right now. I just don't—" She turned to him, a damp sponge in her hand, her voice cracking. "I don't have energy to worry about you, too."

His face creased, and she thought he might cry. Instead, he stepped to her. He took the sponge from her, threw it in the sink, and took her hand, leading her to her bedroom. "Why don't you try letting me do the worrying for a change?"

He tucked her in as if she were a child—and it felt good to let someone else take charge, even if it was only for a few moments. She didn't feel like she was surrendering or giving anything up, more that she was being taken care of. Cherished.

She'd forgotten how good that felt. Decadent. So much better than any spa day indulgence. Just a man caring for a woman.

Her anger and churned-up emotions calmed as she watched him double-check her window locks and turn all the lights on—he knew she couldn't sleep in the dark. But then he surprised her, crawling in on the other side of the bed.

"Seth—"

"Shhh . . . ," he murmured, spooning her, fitting just right. "I'm only going to hold you, be here for you. That's all. It's okay to need something every once in a while. And right now you need sleep."

His words whispered against the back of her head as she finally nodded her assent and relaxed in his embrace. Then, before she realized it, she fell asleep.

THIRTEEN

Friday, 6:32 A.M.

AMANDA WOKE WITH A GROAN. SHE'D PROMISED the Millers she'd stay with Zachary to give them time to go home, sleep in their own bed, see their other children, shower, and feel normal for a few hours at least. That had meant catching a short nap curled up in the vinyl bed-chair at Zachary's bedside.

"Morning," Lucas's voice greeted her. No surprise; the man put early birds to shame, barely needed sleep at all. One of the few things she hated about him. "Let's get you some breakfast."

She glanced at Zachary—the monitor readings were stable—then stood and stretched. "I don't know how parents sleep in those things," she said indicating the combo chair-recliner-bed. "There are lumps and pokes where I didn't even know I had places to poke."

"It's this rotation. You're losing weight. Breakfast?"

"Can't. I have to get my numbers for rounds." She did manage to surreptitiously grasp his hand as she moved past him to look over the ECMO tech's shoulder. To her surprise, he actually held on for a long moment.

"Got 'em." Lucas handed her a sheaf of papers.

"That's cheating. I have to do my own work." Usually the junior member of the team—in this case, Amanda—prerounded on every patient in the ICU, collecting the lab values and vital signs from overnight. It was tedious work, deciphering nurses' notes scrawled on patient bedside charts, but important to facilitate the changeover from the on-call team to the new team.

"It's two minutes on the computer—and you said nothing good would ever come from electronic medical records. C'mon."

The ECMO tech chuckled. "Listen to the man, Amanda. Zachary's cool. You need to learn to grab food when you can if you're going to survive this place."

Amanda glanced at Zachary's peaceful face, then brushed her hand over his forehead. "Okay, let's go."

They walked down the stairs from the fourth floor to the cafeteria, unabashedly holding hands now that they had privacy. Amanda loved the way Lucas treated her like she was Scarlett O'Hara—a lady to be wooed, courted. Sometimes his old-fashioned values and propriety unleashed her impatience, but they never failed to charm her.

"So, you remember Dr. Frantz's patient?" Amanda asked Lucas.

"Which one? The kid I did the LP on, or the kid you're trying to find a diagnosis for?"

"Both. They met last night—really hit it off. It was kind of fun to see, opposites attract and all that. I mean, he's a rich kid, obnoxious, annoying as hell—but with her, he was really sweet, caring. And she's come all the way from Africa to this foreign land, dirt poor, trying to make a new life only to get sick. Of all things, it was spending time with Tank, not any of our medicine, that made Narolie feel better."

"Romeo and Juliet," he said, a sly smile crossing his face. "Be careful. You know how that turned out."

She skipped a few steps ahead, pulling him along with her. She'd hit her postcall, sleep-deprived euphoria, the second wind that would soon die and leave her crashing.

"I know. But you should have seen them." She sighed. "I just hope I can figure out what's wrong with Narolie."

"She still vomiting?"

"Stopped finally, last night. Said she had a headache, but that was better as well. I did a complete history and physical—no aura of migraines and no pattern I can find."

"Hmmm. Are the symptoms worse in the morning? Could be an intracranial process. Mass effect from a tumor or abscess. Sometimes they don't show up on a regular CT, especially if they're in the posterior fossa."

"I know. I wish I could figure out a way to consult you without Frantz knowing about it."

"No can do. I'd love to help out, but I need to be able to document it."

"And you can't do that without an official consult." They pushed open the door to the cafeteria and dropped hands. Amanda missed his touch immediately. Somehow Lucas always made her feel better, smarter, stronger than she really was. "I need to find something this morning before Dr. Frantz kicks her out of the hospital."

Lucas considered. "Maybe that's the answer. Let him discharge her and I'll re-admit her to my service."

Wow. Amanda turned to him, stunned. It was the perfect solution—except she couldn't let him do it. "You don't even know if it is a neuro problem, Lucas. Besides, I can't let you fight my battles. I'll figure something out."

"If that's what you want." Lucas rarely argued with her—he seemed to think she was smart enough to make her own decisions.

Although she enjoyed that he respected her that much,

sometimes she wished he'd pull rank as an attending and step in. Even if she couldn't ask him to.

Damn, had she just let her sense of pride doom Narolie's only chance at being cured?

NORA WOKE CERTAIN OF ONE THING: THAT SHE had to tell Jerry Boyle everything. Then she could find the strength to deal with Seth and, maybe, rebuild their relationship.

But she couldn't face Jerry alone, so after Seth left, she drove over to Lydia's. Nestled at the end of a cul-de-sac, Lydia's house was the old cemetery caretaker's cottage. The mature hemlocks, spruce, and arborvitae surrounding it gave it a Thomas Kinkade feeling, as if it sat alone in the countryside rather than the center of a busy Pittsburgh neighborhood.

Nora walked up the path leading to Lydia's front door. Amanda had planted flowerbeds on either side—partly as a housewarming gift to Lydia and partly to assuage her homesickness for her family's gardens in South Carolina. Nora recognized chrysanthemum, lavender, the spiky twigs of rosebushes, and a lovely winter surprise: velvet-soft pansies in purple and gold. The only Christmas decoration was an evergreen wreath with a large black-and-gold Steelers ribbon that hung on the front door. Trey's contribution, she was sure. Lydia didn't seem the holiday-decorating type.

She hesitated. It was early, but Lydia kept strange hours—Nora had even spied her going for runs alone in the dark after midnight shifts ended. Trey's red pickup truck was parked in the driveway, but it was almost seven, and he'd surely be leaving for his shift soon. As she rang the doorbell she heard voices inside.

They didn't sound so happy. The chimes punctuated the sharp sounds. Were Lydia and Trey fighting? It seemed so unlike them. Lydia always seemed to find something to rile her passions—but Trey? In all the years Nora had known him, she'd never once heard him raise his voice, not even when in the midst of traumas that had descended into chaos.

She wished she could take back ringing the doorbell, leave and come again, but it was too late. Trey yanked open the door, then blinked in surprise. "Nora. What are you doing here?"

"Is Lydia in?"

He scowled and turned to shout over his shoulder, "Lydia! It's Nora." His expression softened as he faced Nora again, ushering her into the living room. "Are you okay? I heard what happened yesterday, that you were the one to find Karen."

"I'm fine. Thanks." Felt weird to offer thanks for anything that happened yesterday.

He shifted his weight, then picked up his gear bag. "Well, I'd best be going or I'll be late. Lydia's in the kitchen." Again the frown. "Maybe you can talk some sense into her."

Before she could ask, he left, slamming the door behind him. A few moments later, the engine of his pickup revved and he squealed out of the driveway.

"Nora, what are you doing here?" Lydia appeared in the archway between the living room and dining room. "Is everything okay?"

No. Everything was not okay. Everything was very wrong. Because in her hand, Lydia held a gun.

Nora froze, not able to take her eyes off the handgun. "Lydia, you have a gun? I don't believe it. You're a doctor, for God's sake—"

"Lots of doctors have guns," Lydia said, looking down at the pistol as if she hadn't even realized she held it. She led Nora into the kitchen, where a gray plastic carrying case and boxes of ammunition lay on the table. "Besides, this is Pennsylvania. Everyone here has a gun. You all have like a state holiday on the first day of deer season."

"That's different. That's hunting. Putting food on the table. This"—Nora gestured at the gun—"this is to kill a person."

"Not kill." Lydia placed the gun into the foam cutouts that lined the case. It wasn't very large; it was black with etched crisscrosses and a silver bull's-eye on the grip, and it definitely looked like it could kill. Nora was glad when Lydia shut the lid on it. "Not necessarily. But definitely stop them."

"Lydia! You're talking about shooting someone. A human being."

"I'm talking about self-defense." Lydia grabbed her gun case. "Anyway, I'm late. Boyle's waiting."

"This is why you're meeting Jerry?" Nora gestured to the case. She'd thought they were meeting to discuss Karen.

"We meet to shoot a few times a month. He helped me get my carry permit."

"What does Trey think about all this?"

Lydia grimaced. "He hates it. Trey thinks the world's problems would be solved by buying a Christmas tree and singing carols."

GINA RUBBED HER EYES. SHE HADN'T EVEN BOTHered with makeup; she'd rolled out of bed and into the shower, thrown some clothes on, and rushed to start her shift in the ER. No sleep last night—she couldn't get Ken Rosen's words out of her mind. That she shouldn't marry Jerry.

The idea wouldn't leave her any peace. Not because she thought Ken was right about Jerry being wrong for her. Rather because she began to think about Jerry—what if *she* was wrong for him? What if she made his life miserable?

Why hadn't she told Ken that she loved Jerry?

And when she had drifted off, it was only to be awakened by nightmares of her running alone down a Homewood street, a car filled with gunmen behind her, no idea where to go. Or worse, the ultimate nightmare: Gina living with her parents again, bowing to their will, trying to appease and please them.

Jerry wasn't like that, she thought as she arrived at the

ER's locker room and changed into scrubs for her shift in the ER. He would never ask her to change just to suit him. But did he really know and understand her? Or had she just put on another act, a different act, for him like she had all her life with her parents? What would happen when Jerry discovered the real her?

Maybe Ken was right. She slammed her locker shut, the thin metal door flying back at her so she slapped it again. It caught this time, shuddering into place with a weird keening noise that made her teeth ache. She stomped out to the ER, shoving aside all existential nonsense. She knew who she was, that was all that mattered.

Wasn't it?

She was barely halfway to the nurses' station when she heard her name called. She whirled around, then wished she'd run the other way instead. Coming down the hall behind her was Tank's mother. Worse, matching her stride for stride, was Gina's mother, LaRose Freeman, looking particularly elegant in a Donna Karan suit the color of pink champagne.

"Regina," LaRose said in a voice of command.

No running and hiding, no escape. Gina waited for them, wrapping her arms around her chest, leaning against the wall, trying to assume a nonchalant stance.

"Thank God we found you!" Mrs. Trenton gushed. Gina cringed—it was much too early in the day for exclamation marks.

"Catherine needs your help," LaRose said.

Gina waited, refusing to get sucked in. Probably they were going to try to send her on a food run for Tank like they had Amanda. But Mrs. Trenton surprised her, grasping Gina's hand as if Gina were a lifesaver.

"You have to help me," she said. "Harold's missing."

FOURTEEN

Friday, 6:53 A.M.

"ARE YOU OKAY? DO YOU NEED SOMETHING?"
Lydia asked Nora, wondering why the charge nurse had
come to her. It was awkward knowing what she knew about
Nora—but Lydia couldn't betray Seth's confidence, wouldn't
let on to Nora that she knew any of the charge nurse's secrets.

Way too complicated. So much easier just staying out of
other people's problems.

"No. I'm fine." Nora mumbled the words as if they'd become automatic.

"I've got to go, I'm late," Lydia said, heading out the door
to the carport.

Nora followed. "Wait. I'll go with you. I need to talk to
Jerry."

Lydia had been planning to take the bike—had even had
small inklings about "forgetting" her helmet. No way she
would ever, ever be able to explain *that* to Nora. An ER doc
riding a "donorcycle" without a helmet? How on earth could
she explain the thrill of it? The way riding the Triumph or

shooting her nine-millimeter made her feel alive, immortal, death-defying, and fearless.

Almost better than the adrenaline rush of a fresh trauma.

The moment of self-indulgence was brief. "Sure," she said to Nora, tugging her gloves on, snugging Maria's charm bracelet inside her left one. She wasn't sure why she'd been drawn to wearing it today, but it felt right. "Come along."

Without breaking stride, Lydia headed for her Ford Escape, which was parked in the driveway. "If you don't want to be alone, I can call Elise," she suggested. She was pretty sure the flight nurse had the day off. And because Elise had been there with Nora in the cemetery yesterday, she'd understand what Nora was going through. "You two can hang out, go shopping or something."

"You trying to get rid of me?" Nora said it with a smile, but Lydia heard the hurt in her tone.

"No. Of course not. You and Elise have known each other longer; I figured—"

"Look. Lydia. It's all right. You don't have to babysit me. I'll be fine. Just tell me where to find Jerry. I can find my own way from there."

Lydia didn't like the jagged edge Nora's voice had taken on. "Hop in, you can ride with me."

They drove through Highland Park in silence. "Would you use it?" Nora asked, nodding at the gun case. "Really?"

That was an easy one. "Yes. When I was attacked, in my own home—I felt so . . . helpless. I never want to feel that way again."

"I read somewhere that women carrying guns are more likely to have them taken away, used against them."

Lydia choked back a laugh. After living on the streets of L.A., hustling with her mother, and then spending the rest of her youth in foster care, she knew every dirty street-fighting trick in the book. Hell, she could write her own book. Those were the skills that had saved her life in October. "Let them try."

After a long silence, Nora said, "I think that's why Trey

doesn't like it. He doesn't like seeing that side of you."

"What side of me?"

"The side that put that man in the hospital."

"He tried to kill me." Why did everyone always forget that? "Besides, I've never hidden who I am from Trey." Except for telling him next to nothing about her childhood or her mother or the fact that Jerry Boyle was reinvestigating Maria's murder. Guilt left a bitter taste in her mouth.

"Lydia, you need to be careful. I've seen the way Trey looks at you. The man has fallen, fallen hard."

"Who asked him to?" Lydia muttered, hoping Nora wouldn't hear. As if by blaming Trey she could make the problem go away. Hah.

She pulled off Washington Boulevard into the Pittsburgh Police Training Center. "We're here. You'll need your driver's license, but leave everything else in the car."

Sandy McKenna was manning the desk as usual.

Lydia signed in and opened her gun case for McKenna to inspect her Para Carry 9. "Is Boyle here yet?"

"Nope. Called and said he'd be a few minutes late. Who's your friend?" Running a hand through his military-cropped silver hair, Sandy beamed at Nora.

"Nora, this is Sandy. Watch out for him, he bites." Lydia made introductions with a smile. After an upbringing where distrust of the police had been pounded into her, she was pleasantly surprised to find herself at ease with men like McKenna and Boyle, even to the point of calling them friends.

"Hi, Nora," Sandy said, flirting shamelessly. "This your first time at a range? I need you to fill out this form, and then I'll go over the safety briefing with you while we wait for Boyle. Are you going to be shooting today?"

"No. No shooting, not for me." Nora jumped as the sound of gunfire came from beyond the thick Lexan window that looked out onto the range.

"She's here to try to talk me out of owning a gun," Lydia told him.

"You gotta be kidding. Lydia's a natural. Are you going to be doing those weak-hand drills again? I'll put you in the center stall so the cadets can see how it's really done."

Lydia was left-handed by birth and right-handed by the grace of the nuns who had taught her how to write. Her nine-millimeter was set up for a right-handed shooter, but she liked to practice with her left as well. Never knew when it might come in handy. She'd gotten good enough that she could beat almost everyone except McKenna and Boyle. Given that Sandy was a former SWAT team commander, and before that an army sniper, that was saying a lot.

Boyle came rushing in from the parking lot, toting a box of ammo and his two off-duty weapons. His hair was still wet from a shower, and he looked as if he hadn't slept.

"Nora." He stopped short when he saw the charge nurse. "What are you doing here?" He dumped his ammo and guns on the counter before folding Nora into his arms with a gentle embrace. "You doing okay?"

Lydia shook her head, constantly amazed at the way Boyle did his job so well yet still allowed his vulnerabilities to show through. He was unlike any cop she'd ever known. He gave Nora a tight squeeze, one hand ruffling her auburn hair before releasing her.

"I need to talk to you, Jerry," Nora said, her voice breaking. "It's important."

"Sure, no problem."

"Do you want me to leave?" Lydia asked, feeling uncomfortable with the emotions roiling off Nora. She shifted her weight, anxious to flee to the comfort of the firing line, but to her chagrin, Nora grabbed her wrist.

"No. Please, Lydia. Stay."

Where was Amanda, or Elise, hell, even Gina, when she needed them? Lydia was no good at this.

Sandy cleared his throat, obviously also embarrassed by Nora's sudden emotional outburst. "Yunz can use my office."

Boyle nodded his thanks and opened the door to the small

cinder-block-walled room decorated with brass plaques and mounted handguns. Nora tugged Lydia inside with her, not dropping her hand as she sank onto the well-worn leather loveseat across from Sandy's desk. Lydia tried to keep her distance by perching on the arm of the couch, but Boyle had no compunctions, plunging straight into the heart of things by crouching down so that he was knee to knee with Nora, taking her free hand.

"Nora, what is it?"

The charge nurse looked up, tears spilling freely down her cheeks. "I lied. I'm sorry, Jerry. It's all my fault. Karen's dead because of me."

AMANDA GOT BACK TO THE PICU JUST IN TIME for rounds. She felt better after eating, but guilty about not personally checking on her patients before rounds started. She was surprised to see the team clustered around Tank's room. Had he crashed?

More guilt hit her as she jogged across the unit to the isolation room. Damn, she'd thought he was just a goofball kid, not really sick. More lonely and upset about his mom and dad than anything.

Then she stopped short. His bed was empty. His room was empty.

Dr. Frantz was berating the charge nurse, who was having none of it. "We have critical patients here," the nurse was saying. "If yours is healthy enough to disobey orders to remain in his room and abscond, then he doesn't belong here in the first place. We do not provide a babysitting service, Doctor."

Bravo, Amanda echoed the sentiment. But that didn't answer the question of where Tank was. Probably run off to play his Game Boy . . . or down to Narolie's room?

She edged back from the crowd. Before she could escape to the nurses' station and call down to Narolie's nurse, Dr. Frantz spotted her.

"Amanda Mason." His tone was sharp, and suddenly all eyes were on her. "Do you know where Harold is?"

"No, sir."

"He's your responsibility. Go. Find him."

Amanda blinked. Suddenly she was responsible for Dr. Frantz's mistakes? Bad enough the man thought he could use and abuse her, but she had patients up here whom she was responsible for. "Sir, I can't. I have rounds. And then I need to help with Zachary's next treatment."

Dr. Frantz turned on her as if he were a pit bull. "Did you not hear me? A critically ill boy is wandering the halls, potentially contagious with a life-threatening illness—"

"Actually the latex agglutinations came back negative for meningococcemia," Terry Wyshkoff, the PICU fellow, put in. "He's been afebrile since two a.m., and his white count is normal."

Dr. Frantz brushed her comments aside. "Just means I was right and the antibiotics are working. We need to find him—"

"Which hospital security is already working on," Terry said. "We know from security that he hasn't left the hospital and every nursing unit is in lockdown, so what makes you think my medical student can find him faster?"

Now Amanda felt like a piece of meat torn between *two* pit bulls. Dr. Frantz glowered at Terry, not relenting. "Are you saying that Ms. Mason's services are so essential that you can't spare her long enough to find a missing patient?"

"Have you called the police?" Amanda asked.

Both physicians stared at her—Dr. Frantz with a withering glare and Terry with a smirk. "The family requested that we not call the police," Dr. Frantz said.

"Because if we do, we'd need to let them know about Harold's positive tox screen and the joint the nurses found in his pillowcase," Terry added.

"Ms. Mason was with Harold yesterday," Dr. Frantz said. "She bonded with him. If he's confused or agitated, she may be able to help."

Terry ignored Dr. Frantz to turn to Amanda. "It's your choice, Amanda. If you think you can help find Tank faster, I'll cover Zachary for you. If not, you don't have to."

Amanda considered. "Well, I am watching another patient of Dr. Frantz's. One who needs a brain MRI and neuro consult ordered. So while I'm waiting for those, I maybe could look for Tank."

Dr. Frantz met her gaze, then gave her a slow nod. "Thanks for reminding me, Amanda. I'll take care of those orders right away."

"Then I'll get started looking for Tank right away." As Dr. Frantz strode over to the nurses' station, Amanda turned to Terry. "Call me if the Millers need anything."

"No problem. You do realize Frantz is using you as a scapegoat. If anything goes wrong, it's your head on a platter."

Amanda glanced over her shoulder to where Dr. Frantz stood talking on the phone. Hopefully ordering an MRI on Narolie. "That's okay. I'm using him, too."

NORA DREW IN A DEEP BREATH, ALMOST CHOKING on the smell of gunpowder and an acrid oily scent—cleaning fluid? She was so tired of tears, the way they leached her strength, sucked her dry. Sitting up straight, she folded her hands carefully into her lap.

"Two years ago, on New Year's Eve, I was raped," she started.

Jerry remained crouched in front of her, his hands on her knees, gripping them tight to quiet her trembling.

Nora kept her gaze focused on a photo mounted above the desk in the place of honor. In it a dozen men bulky with the weight of their combat SWAT uniforms held rifles aloft in a posture of victory. She recognized Sandy McKenna, the man from out front, and to her surprise, on the far end, Jerry Boyle.

"I didn't know you were on the SWAT team," she said, glad for the distraction.

Jerry squirmed, whether from irritation at her stalling tactic or embarrassment, she wasn't sure. "Long time ago. Messed up my shoulder, transferred to hostage negotiation then to Major Crimes."

He waited, his gaze on her face even though she still couldn't bring herself to meet his eyes.

"Hostage negotiation? You'd be good at that."

He only shrugged in response.

"I'm sorry," Nora said, forcing herself back on track. "I've never told anyone—except Seth. Look what came of that." She flinched at the bitterness in her voice. It wasn't Seth's fault. It was hers. "You see, the man who attacked me, he's the same one who killed Karen."

"Are you sure?" Lydia asked, sliding down from the arm of the couch to sit beside Nora, their thighs touching. She laid her hand on Nora's forearm, not forcing the contact, just there. Nora appreciated that, the way Lydia seemed able to get involved without getting sucked in too deep.

"Yes. He left me, naked, spray-painted, eyes glued shut, hair chopped—"

"Did he cut you?"

Nora shut her eyes before answering Lydia's question. Jerry remained silent, waiting, allowing her to pace herself. "No. But he had a knife. He—he touched me with it."

The room was quiet except for the faint sound of gunfire from beyond the walls.

"Start from the beginning," Jerry suggested as the silence grew.

Nora nodded, eyes still closed, telling them everything. That she'd gotten a new dress; how it was only her second date with Matt—they both knew the relationship was going nowhere, but who was going to pass up a date for New Year's?—and how they'd spent the night drinking champagne and dancing; the cab ride home; Matt too drunk to escort her to her door; watching him drive off . . .

"I never saw the man. He came up behind me, put the

knife to my throat, and I froze. He made me walk to where his car was parked behind a Dumpster, made me kneel down. I remember there was ice and slush on the street; I worried about getting my new dress dirty."

A strained laugh circled around the room. It took Nora a moment to realize it had come from her. She inhaled, opening her eyes. Jerry hadn't moved, although surely his legs were cramping by now. Lydia sat twisted so that she faced Nora, her hand stroking Nora's arm, but Nora couldn't feel it. It was as if she drifted above them all, far away from her words or the memories they described.

"Of course, my dress was the least of my worries. He yanked my head back and that was the only time I caught a glimpse of his face—he wore a black ski mask. Then he poured superglue into my eyes and I didn't see anything else. He used duct tape to tie my hands and cover my mouth before shoving me into his trunk. We drove for a long time, around and around. I remember praying I wouldn't throw up and aspirate and choke to death."

Her hands tightened their grip on her knees, digging in, holding on for dear life. "That's when I knew I would do whatever it took to get out of there alive."

FIFTEEN

Friday, 7:22 A.M.

"I'M SURE TANK'S FINE," GINA SAID, LEADING HER mother and Mrs. Trenton to the nurses' station, where she picked up a patient's chart. "Do you need me to call security for you?"

"They're already looking."

"Then I don't understand. What do you want me to do?" She met her mother's eyes straight on as she said this, waiting for LaRose to ask her to call Jerry. As embarrassing as it was for her parents to have her "associating" with a cop, she was glad for the opportunity for them to see how good Jerry was. Not to mention the groveling she intended to coax from LaRose.

Mrs. Trenton grabbed for her arm. "We want you to find him!"

"Me? How would I know where he went? Besides"—she gestured to the stack of charts—"I have patients to take care of."

"You've worked in this hospital for three years," LaRose said, acting as if Gina had been exiled to a dungeon for a life sentence. "Surely you know where a teenager might run off to."

Gina knew a lot of places—the medical center had two large towers built onto the original infrastructure, which dated back more than one hundred fifty years. "The guys in security know this place even better than I do."

"But we're—*I'm*—asking you to help. It's not like they don't have other doctors around here. This is Catherine's son we're talking about." LaRose laid her hand on Gina's arm, the closest she got to an affectionate hug.

And, like always, Gina found herself seriously considering abandoning her duties to do her mother's bidding. She didn't want to—in fact, the impulse to tell her mother to go to hell was almost as strong. A few months ago that was exactly what she would have done.

But neither was the right thing—for her or her patients. Ken Rosen was right. She needed to start acting like she had her own life to live, not someone else's. Even if it meant screwing up the always tenuous relationship she had with her parents.

She squeezed her eyes shut for a moment, then sucked in her breath. "I'm sorry. I can't help you."

When she opened her eyes, Mrs. Trenton was staring at her with eyes welling up, smudging her mascara. LaRose merely shook her head in dismissal, removed her hand from Gina's arm, and straightened. "Very well."

Before Gina could try to explain or apologize or do anything to wipe the look of outrage from her mother's face, Rachel, the charge nurse, interrupted. "Gina, we need you in Trauma One. They're bringing in a cop who's critical."

Shit, a cop. Jerry was working today—detectives were usually safe from danger, but a few months ago he'd been stabbed by an angry pimp he'd been questioning. "Did they say who?"

"Said it was an officer named Boyle. All I know is blunt-trauma injury and a GSW to the head."

What? No, no. Boyle was a common name, there had to be more than one on the police force. It wasn't Jerry. It couldn't be. All of this passed through her in a flash as she dropped the chart she held, abandoned her mother and Mrs. Trenton, and grabbed a gown and mask from the cart beside the trauma room. She dashed down to the ambulance bay, the gown flapping behind her. *Focus. ABCs, ABCs. You have a job to do, you can't lose it, not now.*

Sirens screamed the arrival of the ambulance. Gina ran out, wrenching the rear door of the ambulance open before it stopped. The December wind sliced through the thin Tyvek gown, but all her attention was on her patient. She couldn't see his face because the paramedic doing CPR blocked the way.

"What's his name?" she asked. The second medic glanced at her—the patient's name wasn't the first question an ER doctor wanted or needed answered on a fresh trauma.

"Jerry Boyle."

Ice flooded Gina's veins, flash-freezing her heart in mid-beat. *No!*

"Found in his town house over in Friendship," he continued as they hauled the cot out of the ambulance. "Looks like a victim of a home invasion, beaten to a pulp, then shot. We had agonal respirations and a pulse when we arrived, but just lost both."

Gina forced herself to step forward so that she could see clearly. The man on the gurney had been beaten so badly that she doubted his own mother would recognize him.

But he definitely was not *her* Jerry. *This* Boyle's hair was red; he had a beer belly and on his right deltoid was a tattoo of an eagle clutching a flag.

"Let's get him into Trauma One," she ordered, back in command. "Any penetrating injuries other than the head wound?"

"No. But bruises from here to Philly and back again. This guy took one hell of a beating."

As they rushed the stretcher down the hall, Gina wondered what kind of idiot robber would pull a home invasion on a cop's house?

"TELL ME WHAT YOU WANT, NORA," HE WHISPERED as his lips caressed her neck. Outside, his voice had been harsh, muffled. In here, wherever "here" was, it was tinny, mechanical, echoing as if he were everywhere at once.

"What I want?" Her voice was choked with tears she didn't dare shed.

"Yes. I want this night to be perfect. Your wildest dreams come true."

He moved her in a parody of a waltz. His voice echoed, then faded as if they were in a small space. Her shoes tapped against a hard surface, concrete or tile, she guessed.

"What if I want—" She stopped herself before she could beg to go home, to be let free. She couldn't afford to anger him, not with his knife pressed into her back, over her spine.

"What if I want to touch you?" She tried and failed to give her voice a seductive edge. He didn't seem to notice.

"Touch me where?" The mechanical disembodied whisper amplified his excitement. "Touch me where?"

"All—all over."

He rubbed his face against her cheek, his tongue lapping at her skin as if tasting her terror. "I love it when you blush like that. It makes your freckles come out. Enchanting."

His hands slid around to caress her breasts. "Do you like that, Nora? Ah, you do, I can feel it. What are you wearing under this dress? I know you picked it out with me in mind. Blue, my favorite color."

She froze, her breath trapped in her throat as his knife rasped against the back of her neck. There was a tug and then the snick *of her halter strap parting. Followed by the soft shiver of fabric sliding to the floor. His hands left her and she was suddenly disoriented, not certain where to face, where danger might attack from.*

Then she heard his breathing. Fast, heavy, not quite panting.

"Very nice," he said, his voice surrounding her, making her dizzy. She spun around, trying to center herself. "You read my mind. Is that your secret, Nora? You read men's minds, drive them wild with thoughts of you?"

"What do you want?" she asked, praying for him to just tell her, to stop playing games, tormenting her. "I'll do whatever you want."

It came out as a whimpered plea and she hated that. But she didn't want to die, not tonight, not at the hands of this creep. Visions of her mother and father weeping over a closed casket, of her younger brothers and sister broken, inconsolable, filled her mind. No. She'd live, do whatever it took to make it out of here alive.

"I want to please you, to make this the best night of your life, Nora. That's all I want."

His hands reached out from behind her, pulling her to him, her restrained hands pressing against his crotch, unable to escape the knowledge of his erection. He held her there, his knife pressed against her throat. She was afraid to move, to even breathe, holding her breath until she thought she'd black out. When the pressure grew too much, she tried to sneak in a breath, slow, shallow.

He laughed. Fabric whispered against her ankle and vanished again as he kicked her tangled dress away. "Don't worry," he said, his mouth close to her ear. "I won't let you fall. I'm here for you, Nora. I'll always be here."

He spun her to face him, his hand resting on her breast, his knife sliding over her bare skin. A ripping noise, a swish of air, and her strapless bra fell to the floor with a soft thud. Her lace panties soon followed. She trembled, naked now except for thigh-high stockings and her heels. She stood, frozen as his hands and mouth and knife explored every inch of her bare skin.

It had taken all her energy not to flinch as she imagined herself somewhere, anywhere else. . . .

Lydia's hand squeezed hers, and Nora jerked back to the here and now: a small cinder-block office reeking of gunpowder and testosterone. Jerry was still crouching before her, leaning close, too close.

Nora shook herself, pulling away from Jerry. He seemed to understand, stood up straight, his joints creaking, and settled against the desk a few feet away from her.

"Anyway, he kept me there for two days and nights. Long enough that he fed me—microwave burritos, some pop. I remember when I had to use the bathroom, that embarrassed him, he wouldn't help me or touch me, even though I was blind and my hands were tied. He kept the door open, but I'll bet he didn't watch. And he had to be using Viagra or something because every time I thought it was over, he'd . . . well, he'd be ready again."

"All this time he acted like you were on a date?" Jerry asked.

She nodded, her gaze fixed on the frayed edges of his pants cuffs. "Like we knew each other, were lovers." Her voice drifted off. "Then it all changed. He couldn't—perform anymore, blamed me. Screamed that I'd wasted his precious time. Began to hit me, hurt me. He stopped talking, and that was the scariest part of all."

Her body shook as she rushed to finish before she lost her courage. "He threw me naked into the trunk of his car. We drove and drove, and then he made me get out, walk barefoot through the snow and ice up some steps and into a building. It smelled so bad I almost threw up, but he told me if I did he'd kill me.

"He made me walk up more steps; they were old and creaky and I could feel the dirt and trash beneath my feet. Then he began to hit me, kick me. He chopped off my hair and grabbed some spray paint. I think it must have been left there because I don't remember him carrying anything except his knife. He held one hand around me and had the knife in his other. Anyway, he sprayed the paint on me; it got in my mouth and burned. Then he found a piece of plastic and put it over my face, suffocating me. I'd pass out, then come to, and he'd do it again and again and again."

She dropped her gaze, now concentrating on Jerry's polished leather loafers and his hideous green and purple tartan socks. Only Gina could have persuaded a man to wear those socks.

"That's when I thought I was going to die. I passed out one more time, and when I woke up he was gone. I worked my hands free of the duct tape, pried my eyes open, used some old newspapers and trash bags to cover myself, and ran home in the dark."

"You never reported it?"

Nora shook her head. "He said he'd kill my family—he knew their names, where they lived, everything. He laughed about how easy it would be. I was so scared and ashamed, I couldn't, I just couldn't. I never told anyone until I told Seth. I couldn't risk him targeting my family or coming after me again."

Tears threatened to overwhelm her and she buried her face in her hands, trying to pull it together. Damn it, there had to be a statute of limitations on crying, didn't there? She hadn't even cried this much when it happened or when she'd told Seth the barest of details, letting him draw the wrong conclusions.

"You can't blame yourself," Jerry said.

"We always blame ourselves, it's human nature," Lydia replied, even as she circled an arm around Nora's shoulders protectively. "That's why you became a sexual assault examiner, isn't it? Because you felt guilty."

Nora nodded, surprised Lydia understood. She raised her head. "Then when I found Karen—I knew. If I had told someone, back then, maybe—"

"Probably not," Jerry said. "You never saw him. He disguised his voice, used condoms. Made you bathe in bleach. I doubt he intended to use the spray paint to destroy evidence, although it's pretty damn effective. That feels like an afterthought, at least the first time with you."

"How did you know about the bleach and condoms?" Nora asked, now facing Jerry straight on. Her stomach did a slow, curdling flip-flop. "I didn't tell you that. And 'the first time'—you mean there were others after me, before Karen?"

He met her gaze, his lips pinched. She saw the ugly truth in his eyes before he nodded. "At least two more that we know of. So far. I'm waiting to hear back from the FBI's ViCAP. One was attacked last year, the other seven weeks ago."

Guilt slammed down on her, stealing her breath. "Are . . . are they alive?"

"Yes. Both found naked, abandoned, spray-painted with graffiti. One in a Dumpster in Uniontown and the other near the old Rolling Rock plant in Latrobe. No usable forensics from either case. Both blitz attacks and only held for a few hours, as we suspect Karen was."

Nora hugged herself, desperate to feel warm again, desperate to feel anything. "Two more. But I was the first."

"And he took a lot more time with you," Jerry continued. "I haven't interviewed either of the other victims yet—we just learned about the Uniontown victim this morning, in fact, but the investigating officers said both victims worked at health care facilities. One in the kitchen, the other as a secretary. If they'd all been within Allegheny County, we would have figured it as the same actor from the start. But three different jurisdictions—"

"Uniontown, Latrobe. And now he's back here in Pittsburgh," Lydia said.

"Now he's back."

SIXTEEN

Friday, 8:02 A.M.

AMANDA LEFT THE PICU AND IMMEDIATELY headed down to peds. She had a pretty good idea where Tank might be and wanted to get to him before any nurses spilled the beans to Dr. Frantz and all bets were off. She had no doubts that Dr. Frantz would renege on his deal and kick Narolie out if he found Tank before she did.

She pushed through the stairwell door and jogged past the clump of peds residents making rounds, finally reaching Narolie's room.

The bed was empty. As was the bathroom. No signs of Narolie anywhere—nothing except an IV pole with the bag of fluid hanging empty above the pump and the intravenous line dangling over the side of the bed rail.

"Sugar!" Amanda swore. She would have said what she was really thinking—words she'd learned by listening to her older brothers—except this was the pediatric floor and you never knew who could be listening. She spun around in a circle once more, as if Narolie and Tank would magically appear, then tapped her foot in an irritated staccato as she thought.

During her pediatric rotations, she'd quickly learned that the ward clerks were the all-seeing, all-knowing eyes of the floor. Reversing her path, she headed out to the nurses' station.

"Monica, have you seen Narolie Maxeke?"

"Hey, Amanda," Monica said, typing and juggling the phone as she smiled a greeting. "Thought you were in the PICU this month."

"Following up on a patient. Room three-twelve?"

Monica shook her head. "Sorry, no. But I just put in a few orders for her, so she can't be far. Did you try the teen lounge?"

The teen lounge was a locked area on the opposite end of the floor from the younger kids' playroom. Only staff and teens with lounge privileges were given the code. "Good idea. Thanks."

Waving at a few of the day-shift nurses, Amanda made her way down to the teen lounge. She entered the code—a not-so-hard-to-remember 4-3-2-1—and walked in. An emaciated boy in a wheelchair equipped with an oxygen tank was bobbing his head to technofunk while watching one of the X-Men movies and playing a handheld video game.

Otherwise the room was empty. "Have you seen a black girl?" she asked. "Tall, skinny, her name's Narolie?"

The boy shook his head without looking up from his game. Amanda turned the boom box off and stood in front of him, blocking his view of the TV. Deprived of two-thirds of his sensory overstimulation, he glanced up in annoyance. "What?"

"I'm looking for two kids. A girl named Narolie and a boy called Tank."

"Oh, them. They left. Pair of emos, didn't like my tunes. I told 'em to get a room—way they talked you'd think the world was ending or something."

"Do you know where they went?"

He shook his head. "Nope. They spent all their time looking out the window. Said something about watching the storm."

"Thanks." She turned his music back on, but at a slightly less deafening volume, and looked past him, out the windows. The lounge faced out onto the visitors' parking garage—not a very romantic or colorful view. A few drops of rain streaked the window; thick, heavy like it had started as snow but melted as it fell.

The lounge door opened. Lucas Stone stood there, his gaze sweeping the room before coming to rest on her. "Heard my consult might be down here."

Amanda smiled. Dr. Frantz couldn't discharge Narolie now—not while he was waiting for Lucas's consult. She led him from the room.

"How did you get Frantz to change his mind?" he asked.

"His PICU patient went missing. He said he'd schedule a neuro consult for Narolie if I found Tank."

"Very Machiavellian. Of course, now we have two patients missing. Coincidence?"

She shook her head. "Doubt it. Anyway, sorry to waste your time. I'll call you as soon as I find Narolie."

Instead of leaving, he kept pace with her as she entered the stairwell and headed downstairs. "I'll help."

"Lucas. You're busy. I can clean up my own mistakes."

"Two lonely, sick kids who found something in each other. Doesn't sound like a mistake to me."

"Try explaining that to Tank's mom or Dr. Frantz."

"Anyway, I have ulterior motives. This consult is keeping me out of a very tedious IRB meeting. And besides"—he slipped his hand into hers—"I haven't had much of a chance to see you this month."

She paused on the landing to turn and look at him for a long moment. No kiss, no words, just look. Those old-soul blue-gray eyes, the strong jaw that spoke of a stubbornness as irritating as it was charming, the shadow of a smile hovering at his lips.

A lot of people saw Lucas as aloof, even arrogant, because of his superintelligence, disregard for social niceties, and obsessive-compulsiveness. They didn't know the man she knew. The man who had spent a lifetime as an outsider and who'd paid a high price for his talents.

Lucas hadn't changed because of her—thank God, because she loved him as he was—but he had lowered his defenses, invited her inside the barriers he had built around his true self. And that was a gift both unexpected and precious.

"What?" he asked, breaking contact and looking back when she didn't continue down the steps with him. "Did I say something wrong?"

She skipped down three steps to join him. "No. You said something right."

GINA AND THE PARAMEDICS RAN THE STRETCHER with the wounded cop into Trauma One. Waiting for them was an array of nurses, residents, and the surgical attending on duty, Diana DeFalco.

"What have we got?" DeFalco asked, staking her claim to the position at the foot of the gurney where she could see everything and bark out commands.

Gina hadn't worked much with the new trauma surgeon, but she had seen her in action. DeFalco didn't trust the emergency medicine residents yet. She always took over as command doc when no other attendings were around. Normally Gina would argue the point; after all, how was she supposed to learn how to run a trauma if no one gave her the chance? But not today, not with a cop without a pulse on the table.

Instead, Gina let the medics give DeFalco the bullet points while she quickly assessed the ABCs: airway secured;

breathing—no breath sounds on the right, trachea deviated. Which meant no time for C, circulation, until she got a chest tube in place.

"Tension pneumo on the right, give me a thirty-six French chest tube," she ordered as she poured Betadine over the right chest and grabbed a scalpel. The nurses, as always, were a step ahead of her; as soon as she said the magic words *tension pneumo* they were there with an open instrument tray, one handing her a chest tube as the other grabbed the pleurovac.

Gina palpated the space over the fifth rib, sliced the skin and muscle, and used the large curved hemostat to push her way into the pleural cavity. Immediately a *whoosh* of air greeted her. As she threaded the chest tube through the hole she'd created, the paramedic doing CPR stopped.

"We have a pulse," DeFalco announced.

Gina confirmed the rhythm on the monitor. A familiar flush of pride flowed through her—she'd literally just brought Officer Boyle back from the dead. "Let's get labs, four units of O neg, and place a Foley and NG while I start the FAST exam."

She reached for the ultrasound, but DeFalco blocked her way. "No need for that."

"What are you talking about? I need to find where he's bleeding from."

"Check out his head. There's no exit wound. Both pupils are blown."

Gina frowned at the attending. No exit wound meant the bullet had remained inside, ricocheting within the skull, tearing through brain tissue.

"Let me see," she said, jostling past the respiratory tech bagging air into the cop's lungs to check the pupils herself. Both were dilated, unresponsive to light. She checked the nostrils. "CSF leaking."

"Positive Babinsky, his toes are upgoing," DeFalco said from the foot of the bed.

"Let's see what the CT shows," Gina pleaded. Damn it, she hadn't saved the man just to declare him brain dead.

The monitor alarmed. "Lost his pulse," a nurse called out as she began CPR.

The team scrambled to run the code. In between pushing drugs and trying to shock the cop's heart back to life again, Gina checked for other injuries—anything she could fix.

It seemed like only a few seconds later that she felt De-Falco's hand on her arm, gently tugging her away from the frenzy of activity surrounding Officer Boyle. "It's time to call it."

"No, we can't call it! Not yet."

"We've done everything possible."

"We can't stop yet. Give him more time."

"Gina, no amount of time is bringing him back. Call it."

"He's a cop, we need to try."

"You're taking this personally. I'm sorry, did you know him?"

Gina stared down at the naked body of Officer Boyle. "No. No, I never met him."

"Anyone else with objections? No? Then call it."

Gina opened her mouth, tried to form the words, but Jerry—*her* Jerry Boyle—kept staring back at her from the gurney. It could have been him. What if someday it was him?

Shaking her head, she tore her mask off and backed away from the lifeless body.

"Time of death, eight thirty-six."

LYDIA RETRIEVED HER NINE-MILLIMETER AND AM-munition and waited with Nora in the foyer of the shooting range while Boyle called his partner. Nora was going to show him the building where she'd been abandoned. Even though it had been over two years and there was no hope of any usable evidence, Boyle said he wanted to see it, get a feel for this "actor"—the word he used for the killer.

Lydia bounced back and forth on her toes, wishing she could stay here and shoot. But she couldn't—wouldn't—abandon Nora. She just wished she had the right words of comfort to offer. It seemed to only make things worse when she did say anything.

So, here she was, Nora gripping her hand like a lifeline, getting ready to drive to an East Liberty crack house and see firsthand the place where her friend had been beaten, raped, and left for dead.

She'd always admired Nora for the way the charge nurse could handle even the craziest of emergencies, the most chaotic shifts, for the way she fought to protect her patients . . . but now it seemed there was more to Nora's strength than Lydia had ever imagined.

Nora needed her help, and Lydia felt shamed by her own inadequacy. She didn't know how to do this. Should she act strong, say nothing, wait for Nora to say something? Or ask questions, help Nora let it all out and talk about the nightmare she'd kept bottled up for two long years?

She liked it better when she had no friends. No, that wasn't true, but *mierda*, did it have to be so hard?

"We're set," Boyle said, stepping out of Sandy's office as he snapped his phone shut. "Janet is going to run down Matt Zersky and cover the PM."

He was in high-energy mode, but after glancing at Nora, he toned it down. Even Lydia flinched a bit at the thought that Janet Kwon was on her way to watch poor Karen's already mutilated body be cut apart even more during the postmortem.

The air outside felt dark and heavy with the added weight of moisture. Cold, sticky, slushy. Although she'd lived her whole life until now in L.A., Lydia had visited winter climates—hiking in the Grand Tetons, skiing at Tahoe. That air had been brisk and clean, a pleasure to inhale. Full of light and energy.

Pittsburgh winter seemed a far cry from that. Pittsburgh

winter was coal-dust skies and Scrooge-like shivering that wore her out no matter how many layers she put on.

"You okay following me?" Boyle asked Lydia as he helped Nora into the passenger seat of his Subaru Impreza.

Lydia shot him a glare. *She* wasn't the one he needed to worry about.

She walked past him to her Escape.

The morning traffic had died down, and it seemed no one was in a rush to be out and about on a gray day hazy with thunderstorms alternating between rain and sleet. Lydia had no trouble following Boyle's silver Impreza as he led her through Highland Park and into East Liberty.

When they finally turned onto Alhambra Way, she realized that the medical center was only a few blocks away. They were near the church where the riots had started last summer. Alhambra hadn't been spared.

The buildings surrounding the yellow-brick three-story tenement Boyle parked in front of were partially burned. Up and down the block it seemed there wasn't a window intact, many boarded up with plywood serving as blank canvas for graffiti artists, the rest left with jagged glass knifing through empty air.

Boyle got out of the Subaru, talking on his cell phone as he walked around to open Nora's door. By the time Nora had stepped out of the car, Lydia had joined them on the soot-stained sidewalk, carrying a flashlight, her nine-millimeter close at hand in her parka pocket.

Boyle's jacket was unbuttoned, pushed back to reveal his gun and badge to any prying eyes. He need not have bothered. The block felt deserted. It was the house itself that radiated malevolence.

Below the slant of a narrow porch roof missing a support beam, the front door gaped open like a lopsided leer. Darkness inside beckoned; there were no signs of life.

Thunder pealed. The rusted tin roof shook as if laughing. Rain began to pelt them. Nora's teeth were chattering.

"You sure about this?" Lydia asked Nora.

"Yes."

Impervious to the rain, Boyle hung up his cell phone and led the way, his hand on his gun. Nora hugged her chest as she climbed the porch steps. She almost lost her balance, but Lydia steadied her.

Boyle stepped through the door's opening. A loud pop sounded. Nora jumped, hugged herself tighter.

"Stepped on a crack pipe," he called back. The only sign of life was his flashlight beam. Then that vanished into the darkness.

"Place is empty; there's no one here," he called out a few minutes later.

Once Boyle sounded the all clear, Nora stepped over the threshold and Lydia followed, one hand holding her Mag-Lite. She didn't even realize she had drawn her gun until she felt its grip sliding against her sweat-slicked palm. Right now she wasn't sure whether the adrenaline jazzing her nerves was from fear or the thrill of danger. Nora clutched at her wrist and Lydia reluctantly put her gun away, allowing Nora to hold her free hand instead.

The smell became overwhelming after a mere two steps away from the open door. The rancid stench of decay, human waste, alcohol, stale sex, marijuana, and mold was enough to make Lydia gag. She wrinkled her nose, wishing she had a hand free to cover it, and breathed shallowly through her mouth.

Other than a pile of half-burned, broken furniture, the front room was empty. The whole house felt empty, the only signs of life the brightly colored graffiti that glared in the beam of her and Boyle's flashlights.

She remembered the words painted onto Karen's skin and wondered if it was the same artist. Then shuddered as she tried not to imagine Nora going through that same hell on earth.

Boyle quickly glanced through the rear rooms on the first

floor, his flashlight dancing its way over the moldering piles of debris. "Nothing down here." He turned to Nora, catching her face in his light like a deer on a dark highway. "You said he took you upstairs?"

Nora nodded. They rounded the corner and shone their lights on the staircase leading up to where Nora had said she'd been abandoned. The banister was missing, but the steps appeared intact. Graffiti overlapped graffiti, covering the steps, the wall, and the ceiling overhead, an effect that made the darkness more disorienting than ever. No sound except the occasional scurry of rodents and the hollow echo of the storm raging.

Boyle motioned for them to wait where they were as he climbed the steps and vanished into the black shadows beyond. Lightning arced outside the front window, blinding Lydia with its brilliance. Thunder followed, rattling the little glass remaining in the window.

When her eyes adjusted again, Lydia could see Nora standing at the foot of the stairs, her gaze focused on the darkness at the top. Anguish twisted her face, made even more ghostly in the flashlight's sharp scrutiny. Lydia laid a hand on Nora's arm. Goosebumps rippled across Nora's flesh.

"Let's get out of here," Lydia said. "We can wait for Boyle outside, in the car."

Nora took a step forward, shaking her head, her lips trembling.

"No. I need to see . . ." Her voice trailed away.

Boyle's light returned to the top of the steps. "Which room, Nora? It's like a maze up here."

"Hold on," Lydia hollered, covering for Nora as the other woman pressed her body against the wall and took several deep breaths. "We're coming."

The sound of Boyle's cell phone made her jump. Someone—Gina, no doubt—had programmed it to play the "Bad Boys" theme from *COPS*. Even Nora managed a faint smile as she continued climbing up the steps.

Jerry called down from the landing. "Nora, have you seen your New Year's date, Matt Zersky, since the night you were abducted?"

Nora shook her head, eyes creased in puzzlement. "No. But it was only our second date, we weren't serious. And after what happened, I didn't exactly seek him out. Why?"

"His parents reported him missing a week after you were abducted. No one has seen him since."

SEVENTEEN

Friday, 9:03 A.M.

GINA TRAILED AFTER DIANA DEFALCO AS SHE WENT to talk to Officer Jeremiah Boyle's family; an ex-wife and a college-aged son surrounded by a crowd of black uniforms that filled the hallway.

"What happened, doc?" One of the police officers rushed forward when he saw them approaching. An advance guard.

Dr. DeFalco met his gaze and merely shook her head. The officer's face blanked for a moment, and then he turned to face the others. Before Gina and DeFalco could say a word, the wife was crying, clinging to her son. The son was trying hard not to cry, to stand up straight and bear his mother's weight.

"I'm sorry," DeFalco began.

"The son of a bitch," a cop muttered behind her, his words undercut by the sound of armed men adjusting their gun belts, preparing for war.

"We did everything we could," DeFalco continued.

The wife nodded her head without ever looking up, her

shoulders sagging. "I know," she whispered. "I always knew it would be like this. Every night I went to bed dreading this moment."

"Mom—" The son couldn't say anything more, his face twisting in pain.

"We have a counselor—"

"No." One of the officers stepped forward. "We can take it from here. Thanks, doc."

"If you have any questions, please feel free to ask. Anytime." DeFalco backed off, but the ex grabbed at her sleeve. She missed, and caught Gina instead. Gina flinched, looking down at the woman with panic.

"Tell me," Mrs. Boyle choked out the words. "Did he suffer?"

Gina opened her mouth, but a dry sputter was all that emerged. She couldn't lie—she should, by all mercy, she should—but she couldn't. But the son had already grasped his mother's hand, releasing Gina.

"Not as much as we're gonna make the bastard who did this suffer," one of the men muttered as Gina backed away.

She pushed her way through the sea of uniforms, ignoring the sound of her name being called.

She found herself in the clean holding room. It was empty, and quiet except for the drip of a faucet. Gina sagged against the shelves, her vision blurred. Her legs trembled, then weakened, and she slid to the floor. She hugged her knees to her chest, burying her face.

The door opened and she glanced up. Ken Rosen stood there. Assessing her with the same unemotional scrutiny he brought to everything. "You look like you could use someone to talk to."

"I look like a baby." She swiped her fist across her eyes. "Go ahead and say it. It's what Diana DeFalco thinks, it's what everyone thinks, it's what Jerry will think."

"Jerry? What's he got to do with this?"

"The cop who died? His name was Jeremiah Boyle—Jerry Boyle. I freaked. Still am. Can't stop thinking—what if that had been my Jerry? What if I do marry him and someday he walks out the door and never comes back? What if I let him into my life, into my heart, and then lose him? Forever."

Gina shook her head, her fingers massaging her throat, tangling in the chain where Jerry's ring hung around her neck. "I don't look good in black."

The joke fell flat.

"You can't think like that." Ken finally broke the silence. "Bad things happen to all of us. And, as silly and awful and inconceivable as it sounds, life does go on. You will go on. Time has a way of healing things that even medicine can't."

"You sound like a freaking Hallmark commercial."

He didn't take the bait, but instead sat there beside her on the floor, holding her hand, saying nothing. As if their conversation yesterday—and the slap that accompanied it—had never happened. As if it didn't matter. She blew out her breath, an unaccustomed feeling settling over her. Not quite serenity, not quite acceptance, not quite clarity . . . but almost.

"You know what the worst thing is?" Why couldn't she stop talking? She didn't want to say any of this, expose secrets she didn't even allow herself to see. "When I imagine it—Jerry gone—I can't even think of how it might happen or what he might suffer. All I see is me. Alone. All I can think is: Who would take care of me?"

She yanked Jerry's ring free, holding it up to the light. It glistened like a star in the light of the single sixty-watt bulb. "Pretty selfish, huh? Selfish and stupid. But that's me. That's the kind of woman he's getting."

She tucked the ring away, stood, and brushed off the back of her scrubs.

Ken got to his feet as well. "You're afraid he'll regret his choice?"

"No," Gina said, rearranging her stethoscope around her neck and adjusting her expression to her usual armor-plated banality. "I'm afraid *I* will."

AMANDA AND LUCAS SCOURED THE CAFETERIA and gift shop looking for Tank and Narolie. "I thought the way he was complaining about the food, he'd come down here looking for something better."

"Where else?"

"The kid in the teen lounge said something about they were watching the storm, but I don't know where—" She stopped. "The research tower. It's taller than the patient tower, has more windows, better views."

"Okay, we can start at the top, work our way down." They headed toward the elevators. Usually Lucas avoided elevators—microincubators, he called them—but Amanda had lost her postcall second wind and was starting to drag. No way was she about to climb up to the eighth floor where the pedestrian skyway connected the two buildings. Luckily they caught an empty elevator car.

"If we don't find him, Dr. Frantz is going to kill me," Amanda said as she pushed the button for the eighth floor. Until a few years ago it had housed all the call rooms and the helipad. After the research tower was built, the helipad was moved to a paved area beside the ER and now each floor had its own tiny call rooms.

"Stop worrying about Frantz," Lucas said.

"What if I don't match here at Angels?"

"Then we'll go someplace else."

"Are you crazy? How can you think of leaving? Except for medical school you've never lived anywhere else. Your dad's here. Your research. Your career."

"You go, I go. Besides, what medical center could resist hiring a double-boarded neurologist *and* a brilliant up-and-coming pediatrician?"

Even through her haze of fatigue, she realized what he was offering her. Change didn't come easily to Lucas; he preferred his life predictable and well ordered. She turned to him, touching his arm. "When we first met, I thought you were the heartless logical one and I was the hopeless dreamer."

"And now?"

"Now I think we're both dreamers."

"But not hopeless."

"Not hopeless. Never hopeless."

"I can live with that." A whisper of a smile curved his lips.

Since when had she become the practical one in this relationship? But Amanda enjoyed seeing this whimsical side of Lucas. As if everything were meant to be—as if they were meant to be. No worries.

The elevator doors opened. Lucas turned left toward the skyway over to the research tower. Amanda stopped, noticing that the fire door leading out to the old helipad was loose, rattling in the wind. The large picture window beside it was smeared with sleet, but she saw movement outside that didn't come from the storm. A crack of lightning illuminated two slim forms on the helipad, one lunging, the other grabbing.

"Lucas! They're here!" Amanda wrenched the fire door open—a rock had been positioned to keep it from latching shut and locking. A gust of wind and sleet pummeled her, but over the noise of the storm she heard a boy's voice.

"No! Stop it, stop it!" It was Tank, dressed in his school clothes, soaking wet, struggling against the wind as he ran after Narolie.

Narolie wore hospital scrubs with one foot bare, the other wearing a hospital slipper. Her hair was whipping in every direction, making her look like a force of nature, part of the storm. Then she looked back over her shoulder. Her face was twisted, eyes so big the whites shone all around, mouth open, screaming even though no sound came.

Amanda ran out onto the cracked concrete and gravel roof. The wind was stronger here, eight stories off the ground, and what was rain down below was frozen up here, biting, stinging as the wind hurled it at her. Twenty feet in front of her, Tank caught Narolie, hugging her from behind, trying to pull her away from the ledge.

"Narolie, you can't fly home. Listen to me!"

A wordless screech came from Narolie, a sound that rippled its way down Amanda's nerve endings, primal and terrifying. Narolie kicked and flailed, fighting Tank. Lucas caught up with Amanda, and together they herded the two teens back from the edge. Narolie's hair was torn loose from her braids, matted around her face as she clawed at the air before her.

"What happened?" Amanda asked Tank as Lucas grabbed Narolie in a bear hug and hauled her inside.

Tank's cheeks were flushed with cold, his eyes wide with fear. "It was just a little pot, that's all. Just one little joint."

She ushered him inside to the elevator bank and wrestled the door shut behind her. "How'd you get out there?"

Tank shrugged, his gaze fixed on Narolie, who was still fighting Lucas, lunging for the window. "All the door codes are the same. Wasn't hard."

"What do you think?" Amanda asked Lucas, who had resorted to sandwiching Narolie between the wall and his body to keep her from hurting herself. "Psychotic reaction to the marijuana?"

"Could be. How was she before?"

"Okay. She wanted to see snow," Tank answered. "But then we got up here and she said her head hurt, she pulled at her hair, was hitting herself on the side of her head, crying for it to stop. So I gave her a joint and we went outside to smoke it. Thought it'd help. But she went nuts, ran away, wanted to fly." Tank scuffed his foot against the floor, twisting it as if the linoleum were a worry stone. "She gonna be all right?"

"I don't know yet," Amanda answered, stabbing at the elevator call button again. "Where'd you get the joint, Tank?"

"Why?" he asked, suspicion edging his voice.

"Because it could have been dipped in PCP or LSD or combined with cocaine or anything."

He shook his head. "No. It's clean."

Amanda wasn't as sure as he was. Before she could ask more, Narolie slumped into Lucas's arms, her body shuddering as a seizure overcame her.

Lucas supported the girl and did something Amanda had never heard him do before. He swore. "Damn."

The elevator doors opened and Lucas scooped Narolie up into his arms, rushing inside. Amanda pulled Tank, who appeared frozen in shock, in with them.

"Where to? Should we take her back to peds?"

"No. The ER," Lucas said, sitting on the floor and draping Narolie over his lap to protect her head and keep her airway open as her limbs flailed. "They're better equipped."

A few minutes later they were rushing through the hall to the ER, Lucas shouting orders as they reached the nearest exam room. Amanda worked beside him, helping to get oxygen onto Narolie, hooking up the IV, and pushing the anticonvulsant medication. Once the meds took effect, Narolie lay on the bed, unresponsive.

Amanda stroked Narolie's hair back, untangling it from the oxygen mask. "She's burning up."

"Temp's one-oh-four," a nurse said.

"What's wrong with her?" Tank said, clutching Narolie's free hand. Amanda had to give him credit—despite the seizure and the frenzied activity, he'd stayed with Narolie.

"I wish I knew."

NORA CLIMBED THE STEPS IN A HAZE. SHADOWS clung to her vision as Lydia's and Jerry's lights danced through the blackness.

Matt Zersky. She remembered he'd been twenty-four, a MBA student at Pitt. A friend of a friend had introduced them at a party. He rented a house in Squirrel Hill with several other students, but she'd never been there or met them—in fact, she hadn't even really *liked*-liked Matt.

But he was fun and it was the holidays and he said he'd love to take her to the nursing school's annual alumni New Year's ball. She'd thought at the time that he might be more interested in the chance to meet her fellow nurses than being with her, but she'd been dreading going without a date, so it seemed like a win-win.

At the time.

She couldn't for the life of her remember his face, his voice, his smell, the way his hands had felt helping her into and out of their cab. . . . She strained to reclaim him as a person, struggled for the most minute details.

His ringtone had been the Steelers' fight song. He drove a black Miata. She remembered thinking what an impractical car for western Pennsylvania and what a waste that it was automatic instead of manual. . . . That was it.

Her foot twisted on something soft and slimy. She careened to the left, hugging the wall and not looking down. Panic closed in around her and suddenly she was certain that her attacker was up there in the darkness, waiting for her. It had to be hovering around freezing inside the house, but sweat coated Nora's flesh.

Lydia's hand pressed against the small of her back, supporting her. "Here," she said, "take the light. I can see fine without it."

Nora didn't argue. She fastened her fingers on the light and aimed it in front of her. She stumbled to the top of the steps, where Jerry waited, still talking on his cell phone.

"Did they find Matt?" she asked as if a miracle of modern police investigation could have taken place in the last three minutes.

Jerry merely shook his head. Nora's heart sank. Lydia moved past her, glancing into the two rooms that opened off the top of the landing. Nora followed her with the light, illuminating more graffiti and debris, trying to still her shaking hand. Her teeth were clenched as she fought against their chattering.

Lydia disappeared into a room, Jerry a few steps behind her. Nora was tempted to turn the light off and follow her memory, but settled for half-closing her eyes, simulating blindness. Yes, they had moved to the right, down the hall, to the room at the far end, in the rear of the building.

She held one hand out in front of her as if she were blind, her fingers trailing along the fraying wallpaper. She stopped short in front of a wood-paneled door that perched halfway open, inviting her into the blackness beyond. Her mouth was dry, but when she tried to swallow, to find some moisture, all she tasted was the acid bite of the bleach *he* had made her swallow.

Her hand brushed against the door. It opened the rest of the way. She didn't step inside, but instead swung the flashlight around, searching for the danger every nerve in her body alerted her to.

The neon glow of graffiti greeted her, reflected eerily in the small, intense beam of light. Her chest was tight and she realized she was holding her breath. She released it as the light hit the far wall.

Caught in the light, the colors faded but still vivid in her mind's eye, was her own bloody handprint.

Nora didn't hear the thud as the flashlight fell from her hand. She sank to the ground, the room swimming in darkness, unable to stop the sensations bombarding her as her mind raced back two years.

His hands tightening around her throat, the pressure building in her chest, her head pounding as she lay crushed beneath his weight. The giddy euphoria, the last defense of an oxygen-starved brain when he didn't let go. Her prayers echoing through her mind as she begged for release. His breath against her cheek as he prolonged his deadly embrace.

Her final gasp as she slipped away, thanking God that it was finally over . . .

EIGHTEEN

Friday, 9:42 A.M.

GINA AND KEN LEFT THE STOREROOM ONLY TO find Gina's mother pacing the hallway in front of the nurses' station.

LaRose rushed toward them, actual worry lines marring her creaseless skin. "Regina, are you okay?"

"What are you doing here?" Gina asked. "Thought you went to find Tank."

LaRose didn't answer her. Instead she was staring at Ken. More specifically at Ken's name tag. Ken silently accepted the scrutiny, his face as indecipherable as a Rosetta stone.

"Ken, this is my mother, LaRose Freeman," Gina said, even though it was clear both of them had already figured that out.

"Dr. Rosen," LaRose said, her voice strong and loud—a little too loud. "It is a pleasure to meet you."

Gina noticed that LaRose didn't extend her hand. Neither did Ken. Instead Ken squared his shoulders, bracing for a blow.

"Your daughter is an excellent doctor," he said. "You should be very proud of her."

Then he left—turned and strode down the hall, shoulders hunched as if waiting to get shot in the back.

Gina stared after him. Even when they were both under fire in the drive-by last summer, she'd never seen Ken so rattled.

"I didn't know he was so young," LaRose murmured, clutching her handbag to her chest.

"Ken? He's thirty-six. That's not so young," Gina protested. "Jerry's thirty-seven and you keep telling me he's too old."

LaRose shook her head as if only half-hearing her. "So he would have been only thirty-two when it happened—barely older than you are now."

"When what happened? Is that when Moses took Ken to court?"

LaRose nodded. "It's so rare for your father to admit a mistake. And you know how passionate he is about exploring the gray areas of the law."

"Ken is practicing, getting grants, on the tenure track—so even if he lost a malpractice suit, it obviously didn't hurt him. Not like that doctor who killed himself after Moses shredded him to pieces in court."

"That was a car accident. A very unfortunate accident. Had nothing to do with your father."

Yeah, right. "So what did Moses do to Ken?"

LaRose looked at Gina, then back at the empty hallway where Ken had last been seen. "I'll tell you if you help me find Harold."

Gina hated the way every conversation with her parents became a negotiation. Nothing was ever free, Moses would say. Not even a parent's love.

She was ready to walk away, let LaRose waste her time running all over the hospital searching for Tank. Would serve her right, seeing how people with *real* problems lived. But

Gina wanted to know what had happened between Ken and Moses. Then she spied a familiar figure in the exam room down the hall.

"Come with me," she told LaRose, leading her to the dictation room behind the nurses' station. LaRose followed, holding her purse against her chest, elbows into her sides as if fearful of contamination. "So, what happened?"

"Dr. Rosen didn't lose his case. But sometimes there are unintended consequences."

Gina faced her mother across the tiny space. "What did Moses do?"

"His job." LaRose bristled with defensiveness. "It was really bad timing, that's all. No one could blame your father."

"What happened?"

LaRose sighed, actually pursing her lips enough to allow wrinkles to appear at the corners of her mouth. It was the most upset Gina had ever seen her. "You understand enough about your father's work to know that he often must list several defendants before he can get to the truth of who is responsible. Well, he made a mistake accusing Dr. Rosen—a mistake compounded by tactics the hospital took in defense of the other doctors, trying to shield them."

"You mean he dragged Ken through a trial, knowing he was innocent? Do you have any idea what that can do to a doctor, facing those kind of accusations?"

LaRose looked away as she continued. "During the trial, there was an—accident. Dr. Rosen's family was killed."

"His family?" Gina slumped against the wall, remembering the anguish in Jeremiah Boyle's ex-wife's face. She knuckled her fists into her thighs, trying to grind out any feeling.

"His wife and daughter. They were on vacation, but because the trial went longer than expected, Dr. Rosen had had to stay in Pittsburgh."

Jesus. A wife and a kid. Gina dug her knuckles in deeper, the pain keeping her anger at bay. "For the trial."

LaRose only nodded.

"A trial that Moses had no right involving Ken in in the first place."

LaRose was silent.

"Did Moses ever apologize? Say anything to Ken?"

"To my knowledge, they've never spoken or met outside the courtroom."

"How could he? He destroyed a man's life."

"Your father did no such thing. He did what he thought was right—for the law."

"For himself."

"Regina Freeman, show some respect."

"What about respect for Ken? For the hell Moses put him through?"

"You can't understand. There are some things you cannot apologize for. And your father was never one for apologies—especially not when he was doing the right thing." She smoothed invisible wrinkles from her Donna Karan. "Now, let's find Harold."

"Wait here. I'll go get him."

"You know where he is? Let me call Catherine."

"No. We do this my way or not at all."

LaRose frowned, eyes narrowing as if suspecting her daughter of something criminal. "Very well, if you insist."

A SOUND PRIMAL AND RAW SCREECHED ITS WAY up Lydia's nerve endings. It wasn't loud, but still it made every hair on her arms stand up.

Before she could do more than pinpoint where it came from, she was running in that direction. Despite every instinct telling her to stop, turn around, go the other way. That sound meant pain, anguish . . . death.

She slammed into the room, her hand gripping her gun, her pulse thudding in her fingertips. Boyle ran in right behind her—a good thing, because he had a light.

Nora was balled up on the floor, one hand splayed against a red mark darker than the rest of the graffiti on the wall. She was rocking her body, trying to curl it up tighter, chin tucked against her knees, eyes squeezed shut.

Making herself into a smaller target.

This was where it happened.

Lydia met Boyle's eyes, dilated wide despite the bright LED light, and knew he also understood. He holstered his weapon as she returned hers to her pocket. Her breath was coming so fast it fogged the air, but she didn't feel the cold. She knelt beside Nora and took her into her arms, pulling her away from the wall she was huddled against.

"It's okay," she whispered over and over, knowing the words were nonsense. It wouldn't be okay, not until this guy was locked up. For good. Even then, there was no way to repair the damage he'd done. Maybe heal it—with time—but never make it go away, make everything okay. Not for Nora.

Boyle aimed the light past Nora to the wall. There was a faint outline of a palm print in what looked like dried blood.

Lydia gripped Nora hard, hauling her back as fast as she could. The rapid motion snapped Nora out of her trance. Nora's soft keening stopped, and her eyes opened. Her face was pale as she and Lydia knelt together on the floor in the dark.

Boyle stepped away from them, keeping silent. He seemed to recognize how fragile the moment was. Lydia panicked, not quite sure what was best to do for Nora. Thankfully Nora quickly regained control. After squeezing Lydia in a tight hug for a moment, she pulled back, brushing her fingers over her jacket as if brushing away the tenement's dirt and grime that had contaminated her.

"I'm okay." Her voice was flinty, ready to break. But it didn't.

Lydia stood, offering a hand up. Nora's fingers were cold, her arm trembling as Lydia pulled her to her feet. She swayed, then took a breath and steadied herself. "Thanks."

Lydia put an arm around Nora, as much for herself as for

Nora, and led her to the door. "We'll wait in the car," she told Boyle without looking back.

Once inside the SUV, Lydia was prepared for hysterics, ready for another breakdown—after everything Nora had been through, she deserved one. Instead, she was amazed at Nora's calm. Wondered if, like the storm raging around them, something would soon break loose.

Thunder rocked the Escape; between it and the pounding sleet there was no chance for conversation even if either of them wanted to talk.

Lydia sure as hell didn't. What could she say? She had no words of comfort, could do nothing to erase the horror of Nora's attack two years ago. She offered to call Nora's parents, Mickey, Amanda, Seth, or even Gina, had volunteered to go get Tommy Z, but Nora merely shook her head in silence with each alternative.

So now they sat. Lydia drumming her fingers, tapping her feet, shifting her weight as water from her soaked jeans seeped into the seat. Nora curled up, arms hugging her knees, shivering, and Lydia turned the heat up higher.

"I thought you said he didn't cut you," Lydia finally blurted out. She couldn't help herself; as much as she didn't want to know the details, she just *had* to know. As if by knowing, she could tamp down the fury building in her. In the ER she could have shut her emotions off, but this wasn't the ER. This was her friend.

Nora didn't look up. "He didn't. I did. I used a nail in the floorboard to cut myself free of the duct tape. Made a bloody mess."

Lydia shook her head at the way Nora said it. Like they were talking about forgetting their umbrellas. "What you went through. What you've been through. I don't know if I could have handled it as well."

There was a long moment in which the only sound was the drumming of the rain. Lydia worried that her words had been presumptuous, that she had said the wrong thing.

But then Nora unfurled her body and turned to look at Lydia. Shadows from the rain played over Nora's face in gray streaks like tears. "That means a lot. Coming from you. Thanks."

"You're welcome. Are you sure there's nothing I can do to help?"

"You're here. That's a huge help." Nora stared through the fogged window. "I thought I'd put it all behind, buried it, somehow moved on. Re-created myself. But now I realize it was all just a wall of denial. The wall is crumbling down and there's nothing I can do about it."

"You're facing it. You're strong enough to face it. Maybe you weren't two years ago."

"Maybe I wasn't. Maybe I'm not. I wish I knew for sure." Nora blew her breath out, then focused on smoothing the wrinkles from her wet khakis. "In the fall, when that man attacked you, do you think—would you have—killed him?"

"Yes."

Nora tilted her face to squint up at her, as if Lydia were an alien from another planet. "Really? See, I don't think I could. Ever. Kill someone. Does that make me a victim?"

God, how was she supposed to know? All Lydia knew was the life she'd lived, and that life left no room for weakness or vulnerability—taking care of Maria, living on the streets had taught her that early on. Didn't make Lydia a hero, didn't make her way the right way—in fact, it was a pretty warped way of looking at the world, assuming that no one around you could be trusted, your guard always up, ready for a fight.

Not a whole lot of room for anyone else after you'd walled yourself in, ready for a siege. Even after her attack, Nora had been able to build relationships, had found Seth, found friends—that had to be the healthier way to live.

"You know why I wanted a gun?" Lydia asked.

"To protect yourself?"

"No. To fight back, to make sure no one could take what was mine."

"What's the difference?"

"The difference is that you found a way to survive, without taking someone else's life. I could have killed that man two months ago when he came into my home and attacked me. I *will* kill anyone who tries that again. Who tries to hurt anyone close to me."

Nora leaned back against the door, her gaze never leaving Lydia's face. "That's why Trey hates the gun."

Lydia nodded. "It has nothing to do with safety—hell, half his family are cops and have guns around. It's because he doesn't want to admit who I really am, what I am capable of."

"Because he's not."

"No. He's not."

"I think maybe that's not a bad thing. A man who doesn't embrace violence as an option." Nora's words emerged slowly, with consideration—as if she realized that she and Trey were in the same category.

"It's not a bad thing. But can a man like that be happy with a woman like me?" Lydia immediately wished she hadn't let that last bit escape. It hit too close to home. "So what happened with Seth? Did you listen to him?"

Nora frowned as if irritated with herself. "Yes. No. I let him stay, but we didn't really talk. Not about what really matters."

"I'm glad you're giving him a chance."

"Why's it so important to you?"

"I'm not sure. But Seth's one of the good guys."

"Hmpf." Nora didn't sound too convinced.

Lydia didn't push the issue—this was exactly why she tried to stay out of other people's problems. She stared at the sleet that had iced the windshield into an impressionistic grayscape.

"Maybe he thought that, too." Nora's voice came tightly, as if she were straining against something.

"Who?"

"The killer. Maybe he thinks he's one of the good guys, too. But that doesn't stop him from torture, rape, and murder."

"What do you mean?"

"I mean, maybe you can't ever truly know anyone. Maybe it's not even worth trying."

"You don't believe that."

Nora rested her head against the window, her expression blank. "I don't know what I believe anymore."

NINETEEN

THE SEIZURE STOPPED, BUT THEN NAROLIE BE-
came more combative, despite the sedatives in her system.
"This isn't just a reaction to smoking marijuana," Amanda
said as she helped the nurses fasten padded Velcro restraints
to Narolie's bony wrists and ankles.

"I need that MRI." Lucas dodged Narolie's gnashing teeth
as he tried to get a good look at her pupils.

"Just do something," Tank pleaded, backing away from
Narolie's bed, his entire body shaking. "Please help her."

To Amanda's relief, Gina appeared in the doorway. "Mind
if I borrow Tank?"

"No. I want to stay."

"We'll be taking her for an MRI, Tank," Amanda explained. "I'll come find you as soon as we know anything."

His gaze clutched at hers. "You promise?"

"I promise."

Reluctantly he turned and went with Gina. Amanda looked
at Lucas, who was frowning, squinting one eye like he always did when he was puzzled—which wasn't often.

"Did they do a thick prep for malaria?" he asked. "It would be a strange presentation for cerebral malaria, but—"

"She's been tested three times. Evidence of past infection, no evidence of any reactivation. No other ova or parasites, no signs of immunodeficiency, normal head CT, normal everything. That's why they called in psych."

He shook his head. "It's not psychiatric. Make sure there's a tox screen—in case Tank gave her anything besides the marijuana."

"Already done." Amanda stroked her fingers along Narolie's arm, trying to calm the girl, who was tossing and grimacing as if caught in a nightmare. "What else can we do?"

"Nothing. Not until I see what the MRI shows."

"And if it's normal as well?"

Lucas didn't answer. Usually Amanda appreciated the fact that he never gave his patients false assurances, but right now she could've used a little hope.

BOYLE RAPPED ON LYDIA'S WINDOW, GESTURING for her to join him outside. He'd grabbed a stray piece of corrugated cardboard and held it overhead against the sleet so they each froze only half their bodies.

"I'm headed back to the station house," he shouted over the wind, leaning forward so that their foreheads almost touched. "I need to get a formal statement from Nora."

Lydia glanced back over her shoulder at Nora's shadowy figure swimming in the rain-streaked window. "I'll take her, meet you there."

"Has she said anything?"

"Nothing about what happened."

He grimaced. "Normal reaction. A lot of victims try to disassociate themselves—"

"Don't. Boyle, don't. She may have been a victim of a crime, may still be wrapped up in its consequences, may never be the same after this, but don't you dare try to pigeonhole her or treat her like this is anything normal. She's a friend. She's your friend. So"—her voice caught and she was glad for the rain that masked the tears knotted in her throat—"just don't. Okay?"

He was silent for a long moment, his gaze paralleling hers as he stared at Nora. Then he nodded. "Sometimes when a case hits too close to home, *we* have to disassociate ourselves as well."

"I know. Believe me, I know." She gave his arm a squeeze. "I'll meet you at the station."

"All right."

He left. She stood in the sleet, watching him walk away, and knew she shouldn't have lashed out at him. Boyle was the last person who could be accused of being unsympathetic to a victim or a friend. She opened her car door, wondering if it wasn't herself and her clumsy inability to help Nora that really upset her.

"We're going to the police station," she explained to Nora as the Escape plowed through the storm water runoff that had formed a series of rapids along Penn Avenue. "Boyle will need an official statement."

"I know."

"Are you sure you don't want me to call anyone?"

Silence. Lydia shivered, but the heat was already on high. It wouldn't help anyway. She could have a furnace blasting heat from the vents and she would still be cold.

The precinct house wasn't far. It wasn't until they drove around Penn Circle and Lydia spotted the officious yellow-brick building ringed in chain link and razor wire that she realized she'd have to go inside. Couldn't just dump Nora at the curb like a drive-by, could she?

Now she was sweating. Walking into a building filled with cops . . . All those men in uniform, carrying guns and nightsticks—just like the man who had murdered her mother, not knowing that twelve-year-old Lydia had seen everything from her hiding place.

That was eighteen years ago, and she had worked with many fine police officers during her time as a medic in L.A. and as an ER physician. She no longer fought head-reeling nausea at the sight of an uniformed officer—hell, here in Pittsburgh she even counted Jerry Boyle as a friend.

But one-on-one was a lot different from entering a building designed to leave civilians helpless and at the mercy of the police's power. Her breath came shallow and fast as she pulled into a visitor's spot and ushered Nora inside the public entrance.

Nora shuffled like a woman fifty years her senior, the events of the day finally overwhelming even her seemingly boundless reserves of energy. Lydia parked her in a chair in the lobby and went to explain to the sergeant stationed behind inch-thick bulletproof glass who they were and why they were there. She was surprised to see Seth Cochran also waiting at the counter.

"Seth, what are you doing here?" she asked.

"A detective called, said I needed to come down and answer some questions about my relationship with Karen." He frowned. "What are you doing here? I thought you were with Nora. Is she all right?"

Lydia gave him a rough sketch of their trip to the tenement.

He turned, his gaze roaming past her to zero in on Nora's still form at the far end of the lobby. She was staring out the window at the rain, her back to them. He rocked forward as if wanting to go to her.

"I wish I knew how to help her," he said, his voice as low as a whisper.

"You do. Better than anyone else."

He sucked in his breath, squared his shoulders, and strode across the lobby to sit down beside Nora. She jerked her head up when he placed his arm around her shoulder, then turned to him and buried her face in his chest, clenching him so tightly that her knuckles went white. Lydia watched them, surprised by the tears that ambushed her.

"Hey, glad you're still here," Boyle said as he pushed through the secure doors separating the lobby from the inner workings of the station. Lydia swiped at her eyes with a furtive wave of her hand. "How's she doing?" He nodded in Nora's direction.

"Better than I would be. I'm worried she's going to pay the price, sooner or later."

"Someone staying with her?"

"Yes."

"Good." He paused. "Listen, before you leave, I wanted to apologize for springing that stuff about your mom on you. It was a long shot that Epson, my friend in California, would find anything new, but I thought you should know that the L.A. cops tried."

"I know."

"Last I talked with him, he said he was going to run your mom's prints again, see if anything pops now that more databases are digitalized. I have a call in to him, but he's not answering. He's retiring this month and with the holidays and all, he's probably using up anything left on his vacation time—"

"It's fine. Don't worry about it." She glanced back over her shoulder at Nora and Seth. "You've got more important things on your plate than an eighteen-year-old homicide. Let it rest."

AS SHE ESCORTED TANK DOWN THE HALL TO THE family room, Gina scanned the board. A bunch of fever and body aches, a few fender benders—nothing serious enough to require a trauma alert—a preterm labor OB-GYN was down for, an ACS on his way to the cath lab, and a kid with a asthma attack. She spotted Jim Lazarov chatting up a nurse in the far corner.

"Hey, Lazarov," she called. "How's the kid in two?"

"Haven't seen him yet," Jim said with a grouchy scowl. "The nurses are still getting his vitals."

"You don't wait around on an asthma attack. Get a move on. That way respiratory can get a treatment started while you're mucking around with the rest of the history and exam."

His scowl deepened but he did grab the chart from the rack. Gina kept going, dragging Tank into the family room and closing the door behind them.

"She's never seen snow," Tank muttered as he sank into one of the chairs. "It's all my fault. I just wanted to show her snow for the first time."

"So I see." Gina gestured to his wet clothes. "What happened?"

Tank hung his head and seemed to crawl inside himself. "She started to get this headache—at first she didn't say anything, but I knew something was wrong. I told her we could go back, get a nurse, but she said no, she wanted to stay and watch the storm. Even though it wasn't really snow—not the pretty kind, anyway."

Gina started to interrupt, to tell him to forget about the snow, but then she remembered how Lydia often got people to spill their guts just by listening. Worth a try. So she said nothing, but merely perched on the arm of the chair beside him.

"But she was crying because of her headache, so I gave her a joint. I didn't know it would hurt her, honest!" He looked up at her, pleading.

She almost gave in, almost did what Jerry and everyone did whenever she screwed up: tell him it wasn't his fault, tell him everything would be okay. But one look at Tank and she knew he'd had a lifetime of that, just as she had, and he wouldn't be fooled. Instead, she took another page from Lydia's book—and Ken Rosen's as well.

"You didn't think sharing an illegal drug with a thirteen-year-old girl with a serious medical illness would hurt?" Her voice was more accusing than either Lydia's or Ken's, so she backed it down a notch. "Or you just didn't think?"

Tank looked up at her in surprise, ready to argue, but she merely stared back. He looked away, miserable as he hugged himself, scratching at his arms. "I did think," he said defensively. "I thought about how a little pot gets me through the rough times, makes everything feel okay."

"No one is accusing you of trying to hurt Narolie," Gina said. Tank scratched more furiously, his nails digging into his forearms and palms. "But we all know you weren't using your best judgment. You're smarter than that, Tank."

"Says you."

Gina could take his itching no longer. He didn't even seem to notice he was doing it. She grabbed one of his hands and stretched out his arm so she could look at his forearm. The rash he'd denied noticing yesterday was more prominent today—now scratched and scaling and with a definite pattern. "I thought you said it wasn't itchy."

He shrugged. "It wasn't."

"When was the last time you used marijuana?"

"Yesterday morning before class. The Nazis up in the ICU have smoke detectors in the bathrooms, and I gave Narolie the last joint I had on me."

Gina held his hand palm up, spread his fingers wide, and scrutinized the spaces between them. She smiled. "I think I know what's wrong with you, Tank."

"Can you fix it? So then I can go see Narolie?"

"I can fix it. But I guarantee your mom's not going to like it."

He met her gaze and grinned. "Cool."

TWENTY

Friday, 11:01 A.M.

"IF YOU TWO WILL COME WITH ME . . ." JERRY Boyle's voice broke through the white noise that filled Nora's brain. She pushed back from Seth, swiped at her eyes with one hand, and stood up.

"Janet Kwon is waiting to speak with Seth." Jerry led them through the secure doors and upstairs to the Major Crimes squad room. "We've finished interviewing the other two local victims. At least the other two that we know about."

"Local?" Seth asked. "You mean there are more victims out there who aren't local?"

"Looks like there could be. The FBI found three more cases—two in Baltimore and one in Cleveland. Same MO."

Nora clutched at Seth's arm. "Are—are they dead?"

"No. I'm waiting to get more information from the investigators working their cases, but sounds like the same actor. They were all redheads, all worked in health care facilities, all attacked in the last fourteen months. In the meantime, I was hoping that you could help out here. Talk with our local victims."

"Me?" She couldn't face those women—women hurt because of her cowardice.

"With all three of you together, you might come up with some detail that might help. Because right now we have nothing." His shoulders slumped. She'd never seen him this tired. "Wait here. I'll get Janet."

Nora gripped Seth's hand. "I can't do it. How can I face those women, knowing that I might have prevented what happened to them?"

Seth pulled her to him, almost smothering her against his chest. Being close to him felt good, safe.

"You can do it. You can do anything."

His words surprised her, with their simple faith in her. Seth ignored the past and focused on what was possible in the here and now.

He kissed the top of her head, his fingers ruffling through her hair before separating from her. "I believe in you, Nora. Never forget that."

Jerry returned, accompanied by his partner, Janet Kwon. "You ready?"

"Can Seth come with me?"

"No. Sorry. Like I said, Janet needs to clear up a few things with him."

Nora caught an unfamiliar edge to Jerry's voice, but before she could say anything, Janet had separated Seth from her and was leading him into a small interview room down the hall. Jerry touched her on the arm. "Here we go."

He led her through the door into a small room furnished similarly to the family lounge at Angels. Two vinyl love seats created the outside walls of a square with two more identical vinyl chairs at top and bottom. A low coffee table with two boxes of tissues and an assortment of sodas stood in the center of the square.

The chairs had already been taken. A woman with short, spiky strawberry-blond hair sat in one, legs crossed, top leg bobbing in time with her hand as she awkwardly tapped a cigarette free from a pack. The action was difficult because her left arm was in a cast.

"When's it come off?" the second woman asked. She had no obvious injuries. Her hair was shoulder length and dyed onyx. But her eyebrows were lighter, almost the same shade as Nora's own.

"Next week," the smoker said as soon as she inhaled several puffs, stacking them one on top of the other, ignoring the NO SMOKING sign across from her. Her foot never stopped its motion.

"Ladies," Jerry interrupted, easing Nora forward until she had no choice but to take a seat on the nearest love seat. "This is Nora. Nora, this is Meg and Amy."

"Hi," she said, nodding at each, barely catching that the strawberry blond was Meg, and Amy was the one with the bad dye job.

"Welcome to the club," Amy said. "When did he get you?"

"Two years ago," Nora answered, startled by her frankness. "Almost three, now."

"I was fourteen months ago," Amy feathered her fingers through her hair, "and she was—"

"Seven weeks ago." Meg had already sucked her cigarette down to the filter, but she kept on inhaling, her lips pursed so tight that her lipstick bled into the skin around her mouth.

"Guess that makes you the first one. Lucky you." Amy turned to Jerry. "How's this going to work?"

"First, thank you both for agreeing to this. It's not how we usually do things, but—" Jerry sank into the last love seat, elbows on his knees, leaning forward, mirroring the anxiety of all three women. "I know this is a lot to ask. And I appreciate your helping us. I've read your statements, but I thought that getting you three together, you might be able to fill in the gaps, maybe spark a memory—anything to help us nail this guy."

"Uniontown cops said it couldn't be done." Amy interrupted him, obviously wanting to be in control. "Not without evidence."

"That was when they thought they only had one victim. Now we have four in the area. And a pattern. What we call a—"

"Signature," Amy put in. "Yeah, we get it. We watch *CSI*, you know. Is this legal, us talking together?"

"The fact is, that with no forensic evidence and no way for any of you to identify your attacker—"

"You can't convict him even if you do catch him. Right?" Amy shifted her weight to the edge of her seat, planting her feet, ready to bolt. "So what are we even doing here?"

Nora wanted to tell the other woman to just shut up and let him talk, get this over with, but she didn't. Instead, she opened a can of Sprite and sat back, concentrating on the way the condensation dribbled off the can and onto her hand. The bubbles scratched against her throat, felt sharp, and she remembered feeling that same tightness when she'd been taken, the rapist's knife against her neck.

Jerry didn't seem to mind Amy's power play. He kept his voice low and steady, nonconfrontational. "If you can help me find him, maybe we can convict him for murder."

"Murder?" Meg gasped.

"I'm afraid so. His last victim died."

Silence swirled between them as each woman reluctantly settled back into her chair and met the others' eyes.

"How's this gonna work?" Amy asked.

"I thought we'd start from the beginning, each of you chiming in as you remember events. Amy, do you want to describe how he initially approached you?"

Amy pushed back in her chair, as far back as she could get without toppling it over. "Why doesn't *she*? After all, she was the first."

It took Nora a moment to realize that both Meg and Amy were staring at her, waiting for her.

She swallowed, the soda scratching and almost choking

her. Coughing, she put the can down on the table. Swirling it around the smooth veneer, she traced wet spirals as she spoke.

"It was New Year's Eve. My date and I were both a little drunk, so we took a cab. He dropped me off in front of my building, and I was walking up the steps." One of the other women made a sharp, gasping noise, but Nora didn't look up to see who it was. "He came up behind me; I never saw him. Put a knife to my throat, dragged me to his car, made me kneel down, put glue in my eyes so I couldn't see, duct-taped my hands, and threw me in the trunk."

"With me it was a gun." Meg's voice was raspy from more than smoking, Nora realized. She looked closer and saw that she still had red marks, thin like wire, along her neck. Maybe they were permanent; maybe he had damaged her voice box when he choked her?

"Me, too," Amy said. "But after we got there, to the first place, it was always a knife." She shivered, pushing up her sleeves, revealing thin lines of scars arcing over her arms. "He liked cutting. A lot."

"He liked a lot of things," Meg said, lighting another cigarette. "Cutting, pinching, choking, hitting. Talking. God, that made it worse—he wouldn't shut up."

Nora found herself nodding in unison with Amy.

"Tell me about his voice," Jerry said in a low voice, now leaning back, keeping out of their way.

"Weird, mechanical."

"Tinny—not a robot's, but like the voice on the elevator that tells you what floor you're on," Amy added.

"Not human," Nora said. Both women looked at her, making eye contact before quickly looking away.

"Could it have come from a computer?"

"It was like in surround sound, so yeah," Meg said, eyes drifting shut, body rocking as she remembered. "And he had a headset or Bluetooth thingy on—I knocked it off once and it made a noise when it hit the floor."

"After the car ride, the first one, can you remember anything about where he took you? Did he carry you from the car? Did you walk? How far was it? Any sounds, smells?"

As Jerry led them each through their captivity, it became clear that they had all been kept in the same place before being dumped elsewhere. But Nora's experiences were quite different from the other women's. The other two women hadn't had the "date" at all, hadn't been forced to pretend to make love with their captor, nor had he worked to pleasure them.

He had beaten them, used them, cut them, done unspeakable things to them, heaped verbal abuse on them, called them harlots, whores, sluts, bitches, had repeatedly strangled them using his hands, wire, plastic bags, and their own hair after he chopped it off, had carved words into their flesh along with spray-painting them with graffiti . . . the list of atrocities went on and on.

The only thing he didn't do was actually have sex with them.

"Do you think that was because you fought back or because he couldn't?" Jerry asked Amy when she finished describing her attempts to kick and head-butt the attacker.

"He couldn't get it up," Amy said triumphantly. "Maybe 'cause I kneed him in the balls hard enough to rupture them."

"He couldn't—er—perform with me, either," Meg put in, her head turned to focus on a distant corner of the ceiling. "But I didn't fight. I just lay there limp, let him do whatever he wanted. I just wanted it to be over."

Nora felt Jerry's gaze on her and knew he also was seeing a disturbing trend. Nora had been a love interest. She had been forced to be an active participant. Only with Nora had the attacker been able to perform sexually.

She'd been the first. The attacker hadn't selected her at random, stalked her, and then attacked her as part of a pattern. He had wanted her. Chosen her.

Then when she disappointed, he had thrown her out like garbage and began to vent his rage on other women. Women who looked like her. Same build, hair in the reddish spectrum, same pale complexion, same upturned nose, same lips that her father called a Cupid's bow.

Nora retreated to a corner of the love seat, curled up, knees to her chin, her chest heaving as she tried to stave off a panic attack.

Concentrating on her breathing, head rushing with noise that had nothing to do with the words the other women were saying, she felt herself drifting away in a sea of gray, until Amy's voice cut through.

"He kept talking about how I needed to be taught a lesson, that I had no idea what love really was, that I was just a cheap whore. Acted like it was my fault he couldn't get it up."

"Yeah," Meg said, pulverizing her cigarette against the bottom of the ashtray. "Same here. Over and over, about how he had sacrificed everything for love, and I wasn't worthy. He used that word a lot. *Worthy.*"

Amy was silent for a long moment. When she spoke, it wasn't with her previous strident anger. "He knew things about me. Where I lived, my boyfriend's name. Where I worked. Said if I disrespected him again, he'd know, come back."

Meg shuddered, looked away, and blinked hard. Her foot stopped bouncing for a long moment. "I still live in the same place," she said in a small voice. "Don't have money to move."

"Is there someone who can stay with you the next few days?" Jerry asked. "Or somewhere else you can—"

"She's coming home with me," Amy said, standing up and brushing her hands against her jeans as if shooing away Jerry and the memories his questions dredged up. She walked around the coffee table and placed her hands palm down on Meg's shoulders. "Come on, Meg. We're done here."

Nora heard the door shut behind them but didn't turn her head. She sat there, arms hugging her knees to her chest, not blinking.

Jerry must have escorted the others out because the door opened again a few minutes later and he sat down beside her.

"You okay?" he asked without touching her. Like he was afraid she would shatter. She wondered if maybe he was right.

"It was me. He wanted me—something from me." Her eyes were half shut, giving her a narrow view of her gray world. "Something I couldn't give him. It pissed him off and he kept going after other women—" She stopped herself, resting her forehead on her knees.

Jerry was silent, merely wrapping his arms around her shoulders. Somehow it wasn't as comforting as Seth's embrace. But then again, nothing was.

"Why me, Jerry?" she asked, her voice shredded with tears. "What does he want from me?"

TWENTY-ONE

Friday, 11:23 A.M.

NAROLIE'S FACE APPEARED CALM AS THE SEDATIVES finally took effect. Amanda only wished she felt as calm. She hated coming down to MRI ever since one of her patients, a little baby, had almost died there. No one blamed her, but she couldn't shake the guilt or the sense of doom that settled on her every time she watched a patient enter the MRI chamber.

Lucas leaned forward, squinting into the computer screen as the machine chugged and clanked and clanged. Views of Narolie's brain appeared.

"Anything?" Amanda asked, knowing Lucas could pick up subtleties that no computer ever would.

"No," said the radiologist sitting beside Lucas.

"Yes," said Lucas. "Hyperintensity in the hippocampus."

The radiologist frowned, glanced at where Lucas was pointing the tip of his pen, then slowly nodded. "You're right." New images appeared, magnified, and the radiologist twisted his mouth into a wry smile. "Damn it, Stone, I hate it when you do that."

"What is it?" Amanda asked, her hand wrapping around

Lucas's arm, forgetting all about protocol or propriety. Lucas didn't seem to mind; he covered her hand with his and gave her a quick squeeze.

"Encephalitis," he said.

"Right," the radiologist agreed. "Definite signs of meningeal enhancement. Usually I see this with herpes virus, but there are others."

"West Nile, Rift Valley, Eastern equine, Chikungunya," Lucas supplied. The litany of diseases sounded like a death knell.

"Is there a cure?"

Both men swiveled in their chairs to stare at her. "No."

LYDIA PULLED THE ESCAPE INTO HER DRIVEWAY and took her gun case out of the back with regret. Shooting something would feel so good right now. Much better than this pent-up, churning anxiety—all about things she had no control over.

She jogged into the house and tossed the case onto the kitchen table, startling Ginger Cat, who was sprawled out napping in the center of the empty dining room floor. Ginger Cat deigned to flick an ear at her, then closed his eyes again.

The expression on Nora's face still haunted her. Was there a word for *more than terrified*? *More than exhausted*? The closest she could come was *despair*.

Lydia banged around in the kitchen, more for the chance to make noise than actual cooking. She ended up chopping up an avocado and a tomato and tossing in some shredded carrots and cheese for her own version of guacamole and ate it scooped onto some Black Russian bread from the bakery down on Penn.

She ate standing up, as usual, wandering through her house, plate in hand. The empty corner of the dining room beckoned to her. Her long board used to stand there, a Kalama eight-foot, six-inch board with a polycarb tri-fin. If she closed her eyes she could feel the wind and surf on her face, the roll of the board beneath her feet. . . . She'd been here only a few months, but already L.A. seemed a distant memory.

She wished some of those memories would stay buried. Like the memory of the day her mother was murdered. Reading the LAPD's report, going to that crack house today . . . she couldn't stop the memories from resurfacing. Somehow Nora's torment and her mother's were becoming all tangled up, screams and pain and terror mangled together, and all Lydia could do was stand by and watch, helpless.

She shuddered and stepped into the center of the empty room. Why was everyone saying she needed more stuff? she wondered as rain-cast shadows played over the polished red oak floors and the bare vanilla-apricot plaster walls. More stuff just meant more things you could lose, more stuff to be taken away from you, mourned over. . . .

Ginger Cat sensed her restlessness and wound between her legs, brushing his body against her. She sat down on the bare floor, scratched him behind his ears, and was soon rewarded with a jangled rumble that was his version of a purr. Even that was no comfort. When she'd first come to this house and found Ginger Cat, he was an exotic creature, a graveyard cat that resembled a wild panther.

But now he seemed to have adopted her—had even come to accept Trey—and was spending more time inside the house. If she was around he wouldn't let her out of his sight, as if he'd anointed himself her protector.

Domesticated.

Caged in. By walls, by people, by duty.

"This was a mistake," Lydia said, standing up, disrupting Ginger Cat's purr-fest. She opened one of the French doors, ignoring the frigid wind that sliced through her still-damp clothing. "Go on, shoo, you don't belong inside."

The cat sat back on his haunches and looked at her as if she were the crazy one.

"You should be running around, free, not caught up here—"
She waved her hand at the empty space, the empty walls that
created Ginger Cat's prison. Her prison? Maybe she was the
one who'd made a mistake. Maybe she was the one who
wasn't compatible with domestic life.

Maybe she was the one who needed to return to the wild.

Instead of leaving, Ginger Cat padded over to her, wound
his body around her legs, placing himself between her and
the door, and nudged her away from the opening with his
head. Herding her. Away from danger. Back to comfort and
safety.

She let go of the door, a final gust of wind swirling through
the room, whistling like a banshee as it slammed the door
shut. Leaning her forehead against the chilled glass, she ignored the winter wind rattling through her body and stared
out at the gray.

"Why won't you leave?" she pleaded with the cat, who
answered by rubbing the side of his face against her leg.
Tears pricked the back of her eyes, and she blinked furiously.
Everything she'd seen and heard today and it was a damn cat
who finally made her cry?

"SO I DON'T HAVE THAT MENINGO THING?" TANK
asked as Gina led him from the family room. "I'm not going
to die?"

It had to say something hopeful about the boy that his first
thought had been about Narolie and only now was he worried
about himself. Gina smiled at the skinny teen, taking care not
to touch him—not now that she knew what he had.

"No, Tank. If I'm right, you're going to be just fine." A
screeching noise down the hall made her look up. It was Tank's
mom along with LaRose, both clattering as fast as their heels
would take them. "Shit."

"Harold!" Mrs. Trenton's exclamation points hit mezzo-
soprano as she launched herself at her son, half-hugging him,

half-hauling him away from Gina. "What have you done? I was so worried!"

"He's fine," Gina said firmly. "Come in here, please. I'll explain everything." She pulled the curtain back on an open bed space. Mrs. Trenton balked at the less-than-executive-suite surroundings, so Gina added, "I'm sure you don't want to discuss this in the middle of the hallway."

That did the trick. Tank's mother practically shoved him behind the curtain. LaRose tried to follow, eyes gleaming at the prospect of insider info, but Gina intervened, blocking her path. LaRose relented and turned away.

As LaRose walked toward the nurses' station, Gina spotted Ken Rosen.

"Gina, have you seen Narolie Maxeke? Lucas Stone called me in to consult on her case."

"Last I heard, they were still down in MRI. What did Lucas find?"

"Looks like encephalitis."

"Really? That stinks. Hey, can you give me a hand with Harold Trenton? I think I figured out what's going on with him."

"What's he doing back down here? I thought he was in the PICU."

Instead of answering, Gina ushered Ken inside the curtained space and pulled the curtain shut behind her. Tank sat on the bed, legs dangling, hands clenching the mattress with a death grip. His mother hovered alongside him.

"I'm not going back up there," Tank was saying. "Not until I know Narolie's okay."

"Harold, you'll do as we say. You've caused enough trouble already. If your grandfather hears of this—"

"I'm sure you remember Dr. Rosen, our infectious-disease expert," Gina interrupted. "I've asked him to confirm my findings. Tank, show Dr. Rosen your palms." As Tank complied, she handed Ken a pair of gloves. "You'll want these."

"Findings?" Mrs. Trenton said. "What findings?"

"Tank doesn't have meningococcemia," Gina said, while Ken examined the area between Tank's fingers and then used a scalpel and slide to take a small scraping. "In fact, I think Dr. Rosen will be able to give us the answer in a few minutes." Ken nodded at her, then left, taking the slide with him.

"But Dr. Frantz, everyone said—"

"Dr. Frantz was mistaken. Misled, actually. You see, Tank uses marijuana. And I'm not sure what other drugs."

"How dare you! My son doesn't—"

"So I toke up? What's that got to do with anything?" Tank said, straightening up and giving his mother a rebel stare.

"Harold!"

Gina continued, keeping her tone professional. She wanted to feel some satisfaction, at least a little, but instead she felt sad. For Tank. "Because of the marijuana use and maybe some other factors, Tank couldn't remember how long he'd had the rash and told us it wasn't itchy. Given the fever, and because none of the adults in his life could say when it started, the nurse jumped to conclusions. But if I'm right, Tank's rash has been there several days rather than the few hours we'd see with meningococcemia."

"What about the fever?"

"Probably a virus," Gina explained.

"So all this is for a case of the flu?"

"No, there's more."

Ken returned, right on cue. "You're right, Gina. Mites were present on the wet prep."

"Mites? What's going on here?"

"Tank has scabies."

"Scabies!" Mrs. Trenton jumped away from her son and gave him a look of horror. "That's like lice! People like us can't get scabies!"

LUCAS AND THE RADIOLOGIST TOOK THEIR TIME, getting more views of Narolie's brain after giving her some intravenous contrast. As they nattered on about FLAIR intensity and attenuation versus enhancement, Amanda pressed her face against the window separating them from Narolie. How was she going to explain to Narolie that she was going to get worse, that there was no cure, that she was dying?

It was wrong, all wrong. Anger seeped into Amanda's veins, chasing away her doubts. There had to be something they'd missed. She wasn't about to let some nameless disease steal a girl's life.

Finally the machine stopped clanking and the tech wheeled Narolie out of the magnet's field. Amanda rushed out to meet her. The sedation was beginning to wear off. Narolie's eyelids fluttered, then opened. She looked around, eyes wide, pupils dilated.

"It's okay, Narolie," Amanda said, leaning over the stretcher so that Narolie could see her better. "I'm here."

"What—" Narolie's gaze darted to and fro. "Who are you? What do you want?" She yanked against the restraints holding her in place. "You want to kill us! Help! Stop!"

Lucas came running from the control room just as Narolie managed to get one hand free and grabbed Amanda's throat with deadly force. Amanda clawed at her, but Narolie seemed possessed with an unimaginable strength.

"I won't let you hurt my brother." Narolie spit the words through clenched jaws in a tone that resembled a growl. Then she began to scream in another language—Swahili?

Amanda's vision dimmed as she struggled. Narolie's screams pounded through her brain in time with her pulse. Then Narolie slumped back. Amanda blinked, saw Lucas holding a syringe, standing near the IV on the opposite side of the bed.

"Are you okay?" he asked.

"I'm fine." Amanda massaged her neck and swallowed twice. It hurt, but no more than a bruise. Before she could say anything else, Narolie's monitor sounded an alarm. "Blood pressure dropping." She turned to Lucas. "What did you give her?"

Lucas was shaking his head. "Only another two of Versed. It shouldn't have this effect."

Amanda listened to Narolie's heart. Its rhythm was slowing, and then there was silence. "No pulse!"

TWENTY-TWO

Nora spent the rest of the afternoon with Jerry, dissecting every moment of her attack. Somehow she choked down a chicken salad sandwich that tasted like paste, but she barely noticed. It was as if talking about those two days, reliving them, had transported her mind back in time. Occasionally as she spoke, she'd forget Jerry was even there, could instead almost smell, hear, and feel the rapist with her.

Once Jerry's cell phone went off, startling her so badly that it triggered a panic attack. She'd excused herself, somehow making it to the bathroom before breaking down, then sat in the stall, knees drawn to her chest, rocking back and forth until she could breathe again. When she shakily emerged, the bright light reflected in the mirror seared her vision just as it had after those two days when she'd been blind to the world, her eyelids sealed shut, the glue scratching her corneas.

She'd washed her face, wiped away some of the sweat and stench of terror that covered her, rinsed the acid taste from her mouth, and finally exited to find Jerry waiting.

"You sure you're up to this?" he'd asked, even as he steered her back into the interview room.

What choice did she have? She'd simply nodded and resumed her seat, beginning to describe once more the details of the two days she'd tried her best to erase permanently from her memory.

Finally, they finished. She'd answered all of Jerry's questions, at least all the ones she had answers to. He looked wrung out, his hands hanging lifelessly between his knees, his expression grim, and she knew that after everything she'd been through, it still wasn't enough.

"None of that helped, did it?"

He shook his head. "Of course it did. Even if it doesn't give me any concrete evidence about where to look for this guy, it gives me an idea about how he thinks."

"I'm not sure that's such a good thing. Understanding how his mind works."

"Maybe not. But right now, without any forensic evidence, it's the best weapon I have to hunt him down. I wish we could explain the eighteen months between your attack and the next victim." He scrubbed his palms over his face and glanced up at her. She suddenly had the sinking feeling that maybe they weren't finished after all. "I have to ask—"

She slid to the edge of her seat, hanging on to the weathered upholstery. "What?"

"Seth. When did you first meet? We know he was working at Angels during the time of your attack."

"No." Her voice emerged a hoarse whisper. She cleared her throat, met his gaze. "No. We didn't meet until a year later. It couldn't have been Seth."

"I want to think that. But he knew both you and Karen, he knows hospitals, he could move around one without anyone noticing."

"No. Jerry, you know Seth. He'd never hurt anyone; hell, I can't even get him to kill a spider. It's not possible."

"I'd feel a lot better about things if he had come forward about his association with Karen."

Silence circled the room. "It wasn't him. Besides, he was on call the night Karen was—" *Taken, raped, tortured, violated, murdered . . .* there was no one word large enough to encompass everything she'd experienced.

"Janet is verifying his alibi now."

"There's no way. It wasn't him." Nora tried to focus her vision as she was catapulted back in time, felt the breadth of her attacker's hands pressed against her, inhaled his odor. . . . Her stomach churned, and she regretted the sandwich Jerry had made her eat.

She thought of Seth, the way he moved, the way he made love, his scent, his touch, his taste. "Trust me. It wasn't Seth."

"You think it's a coincidence this guy targeted both you and Karen?"

The question had been nagging at her since yesterday. "No." She finally met his gaze once more. "You think he's going to come after me again."

Jerry blew his breath out, obviously frustrated. "I wish I knew. This actor has a thing for women and hospitals. Knows their routines, is comfortable inside them. He takes the time and effort to learn everything he can about his victims before he attacks. But what worries me is the extra time he took with you. That and the way the others look like you."

"Except for Karen. Maybe he's changed the type of woman he's targeting? Tall blondes instead of petite redheads?"

His look of doubt said it all. She knew it couldn't be that easy.

"I wish I could say for sure one way or the other. Whatever's going on in this guy's head, it makes sense to him— even if not to us." He stood, shaking the creases from his trousers. "If you think of anything, call me."

She pushed out of her chair, hoisting herself back onto her feet, feeling a bit breathless and dizzy as her thoughts collided. "Why? Why me? I've read about stalkers, what do you call them, the ones who are delusional and make up a relationship out of nothing?"

"Intimacy seekers."

"Right. But I'm not famous or anything. I'm not beautiful. Why me?"

"We may never know. And it may not really be all about you—I don't have enough information yet. Maybe it's something to do with the hospitals; maybe that's what set him off. The important thing is, you shouldn't go home alone. Get out of town, visit family, or—"

"No." She was shaking her head. "No. I've been running from this for two years. I can't keep running—if he *is* after me, he'll catch up with me sooner or later."

"Nora. At least give me some time. This isn't the movies; we can't arrange around-the-clock protection for you."

"Even if you could, for how long? There were months between Amy and Meg and Karen's attacks, not to mention the out-of-state victims."

He nodded and opened the door, leading her to the elevator lobby. "And there might be more victims out there that we don't know about yet."

Nora hoped that wasn't the case. But she knew all too well that most sexual assault victims never reported their assaults. Which meant who knew how many other women could have fallen prey.

The elevator dinged, and its doors opened. "So, what should I do? I can't put my life on hold forever." She turned to face him. "What would you do if it were Gina who might be in danger?"

His eyes took on a vacant look as a smile creased his features. "I'd take her to Vegas for a quickie wedding, then off to a Greek island for a honeymoon that would last as long as it took for them to catch the creep." He blinked, and his eyes clouded. "But that's not going to happen. Because you're one of those hyper-responsible, take-charge, independent types who will insist on standing her ground, aren't you?"

"I'm no fool, Jerry. Just a realist. This guy is obviously patient, has some plan of his own. *If* he is after me, running and hiding will only delay the inevitable. And he might target someone else—maybe even my family or friends—in the meantime."

He surprised her by giving her a quick hug. "At least do me a favor and stay with someone else for now. Keep a low profile. The less attractive a target you are, the less likely he is to make a move, and the more time I buy to investigate."

She stood on her tiptoes and kissed him on the cheek. "Thanks, Jerry."

They arrived on the first floor and she was surprised to see Seth waiting, pacing the public lobby beyond the large, bulletproof, glassed-in desk. Jerry escorted her through the locked doors, and she felt a weight leave her chest as if she were a prisoner being paroled early for good behavior.

When Seth caught sight of her, he froze midstep. The look on his face was a mixture of relief and concern. He rushed forward, wrapping his arms around her. "Are you all right?"

She pushed away; it was too hard to breathe, being that close to him. "I'm fine."

Seth squared off against Jerry. "It's been hours."

"No one told you to wait." Jerry placed a hand on Nora's arm. "Nora, do you want me to take you to Lydia's?"

"She's coming home with me," Seth protested. Nora backed away from both men, too tired to interfere. Better to let them run the course of their testosterone-driven standoff.

"That's up to Nora," Jerry said, although Nora considered it a good sign that he no longer considered Seth a viable suspect. "How did your chat with Janet Kwon go?"

Seth bristled. "Yeah, she's a real peach. If I ever need a prostate exam, I'll know who to call."

"Hey, you're out here, not locked up, that says a lot. Like the fact that your alibi checked out." Jerry smiled, but it didn't make it to his eyes, which were still filled with worry.

"What do you say, Nora? You going home with this mutt, or you want me to take you somewhere else?"

Seth beseeched her with his gaze. She never could resist those big, dark eyes. "I'll go home with Seth."

"Okay. You think of anything, see anything, hell, you even feel like this guy has eyes on you, I want you to call me right away. Night or day. Understand?"

She squeezed his arm in gratitude. "I will. Thanks, Jerry."

"So you guys still don't know who this nut job is?" Seth demanded. "What about those flowers from a few months ago; can't you trace him through the florists or something?"

Nora frowned at Seth. "What are you talking about? *You* sent those flowers."

"What flowers?" Jerry asked.

"Back in October some creep was sending Nora flowers all the time." Anger simmered through his words. "She thought it was me—I told her to call you guys." He turned to Nora. "I told you it wasn't me, except for the one time. After you refused to talk to me."

Nora's head was pounding. "But I—you really didn't send the others?" She thought for a long moment, a stray memory nagging at her for attention. Something recent—something from last night. "Seth, did you bring flowers with you yesterday? When you came to my place?"

"No. I brought the DVD, that was it."

Nora grabbed Jerry's arm. "Call Mickey, send someone over there, please. Make sure she's okay." She quickly explained to Jerry about the bouquet of lavender daylilies and the anonymous flowers she'd gotten in October. She could kick herself for being such a fool, but it had made so much sense back then that they'd been sent by Seth. Besides, it wasn't like they were threatening—more like an awkward form of courtship.

Jerry caught on quickly, interrupting her to send a patrol car over to check on Mickey and gather any evidence that might be left.

"You know, this changes everything," he said once he hung up from talking to the other officers. "This guy hasn't forgotten you."

"Sending flowers isn't exactly a threat," Nora said, relieved that Mickey was okay. "Besides, maybe it's a good thing—finally some evidence for you."

"Come on, Nora," Seth said, taking her arm. "I'm taking you home with me tonight."

Jerry gave Seth a measuring look. "You watch out for her, you hear?"

Seth rose to his full height as if rising to a challenge. That still put him a few inches shy of Jerry's six-one, but he didn't back down. "I will. And you guys do your jobs. Stop wasting your time talking to people like me and find this son of a bitch, why don'tcha?"

Jerry jerked his chin in a brusque nod and walked back through the barrier that separated the police from the civilians. Seth took Nora's hand in his, and she finally felt warm again. Felt something at least. Better than fear and guilt and regret, Seth's touch made her feel hopeful.

He led her out into the parking lot, where his vintage Mustang shimmered with a thin coating of ice and snow. The driver's-side door had been scratched up again. For some reason, the classic muscle car was a magnet for vandals. No matter what kind of security Seth put on it, it was constantly being keyed or dented and twice had its windows smashed out.

"You sure you're all right?" he asked again, turning her attention away from the Mustang and to him, both of his palms resting on her shoulders as he scrutinized her.

Instead of answering, she fell into his arms, holding him tight, inhaling his scent, and letting his strength support her.

GINA AND KEN LEFT TANK AND HIS MOTHER awaiting their "second" opinion from Dr. Frantz. LaRose had vanished—after eavesdropping in on Tank's diagnosis, no doubt—and the ER seemed relatively quiet.

"Nice call," Ken told her as he added the results of the wet prep to Tank's medical record. "Can't believe we all missed that yesterday."

"Fever, a piss-poor history, and without any scratching they looked like petechiae. Besides, who ever heard of scabies that didn't itch?" Gina said graciously, although she was rather proud of herself. Not even Lydia Fiore or Lucas Stone had thought of scabies. Poor kid probably caught them at school—oh boy, she wished she could see the look on Nurse Pritchard's face when they told her.

She watched Ken type and thought about what her mother had told her about his family. She should say something. Or maybe she shouldn't.

Before she could decide, Amanda and Lucas rushed a gurney down the hallway at a breakneck pace. "We need a room," Lucas called out as Amanda bagged oxygen into their patient.

Gina glanced at the board. "Take Trauma Two." She jogged over to join them. "What's going on?"

"Intermittent asystole," Lucas said as the nurses quickly reattached Narolie to the overhead monitor. "She keeps bradying down and losing her pulse."

"Let's get some atropine on board," Gina ordered, moving to assess Narolie. She watched the monitor. The heart rate was fluctuating from a rapid rate over one hundred to a much-too-slow rate of thirty . . . twenty . . . "Flatline. Is there a pulse?"

"No pulse," Amanda said, her fingers on Narolie's carotid. Then a blip appeared on the monitor, followed by another. "Wait. Now I've got one."

"Must be some kind of autonomic dysfunction," Lucas said.

Gina couldn't care less—it wouldn't do Narolie any good to have a diagnosis if they didn't stabilize her breathing and heart rhythm first.

"Amanda, set up for intubation," she ordered. "Get me a twelve-lead and a rhythm strip."

"We should call her aunt," Amanda said as she grabbed a laryngoscope and endotracheal tube.

"I already did," Lucas said, "when I saw the MRI. I think they understood me—their English wasn't very good."

"Let's focus here, people," Gina snapped. Who cared about language skills when the patient was trying hard to die on them? "Amanda, can you do the intubation or should I?"

"I can." Amanda double-checked her equipment, then stepped alongside the respiratory tech who was bagging oxygen into Narolie through a mask. "Stop bagging."

Gina watched, nodding in approval as Amanda swiftly forced the endotracheal tube through Narolie's vocal cords. A few months ago Amanda would have fumbled her way through the procedure, or worse, would have avoided it for fear of failure.

Before she could say anything, the door burst open and a fine-boned black woman in African tribal clothing accompanied by another woman in a business suit appeared. The first woman took one look at Narolie and began crying, pushing past the nurses to rush to her side. She began to speak in a rapid-fire language that was both melodic and harsh at the same time.

"Matokeo ya utafutaji kwa!"

"She's saying, 'Oh, my poor, dear girl,'" the other woman translated. "She wants to know what happened to Narolie."

"And you are?" Gina asked.

"Tracy Steward with Catholic Relief Services. We facilitated Narolie and her brother's arrival here on a P3 visa."

The aunt began to speak again, this time clutching at Amanda's arm.

"She wants to know what's wrong, what she should tell Narolie's family," Tracy said.

"I thought she *was* Narolie's family," Amanda said. "Isn't she her aunt?"

Tracy frowned. "That's what I was told." She exchanged words with the aunt, who was now crying, shaking her head. "No, not blood relation. It's an honorary term. Their families are from the same small village; they treat each other as family even if they aren't really."

"If the aunt isn't a blood relative, does she have legal custody? Can we treat Narolie?" Gina asked.

"It's an emergency, so that's not an issue," Lucas said.

"Of course we'll treat her," Amanda put in.

"I'm more concerned with her immigration status," the translator said. "P3 visas are granted only to blood relations. If her visa is voided, she'll lose her benefits, could even be repatriated."

"Repatriated?" Gina asked, not liking the idea of the government interfering with her patient. "Does that mean what I think it means?"

"It means she could be sent back. And not to the refugee camp in Kenya, but to Somalia, her country of birth."

"How could they possibly send a sick girl back to a place like that?" Amanda asked.

"Don't worry," Lucas assured her. "No one's going anywhere. Not while she's my patient."

"That might be a problem," Gina said. "She's not your patient. Technically, she's Frantz's patient."

TWENTY-THREE

Friday, 2:02 P.M.

LYDIA FOUND HERSELF SITTING ON THE FLOOR, the cat pressed against her body, as she watched the storm outside, one side of her face numb from the cold as it pressed against the glass. The drops of moisture slipping down the glass were just condensation. At least that's what she told herself.

She hated feeling like this: churning, empty, uncertain, anxious. She wanted to run, escape the confines of the house, of her memories, and head out into the wind, challenging it to a race. But Ginger Cat was asleep on her lap, weighing her down.

Poor excuse. She wondered if maybe the real reason was the fear that once she started to run, she might never stop.

A sharp rap on the front door broke through her thoughts. She slid Ginger Cat onto the floor, earning a glower, then stood and walked to the door. Tommy Z waited on the other side.

"What do you want?" she asked, stepping onto the porch, resisting the urge to hug herself against the cold.

Tommy was alone. He backed up, yielding to her, one hand fidgeting with the scarf knotted tight around his neck. "Mr. Tillman asked me to come speak with you. He's concerned—er—about your well-being."

Lydia stared at Tommy so hard that his rosacea, already blossoming in the cold, flared scarlet. "Mr. Tillman, the CEO of the hospital, told you to come here to my home?"

"Well, no, not exactly. I checked with Glen Bakker and he said you lived over here." He unbuttoned, then rebuttoned the top button on his coat. "Can we talk?"

She nodded to the porch swing, although she knew he really wanted to get inside the house—both for the warmth as well as for the chance to snoop around. He smiled his thanks and settled into the swing. Lydia sat opposite him. Surrounding the porch, tall hemlocks swayed in the wind, their branches coated silver with the sleet. The rain had slowed and now seemed intent on changing into snow. She was freezing, but refused to let Tommy see.

"What exactly worried you so much that you felt you needed to come to my home on my day off, Mr. Zywchez?"

He winced at her butchering his name. "Zwyczaje. But please, call me Tommy. Everyone does."

"So you've said before. Is that what brought you here? Clarifying your name?"

"Boy, you don't cut a guy a break, do you? I knew you'd be a tough one, but I've counseled plenty of cops and firefighters—even did a stint working with prisoners once. I thought I could handle you, Dr. Fiore. Guess I was wrong."

Lydia allowed his pause to lengthen. She knew he expected her to jump in and apologize, start talking, but to hell with that. She didn't like anyone messing with her business—or her head.

"Maybe this wasn't such a good idea after all," he finally said, climbing to his feet once more. "I promised Mr. Tillman I would personally evaluate everyone involved in yesterday's resuscitation, so I guess we'll consider you evaluated."

"What will you tell Tillman?" she asked.

He met her gaze with a sigh. "Mr. Tillman may be my boss, but I don't work for him," he said. "I work for what's best for my clients."

"Really? Is that why you told Tillman about Nora Halloran's assault two years ago? Because that was in the best interest of helping Seth Cochran, your client?"

His mouth opened, then closed, like a fish out of water. The color on his cheeks flared to purple. "How dare you! I never—"

"Seth said you implied that you had, said Tillman was gunning for Nora after the rape kit went missing."

He twisted his scarf so tightly she thought it might choke him. "I'm sorry Dr. Cochran had that impression. I assure you, I never divulged my knowledge of Nora's past to anyone, including Mr. Tillman."

She scrutinized him. He seemed truthful. Hard to tell what was hiding behind that snake-oil salesman exterior. "And what will you tell Tillman about our conversation?"

"All I can tell him is that we spoke and that I'm satisfied that no more intervention is necessary."

"He's not going to like that. Tillman wants to see me fired. Has ever since I got here."

"None of my affair. Although given your involvement in recent events, I would suggest that you might consider counseling. It's not a weakness. Everyone needs someone to talk to. To anchor them."

"I have someone," she said, aiming a glance through the windows at Ginger Cat, who watched from the windowsill. Cats counted, didn't they? And Trey; she had Trey, of course.

Two anchors. More than she'd ever had before in her life.

Tommy's cell phone rang. "Excuse me," he said, glancing at the display. He turned his back to her and spoke for a few minutes, then faced her again. "I need to get back to the hospital. There's a Somali patient having problems and they need my assistance."

"Narolie Maxeke?" she asked. "Thirteen-year-old girl? I admitted her yesterday."

"Apparently she's not doing so well." He hesitated. "Thank you, Dr. Fiore. Take care. You know where to find me if you need me." He cast a worried look up at the clouds hovering overhead and dashed down her porch steps dodging heavy, wet snowflakes.

Lydia watched him go, wondering at his intentions and his sincerity. He was hiding something, she was certain of it.

She paced the porch, then went inside, her cheeks burning as the warmer air hit them. There wasn't time for them to thaw, though. Grabbing her parka, she headed back out into the cold, heading for Angels of Mercy.

THE DRIVE TO SETH'S BLOOMFIELD TOWN HOUSE— Seth and Nora's old town house—was spent in silence. The rain had turned to snow that glazed the city streets silver. Seth pulled into the drive. Nora took a moment to look at the place she used to call home.

There were no holiday decorations, but the leaves were raked clean and the flowerbeds she'd planted looked freshly mulched, ready for winter. Usually Seth needed constant reminders to mow the lawn or to do any yard work. But somehow he'd managed to remember without her there.

Nora wondered how much of her nagging he'd ever needed. Or why she'd felt the need to be the "responsible" one in their relationship. Why she couldn't trust that Seth would act like an adult without her playing mother hen.

So many things she had accepted without thought— reaching back long before the attack on her two years ago. Being the eldest of four with two working parents, she'd always taken on more than most other kids her age. Taking care of her brothers and sister, cooking, cleaning while her parents were at work, helping with homework, disciplining, keeping straight As herself, getting her first job when she was thirteen . . . now that she thought about it, she honestly couldn't remember having a childhood. It was as if her adulthood had begun before adolescence and she'd never questioned why.

Seth led the way up the front porch, east facing and shrouded in shadows. He unlocked the door and reached inside to turn on the light before stepping aside for her to enter. One of their many rituals: Seth always preceded her into a room and turned on the lights for her.

This time he paused on the threshold, turning back to her. "You weren't really afraid of the dark because your brother accidentally locked you in a closet when you were kids playing hide-and-seek?"

Nora shook her head. Looked like Seth was also beginning to question their life together. "No."

His lips flattened. He glanced around the inside of the house before escorting her through the door, one palm pressed against the small of her back.

The place was fairly clean for a bachelor keeping the kind of hours Seth did. Photos of the two of them together greeted her from the mantel and walls of the living room. "Where's DeBakey?"

"I finally finished fencing in the backyard," he explained. She followed him into the kitchen.

Standing on his hind legs, his nose pressed against the window of the back door, was the Labrador retriever she and Seth had adopted. Their "baby," Seth had kidded at the time.

Seth grabbed a large beach towel from a hook and opened the door. DeBakey launched himself inside, spraying mud and water over the floor, the cabinets, and both Seth and Nora. The dog ignored Seth, lunging for Nora, whining when Seth tried to hold him still long enough for a rudimentary drying-off.

Nora was bowled over by the dog's weight and soon found herself covered in puppy kisses and drowning in dog breath. God, how she had missed this.

"Off! Down, boy, down!" Seth was futilely trying to haul

DeBakey off her. The dog ignored him, his full attention concentrated on Nora, his long-lost human.

"It's all right," Nora said when she could take in a full breath. "DeBakey, sit!"

The dog immediately sat, his haunches and tail wiggling happily.

"Jeezit, he never listens to me like that." Seth swiped at the larger puddles of mud with the towel.

"You don't have the magic Mommy voice," Nora said, patting DeBakey and scratching behind his ears. "Good boy, DeBakey, good boy."

Seth joined her on the floor, the dog between them. A circle of family, love, and wet dog fur. Nora's stomach clenched at the aching familiarity of the scene. *Just one night,* she reminded herself. She was only here for one night.

"So you lied about why you were afraid of the dark," Seth said as he scrubbed DeBakey dry with the towel. "I lied, too."

Nora jerked her head up. "You did?" She hated that her first thought was to wonder if he'd lied about being on call when Karen was attacked. No. It couldn't be. She hugged DeBakey closer. "When?"

"The first time was right after you told me you were—assaulted. Remember when I told you I'd sprained my wrist playing basketball?"

Relief washed over her. "You moped around all weekend acting like a baby until the swelling went down and you knew you would be able to operate."

"It wasn't playing basketball. I was angry and upset and I didn't want you to see it, so I went to a bar, had a few. Only made things worse."

She rolled her eyes. Seth was a lightweight when it came to alcohol—something he hated to admit, coming from a family where beers were tossed back as fast as pretzels.

"There was this guy, he was kind of drunk, too, and he was trying to hook up with the waitress, only she wasn't interested, but he kept pushing and pushing. So I pushed back. Actually I almost hit the guy." He still wasn't looking at her, his hands rubbing DeBakey so hard she was surprised the dog had any fur left. "I slammed the bar instead."

"That was stupid. You could have broken your hand, ended your career."

He shrugged, stood, and carefully hung the towel on the hook beside the door. DeBakey stayed on the floor with Nora, rolling onto his back so she could rub his belly.

Silence as Seth fiddled with the ends of the towel, making them perfectly even. They both knew it was her need for perfection that had instilled the habit—he couldn't care less if a towel hung crooked or was wadded up in a corner on the floor.

"Guess we're both liars," Seth said, his voice low, his face still turned away from her. "When we made love, you weren't crying because you were giddy with passion, were you?"

"No." The single syllable fell leaden between them.

"Did I ever make you happy?" He spun around to face her, his hands stretched out at his sides.

"Yes." She remembered the first time they had made love, how awkward and nervous she'd been, but he hadn't rushed her, had worked with her, leaving the lights on, going slow— she couldn't even do it the first time, had broken away half- way through, gone to the bathroom, and returned feeling embarrassed and ashamed, but Seth had held her, calmed her, until she relaxed enough to start again. Her throat tightened. "God, yes."

"When? Please, Nora, I need to know that we weren't liv- ing a lie the entire time we were together. Tell me I managed to do something right."

The pleading in his voice tore at her heart. "Seth . . ." She trailed off, unable to put her feelings in words, not after so many words had betrayed them both. She settled for facts instead. "When you picked out DeBakey."

The dog thumped his tail against the floor.

"He was a broken-down, mangy wreck, so skinny his ribs showed, that godawful eye infection that trailed pus everywhere, the way he wouldn't make eye contact or even stand up. He lay there like he'd lost all hope, given up, but you took one look at him and said, 'There's a dog with the heart of a lion.' You crawled into his cage and stroked him and sang to him until he found the willpower to get up and follow you out." She choked at the memory, her eyes welling up. "You won both our hearts that day."

Stray tears slid down her cheeks. Seth blinked as if he were about to cry as well. Then he fell to his knees and gathered her into his arms, holding her for a long moment.

"I might have picked him out," he said, stroking DeBakey behind the ear as he intertwined his other arm in hers, "but you're the one who got him to eat and gave him his medicine." He shuddered at the memory of the eyedrops that had to be given four times a day.

"He was a good patient. Better than most of the humans I've dealt with." She squeezed Seth's arm. "Including you."

He turned and kissed her. As their lips met, a familiar warmth spread through her, enticing her like a drug. She opened her eyes and pushed away.

Damn it all, she'd spent two long years mastering her emotions, staying in control. She wasn't about to forget the fact that Seth had hurt her—no matter how loving he acted now. She stood, leaving Seth and DeBakey behind, and washed her hands in the kitchen sink, running the water so hot the steam fogged her vision.

"How about if I make us all some dinner?" she asked, her voice crisp and cheerful as she regained control. Never again would she allow someone to sneak below her guard, let them hurt her.

Never again.

TWENTY-FOUR

Friday, 2:13 P.M.

GINA AND AMANDA HAD REMAINED WITH NAROLIE, along with the PICU team, while Lucas took her aunt and the translator to the family room to discuss the situation.

"What the hell is going on here?" Dr. Frantz said, slamming the door against the wall as he barreled into the room. "Who told my patient that he had scabies and could go home?"

"Here to check on your other patient, Dr. Frantz?" Gina said, backing away as the PICU team prepared Narolie for transport. "She's taking Tank's bed in the ICU."

"Who?" Frantz frowned, then did a double take as he looked at Narolie, barely visible amid the array of technology. "She was supposed to be discharged this morning." He scowled and took a step toward Amanda. "What did you do?"

"She did nothing," Gina said, inserting herself between Frantz and Amanda. "Except protect her patient. Maybe you should consider transferring her to Dr. Stone's service—wouldn't want the lawyers to see your name all over the chart."

"What are you implying, young lady? I don't care who your father is—"

"You might want to rethink that when I give his name to Narolie's family. And explain to them how you were going to send a critically ill patient home."

"How dare you!" He spun on his heel, ready to stalk out, but Gina wasn't letting him off that easy.

"By the way, I'm the one who discovered Tank's scabies. You'd better let the folks at Heinz Prep know. I think you'll have a lot of angry parents on your hands."

LYDIA RUSHED INTO THE PICU AND HEADED straight to the nurses' station, avoiding the gazes of the parents sitting vigil at the bedsides of young children. She hated coming here. Too much hope, too much despair, not enough that doctors, nurses, anyone could actually control.

And way too much time to think about it all.

As she rounded the desk and approached the chart rack, she spotted Lucas in the dictation area, talking with someone. The nurses in the ER had filled her in on what had happened in the MRI and how Lucas had taken over Narolie's case. Thank God, finally Narolie was in the hands of a doctor who'd think twice about her care.

She grabbed Narolie's chart and scanned the notes from the MRI and the resuscitation that followed. Encephalitis? A catchall term for so many diseases, all of them bad. Very bad. The fact that she'd deteriorated so quickly was more bad news.

Lydia glanced inside the dictation room, trying to gauge whether this was a good time to interrupt, to ask questions about Narolie. Then she saw who Lucas was talking to. The CEO, Oliver Tillman.

"I told you, it's too early for me to give you a prognosis." Lucas had raised his voice.

"But most cases of encephalitis require long-term care and rehab, correct?"

"Well, yes. But every patient is different—"

"That's okay, Dr. Stone. All I require to institute repatriation procedures is a general overview of the situation. Thank you for your time."

"You can't just ship her off—"

"It's in her best interests to be reunited with her family. I'm working to make that happen." Tillman brushed past Lucas and strode out of the nurses' station, heading out the doors without a glance at any of the families or patients around him.

"He wasn't talking about Narolie, was he?" Lydia asked. "What does he mean, reunited with her family? Her family is here."

Lucas scowled. "Seems the U.S. government's definition of *family* differs from the Somali one. Narolie isn't really related to her 'aunt' at all. And her P3 visa was based on her entering the country to join blood relatives."

"So we'll deal with that later, after we know what's going on with her. It takes years to deport someone, doesn't it?"

"If she's not a valid immigrant, she loses her medical assistance. Which means the hospital will foot the bill for all her care—and unfortunately, given her deterioration, it might be care for a long, long time. Not to mention rehab, if she does improve."

"She's that bad off?" Lydia knew that's what the chart said, but she couldn't believe that the vibrant girl she'd met yesterday was now lying in a coma.

"Yes. And there's a loophole in the law that allows hospitals to 'repatriate' patients to their native countries. It's done in the guise of reuniting them with their families to facilitate long-term care, but really it's all about saving money."

"You've got to be kidding me." Lydia turned to stare at the doors Tillman had exited through. "Son of a bitch."

"Tillman says it's to protect the medical center—the money spent on Narolie if she remains in a persistent vegetative state could be used to care for hundreds of patients."

"Hundreds of nameless, faceless, future patients. We've got to concentrate on the one we know, the one who came to us for help. Here and now."

"That's the problem. I'm not sure there is anything we can do to help her."

AMANDA FUMBLED THE SUCTION CATHETER. AS IT flew from her fingers she tried to catch it, but it ended up on the floor beside Zachary's bed.

"Sorry," she told the respiratory tech as she bent over to pick it up. Too late she realized that she should have let it go—now she had to wash her hands and change her gloves.

"Forget it," Michael said as he opened a new catheter and deftly threaded it down Zachary's endotracheal tube. "I've got it. Weren't you supposed to go home—like hours ago?"

Amanda's sigh sounded loud and pathetic. But she couldn't help it. Her entire body drooped with fatigue. "I feel like I neglected Zachary and his folks today—I was so caught up with Narolie's case. And now she's . . ." She trailed off, her gaze fixed on the closed doors to Narolie's room.

"You're good at this, Amanda." He reattached the endotracheal tube to the ventilator, discarding the catheter and his gloves in one smooth movement. "But you need to learn to pace yourself. You can't give everything to any one patient— you won't have anything left."

She squirmed under his compliments. "Yeah, I guess you're right." She helped him finish cleaning up. "I'll go talk to the Millers and then call it a night."

"See you in the morning."

Amanda almost tripped over the threshold of the family waiting room as she sought out Zachary's parents. They were huddled in the far corner, the dad staring out the window at the angels in the cemetery, the mom pretending to read an out-of-date *Redbook*, her gaze unfocused, her face wet with tears.

"We're done," Amanda told them. "He did fine." She sat down on the chair beside Zachary's mother. "How are you guys holding up?"

"Fine," the mother echoed. The dad didn't respond, seemed lost in the night beyond the window. "I still can't believe this happened. That we were distracted—that a simple thing like a pop bottle could be so devastating."

"It's no one's fault. Zachary couldn't have known that the kerosene was in the bottle and your father couldn't have known—"

"It's his arthritis. It's so bad in his hands that he couldn't handle the childproof lids." Mrs. Miller swung her head, searching the far reaches of the room for an explanation. "He feels terrible. If Zachary—if anything happens—I don't know how he'll, we'll, face it." She grabbed Amanda's hands. "It was only a sip, just a swallow; such a little thing can't kill my boy, can it?"

Amanda said nothing. They both knew that even a tiny sip was enough to poison a child's lungs. And they both knew there was nothing they could do except wait and see if Zachary's lungs could heal.

"You can go in and see him now."

Mrs. Miller stood. But her husband remained frozen in place. "We'll be there in a minute."

"I'll see you tomorrow, then." Amanda left them and returned to the PICU. She stopped inside the door, watching Zachary, dwarfed by the machines keeping him alive.

Her entire body felt numb, and she was desperate for sleep, but she wanted to check on Narolie one last time before going home. To her surprise, she found Lydia at Narolie's bedside, reading the chart.

"We don't have much time," Lydia said when Amanda entered.

"Is she getting worse?" Amanda glanced at the monitor. No, everything seemed to be stable—vital signs all normal. The only problem was that Narolie wouldn't wake up. Even now that the sedatives were out of her system, she remained unconscious. The EEG machine at the base of the bed made a scratching noise as its pens traced out Narolie's brain-waves: almost flat.

"Tillman found out that her visa might not be valid. He wants to deport her. Already has the hospital attorneys working on it. I figure they won't get much done over the weekend, but come Monday—"

"Are you nuts?" Amanda's exhaustion fueled her anger. She jammed her fists into the pockets of her lab coat in an attempt to keep from lashing out and breaking something. "They can't do that! She's a patient, helpless—look at her."

Her voice was sharp with frustration and fatigue. Lydia didn't seem bothered by it. Instead she merely closed the chart on her finger to hold her place and waited. "Yelling isn't going to help her. If we can find something we can treat—some medical reason for her to stay—then we can help her."

Amanda slumped against the glass wall of the cubicle, not caring who saw. "I've been through the chart. There's nothing there. I have no idea what's causing her encephalitis."

"You're exhausted. Why don't you go home, get some rest? Tomorrow, maybe things will make more sense."

"I hope so." Amanda brushed her fingers against Narolie's cheek. The girl didn't respond.

FRUSTRATED THAT THERE WAS NOTHING MORE she could do to help Narolie, Lydia finally left the ICU and headed home. She zipped her parka up tight and dug her hands deep into her pockets as the wind pummeled her. The sleet and snow were gone, leaving patches of black ice in their wake. The sun was also long vanished—if it had ever made an appearance today, Lydia had missed it. Even in the darkness she could feel the moisture-laden clouds pressing down on her, trying to smother all warmth and light.

How did people live like this for five months out of the year? Like moles trapped in a cave, never seeing the light of day. Shivering, she pulled the hood up on her parka, even though she knew it made her look like a wimp—most Pittsburghers were still wearing midweight fall jackets. Maybe she wasn't cut out to be a Pittsburgher, as tough as the steel the town was famous for.

Like Ruby, Trey's mom. Now there was a tough lady. Or Nora—Lydia couldn't even begin to fathom what it had taken to rebuild her life after what had happened two years ago.

She crossed the street and saw that the memorial to Karen now filled most of the block, offerings heaped up against the cemetery fence, flickering votives illuminating them. The police officer was gone, but the cemetery gates were chained shut. She stopped, peering through them at the forlorn angel shrouded in crime-scene tape.

"Kinda scary, ain't it?"

Lydia jerked around at the sound of Pete Sandusky's voice, her hand halfway to his face, ready to do some damage. She pulled it back just in time and thrust it back in her pocket, half-embarrassed by her violent reflex. "What do you want, Pete?"

"Same as yesterday. Confirmation before I run a story. Only this time I have more facts." He walked beside her as she moved down the sidewalk, dodging stuffed animals and flowers. "I saw the photos, Lydia. Heard about how Nora was the one to find Karen. How she lost the rape kit. That the killer could go free because of her incompetence."

Lydia pushed her hood down so that her vision was unobstructed. She'd told Boyle about Pete and her suspicions that Jim Lazarov had stolen the rape kit, but her vague innuendoes and hearsay weren't enough for the police to act on. "Nora didn't lose the rape kit. Whoever showed you those photos stole it. You need to tell the police."

Pete merely smiled, an infuriating, smug smile. "I don't reveal my sources to anyone. And my source says he found the photos, that he has no other evidence. So, what's it going to be, Lydia? You gonna give me the full story, or do I run with what I have?"

He obviously thought she had information that would help Nora. Which was good; it meant he had no idea about Nora being a victim of the same rapist. Not that that would help her if Pete published his story.

Lydia thought furiously. The only thing she had to offer, the only way she could get Pete to quash his story, would be to offer him something more salacious. Would the fact that the CEO of the medical center was having an affair with a murder victim be enough?

"What makes you so certain your source isn't the killer himself?" she asked, trying to buy time as she thought things through. As much as she despised Tillman, she couldn't ruin his reputation based on gossip.

"I don't really care," Pete answered. "If he is the killer, then I have an inside track. If he isn't, I still have a story no one else has."

Maybe Pete's questionable ethics were contagious. Because Lydia thought of another way she could use her knowledge of Tillman's affair. She looked past Pete to the lights of the hospital, zooming in on the fourth floor. The floor where Narolie was. Blackmail? To save a patient. Did that make it worth it?

It would mean sacrificing Nora. Lydia couldn't tell Pete about Tillman without losing the ammunition she'd need to make the CEO stop Narolie's deportation.

Nora was a friend. She'd already suffered so much—could Lydia stand by and let her suffer more if she could stop it? But Narolie had no one, and she was helpless, couldn't fight her own battles.

"Damned if I do, damned if I don't," she muttered.

"Whatever you're gonna do, make it fast. It's freezing out here."

Lydia stared at Pete's rapacious expression. It didn't inspire trust. No guarantee that even if she gave him Tillman, he wouldn't still run the story about Nora.

Cold sliced through her like a dagger shoved between her ribs. "No comment."

As soon as her shift was finished, Gina called her parents' house and left a message for LaRose and Moses that she was coming to dinner. A message was best—they couldn't force her to change her mind or say no that way.

She changed from her scrubs and headed west out of the city to her parents' Sewickley Heights home. *Home* was probably the wrong word—*estate* was more like it. Perched on a hillside overlooking the Allegheny Country Club, the white-brick mansion sprawled across the horizon with a sense of entitlement.

The drive leading up to the house was curved to make it feel twice as long as it was, and tree-lined so the house itself was hidden from view until the last curve was rounded. Then it sprang out at the unsuspecting visitor, dominating their view. As it was meant to.

Gina had outgrown such architectural sleight of hand, or so she thought. She was smarter now; she could handle her parents, deal with them on an even playing field.

"Where's Moses?" she asked when she found LaRose alone in the drawing room.

"I sent him to the club. Thought we could have a little mother-daughter talk."

"But I need to talk to Moses—"

"No, Regina, you don't. Your father won't be taking that girl's case."

Gina felt her cheeks chill as the blood rushed away from her face. "Why not?"

"Don't be silly. You know very well why not. It's totally inappropriate. Besides, it's a frivolous case."

"Frivolous? Frantz could have killed that girl. If Amanda hadn't forced the issue—"

"Yes, your friend is quite passionate. She's also very young and extremely naïve. Catherine told me Amanda was instrumental in introducing Harold to that girl. She was supposed to be taking care of critically ill patients, not playing matchmaker."

"Harold wasn't critically ill—and according to your buddy, Frantz, neither was Narolie."

"You're missing the point. It's all that time in that place, it's warped your perspective. I mean, did you have to humiliate Catherine like that? In front of everyone?"

"I'm a doctor; I made a diagnosis, asked a colleague to confirm it, and treated the patient appropriately. What's to be humiliated about? How do you know about Tank's diagnosis unless you were eavesdropping?"

"My point exactly. Pulling a curtain shut doesn't guarantee a patient privacy—and for such a delicate issue, you should have taken them back to a real room, had some consideration—"

"Right. It was so inconsiderate that the patients using those rooms were there first. Or I could have left my patients, taken your friends back up to the ICU, and used the private room there. The room that Amanda's patient should have had to begin with."

"You have no idea what Catherine has been through. She's trying to save her family—"

"She might try starting with listening to her son, seeing what's really going on with his life!"

LaRose waved away Gina's concerns about Tank. "Regina, your attitude, please. I'm trying to help here, I really am. You need to understand that every decision your father and I make is for the good of the family. That includes you."

"But when do I get a say? All I'm asking is for Moses to—"

"That place, it's sucking the life out of you," LaRose continued without pause, steamrolling over Gina's words as if they were empty air. Which, of course, to LaRose, they were. "Look at you. Where has my beautiful, vibrant little girl disappeared to? Everything will be better when you start working with me at the foundation."

"What if I don't join you at the foundation?" Gina could barely believe she'd spoken the words aloud—she'd thought them so often, she wasn't even sure they'd made it past her lips until she saw LaRose's expression harden.

"Are you trying to blackmail your father into taking this ridiculous case? Do you seriously think those kind of bully tactics will work? Really, Regina."

Right. Leave the bullying to Moses. Not that LaRose wasn't as practiced—she was just more subtle about it. Gina crossed her arms and settled into a slouch that earned her another disapproving glare. "Maybe I like working in the ER. Maybe I don't want to leave."

"Ridiculous. Surely after two years of that place you've realized your mistake. A girl of your sensibilities isn't suited to a life dealing with the dregs of humanity. I was watching you today, Regina. That place has ground the life out of you." LaRose paused. "I'm worried about you."

Gina tried to think of a smart comeback, but couldn't. Mainly because sometimes she thought the same thing. Life in the ER was grueling, and she wasn't sure she was cut out for it. Worse, these past few days, after Ken's talk, damn him, she realized that she wasn't gambling with only her own life and happiness. She was gambling with the lives of her patients. And with Jerry's happiness.

"Once you leave that place and begin working with the

foundation, you'll see how much good people like Dr. Frantz really do. It's important to reciprocate when possible."

"Like Moses refusing to sue Frantz in return for a juicy contribution to the foundation?"

"It's all about saving lives, helping people. Isn't that why you went into medicine to start with?"

"Tell me, Mother. What's the going price on a girl's life?"

TWENTY-FIVE

Friday, 7:26 P.M.

THIS WAS A HUGE MISTAKE, NORA DECIDED AS they finished an awkward dinner in silence. Even DeBakey seemed upset, pacing back and forth between his two humans, resting his chin on their knees, each in turn.

She'd begun to clear the table when Seth jumped up to help and they collided, spilling the tray of leftover meat loaf.

"Damn it!" She threw up her hands and stalked out to the living room. "This isn't going to work."

"Don't leave," Seth said, following her, abandoning the mess for DeBakey to slurp up. He tried to circle his arms around her in an embrace. She batted him away.

"This was all a mistake. We were a mistake. I should have never told you. Should have never expected anyone could love me, not after—I mean, it haunts you, doesn't it? Every time you touched me, you saw him, thought of his hands being there before you, his mouth . . ."

"Nora, shut up!" Seth yelled.

Nora stopped, her entire body shaking with anger, fear, loathing, emotions she couldn't even begin to identify. But his tone quelled them all. Seth never yelled. Never. He might cuss a blue streak, whine, or moan and groan, but he never raised his voice—not to her, not during a trauma, not even when someone screwed up and things started to go wrong in surgery.

"I'm sorry," he said. He stepped back and dropped into the sofa. "I'm so sorry. I kept trying to tell you . . ."

"Tell me what, Seth? You going to confess to more lies? Why don't you tell me the truth: that you didn't want to stay with me after I told you about the rape? It would have saved us both—"

"Because that's not the truth. Whatever you believe or think about me, please believe me when I say that had nothing to do with it."

"Then what, Seth?"

"It wasn't you. It was me."

She groaned at the old chestnut but he ignored her, getting to his feet and pacing the room. DeBakey swung his head to and fro as he watched, clearly uncomfortable with the vibe given off by his two humans.

"You know my family and their history with marriage. My dad's on his second wife and they're already separated. Mom's on her third marriage. Both my sisters are divorced. None of them can get it right. And everyone gets hurt in the end. I kept thinking, what do I have to offer a woman like you? How the hell can I ever expect to make a marriage succeed when I don't even have any concept of what a good relationship is?"

He placed his hands on her shoulders and looked her in the eye. "I couldn't face myself if I let you down, if I ever did something that hurt you so much that you'd want to leave me. So, just like with all my other relationships before you, I started to think that the best thing for everyone involved was to leave now, end it. . . ."

"So you decided to just walk out? Decided that you never really loved me? Don't worry, I guess I already figured it out for myself."

"No!" He lowered his voice. "No. I did love you. I *do* love you. That's what I've been trying to tell you for months. I couldn't leave you. I didn't want to, I wanted to stay, to try to give it, give you, us, everything I had. Damn it, Nora. I was going to propose to you on July fourth!"

"The same day I found you with Karen?" She didn't believe him—although she wanted to. She couldn't. It was just too damn easy, and the price she would pay if she was wrong was too damn high.

"That's when I started sleepwalking again. From the stress. I hadn't done it since I was a kid. Whenever my parents began with the screaming, that's when I'd wake up and find myself outside the house—hiding in the car, up in the tree fort, down the block at a friend's house. Anywhere but at home with all the yelling and shouting."

He hung his head, but his hands remained on her shoulders. She felt his weight sag against her as if his words had sapped his energy. "Anyway, believe it or not, but it's the truth. I love you Nora, I want us to be together—married, not married, I don't care. I just know that"—he blew his breath out and raised his face to meet her gaze—"I need you. I don't think I can be happy without you. But the big question is, can you be happy with me?"

Wow. Nora's insides did a slow somersault as if absorbing an unexpected blow. *Double wow.* He was worried about what she needed? About making her happy?

All her life she'd been trained to put the needs of everyone else first, but here was a man, a man handsome enough that he could have any woman he wanted, and he wanted her? He needed her and wanted to make her happy?

"Seth, I—" She stopped, trying to find words.

"Please, don't say anything. Just be with me tonight—even if it's the last time we might ever be together, please stay tonight."

His tone of yearning melted her. She pulled him close and raised her face to his. It was a kiss as sweet as their first one.

He gathered her in his arms, swept her up, and carried her into the bedroom, shutting the door before DeBakey could follow.

AS SHE WALKED HOME, LYDIA TRIED CALLING Nora, but she wasn't answering. Damn, she needed to warn her about Pete's story. Or come up with some way to stop him.

She shoved her phone back into her pocket and drew up short. The porch light was on, which meant Trey had replaced the burned-out bulb. Which meant Trey was home.

She shook her head, trying to displace the nagging sense of disappointment and irritation. She still wasn't used to the idea of coming home to someone else there, in her space. Not that she minded, she really didn't . . . except she'd been hoping to reread the files Boyle had given her on her mother's murder. She had a ton of questions she wanted to have him ask his friend in L.A.

Couldn't do any of that with Trey around. It felt strange to even think about Maria's murder with him in the house. As if somehow the ghosts of her past and the promise of her future were incompatible.

Flinging such poetic nonsense aside, she opened the door and walked in. Ginger Cat sauntered from the dining room to greet her, followed by Trey.

"How was your day?" she asked as she hung up her coat.

He didn't respond with his usual kiss and smile. Instead he looked as angry as he had this morning when he'd confronted her about her handgun.

"When I got home, your gun was on the kitchen table." His words were clipped, eyes narrowed.

"Locked in its case." She didn't tell him that if she hadn't rushed out to the hospital, she would have been carrying the Para Carry 9 instead.

"Lydia. What if I'd brought one of the kids home with me?"

She frowned, puzzled. "Why would you do that?"

"Because they're family." He enunciated each word as if explaining a foreign concept to an alien. "If you're going to keep a deadly weapon in the house, you need to be more careful."

Did he think she was an idiot? Of course she was careful. And when did her house become *the* house—as in his? Anger seeped into her veins, making her flush. She reined it in, resisting the urge to lash back, recognizing that much of her fury had nothing to do with Trey. It was more about Nora, about Karen, about Maria, about Narolie—all victims she could do nothing to help.

Instead of answering Trey, she stalked past him to the kitchen and retrieved her gun case. Then she kept on going and headed out the garage door.

"Lydia, wait!" Trey called from the doorway as she shoved the gun case into the saddlebags on the Triumph and straddled the bike.

She gunned the engine, pivoted the bike, and sped out into the darkness.

SETH SHUT THE DOOR BEHIND THEM AND GENTLY deposited Nora back onto her feet. He kept watching her as if he were afraid of her—no, *for* her. She hated the fear in his eyes almost as much as she hated the reason for its being there.

She took a deep breath and realized that she wasn't worried about what would happen next. How could she be? The worst had already happened. No more fear of being hurt—she'd already survived the worst she could imagine. No more fear of hurting Seth—she'd already done that. No more fear of her lies and secrets being unearthed—they were already exposed.

For the first time in years she faced a night with no fear, no lies, no secrets. She felt giddy, light-headed, not sure of what to do with this newfound freedom.

She turned back to Seth, startling him by pulling him close and kissing him deeply. He tensed at first, so she upped the ante and slid one hand down his chest and below the waistband of his jeans. He straightened, pulling away, although she could feel his arousal at her touch.

"Nora. We don't have to do this."

His words cemented her resolve.

"Yes. We do," she murmured, unsnapping his jeans. This time she was in charge. She held the power.

Seth said nothing, but seemed to instinctively understand her need to take control.

She shoved him back against the wall, her mouth ravaging his as she tore at the buttons on his shirt. He tried to help, but she batted his hands away, impatient to feel his flesh against hers. She pulled the shirt open, a stray button zinging past her as it tore loose, and tugged it halfway down over his shoulders, pinning his arms behind him. He squirmed, just enough to grind his pelvis against her.

A small sound caught in her throat. She felt powerful, like an animal zeroing in on prey. Seth met her eyes, a smile lighting them, and she knew he was enjoying her usurping control almost as much as she was.

Fettered by his shirt, he leaned back against the wall. She grabbed his hair, pulling him forward into a kiss. His mouth followed her fingers down her neck and chest as she eased out of her blouse. He had to bend at an awkward angle to take her breast, but she didn't make it easy for him. She laughed, exulting in her power.

Then she tugged at his jeans, pulling them and his boxers to his knees, effectively hobbling him. Only his mouth was free, trailing kisses over her chest and belly, wherever she steered him. She teased him without mercy, using her hands and mouth until he was so engorged he winced. "Please, Nora."

He was begging *her*. A thrill shot through her. She pushed him down to his knees, his erection jutting out from his hips.

"Me first," she commanded, standing over him, his mouth at her pelvis. Their gazes collided as he leaned forward and used his mouth on her. She braced herself against the wall, slapping her palms against it as the climax overwhelmed her. A cry mixed with giddy laughter sprang free from her lips. She dropped down, bracing herself on his shoulders as she lowered herself onto him. God, the way he filled her.

Now face to face, their bodies rocked together. Her fingers dug into his skin, leaving indentations as she gripped his shoulders. They came together, a strangled gasp from him and a cry of release from her.

The dog banged against the door, yelping at the noise, making them both collapse in laughter on the floor. Once she'd caught her breath, Nora stretched out, smiling as she watched him squirm free of his clothing. He flopped onto his back, one hand reaching out to her, his chest heaving as he caught his breath.

A feeling of warm contentment washed over her. Never had it felt like that before, so free, as if her body and mind had united with Seth's in one glorious, perfect, brilliant moment.

For the first time, Nora knew what making love really meant and understood why so many women lamented their infrequent orgasms. Jeez, she would give up sleep altogether, every night, if this was the way it made her feel.

She glanced at Seth, surprised to see him blushing. And knew she *could* have this again, have it every night—if she wanted.

LYDIA BARELY MADE IT TO THE END OF THE CUL-de-sac before hitting the brakes. The Triumph skidded on a patch of black ice, whirling her around like one of Trey's dance moves. The lights of the neighbor's Christmas lights spun around her as she wrestled with the bike for control. Finally she came to a stop, still upright. Barely.

Idiot. No helmet, no coat, no gloves. What the hell had she been thinking? Even at this slow speed, if she'd hit her head on the curb, she'd be toast. Or at least her brain would be.

Suddenly the icy air didn't seem to have enough oxygen. She heaved in one breath after another, sweat breaking out on her exposed skin and immediately chilling her. Running wasn't the answer—but it had always been her answer in the past.

Running was Maria's answer. Look how well things turned out for her.

Shivering with cold and shaking with fear, Lydia turned the bike around and walked it back toward her house. Time to grow up. Stop running.

Trey met her at the end of the driveway, wearing his coat, carrying hers. He didn't say anything as he draped it around her shoulders and took the bike from her. He parked it in the carport and followed her into the house.

Lydia kept her coat on, hugging herself as she tried to get warm. She walked through to the living room and turned on the gas fireplace, standing right in front of it, needing its warmth. Trey hung up his coat and slowly turned to her. It was difficult to read his expression; it held so many emotions.

"That was stupid," she started. "I'm sorry. I had a crappy day."

His expression cleared and he nodded, taking a step to meet her. "Want to tell me about it?"

"Not really."

He curled his arm around her shoulders and pulled her close. Finally, she began to feel warm again. Her exhaustion and confusion ebbed away, and she told him about the day spent with Nora and Jerry.

"Why is it people keep turning to me for support? I don't know what to say, what to do to comfort Nora. She's been through hell—what can *I* say?"

"People turn to you because you're strong, Lydia." He turned his face to plant a kiss on her forehead. "People can sense that. You're a survivor."

"So is Nora. What that bastard did to her . . ." She shuddered, and he pulled her tighter to him. "I wish I had some answers for her. I never know what to say that won't make it worse. Thank God she has Amanda to talk to. Hell, even Gina does a better job than I do."

He chuckled at that. "Yeah, right. Because Gina just has *so* very much insight into the human condition."

"At least she knows how to fake it."

"See, there's the difference. You can't fake that kind of thing. It either comes from your heart or it doesn't. With you, it's not about the words but about the action. I can't see Amanda or even Elise, forget about Gina, going into that house with Nora this morning. You were there for her; that counts for a lot."

"Just like you're here for me." She eased away from him, shed her coat, and sank onto the couch. "There's something I need to tell you."

He sat down beside her, not touching her, giving her the space she needed. She rubbed her fingers over Maria's charm bracelet, tracing the chilled brass charms as if they held the power to erase memories.

But what had happened to Maria could never be erased. *No more running,* she told herself, heaving in a deep breath.

"It's about my mother. You need to know how she died."

TWENTY-SIX

Friday, 8:53 P.M.

GINA COULDN'T FACE GOING BACK TO HER HOUSE and telling Amanda that her parents weren't going to help Narolie, so after leaving her mother, she drove to Jerry's East Liberty apartment. Inside the foyer was a man carrying an armful of flowers. He was scrutinizing the apartment directory, his finger hovering between "G. Boyle" and "J. Boyen."

"Those are lovely," she said, admiring the spray of lilies and roses. "Need help finding someone?"

He gave her a grateful smile. "Thanks. The name is smudged on the order—got wet in the rain and snow, I guess. It could be either Boyle or Boyen, I'm not sure."

"Well, since Jerry is my boyfriend and I didn't order him any flowers, I'm hoping they're for Jenny Boyen. She lives across the hall from him, 5-F."

He squinted at his clipboard. "You're right, it does look like Jenny in 5-F, not Jerry in 5-E. Thanks."

"Happens all the time—packages are always getting mixed up between the two. Want me to take you up so you can surprise her?"

"No, better not. I don't want any complaints about breaking security rules or nothing. You know how careful folks have to be these days, and my boss is real strict. Thanks, though."

She smiled, glad to finally be able to help someone tonight. "No problem. I'm sure she'll enjoy the flowers. Have a good night."

She used her key to let herself through the security door and took the elevator up to the fifth floor. When she unlocked the apartment, she was surprised to find Jerry home, scarfing down a microwaved bowl of beef stew.

"Gina," he said with a smile, abandoning the stew to embrace her. "God, what a day. How was yours? You're home late, so I figured it must have been as bad as mine. Did you eat? What can I get you?"

Before she knew it, Jerry had her seated at the table and eating his stew while he fixed himself another bowl. Without asking, he poured her a Yuengling and himself a glass of milk—which told her he was heading back into work—and popped some of her favorite comfort foods, Pillsbury crescent rolls, into the oven. He served her the rolls hot before sitting down to his own meal once more.

"So, anything exciting today?" he asked.

Gina jammed an entire roll into her mouth to keep from answering. They always talked about her—her work, her friends, her family, her feelings.

In the silence, she realized she never asked about his cases. She'd used the excuse that he couldn't talk about his work, it was confidential, but that didn't really hold water, did it? Not when she shared all the intimate details of her patients and their care.

She couldn't remember the last time she'd commented on one of his photographs—his favorite hobby was nature photography—or encouraged him to go play with his cameras. And his family, she'd met them a few times, they were great, but she had to rely on Jerry to get their names straight.

Jerry had even done all the Christmas shopping, signing both their names to the gift cards.

"What happened to that kid from yesterday? The one whose parents are friends with your folks?"

She swallowed, twice. The dough had formed a lump in her throat that she had to force down. "Turns out he wasn't as sick as everyone thought," she answered. "Fooled us all."

Just like Gina. Playing the fool. Playing a role—one role for her parents, another for Jerry. Letting Jerry carry the weight of the relationship, taking care of her. Just like Ken Rosen had said. Damn the man for being right. Again.

She tugged at the chain holding Jerry's ring. Was it fair to Jerry for her to continue the act? She could do better, ask about his work, pay attention to what he needed, try not to be so selfish. She could at least try.

No. If she failed, he'd be hurt. If she didn't try, let things continue the way they were, someday they'd both regret it. She couldn't stand it if she woke up one morning feeling about Jerry the way she felt about her father.

She slid the chain over her head and let it slide through her fingers onto the table between them. "Jerry. We need to talk."

AMANDA HAD FALLEN INTO BED WITHOUT DOING anything except stripping out of her sweat-coated scrubs. She'd eat in the morning. Now she needed sleep.

But sleep wouldn't come. Instead she startled awake at every noise: the furnace kicking in, the rattle of a window, the hum of her alarm clock, even the faint buzz of the refrigerator. They all jolted her from sleep as effectively as her beeper did when she was on call.

Each time she'd jump up, fumbling for her beeper and the phone, certain that she'd made a mistake and a patient was paying the price. Adrenaline would shoot through her, causing her to break out in a sweat.

As she lay back down, determined to calm her nerves and fall back asleep, she was haunted by Narolie. She'd missed something, failed the girl. Glimpses of Narolie's clinic chart swirled through her mind, a kaleidoscope of cramped handwriting and medical terms. Something nagged at her, but it wasn't from Narolie's chart or lab results, it was something Mrs. Miller had said.

"Such a little thing, so innocent," the voice in her head whispered. "Causing such devastation . . ."

Innocent, benign, like a container of poison disguised as a Coke bottle. Benign, something small, something hidden in plain sight . . .

Sleep overtook her before she could finish her thought.

LYDIA STARED AT THE TWO PICTURES RESTING ON her mantel, the only proof she had that Maria existed. Trey came up from behind, wrapping his arms around her. She leaned against him for a moment, inhaling his strength, but then released herself from his embrace.

"Sit down," she told him. If she was going to tell him about Maria, she couldn't be held in one place; she needed space to move, to breathe.

Trey sat on the couch, but he wasn't relaxed; he perched on the edge, elbows on his knees, watching her warily. As he should. She placed one hand on the mantel and steadied herself. This felt like a big mistake, going against every instinct.

Maria had taught her to lie, to never tell the truth about who they were. Lessons to keep them alive.

She met his gaze. His hazel eyes were crinkled with concern, but he didn't look away. Instead he waited for her. Trusting her.

If he only knew.

She couldn't face him, so she turned back to the photos. She picked up one, of her and Maria working together in a lettuce field. Lydia was maybe six years old. She'd been playing at picking the lettuce. It hadn't been until years later that she realized it wasn't a game, not for the adults.

"The first thing I ever remember is running," she said, the flames crackling in time with her words. "Maria was chasing me through a field, we were laughing and giggling, and when she caught me, she tickled me so hard we were both crying. Later, she'd always talk about those days working the fields as the good days. When I was small enough that it was easy to move on, when we could blend in with the migrant workers, spend our days out in the sunshine and our nights sheltered, out of sight."

"You make it sound romantic."

"*She* made it sound romantic," Lydia said, the scorn in her voice surprising her. "It wasn't. It was a hard life—backbreaking work, twelve-, fourteen-hour days, little money. I don't even want to think about the things Maria probably had to do, a young girl alone with a baby." She shook herself free of the realities; they weren't memories, but she was an adult now, and she knew the kinds of things that happened when you had too many vulnerable people crowded into a place where a few men controlled their fate. Her hand trembled as she returned the photo with its smiling faces back to the mantel. "She always made it sound like a fairy tale, our lives. It wasn't. Not really."

"Lydia, you don't—"

She turned around, faced him once more. "Yes. I do. Just let me tell it, my way."

He nodded. Slowly. Ginger Cat appeared from nowhere and jumped up onto the couch arm, watching both of them with his eerie yellow-green eyes. Like Trey, he was at full alert, ready to pounce if danger presented itself.

"She was only seventeen when she had me," Lydia continued. "She told me she'd lived in San Francisco, said she'd used drugs but had gotten clean when she found out she was pregnant. Said I was the reason she'd run away, the reason we kept on running. Said it was the only way to keep me safe."

"Safe from what?"

Lydia swallowed. She didn't even know the man's name, knew nothing about him, but he was the bogeyman who had terrorized her ever since she could remember.

"My father." Wind rattled the windows in the silence that followed her words. "He's the reason why we couldn't stop running, could never have a real home, use our real names." She paused. This was harder than she'd imagined. "I don't even know if Lydia Fiore is my real name; I don't know if anything she told me about who she was, who I am, is real. The only thing I know is that when I was twelve years old, we ran out of room to run."

"Your father found you?"

"I don't know if it was him." Her voice tightened and climbed an octave as her mouth went dry. "It could have been someone he hired. Who knows? All I know is that a man came, a man wearing a badge and a gun and carrying a nightstick. He chased Maria into a church, and he used that stick to beat her to death." She stared at the fire, held her hands out to it even though she was too numbed by memory to feel the heat.

"He beat her because she wouldn't tell him where I was. And he kept hitting and hitting and hitting—"

Trey was behind her again, his hands on her shoulders, gripping hard, trying to pull her from the past. He turned her around to face him, wrapping her into an embrace as tears blinded her.

"He wouldn't stop hitting her," she said, her voice muffled as she pressed her face against his chest. "But she wouldn't tell, she never told. And I saw it all." She gagged and had to force herself to swallow. "I saw it, I could have stopped it, I should have stopped it, I should have saved her . . . but I didn't. I just hid and watched. And then I ran."

TWENTY-SEVEN

Friday, 9:13 P.M.

"Wow." Seth breathed the word out as if it were a prayer.

Nora curled her fingers in his chest hair, loving the feel of his sweat, the familiar scent of him. She'd been a fool to leave him. Even more foolish not to trust him long ago, to release herself to his passion, to hers. What they'd had before—not lovemaking, barely sex—seemed dull and mechanical compared to the feelings she had now.

"Wow," he repeated. "Nora, that was—I mean, we never . . . you never . . ."

She raised her head, balancing on an elbow. His eyes were half closed, his features totally relaxed as his fingers idly traced circles on her back.

"You were faking," she accused him.

"What? No, that was wonderful. Honest," he protested, eyes now open wide.

"Not now, before. All the times before." She squinted at him, not sure whether she felt angry, betrayed, or maybe even a tiny bit amused. "How many times have we made love, and you seemed pleased, satisfied, but you were faking."

He shook his head. "Nora, I'm a guy. We can't fake—that. Not like women."

She crawled on top of him, caging him, her arms pinning his wrists, her knees on either side of his chest. "Don't lie to me, Seth. I never satisfied you. Why didn't you say anything?"

"Wait a minute here. If anyone was faking all those times, it was you. Be honest, Nora."

She hung her head, her hair whisking over his face and chest. To her surprise, laughter bubbled up through her, shaking them both.

"You're right," she said when she finally caught her breath. "I didn't want you to think I was—cold, frigid. I just wanted to feel normal. Told myself it *was* normal, that being with you was the best I'd ever feel and that it was better than what most women had."

He wormed one hand free of her grasp, stroked her hair away from her face, tucking it behind her her ear, and left his hand there, his palm cupping her cheek. "I wish you had told me sooner."

"It was after I told you that you stopped touching me," she reminded him. She pulled away from his touch and sat back on her heels, still straddling his belly. "Was that when you decided to marry me? Out of pity?"

He was shaking his head so hard that it bounced off the floor. He reached for her hand, but she pulled it away, wrapping it across her breasts as she looked away. "It's okay. You can tell me the truth. After I told you, you couldn't bear to touch me. But you really never were going to ask me to marry you, were you?"

"Nora. Stop."

She blinked away tears and looked at him. Really at him. His face was dark with anger and regret.

"I made the first payment on the ring back in December. It took me until June to pay it off, but then you told me about—" He stumbled, sweat breaking out over his forehead.

"That I was raped. It's only a word, Seth." She couldn't believe she was talking like this—but as soon as she said the words, she felt empowered, realized they were true.

He sat up so fast, she almost tumbled off him. He caught her and pulled her close to him, his arms around her like steel bands. "Don't talk like that. It's more than a word. I always knew something was wrong, something had happened. After you told me—I couldn't ask you, you would have thought . . . anyway, I talked with Tommy Z, asked him for advice."

"Oh my God. *You* went for counseling?" This from the man who thought any and all of the world's problems could be solved with a scalpel, a cold beer, or a marathon of *Sports Night*?

He nodded. "We talked. A lot. He made me realize that every time we made love, I was the one starting things. Said maybe I should give you time and space, let you set the pace—"

"That's why you stopped touching me?" She slapped her palm against his chest, laughing once more, feeling the giddy freedom of being able to show her feelings without censure. "Those were the worst three weeks—I was going crazy! Do you have any idea how many times I almost jumped you in the middle of work?"

His normal boyish grin recaptured his features, banishing his look of regret. "Really? Guess Tommy Z had the right idea, then."

"Yeah, until I walked in on you and Karen."

"Hey. I explained that." He pulled her close once more, kissing her fears away.

Nora relented, allowing herself to relax into his embrace. When they separated, she slanted a glance at him. "So if I never satisfied you—"

"I never said *never*," he protested.

"Then why did you want to marry me, anyway?"

His sigh resonated through both of them. He angled his lips to kiss her forehead. "Nora, don't you get it? I fell in love with *you*. The sex didn't matter."

She squinted at him, not believing. Sex was the center of the male universe.

Except—he could have had any woman he wanted, but he had stayed with her. He was terrified of marriage, yet he had bought the ring months ago, slowly worked up his courage.

And even after she'd told him that she was damaged goods—even now that he knew the whole story, her lies and deceptions, all her secrets—even now, he was here. With her.

"The sex didn't matter?" she echoed, wanting desperately to believe.

He made his comic face, ready to cut loose with a joke. Her shoulders tensed, her throat tightened. If he started laughing, she'd slap him silly, she swore she would.

He didn't laugh. Instead he drew in a deep breath, framed her face with his palms, and stared directly into her eyes. "Nothing matters except you."

Warmth spread through her chest, her face, down her arms and legs, out to her fingers and toes, until her entire body felt like it was floating, free of the guilt that had anchored her for so long. All the time she'd thought she'd fooled him, convinced herself that he didn't realize anything was wrong, but she'd been fooling herself. He had known—and hadn't cared.

"You mean it. You really mean it."

Now he laughed, and she joined in. "Yes, Nora. I really, really mean it."

LYDIA WASN'T SURE HOW LONG SHE STOOD THERE, clinging to Trey. Usually when she remembered Maria's death, she was frozen with panic, unable to even cry, but somehow telling him had changed that. There was no panic, only grief—and the guilt of a twelve-year-old who had rescued her mother so many times that she couldn't accept that she hadn't been able to save her one last time.

Irrational, yes. But that didn't make it any less real. That secret guilt had steered her entire life.

"You never found your father? Found out who Maria really was?" Trey asked.

She shook her head. "Boyle asked a friend of his in L.A. to look at the case files. This guy, Epson, told Boyle that the case went cold once Maria became a Jane Doe and they couldn't trace her."

Trey tensed. "Jerry Boyle knows?"

"Well, yeah—" Too late, Lydia realized her inadvertent betrayal. She hadn't meant to keep secrets from Trey—hadn't ever meant to tell Boyle; it had just come out when the detective had found her in the midst of a panic attack that had made her flash back to that awful day in the church.

"You trusted Jerry, but you didn't trust me." He still held her, but it wasn't like before.

Lydia pulled away and turned to face him. "Don't be an idiot. Of course I trust you. You're about the only person I can trust."

"But you told Jerry, not me." His voice reflected his pain.

"I didn't *want* to tell Boyle," she floundered, trying to explain. "He just kind of found out." Trey's eyes narrowed; he wasn't buying it. "Damn it, Trey, don't you understand how hard this is for me? You're the only person I've told everything to—the only person I'd ever let see me like this." She ran her hand over her eyes, gathering leftover tears. "Weak, vulnerable."

"Why?" he persisted. "Jerry can help you find your mother's killer. But why tell me? Why now after all these months? Why tell me at all if it's so painful?"

God, she never dreamed it would be so hard. Stubborn male pride—no, that wasn't fair; it was her own pride and stubbornness and distrusting nature that had led them here. Sometimes she wondered why he stuck around at all.

She wasn't sure of her words, so she answered his fears the best way she could. Framing his face between her palms, she kissed him hard, communicating her feelings in the most honest way possible.

He resisted at first, then returned the kiss, his arms wrapping around her. Finally, they parted, just far enough for her to wipe away fresh tears.

"I told you because that's what families do," she whispered. "Isn't it?"

GINA AND JERRY SPENT MOST OF THE NIGHT TALKing. Or rather, she was talking and he was listening—as usual. She'd used her old version of the "I love you, but I'm not in love with you" speech that had always worked on boyfriends before. Felt guilty doing it, he deserved better—but wasn't that the point?

She'd just worked her way up to the "It's not you, it's me" part when he shook his head and left the room. Stunned, she'd sat on the couch, staring at the bedroom door he'd walked through.

It was totally unlike Jerry to walk out like that, avoiding a painful discussion. He met problems head-on, untangled and defused them, clarifying things until the correct path was clear to everyone involved. She should know; she'd dumped enough of her problems on him.

Finally, when he didn't reappear, Gina stood. She could let herself out or she could go after him. Letting herself out was the easy way—no fuss, no muss. She so very dearly wanted to go that route.

But Jerry deserved to have his chance. She approached the bedroom door, almost hoping he would lash out at her, get angry, pay her back for hurting him. She rapped softly. No answer. She pushed the door open.

The room was dark except for the glow of the clock radio. Jerry sat on the edge of the bed, hands dangling between his knees as he leaned forward, staring into space.

"Why'd you leave?"

"You weren't saying anything." He looked up at her, his face a sick greenish hue in the light of the clock. "You don't even know the truth yourself, do you, Gina?"

She shook her head. Slowly, as if trying to shake off a bad dream. "No. I think that's the problem."

Jerry reached for her hand, and she let him take it. He rubbed his thumb along the base of her ring finger. "I can wait. Will you let me know when you find out?"

"What if—" She swallowed hard. "It's bad news. For us."

"I'll still be here. I can't turn my feelings on and off just because you're not sure."

"I don't want to drag things out, give you false hope." She thought she was being noble, but the words sounded hollow and trite.

He stood, still holding her hand in his. "No such thing as false hope," he whispered, his mouth close to her cheek. He brushed his lips against her skin. "There's only hope."

It took all her willpower to step away from him. "Good-bye, Jerry."

WHETHER BY TEMPERAMENT OR TRAINING, SUR-geons were morning people. For Seth, it didn't come naturally. Which was why Nora was surprised when she woke at 4:50 to find him already awake, watching her as his fingers feathered her hair.

"What?" she asked, sitting bolt upright, dislodging his hand, hugging the sheet to her chest as if it would protect her from the next disaster. Adrenaline flashed through her, depositing a bitter taste in her mouth. "What's wrong?"

His forehead creased, but he said nothing. Instead, he

leaned forward and kissed her tenderly. "I missed this," he whispered. "I missed you."

Panic eased from Nora's muscles. She returned his kiss, tentative at first, a hint of fear undermining her passion. Did she really want to get involved with him again, open herself up to that kind of pain? Last night was great, but it was just one night.

DeBakey whomped his head against the door, rattling it in its frame. A canine alarm clock. Seth jumped out of bed, sliding into a pair of boxers as he went to let the dog outside. Nora also left the sanctuary of sleep behind, grabbing one of Seth's T-shirts, falling into their old routine: he'd take care of feeding DeBakey, she'd take care of feeding the humans.

"You don't have to get up," he said from the doorway, where he harnessed DeBakey's morning joviality. "Go back to sleep."

"I have to be at work by seven."

He stopped, ignoring the dog as he turned to face her. She couldn't make out his features in the dim light, but his voice carried his dismay. "Nora, you can't. Are you crazy? There's a madman stalking you; you can't go back to work. It's the first place he'll look."

"*If* he's after me, he's going to keep looking until he finds me. Better to stay in a crowded ER with people watching over me than here alone."

"How could he find you here?"

She shook her head at his naïveté. She'd spent all night—well, part of the night—thinking about it, following everything Jerry had told her about the rapist to its logical conclusion. "He knows about us, Seth. This will be one of the first places he'll look."

"Oh shit." The expletive rang through the empty air, startling DeBakey into a low growl. The dog paced between its two humans, seeking the hidden threat. "I never should have brought you here. I should have taken you out of town, gone to some motel in the middle of nowhere—"

"If I wanted to leave town, I would have gone. I can take care of myself."

"I know. But we're together again, I'll look after you. I want to."

"Together again?"

"Sure, after last night—"

"One time—"

"One? Excuse me, it was four times for you, three times for me. And neither of us was faking it."

"You're keeping score? What is this, some kind of competition?" She should have expected this of him, so typical. "This is serious, Seth. Oh, I forgot, you're never serious about anything."

"I am serious. And last night *was* important."

"One night of sex doesn't mean everything goes back to the way it used to be. I'm not even sure I want that."

"What? Nora, how can you say that?"

He reached for her, but she dodged him. His touch was too addictive, and she needed a clear head. "I don't know what I want. I'm so tired of all the lies and secrets, but now they're gone and I can live my life again."

"And you don't want me in it, is that what you're saying?"

"No. Please, Seth, don't make this harder."

"I want to take care of you, Nora. Be with you. Is that so awful?"

"You're smothering me. I need time. I can't handle facing every decision and thinking about what's best for you or us. I need to think about what's best for me." The words shocked her—she felt dirty, guilty just saying them. How selfish, how self-centered. Putting herself first? That had never happened before.

A tingle of anticipation soared through her, almost as exciting as the way she'd felt last night. Free, she felt free. And damn, it felt good.

"I'm done hiding, Seth." The calm in her voice surprised her. She felt like she did in the middle of a trauma—adrenaline buzzing through her veins but not distracting her, instead centering her on her mission. What did Lydia call it? In the zone. "I'm not running anymore. It's exactly what he wants, and I refuse to give it to him."

"Even if it kills you?"

TWENTY-EIGHT

Saturday, 5:32 A.M.

THE ARGUMENT CONTINUED IN THE CAR ON THE way to Angels. Seth trying to persuade her to stay home, angry that the police couldn't guarantee her safety, threatening to turn the car around and drive out of the city.

Nora ignored him. He hadn't had as much time to think things through, get used to the fact that he wasn't in complete control of his life. She'd had two years of living that way. Two years too many.

A strange calm had fallen on her, displacing the fear that usually ruled her existence. As if, despite everything—because of everything?—she was ready to reclaim her life.

Or maybe it was simply the endorphin rush that cornered animals experienced when there was nowhere left to run.

Seth's phone buzzed. He drove one-handed and answered it. She heard Lydia's voice. "It's for you," Seth said, handing her the phone.

"Why aren't you answering your phone?" Lydia said. "I've been trying to reach you all night."

Nora smiled as she remembered exactly why she hadn't

been near the phone. She took it from her purse and glanced at the screen. Eleven missed calls? She never got that many in a week. "Why is Pete Sandusky trying to call me?"

"Don't answer him," Lydia instructed. "Where are you?"

"In the car with Seth. Driving to Angels. Why?"

"You have time before your shift starts, right? Tell him to drop you off at my place. You can pick up your car after."

"Lydia, what's going on?"

"We need to talk."

AMANDA WOKE FIVE MINUTES BEFORE THE ALARM went off with a sense of *Eureka!* on her lips. But the feeling was short-lived, as she couldn't remember what answer had come to her during sleep. She remembered snippets of a dream about her dreadful OB-GYN rotation last year. The attending, Dr. Koenig, had pimped her mercilessly every chance he got, asking her questions about arcane historical points, obscure case reports, and studies published in foreign journals.

What the heck did Dr. Koenig have to do with Narolie? Or was it Zachary for whom her tangled dreams had found a cure?

Nine hours of sleep had barely touched her exhaustion, and she found herself almost succumbing in the shower. Prying her eyes open, she dressed, grabbed breakfast, and headed back to Angels for another long day and night on call, praying that her fatigue wouldn't kill someone.

Without Tank and Dr. Frantz to disrupt them, rounds went quickly. It was only Amanda and the PICU fellow, Terry, getting the sign out from the postcall team, along with the weekend PICU attending, Dr. Anthony, who joined them, wearing jeans and loafers, sipping a cup of Starbucks as they strolled from one patient to the next. No pimping, but also little teaching, not with the ranks reduced and so much work to be done.

She wasn't surprised to see Lucas waiting for them when

they arrived at Narolie's bedside. He wore the same clothes as yesterday and looked even more worried. "No improvement," he told them. "Her EEG shows diffuse slowing. She's had some autonomic dysregulation; her BP's been bouncing all over the place, heart rate, too."

Dr. Anthony glanced at the nurses' notes. "She's a ticking time bomb. Look at these BP spikes—if we're not careful, she'll stroke out for sure."

"She might have already," Lucas admitted. "I wanted to get another MRI today, but she's too unstable."

"We'll need to staff her one-on-one," Dr. Anthony told the charge nurse. He shook his head grimly. "This one is going to be tough, Lucas. Does her family know?"

"Yes. It doesn't help that Tillman is trying to have her transferred."

"Transferred? She's in no condition to go anywhere."

"Mr. Tillman wants her deported back to her home country," Amanda explained. "Somalia."

"Is he nuts?" Dr. Anthony almost spilled his coffee as he gestured angrily. "That can't be legal."

"Actually," Lucas said, "it is. I saw an article in the *New York Times*—hospitals all over the country are deporting patients who require long-term care or excessive use of their resources. One in Arizona run by nuns sent a traumatic brain injury patient in a coma back to his family in Mexico even though he was here legally."

"Nuns?" Dr. Anthony scoffed. "They have a helluva lot more conscience than Tillman. We're screwed unless you come up with something fast."

Lucas ignored Dr. Anthony to send a resigned glance in Amanda's direction. Then he straightened his shoulders. "Working on it."

LYDIA WAITED AT THE END OF HER DRIVEWAY. Trey was still sleeping, and not only didn't she want to risk waking him, she didn't think it was fair to Nora to have this discussion where anyone else, even Trey, could hear it. She shouldn't have told him about Nora's rape—but somehow she couldn't help herself. She'd needed him to understand, to hear it. But it was a betrayal of Nora's confidence. Another one.

Damn, this was why she hated gossip, getting involved, tangled up in other people's problems. This is what came of letting people get too close.

She was already regretting telling Trey about Maria. He looked at her differently, acted like she was fragile—or worse, broken. She hated that.

As she paced, she twisted Maria's bracelet over the top of her glove. Each charm had a story to go along with it: a church, a brass key, a heart, a pair of ballet slippers, a bridge. They were silly singsong stories that Maria made up, but Lydia had never grown tired of them. Even as a child she'd understood that those stories were as close as she would ever get to the truth of Maria's past. *Tell me more, tell me more,* she'd beg.

But Maria never did.

And then the past came roaring back, stealing Maria's future.

Lydia jerked her head up, realizing that the rumble wasn't only in her mind—Seth's Mustang was turning around in the cul-de-sac, stopping with the passenger door level with Lydia. Nora opened the door and pushed out of the low-slung muscle car.

"You sure about this?" Seth shouted through the open door.

"Go to work, Seth." Nora slammed the door shut. Seth didn't look happy—in fact, he looked downright angry. And worried. He grimaced, threw the car in gear, and sped off.

"Everything okay?" Lydia asked. She didn't want to get involved, she really didn't, but she had been hoping that Nora and Seth would work things out. Nora needed someone to help her through this, and Seth was a good guy.

The taillights on the Mustang disappeared at the end of the block before Nora replied. "Yes. No." She turned to Lydia. "Ever notice how every time you think you have life figured out, things get more complicated?"

Thinking of Trey, Lydia sighed and jammed her hands into her parka pockets. "Guess I'm going to add to the complications, then. C'mon, I'll buy you breakfast."

As they walked through the predawn darkness, Lydia explained about Narolie and Tillman's attempt at deporting her.

"That's awful," Nora said. They reached Diggers and found a booth in the back. The waitress, used to hospital personnel, anticipated their needs and brought a full pot of coffee without asking as she dropped off the menus. "Can he do that?"

"Lucas is going to try his best to stop him, but, yeah, I think he could get away with it. Unless we stop him."

"We? What do I have to do with it?" Nora sipped her coffee, using both hands to steady her mug.

"Well, that's where it gets complicated." Lydia pushed her coffee away. Usually she loved the stuff, but this morning even the smell of it was making her stomach turn. Probably had less to do with the coffee and more to do with the confession she was about to make. "Tillman was sleeping with Karen."

Nora's eyes got big. "Really? You don't think he's the killer, do you?" Her gaze grew distant as if she were comparing the hospital CEO to everything she remembered about her attacker. "I don't know. Maybe. He's misogynistic enough." She shook her head. "It's so frustrating. I didn't see or hear anything helpful. I wish I had; I could have stopped all this—"

"Nora." Lydia's tone was sharper than she intended, but it did the trick. Nora jerked her chin up. "Stop it. You did the best you could. You survived. You can't blame yourself."

"You're right. I know you are. It's just—"

"Pete Sandusky is going to run a story that you lost Karen's evidence kit." There, it was out. Lydia sat back, waiting for Nora.

"How does Pete know anything—" Nora's eyes narrowed. "You told him?"

"No. He already knew. Whoever stole it sold him the photos of Karen from it. Told him that you found her body, lost the rape kit, everything. Including that Seth and Karen were involved. He came to me for confirmation."

"And you gave it to him?"

"I gave him nothing. But I could have maybe stopped him, traded him the story about Tillman and Karen, tried to save you."

"And you didn't." Nora set her cup down without looking, rattling the silverware and sloshing coffee that she didn't clean up. Then she glanced up at Lydia. "You want to blackmail Tillman, make him leave Narolie alone."

Lydia nodded. "I couldn't think of another way, and Sandusky might have ended up running the story about you anyway. But I wanted to warn you before you walked into a hornet's nest."

"The nurses, everyone at Angels, they'll think I did it on purpose, because of Seth and Karen."

"I know. I'm sorry. I tried to think of something I could do to fix things, but"—Lydia opened her empty hands and laid them on the table between them—"I didn't come up with anything."

Nora didn't make eye contact as she nodded. "You're not even going to go through with it, blackmailing Tillman, are you?"

"No. But I'm going to tell Jerry. It might help his investigation."

"Even if it might mean losing Narolie?"

Lydia closed her eyes as a wave of nausea overtook her.

She hated gambling with a girl's life, but it was the right thing to do. "Even if it means losing Narolie."

"Then you're doing the right thing." Nora's voice was strong, confident. "I can take care of myself. And we'll think of some way to help Narolie."

"Are you sure?"

"I'm sure."

"WHAT ARE YOU DOING HERE?" ASKED LAURIE, the night-shift charge nurse, as Gina walked into the ER on Saturday morning. "You're not on the schedule."

"Making up for hours I owe," Gina mumbled in reply as she headed to the locker room to change. Laurie kept staring, like she was a freak or something. Since when was it a crime to work extra hours? It wasn't so strange to show up, wanting to work when it wasn't her shift, was it?

Gina banged her locker door. Of course it was. Residents worked eighty-hour weeks, why in hell would they come back for more if they had any place better to be?

But suddenly she had no place better to be. Not with Amanda on call and the house empty, Jerry's place off-limits, and no way, nohow could she go home to her parents. . . . Suddenly the frenzy of the ER was her safe haven. A place where she didn't have to think about how screwed up her own life was.

She returned to the nurses' station to check the patient board and was surprised to see Tank sitting there, talking with Jason, the ward clerk. "What are you doing here?"

"Hoping to find you." He stood, clutching a backpack, obviously nervous. He wore jeans—too expensive and pressed with a sharp crease—and a lightweight polo shirt under a heavy wool overcoat. He looked like a foreign kid dressing up as an American teen for Halloween and failing miserably. As if without his school uniform he had no idea how to fit in.

Gina could give him some pointers on that—she'd mastered the art of disguise. But apparently Tank wasn't here for fashion tips. "My grandfather was going to throw out the medicine you gave us, but I kept it, used it just like the directions said. So I'm not contagious now, right? I can go see Narolie and not hurt her, can't I?"

"Does your mother know you're here?" He was silent, looking down at the floor. Guess that answered her question. "How'd you get here, Tank?"

He brightened at that. "Took a bus. Well, a couple, actually. Consuela, our maid, lives near here and she told me how." He was beaming, standing up proudly as if he'd just successfully navigated the Kalahari single-handedly. "I stayed up all last night, researching Somalia. Do you have any idea what's happening there? Especially to the Bantu, like Narolie's family? What they do to women, to girls? Even little babies?" His voice rose to the soprano range and cracked. "They cut them up, rape them, kill them—for no good reason. Just because they're girls. They can't send her back to that, Gina. We have to stop them!"

Gina couldn't help but smile at his passion. "You want to see her?"

"Yes. Please."

"You know she's in a coma, and she can't talk, probably won't hear you?"

"That's okay. Look"—he dug through his bag and pulled out a wad of paper—"I downloaded a Kiswahili dictionary. Even printed it out because I knew you wouldn't let me use my laptop or iPhone in the ICU. I translated some stuff." Now he was blushing. "Stuff I want to say to her, even if she can't hear."

"Okay. Let's get you a visitor's pass, make you legit." The smile he gave her made it all the way to his eyes, giving her a glimpse of the man he might become. Someone strong and brave and ready to fight for what he believed in.

Gina turned away and began walking toward the elevators, hoping he didn't see the single tear that escaped before she could blink it away.

Had she ever been like that?

As Nora and Lydia left Diggers and walked the short distance to Angels, Nora was surprised that drivers didn't honk at her or swerve their cars to hit her. She felt like every eye was on her, condemning her.

Foolish thought. No one on the street would know who she was or her role in Karen's death. But once she entered the hospital . . . everyone would know.

They reached the ER entrance and she couldn't help herself. She hesitated.

"You have to face them sooner or later," Lydia said in a low voice. The voice of experience, Nora knew.

"You're right." Nora sucked in her breath, the frigid air burning against her dry throat. Together they strode inside.

"I'm going to go check on Narolie," Lydia said. "You'll be all right."

She left without waiting for Nora's answer, and Nora realized it hadn't been a question. She wished she were as certain.

"Nora, what are you doing here?" Glen Bakker greeted her when she walked into the nurses' station.

"I'm scheduled to work; where else would I be?"

"Thank God," Jason put in. His smile buoyed Nora. Either he hadn't heard the news or he didn't believe it.

But Jason's faith in her obviously hadn't spread to the other staff—several nurses stopped what they were doing to glare at her.

"Yesterday Tillman sent Carlene down, and she spent more time interrogating us than she did taking care of things," Jason continued. Carlene was the head of nursing, and although she'd been a tough-as-nails scrub nurse once upon a time, she'd been behind a desk long enough to be more comfortable with a spreadsheet than a stethoscope. "Oh damn, she's back again."

"Good morning, Nora," Carlene said with false cheer, her heels clicking on the linoleum. She was taller than Nora, with hair dyed so often its real color was a long-forgotten mystery. Today it appeared honey-brown. "I'm surprised to see you here. My impression was that you were taking more time off. After your ordeal and all. Not to mention the unfortunate press we received this morning."

Glen stepped beside Nora. It was nice to have his bulk shielding her from the stares of her co-workers. "That wasn't Nora's fault. That reporter had no right—"

"Nevertheless, it's our problem now. We can't have patients worried that their nurse is putting a personal vendetta above their needs. Or worse, that she's so incompetent that she can't keep track of vital evidence." Carlene glared at Nora, baring her lips in an illusion of a smile. "Not saying either is true, of course."

"Of course." Nora forced a smile to match Carlene's. "But you wouldn't want to validate a false story by preventing me from working, would you?"

"She has a point, Carlene," Glen said.

Carlene raked Nora with her gaze, seeking out her vulnerable spots. "All right. But I want Tommy Z to do a complete evaluation of her response to the recent stress."

"I'd prefer her working someplace where we can protect her," Glen said. "My men are stretched thin."

"Stop talking about me like I'm a child. I'm fine," Nora protested. She was beginning to hate those two words.

Carlene ignored her. "If there are any problems, Tommy will report directly to me. And Mr. Tillman, of course. He won't be happy to hear you're back at work so soon."

"Tillman has a problem, he can take it up with the union.

I'm scheduled, so I'm working. You can't force me to go home."

"If that's the way you want to handle it, fine. Work. We'll see what happens." Carlene's arch smile made it clear that she expected Nora to break down into a bundle of nerves before the morning was out. "After the news this morning, we'll need to keep your exposure to the public to a minimum. You can work utilization review; I'll take your shift in the ER."

"UR? That's your job." Utilization review was the worst—relegated to reviewing charts of ICU and long-term patients to make sure they were still sick enough to qualify for the services they were receiving. It was a way to anticipate denials by insurance companies with a preemptive strike.

"Today it's yours." Carlene's smile was so forced that Nora was surprised she didn't start cackling like the Wicked Witch of the West. "You can start with the Somali girl in the PICU. Mr. Tillman wants her case expedited. I'll call and tell him you're on your way up for the file."

Great. Thanks to Pete Sandusky, not only did everyone in the hospital now hate her guts, but she might be the one who had to sign the order to send Narolie back to Somalia.

AFTER ROUNDS, AMANDA ESCAPED TO THE MEDI-cal library. She was starting to remember more of her dream from last night—and the real case that had inspired it. When she'd been on her OB-GYN rotation, she'd done an ER consult on a college student with abdominal pain and a calcified mass on ultrasound. Dr. Koenig had grilled her mercilessly about the differential diagnosis, which was vast, and had taunted her when she included ovarian teratoma as a possibility.

"And what is a teratoma?" he'd asked.

Amanda had been surprised by the lowball, basic question. "A benign tumor composed of several tissue types, rising from the ovary."

"Benign?"

"Ninety-eight percent of the time. Rarely, like any tissue in the body, they can develop malignancies."

"But if there's no cancer, there's no reason to worry?"

She'd stalled for time, looking to her resident to jump in, but the resident looked as mystified as Amanda. Dr. Koenig had sighed and dismissed them with instructions to catch up on their reading before they saw him in the morning, when he wanted to know all the complications a "benign" teratoma could cause.

That night Amanda had scoured the OB-GYN journals. She'd found lots of information on teratomas, including a single case report from a Scandinavian journal about a woman who had an acute episode of coma that resolved after removal of a benign teratoma.

She'd made notes and shared them with her resident, prepared for the next day's pimping, but Dr. Koenig had forgotten all about his assignment and had instead interrogated them about the enervation of the bladder wall.

Could a single case from halfway around the world hold the key to Narolie's illness? Amanda hoped so.

She was surprised to see Emma Grey, the patient librarian, working in the small cubicle she and the medical librarian shared. "Emma, it's a Saturday morning, what are you doing here?"

The white-haired librarian looked up with a smile. "Good morning, Amanda. Saturday's my busiest day—families visiting, looking for answers."

Emma had transformed the patient library from a mere lending library into a valuable resource for families. The medical staff would alert her to a family's questions about their loved one's care or diagnosis, and Emma would find easy-to-understand information for them to provide. It saved the staff time and effort, and in only a few months

Emma had become an essential part of the medical team at Angels.

"Where's Deon?" Amanda asked.

"In his favorite comfy chair by the radiator, reading." Emma beamed at her great-grandson, a certified genius according to Emma—and the school. "Deon, say hello to Dr. Amanda."

Deon glanced up from his thick book—the last Harry Potter, Amanda saw—to wave at Amanda. She smiled back, envying him the time to read for pleasure.

"Can I help you find something, dear?" Emma asked.

"Yes, I'd love some help if you've the time. I'm looking for a case report of a teratoma causing coma or maybe encephalitis. It was a Scandinavian journal, but I can't remember which one. Only the abstract was translated—I'm hoping to find a translation of the full text."

Emma nodded, already typing search terms into her computer. "Here's one from six years ago. *Acta Obstetricia et Gynecologica Scandinavica.*"

"Yes. That's it! Can you find me a translation?"

"Hang on a second. French, Italian—here we go, the full text in English. I'll print it out for you."

While the paper was printing, Amanda skimmed the essence of the case. She had remembered correctly. The woman's teratoma had been found years before during an ultrasound while she was pregnant. Because it was a benign tumor and she was asymptomatic, it was never removed. Decades later, she began experiencing strange, psychotic behavior and motor tics thought to be seizures. Her EEG and CT scans were normal, but she deteriorated and fell into a coma.

No medications worked, and nothing revived her. She lay comatose for weeks until a feeding tube perforated her small intestine and required surgery to repair. The surgeon found the teratoma and removed it as well. The next day, to everyone's surprise, the woman woke up and was mentally back to normal.

"Thanks, Emma. This is wonderful," Amanda said as she reached the end of the report. "Now all I have to do is prove that Narolie's calcification is a teratoma and find a surgeon willing to remove it." She rushed toward the door, that *Eureka!* feeling filling her once more, buoying her steps.

NORA LEFT THE ER, TRYING TO IGNORE THE SEN-sation that everyone was staring at her. Tillman's offices were on the top of the research tower, giving him an eagle-eye view of the entire medical center. She walked past the cafeteria, intending to cut past the auditorium and cross the enclosed atrium to the tower entrance.

No such luck. She'd forgotten about the gala preparations. The auxiliary had large privacy screens set up, blocking the corridor past the cafeteria doors, with a sign that read PRI-VATE FUNCTION. Past the screens she could hear the chatter of volunteers draping the walls, hanging decorations, and converting the doctors' dining room, auditorium, and atrium into a venue for tonight's black-tie affair.

No way in hell was she going to be able to attend the gala after everything that had happened. And what kind of respect did that show Karen, still having it as scheduled? No doubt Tillman would turn it into a media circus, a public memorial for Karen—raising even more money while trading on the dead nurse's memory.

As she turned around and headed toward the stairs to take the tunnel over to the tower, Nora chuckled at her Scrooge-like thoughts—great way to get into the holiday spirit! Despite everything that had happened, she found herself actually looking forward to Christmas. Even New Year's.

Taking her life back had a lot to do with that. So did Seth.

She wasn't foolish enough to think that figuring out the

sexual part of their relationship meant the rest would magically fall into place, but learning that he hadn't lied to her—
that was a huge step forward.

Her good mood continued as she remembered the things
Seth had told her last night. She didn't want to dive right into
the same mistakes—and there was the little fact of a killer
who might or might not be obsessed with her—but she felt
hopeful.

Something she hadn't felt in a long, long time.

In addition to the executive administration offices, the research tower also held the clinics and research labs and so,
except for the rare lab assistant, should be deserted on a weekend. She was surprised Tillman was in today. Damn, she was
hoping that when Carlene sent her up here for Narolie's UR
chart, the place would be deserted.

As she opened the door to his outer office, she realized it
wasn't only the CEO making an appearance on a Saturday.
His receptionist was there, as was a secretary typing dictation. And through the window behind the receptionist desk
she saw Tillman holding court with several hospital board
members.

None of whom appeared very happy. Pete Sandusky's
story probably had something to do with that. If Lydia was
right, they had Jim Lazarov to thank. She still couldn't believe the emergency medicine intern would stoop so low as to
steal a rape kit and auction it off to the press.

"I'm here to pick up Narolie Maxeke's chart for utilization review," Nora told the receptionist, avoiding giving her
name. She still wore her street clothes, jeans, and a sweater,
and her coat hid her hospital ID hanging from a belt loop.

"Right. I have it here." The phone rang and the receptionist grabbed it and began speaking even as she handed Nora
Narolie's UR paperwork. Nora was about to leave when the
receptionist covered the phone with her hand and called out,
"Mr. Tillman wants that done ASAP!"

Nora merely nodded and left, feeling like a thief escaping into the night as the door shut behind her. Narolie's information was spread throughout the hospital computer system, so it could be reproduced if need be, but usually the UR chart was the definitive collection of all the administrative information.

As vital as the actual medical record, the chart she held now contained the insurance and legal paper trail Tillman would need to deport Narolie. Maybe she could help Narolie after all. At least buy her some time.

Hugging the chart to her chest, she fled down the hall to the elevator bank. With practically no one in the building today, it arrived quickly. Getting to any patient care floor in the other tower meant crossing the eighth-floor skyway, going back down to the first floor, or using the tunnels again. Nora chose the aerial route and hit the button for the eighth floor.

She took her time crossing the skyway. Usually she avoided the eighth floor, which held the rehab units: long-term patients in vegetative states, patients with spinal cord and traumatic brain injuries, stroke victims. The place where a lot of her patients from the ER ended up. The professionals there did great work, but it was no place for anyone used to the instant gratification of emergency medicine.

The rehab floor kind of spooked her, in fact. Patients and medical staff working so hard to achieve so little. Depressing as hell.

When she was a kid, they used to drag the school choir around to all the area nursing homes to sing Christmas carols. She'd always try to find a way out of it, but her folks made her go. All those blank faces, lined up to see the carolers, some tied to their chairs . . .

"Hey, bitch!" Halfway across the skyway, a man plowed into her from behind, sending Narolie's file flying. Nora careened into the glass wall.

Fear stampeded through her. She bounced off the glass and spun to face her attacker, her arms raised in a primitive protective reflex, eyes half closed, anticipating pain.

"You think you can push me around and get away with it?" Jim Lazarov held her against the glass, his hands pushing against her shoulders. His face was an inch from hers, twisted with fury. "How do you like it, bitch?"

TWENTY-NINE

Saturday, 8:54 A.M.

NORA'S FEAR MIXED WITH ANGER—AND THEN THE fear returned, multiplied, as she realized that Jim could be the killer. He'd gone to medical school here in Pittsburgh, would be familiar with hospitals. Jim seemed shorter than her attacker, but she'd been blinded, so she wasn't certain. He definitely had the anger and strength the killer had.

She forced herself to remain calm. That was what had saved her life last time.

"Let me go," she told Jim, using a voice of command. Her tone was a little shrill, so she hauled in another breath and tried again. "Now, Jim."

His chest heaved as he caught his breath—as if he were the one afraid for his life. More likely excited, she thought with disgust. But his expression cleared, and he released her. He didn't move back, though, still blocking her.

"I'm tired of taking your shit," he said, his words accompanied by spittle that sprayed her face. "Humiliating me in front of an attending yesterday."

Nora didn't wipe it off, but forced her hands to remain

open at her sides. She fought for the calm she'd felt earlier today, for the control.

"Understood," she said, keeping her tone level. "Now, let me pass."

"I'd listen to the lady if I were you." Glen Bakker appeared at the far end of the skyway. "Unless you'd like to spend the holidays in jail."

"For what?" Jim said, but he stepped away, finally giving Nora room to breathe. Glen seemed in no hurry as he strode down the skyway to meet them, his hand resting on his gun. Jim puffed out his chest with bluster. "I didn't do anything wrong."

"I guess we'll let Ms. Halloran be the judge of that," Glen said as he arrived beside Jim and clamped one large hand on the intern's shoulder. Jim deflated beneath the larger man's touch.

Nora thought for a moment. There really wasn't anything Jim had done to her that she hadn't done first to him yesterday, when she'd been so upset.

"It's okay," she told Glen. "You can let him go."

Glen didn't release his grip on Jim's shoulder. "You sure?"

Adrenaline leached from her system, leaving her stomach quivering. As were her hands. Nora jammed them into her coat pockets before either man could notice. "I'm sure."

"Get out of here, then," Glen told Jim, who hastened to comply.

Once Jim had fled the skyway, Nora gathered up the scattered paperwork. Glen got down on his hands and knees and helped her.

"Thought you were going to be working in Carlene's office," he said. "You know, keeping a low profile."

"I need to go down to the PICU, check out this patient in person," Nora lied.

Glen didn't fall for it. "Everything you need is on the computer."

She shrugged and stood up again.

"You're trying to pull a fast one on Tillman, aren't you?"

Tillman signed Glen's paycheck, too, so Nora said nothing as they strolled across the skyway to the patient care tower. "How'd you find me?"

Glen pulled out his PDA. "I've got eyes and ears everywhere, remember? Besides, I told you me and my guys were going to keep an eye out for you."

"Good timing. Thank you."

"You're welcome." They rode the elevator down to the fourth floor, where the ICUs and operating rooms were. "I know you're feeling like you can't trust anyone around here right now, but you can trust me." Glen walked her to the doors of the PICU. "Call me if you're going anywhere, Nora. I don't want you wandering around here alone. Okay?"

Nora blew her breath out. She hated the idea that she wasn't free to do what she wanted. But he was right. "Okay. Thanks again, Glen."

LUCAS WAS QUICKLY LOSING POINTS FOR FIANCÉ of the year, not to mention attending of the year. Amanda couldn't understand why he wasn't as excited by her theory as she was.

"Amanda, I have to do what's best for my patient." They were in the dictation area behind the nurses' station, a small alcove that was quickly becoming too crowded between the two of them and their emotions.

"Why can't you trust me? Lucas, I didn't make this up."

"We don't have time for this. Narolie is deteriorating, Tillman could have her deported at any minute—"

"But the case report about an ovarian teratoma—"

"Abdominal masses don't cause psychosis and encephalitis. We need to give the antivirals time to work."

"We need to operate." Amanda stared him down. Even if she did have to crane her neck and look up at him to do it.

"Do you even know if Narolie *has* a teratoma?"

"The clinic did an upper GI when she first began vomiting. It was normal except for a small calcification near her right ovary. I need a CT to confirm it."

"If she's too unstable for me to get an MRI to follow up on a disease process I do know about, what makes you think I'll risk her life on a CT to try to validate something you have a hunch about?"

She hated when he used that officious tone with her. Hated even more that he was right. She looked beyond him to Narolie's room, where Lydia, Gina, and Tank were sitting with her. "Lucas, please."

"No. I'm sorry, but I'm trying to keep her alive."

"So am I."

"No, you're chasing around, trying to find your silver lining. Medicine doesn't always work that way, Amanda. I can't work that way. I have to deal with the scientific facts."

"It's better than doing nothing."

"Waiting for medication to have an effect is not doing nothing," Lucas protested. "Besides, if it's a teratoma, then she was born with it. Why would it start causing her problems now?"

"The case report didn't have an explanation, but the patient got better when the tumor was removed." She thrust her copy at him. He frowned, but took it and skimmed through it. It was only two pages long—hardly an authoritative research treatise.

"Coincidence." He handed it back to her with a skeptical scowl.

"Lucas—"

"I have to go. I have a stat consult in the ER. Let me know if you find anything else."

Amanda stared after him, fuming. She'd asked him not to give her any special treatment, but damn it, she knew she was right about this—even if the medical evidence was lacking. It was a strong feeling, too strong to shake off. And it might be Narolie's only hope.

NORA WAS SURPRISED TO SEE AMANDA AND LUCAS arguing—especially in such a public place. It was totally unlike either of them. She glanced around the unit. Narolie was in the isolation room with Tank beside her. Along with Gina and Lydia.

Well, good. Between the four of them, they ought to be able to think of a plan to keep Narolie from being deported.

Before she could get Narolie's chart from the nurses' station, the PICU doors opened and Seth blew in like a small hurricane. His Penn State scrub cap was crooked, his surgical mask hung from his neck, and he wore his OR clogs. He raced over to her, ignoring the startled looks from the nurses and parents.

"Nora, are you okay?"

She stared at him, puzzled. "Of course I'm okay. Why shouldn't I be?"

"I heard Jim Lazarov attacked you! Why didn't you call me, let me know you were all right?"

"He didn't attack me. It was just a misunderstanding. Who told you, anyway?"

"One of the security guards told an ER nurse who told one of the transporters who told—"

"Seth, I can take care of myself," Nora interrupted him, irritated at the efficiency and inaccuracy of the hospital gossip machine. And that Seth believed she wouldn't have let him know if something had happened. "Tell me you didn't leave a patient."

He didn't meet her eyes. "Pancreatic pseudocyst. I lied, told them I got paged to check on a patient in the SICU."

"Seth Cochran!" Now she was the angry one. "Get back in there and take care of your patient."

"Maybe you should go home." His expression clouded as he remembered why that wasn't possible. Then he spotted Lydia and Gina walking from Narolie's room to the break room. "Or go to Lydia's. No one would look for you there."

"No. I'll be right here doing my job. You go do yours." She remembered her thoughts from earlier this morning, that he might be safer without her nearby. He hadn't listened to her when she tried to explain then; instead they'd ended up fighting. Just like now.

His eyes darkened as he scowled. "Why won't you ever listen to me? I've been totally honest with you every step of the way, but you still don't trust me, do you?"

"Of course I do." She gestured for him to lower his voice. The parents nearby were obviously agitated by their argument. "This isn't the time—"

"No time ever is." His face filled with pain. "I've tried everything I know, Nora. Bared my soul to you. But I can't keep doing it. Not alone."

Before she could say anything, he strode out of the PICU, the doors swooshing closed behind him.

She took a step after him. Stopped. Maybe it was better this way. Safer. For everyone.

No one questioned *Lydia's* presence here at work, Gina noticed. Despite the fact that she wore jeans and a fleece pullover, Lydia didn't look out of place. Instead she looked in command, ready for action. She led Gina into the PICU's break room and pulled the curtains shut, giving them privacy.

"We need to figure out a way to help Narolie," Lydia said.

"Ahh, so that's why you're here on your day off, instead of helping Trey decorate the Christmas tree or some other blissful domestic activity?"

Lydia frowned. "Trey is at his folks' today. Thank God."

"Really?" Gina asked, secretly thrilled to see St. Lydia the

Perfect having a not-so-perfect day. "Something going on with you two?"

"Just normal stuff." Typical Lydia, treating her private life as off-limits. Gina was surprised she'd said as much as she had.

"Yeah, right." Gina was fascinated to learn she wasn't the only one who hadn't mastered the art of cohabitation. "Trey's like the perfect guy. You two are made for each other."

"You're one to talk—you have Jerry."

Gina hid her expression. No sense letting the whole world knew she'd walked out on Jerry. Especially because she knew Jerry and Lydia were close—hell, he saw more of Lydia than Gina some weeks. She'd let everyone else know about her and Jerry when she was certain she knew how *she* felt about it. Right now, better just to avoid the issue altogether. "Yeah, well, at least Trey talks to you. When Jerry's on a case, it swallows him whole. I'm lucky to get two words out of him."

"It's not Trey. Well, a little. Mainly it's his family." Lydia bounced to her feet. "Damn it, why does everything have to be so complicated?"

Before Gina could answer—not that she had an answer, but that wasn't going to stop her from saying something; she was enjoying her unexpected role of confidante too much— the door banged open and Nora entered. "Men!"

Both Gina and Lydia swiveled to stare at her.

"What did Seth do now?" Gina asked. It wasn't often that she was the sanest in the bunch. It was kind of nice for a change. She leaned forward, elbows on her knees in a serious pose, and nodded to Nora earnestly, borrowing a move from the shrinks. "It's okay, go on."

Nora flounced down onto the chair Lydia had vacated. "He thinks he can smother me, protect me from everything. He heard Jim Lazarov was giving me a hard time and even left a patient in the OR to see if I was okay. Like I couldn't handle it myself. Argh!"

Lydia, to Gina's surprise, took Seth's side. "Hey, after

what's happened the past few days, I think he's got every right to be a bit overprotective."

That earned her a glare from Nora. "Like you'd ever let Trey coddle you. You had half of Pittsburgh gunning for you, and you didn't back down and hide."

Lydia sat down beside Nora and grabbed her hand. "I was going to run, was ready to run and hide, let everyone else deal with it."

No way. Gina stared at Lydia, surprised by her confession. St. Lydia was human after all, as vulnerable as the rest of them? "What stopped you?"

There was a pause. Both Nora and Gina stared at Lydia, waiting for her answer. Lydia startled them both by shaking her head and laughing. "Believe it or not, it was Trey. He made me realize that there were some things worth fighting for after all." She squeezed Nora's hand. "So cut Seth some slack. He loves you and he can't risk losing you to some psycho nut job."

Nora blew her breath out in an exaggerated sigh. "I'm so tired of not being able to live my own life. Everyone talking about me, about what I did, judging me. I want it all to go away, to stop being labeled a victim."

Lydia squatted down to pull a package of coffee filters from the lower cupboard. As she did, her top rode up enough to expose a small pistol holstered at the small of her back.

"Where'd you get that?" Gina asked. Jerry had taught her the rudiments of gun safety—had insisted on it—but she'd never liked guns or seen their attraction. Especially after being shot at. "Put it away. This is a hospital."

Both Nora and Lydia jerked their heads at her pious tone. Before they could say anything, the door shot open and Amanda stalked in. "Men!" She looked at them, her eyes widening at the sight of Lydia's gun. "Is that a nine-millimeter? Perfect. Cuz I'm gonna kill him!"

THIRTY

Saturday, 10:11 A.M.

"AMANDA!" NORA SNAPPED. "I CAN'T BELIEVE YOU said that."

Amanda clapped her hand over her mouth, wide-eyed. "I'm sorry. I wasn't thinking."

Lydia tugged her top down, hiding the gun from sight, and busied herself making coffee.

"I don't think you should have that in the hospital," Nora continued. "Especially not up here near children."

Lydia bobbed her head in a nod, still turned away from them, while Gina sat there grinning.

"Yes, Mom," Gina said, breaking the tension in the room.

"Oh, be quiet." Nora slouched in her chair as the coffee maker gurgled and Lydia rejoined them.

"I'm sorry, Nora," Amanda said again, pulling out a chair for herself. "I was just so upset. But after yesterday—"

"It's okay."

"What were you and Lucas arguing about?" Gina asked.

"I had an idea that might help Narolie. But he wouldn't listen."

"Doesn't sound like Lucas," Lydia said. "What kind of idea?"

Amanda slid a paper across the table to Lydia, who read it and passed it down the line.

"Teratoma causing encephalitis," Gina mused. "Never heard of it."

"No one has," Amanda admitted. "This is the only case report I could find. And I'm not even sure if the abdominal calcification Narolie's upper GI showed is from a teratoma. I need a CT of her belly to find out."

"Lydia, what do you think?" Nora asked.

"I think you don't need a CT to confirm an ovarian teratoma. Get OB-GYN up here to do an ultrasound. If their attending is convinced, they can handle Lucas. And in the meantime see if you can find some more case reports—make it easier to convince both of them."

"A portable ultrasound?" Amanda thought for a moment. "I can do that without compromising her care, so Lucas can't get upset."

"Stop worrying about Lucas and worry about your patient."

"You're right. I was just so surprised when he didn't agree with me."

"Get used to it," Nora put in. "I think I can help as well."

"How?"

"By getting rid of this deportation nonsense. I'll get Mickey on the case—she'll have Tillman and his lawyers so tangled in knots that it will be the next millennium before they can think of trying to kick a patient out of the hospital."

"Mickey!" Lydia smiled, rapping her knuckles on the table in approval. "Fighting lawyers with lawyers, it's perfect. I should have thought of her myself. Nora, you're a genius." She brushed her hands together. "Okay, so one problem solved. And Mickey working on the case should give you a reason to keep a low profile, stay out of trouble, right?"

Nora bristled. "I'm not hiding—"

"Never said you were. But you keep getting people pissed off, and it's going to impact patient care."

"Seth said Jim Lazarov tried to attack her," Amanda put in.

Damn, it was like a conspiracy. They all turned to stare at Nora. "I told you, Seth exaggerated. It was nothing. Okay, I'll hang out here, pretending to review Narolie's chart, stall for time until Mickey can get here." She rolled her eyes at Lydia. "Then maybe I'll go walking alone through the cemetery after dark, since you guys obviously think I'm incapable of taking care of myself."

Lydia flashed her a smile of understanding. It wasn't easy trying to live your life under a threat. Lydia's answer was to carry a gun. Nora's was to focus on her patients. On controlling what she could control.

"Nah, you'll come home with me. Run interference between me and Trey's mom. I'm supposed to be at her place today. Baking cookies—some kind of holiday tradition." Lydia made it sound like having a root canal without anesthesia.

"You could go to the gala and pick up my award for me, instead," Gina suggested, but no one paid her any attention.

"Nora, could you keep an eye on Tank, too?" Amanda said, bringing them back to the problem at hand. "Maybe talk to him—poor kid has no idea about anything. If things go badly, I don't know how he'll handle it."

"I'll call Ken Rosen, ask him to talk with Tank," Gina put in. "He's good with stuff like that."

"Ken?" Lydia said. "Really?"

"Sure, why not? I'll see if he's in his lab today—that will give Tank a place to go while Narolie is getting her ultrasound."

"Sounds like we have all our bases covered," Lydia said. "Okay, I'll see you guys later."

"Where are you going?" Nora asked.

"Down to the ER. I have a little research project that needs finishing. I'll call you when I'm ready to go home."

Nora stared after her. She didn't like the smile that played across Lydia's face—it was the same smile she'd worn yesterday when she talked about blowing the heads off targets.

LYDIA TOOK THE STAIRS BACK DOWN TO THE ER. She didn't go through the main emergency department, but rather took the back way around to the hallway that housed the locker rooms and OR 13. The usual Saturday bustle echoed down the hall from the ER, but no one was around as she ducked into the men's locker room.

She didn't close the door immediately, but held it as she listened, ready for a quick escape. The locker room was empty. She shut the door and grabbed the clipboard from the hook beside it. As in the women's locker room, there was a listing of occupied lockers. Jim Lazarov had number seventeen.

She replaced the clipboard and wound her way past two rows of lockers and benches strewn with discarded scrubs, street shoes, and towels. At least the women cleaned up after themselves. Locker seventeen was on the far wall, the second from the end.

Jim had a cheap combination padlock on it—good enough for routine security, not good enough to match Lydia's skills. She glanced over her shoulder even though no one was there, feeling guilty and rebellious and naughty at the same time. She hadn't picked a lock in years, but this one would be easy.

The lock had three dials on the side and was the kind where the owner could reset the combination at will. Great for convenience, not so hot for security. Lydia pulled the shackle bar out, getting a feel for how tight the tumbler wheels were. As she spun the first wheel, her cell phone rang.

She dropped the lock, and it banged against the locker door. She pulled out her cell and glanced at the screen. Ruby

Garrison, Trey's mom. Damn. If she let it go to voice mail, next thing she knew Trey would be hunting her down.

Keeping an eye on the door to the hall, she connected with the call. As she spoke, she sandwiched the phone between her shoulder and ear in order to free her fingers to work their magic.

"Hi, Ruby."

"Lydia, do you have a pound of butter you could bring with you? I'm afraid with these extra Moravian Christmas cookies we'll be running short."

Lydia tugged the shackle and kept pressure on it as she slowly dialed the bottom wheel, waiting for the slight give in feeling when she hit the right number. "Butter? I don't know, but I can stop at the Giant Eagle on my way over."

"Well, it's best if it's at room temperature to soften."

"You can't just put it in the microwave?" Aha, one down, two to go. She began twisting the second dial.

"That will melt it, not soften it." Ruby's tone made it clear Lydia had no idea what she was doing when it came to baking. Which was the honest truth.

The second number fell into place. Keeping tension on the shackle, Lydia turned the third wheel.

"I'll ask Patrice to get the butter; never mind," Ruby continued. "When are you coming over? The girls are all here."

"Oh, I'm not quite sure." The lock popped open in Lydia's hand. "Go ahead and start without me, I might be a while." She pocketed the lock and opened the locker door.

"But the whole idea is for us to bake together, share our recipes." Recipes? Lydia was supposed to bring a recipe? How about, buy the refrigerated dough that's presliced, eat some as you throw the rest in the oven, and bake?

"Sorry, guess I misunderstood. I'll get there as soon as I can." Jim's locker was a mess—street clothes shoved in along with a gym bag stinking with sweaty socks, a bunch of loose-leaf copies of journal articles, a couple of pocket-sized textbooks, and, sitting in the place of honor on the top shelf, a white shoebox emblazoned with a bright yellow evidence sticker.

She cocked a fist and pulled it back in triumph. *Gotcha.*

"Gotta go now. Bye, Ruby."

"WOW, THAT WAS EASY," AMANDA SAID AS SHE entered Narolie's room. "The OB-GYN intern is on his way to do the ultrasound. He actually sounded excited."

"Of course he's excited," Gina told her. "It's the weekend. If there's a surgery he'll get to scrub in. During the week when all the other residents are around, he'd be crowded out."

Amanda frowned at that. She wanted to cure Narolie, she really did, but . . . "I can't get them to do a surgery behind Lucas's back, can I?"

Gina laughed. "Oh, you are *so* not ready for marriage." She stood and grabbed her coat, motioning to Tank, who was whispering sweet nothings in Narolie's ear. "Don't worry, you'll think of something."

Tank squeezed Narolie's hand and turned to Amanda. "I have her iPod set on shuffle and it's right here," he motioned to the music player tucked under Narolie's pillow—the iPod that had been Tank's yesterday. "And you have my cell number, so you'll call, right?"

"Don't worry, Tank, I'll call. When I hear anything."

Gina shook her head and handed Tank his knapsack. Kid acted like they were leaving for Katmandu. "We'll bring you back some lunch," she promised Amanda as she dragged Tank from the room.

"She'll be okay, won't she?" he asked Gina as they waited for the elevator.

Gina marveled at the change in Tank. Yesterday he was the epitome of spoiled brat, and today he was Mother Teresa. "They'll take good care of her. But she's very sick, Tank. You need to understand."

They entered the elevator and she hit the button for the eighth floor. They'd take the skyway to the research tower and go down a flight to Ken's lab on the seventh floor.

Tank sagged against the wall of the elevator as they began to move. "I know. It's just—I never had someone to take care of before."

LYDIA LEFT THE MEN'S LOCKER ROOM, NOT CAR-ing if anyone saw her this time. In fact, she didn't mind if they did. It would only bolster her story. She hurried down the hall to the security office and found Glen Bakker there chomping a sandwich as he scanned the security monitors.

"Glen, I think you should call the cops," Lydia said in a breathless voice.

He looked up. "Lydia, what happened? Are you okay?"

"I went to my locker—well, I thought it was my locker, my mind was on this patient, and I wasn't looking, and when I opened the locker, I found, I saw—" She paused for a breath. Glen stood, abandoning his sandwich. "Well, maybe you'd better see for yourself. I think I found Karen's rape kit."

They rushed back to the men's locker room. "You came in here?" Glen asked as she pushed open the door.

"Yeah, I wasn't thinking. No one was here."

The locker room was still empty. Glen strode inside. "Which locker was it?"

"Seventeen. Same as mine in the women's locker room." The lie came effortlessly, and she knew he'd never check. Why should he?

Glen approached Jim's locker as if it contained a bomb. Lydia had left the door open, so it was easy to see the rape kit, the broken evidence seal, Nora's signature scrawled across it.

"I'll be damned. Whose locker is this?"

"I don't know." Lydia hated lying—she tried not to,

mainly because she knew how good she was at it. Maria had taught her well.

Glen grabbed his radio. "Carson? Get someone to cover the monitor room, and you come down to the men's locker room on the first floor. I need you to protect some evidence until the cops get here."

Lydia pretended to find the clipboard with the locker assignments. "Number seventeen belongs to Jim Lazarov," she told Glen. "I know him. He's an emergency medicine intern. He doesn't like Nora. Seth Cochran said Jim attacked her earlier today."

Glen raised an eyebrow. "Seth said that?" He grabbed the clipboard from her and scrutinized it. "Let's go find this Lazarov."

GINA LED TANK TO KEN'S LAB. HEAD-BANGING rock was blaring from behind the closed door. She tried the handle, but it was locked.

"Ken!" she shouted as she pounded on the door. No answer. Idiot probably couldn't hear them over the music. She grabbed her phone to call him just as he came around the corner, juggling a tray of sandwiches and drinks.

"The cafeteria is closing early because of the gala," he told them. "Why didn't you wait inside?"

Gina rattled the door handle. "Locked."

"Oh. Right, it's the weekend, I forgot." He handed the tray to Tank and swiped his name tag with its magnetic bar across the lock. It clicked open. "Sorry about that." He held the door for Tank to enter, followed by Gina.

"Hey, way cool," Tank said, stopping inside the door to marvel at the lab. Ken's lab resembled a frat house on a Sunday morning more than a scientific endeavor, but because he brought in tons of grant money, no one complained.

"Wait a sec," Ken told Gina. "Hand me your ID."

"Why?" Gina asked, but she unclipped her hospital ID badge and handed it to him. He swiped it against the door lock, punched in a code, and swiped it again.

"Now you can come any time, day or night." He grinned at her.

"What makes you think I want to?" She stepped aside as Tank knocked over a haphazard pyramid of aluminum cans stacked in the recycling bin.

Ken said nothing, but merely kicked the cans out of their way.

"What's in here?" Tank asked, opening a glass-fronted door and revealing shelves of tissue culture. "Is this where you grow the clones?"

"Those are stem cell cultures. Very precious, and," he said as an alarm sounded from his phone, "very sensitive." He closed the door before opening his phone and shutting off the alarm. "I have it set up so any temperature fluctuation sends an alarm directly to me."

"You guys have more security over here than we do in the patient tower," Gina said.

"When they built this place, it was part of the funding deal," Ken explained as he ushered them into the back room where his office was. It wasn't any neater than the lab, but at least they wouldn't be sharing their lunch with stem cells or white mice. "Lots of expensive equipment and research in this building."

"Yeah, all we have to worry about are patients." Gina removed a stack of journals from a chair and took a seat, letting Tank fend for himself.

Ken pulled out a stool for Tank and sat on the desk beside him. "How's Narolie?"

It took Tank a moment to realize Ken was speaking to him, not Gina. "I found an article about music helping people in comas, so I programmed a whole playlist into my iPod for her," Tank said. "It hasn't worked yet, though."

"Tell Ken about Amanda's theory," Gina said, grabbing one of the sandwiches from the tray and dividing it, putting half back to take to Amanda later.

"Oh yeah. Amanda thinks there's a tera"—he stumbled on the word—"teratoma causing Narolie's coma. She wants them to cut it out."

"She has to prove it's there first."

Tank shrugged as he bit into his own sandwich. Ken picked at a salad, frowning at the wilted greens. "A teratoma causing encephalitis? Interesting. From an immunologic point of view, very interesting." He abandoned his salad and jumped up, grabbing a marker from the collection scattered across his desk. "Tank, did they explain what a teratoma is?"

"No. Just said it was making her sick and it needed to come out."

"Gina, grab that Robbins. There should be some good pictures in there."

As Gina rummaged through the overflowing bookshelf, Ken drew a picture on the whiteboard mounted beside the window behind the desk. His picture looked like a lopsided cluster of grapes, and then he added lines to indicate hair, some ragged teeth, and a primitive-looking brain.

"So," Ken began. "Teratomas are tumors that grow only in women. Know why?"

"Because girls have babies?" Tank ventured.

"Exactly. And the teratoma rises from one of those egg cells multiplying when it shouldn't. And because these eggs are totipotential—"

"Toti-what?"

"They're like stem cells," Gina explained. "Cells that have the potential to form any organ or tissue."

"Exactly." Ken aimed a smile at her. "So when the teratoma cells multiply, they form the same organs that are in you and me."

"You mean like a baby? It's a person inside her?"

"No. Not at all like a baby. It's random. The teratoma

cells have all the ingredients of a human being—kidney, teeth, hair, thyroid, brain, whatever—but it's a random mishmash. Like"—he snapped the lid on his salad and shook it—"a tissue salad. All mixed up."

"And that's what's making Narolie sick?"

"No. Usually teratomas are benign, don't cause problems." Ken stepped back, pondering his sketch of the teratoma. "Tank, do you know how vaccines work?"

"They don't. They're a government conspiracy designed to—" Tank sounded like he was a machine reading a prepared message.

"His grandfather is a chiropractor," Gina put in, waving Tank to a stop.

"Okay," Ken said, without missing a beat, "then do you know how your body fights infections?"

"Yeah, we have an immune system. It makes antibodies and other stuff that wipe out germs."

"What if your immune system thought part of your own body was a germ?"

Tank considered that. "I guess it would try to wipe it out. Fight it."

"Exactly." Ken threw his marker down in triumph.

Tank frowned. Gina gave him time to work it out as she perused the grotesque photos of teratomas from the textbook.

"You mean Narolie's own body is making her sick? It's fighting her brain?"

"It's a plausible theory, although a bit simplistic. But if there's brain tissue in the teratoma and she developed antibodies against that tissue, then those antibodies could—"

"Attack her own brain." Tank finished Ken's thought. He bounced off the stool and grabbed Gina's arm. "Gina. They have to take it out. Now."

THIRTY-ONE

Saturday, 12:49 P.M.

NORA HAD TAKEN OVER THE PICU'S BREAK ROOM, spreading out the contents of Narolie's UR chart, pretending to read every scrap of information included. In reality, she was bored sick, but if Carlene or one of her spies asked, they'd be assured that Nora was doing her due diligence.

Thankfully, Mickey Cohen arrived before she ran out of forms to pretend to read. "Nora, when I said take a few days off, I was hoping you'd be spending them with Seth," the lawyer said as she breezed into the break room and helped herself to a cup of decaf. "You guys did make up, didn't you?"

Nora smiled, remembering exactly how they had made up last night. "We're talking," she said, hedging her bets.

"If I had a guy like Seth around, I'd be doing more than just talking." Mickey slid into the seat beside her. "So, I had quite an exciting day of it yesterday, with the police storming my office and all."

"Sorry. I meant to call to check on you. Did they find anything with those flowers?"

"No. And I never saw who delivered them—the guy just

rang the bell and left them there. I forgot all about them until the police showed up asking for them."

"So there was no card or anything?"

"Nope. Just the flowers." Mickey tilted her head, scrutinizing Nora. "You're staying with Seth, right?"

"I don't know. Probably not. I don't want anyone else caught in the crossfire. And besides, things are still—" She stopped, uncertain of how to describe her and Seth's relationship.

Mickey took her hand and squeezed it tight. "Don't worry, everything will be fine. Once the cops catch this guy, you and Seth can take your time, get things right."

Nora forced a smile. "I hope so."

After a moment of awkward silence, Mickey pulled Narolie's chart closer. "So this is our girl, eh?"

"I know it's not exactly your kind of case, but—"

"Are you kidding? If I can't find constitutional grounds against yanking a comatose minor from her hospital bed and dumping her back into a third-world cesspool where she'll be raped, tortured, and likely killed, then I need to find a new job."

Nora blew out a sigh of relief. She'd been worried that Mickey might turn down Narolie's case like Gina's father had. "So you can help her?"

"Give me a few hours of peace and quiet and I think so, yes." Mickey curled herself over the chart, reading and grabbing a legal pad and pen from her bag to take notes. "Oh, and coffee, lots of coffee."

LYDIA WAS VERY SURPRISED WHEN GLEN BAKKER elected to question Jim Lazarov in his office before the police arrived. Then Oliver Tillman showed up, and she realized they were simply trying to get a jump start on any CYA maneuvers necessary to limit the medical center's liability if Jim was the killer.

Idiots. Jim was no killer.

She knew the police would never be able to get a warrant to search Lazarov's locker based on her suspicions. And that finding the rape kit there changed nothing, legally. No lock on the locker (supposedly) meant anyone could have left it there, trying to frame Lazarov. And the seal on the kit was broken, thanks to Jim's opening it to extract the pictures he sold to Pete Sandusky.

All she wanted was to stop him from leaking anything further to Pete. Now that Jim was exposed, his career on the line, he'd think twice before giving the reporter any more insider information.

Sitting outside Glen's office, the door strategically cracked so she could listen to everything, she wrote out her "statement." Tillman looked ready to stroke out, his face was so red, as he shouted at Lazarov, threatening to remove him from the residency program. Lazarov blustered his way through, insisting that he was being framed, denying any knowledge of the rape kit.

By the end, even Lydia began to believe him, wondering if maybe she'd stumbled onto the evidence someone else had planted and was getting ready to "uncover." Lazarov was a jerk, but he was no fool. Why would he leave the evidence there in his locker, practically in plain sight?

She finished her statement and handed it to the guard sitting at the front desk. On her way back to the PICU, her phone rang again. Trey this time.

"Where are you?" he said. "My mom's getting worried."

"I'm still at the hospital. I'm not sure when I'll get over to your mom's."

"So you're not going home anytime soon?"

"I doubt it. Why?"

"No reason. Just do me a favor and let my mom know when you leave the hospital. You know how she is."

Lydia hung up. Suddenly, spending the day watching

over Nora in the PICU seemed more appealing than baking cookies.

AMANDA PAUSED OUTSIDE DR. KOENIG'S OFFICE door before knocking. She was surprised how nervous she was about approaching the cantankerous OB-GYN attending. Gathering up her courage, she knocked and opened the door.

"I'm not sure if you remember me, Dr. Koenig. I'm Amanda Mason; I did my rotation with you last year."

Dr. Koenig didn't even look up. He was reading a journal, highlighter in one hand, pen in the other, scribbling notes. "Of course I remember. Your car had trouble making it to work on time with the snow, so you started sleeping in the hospital even when you weren't on call. And unlike many of the other students, you seemed to appreciate my Socratic teaching methods, rising to the challenge a number of times. In fact, I gave you a B-plus, my highest grade for the year, if I recall."

Amanda was stunned. She didn't think anyone but Gina knew about her sleeping in the hospital during her rotation. And she'd been upset with the B-plus after all the work she'd done, but had had no idea that Dr. Koenig never gave anything higher.

"My resident, Dr. Richards—"

"Roberts," Amanda corrected without thinking, though Dr. Koenig didn't seem to notice.

"—was telling me about your case. Tell me, what made you think of teratoma-induced encephalitis?"

"It was a case report I read while on your service. You had asked me to investigate the number of ways a benign teratoma wasn't benign. Unfortunately that case report is the only one I've found so far."

"So far." He leaned back, finally looking at her, smiled, pulled open a file drawer, and tossed a handful of files onto his desk. "I've the largest unpublished collection of cases in the country. Maybe even the world."

Amanda leafed through the files. All women in comas, all with incidental finding of teratomas, all revived "miraculously" when their teratomas were removed. The cases came from all over the country.

"My colleagues know it's an interest of mine," Dr. Koenig said. "I've been waiting for years to find a patient of my own. And then I can finally publish definitively." He stood and opened the door. "Hurry along, Ms. Mason. Our patient is waiting for us to make medical history."

NORA WAS MORE THAN READY TO LEAVE THE PICU by the time Lydia arrived and told her about finding the rape kit in Jim's locker. They began walking down the hall, hoping to grab lunch from the cafeteria.

"So you think Jim was telling the truth?"

Lydia hesitated. "Hate to say it, but yes."

Nora paused as they approached the corridor leading to the surgical call rooms.

Lydia stopped as well, her gaze zeroing in on the trauma resident's room. "You should probably go talk to him."

"I can't—it will just end up hurting both of us. Again."

"Ever stop to think that maybe he's worth a little pain? You've sure put him through hell these past few months, refusing to listen to anything he had to say."

Nora's shoulders hunched. She knew shutting Seth out of her life, especially right now, was the best thing. The safest thing. But suddenly, *safe* no longer seemed as important as it used to. The feelings she and Seth had shared last night—those seemed much more vital.

"You're right."

Seth's room was the first door. She knocked but didn't hear him answer. Then came the sound of a thud, like someone had knocked something over. "Seth? It's me."

She knocked on the door again, then opened it without waiting for a response.

The smell slapped at Nora. She jerked back, her pulse stampeding. The copper scent of blood fought with the sickly sweet smell of fresh spray paint.

Blood mixed with neon colors in a kaleidoscope of carnage. There was blood on the floor, blood on the walls, blood on the bed, blood still bubbling from Seth's slit throat.

THIRTY-TWO

Saturday, 1:47 P.M.

SETH WAS SPRAWLED ON THE BED FACE UP, SPRAYS of blood coloring his pale blue scrubs. His eyes were open, staring unseeing, one hand pressed to his throat, the other flung out to the side as if reaching for a lifeline.

Above his head, in fresh angry orange spray paint splattered with blood over the top of it was written *MINE*.

Nora stood frozen at the doorway, hand to her mouth, trying to blink away the scene as a nightmare. But it was real. Her breath coming in gasps, she took a step forward.

From the blood spatter, it was clear there'd been a struggle. Blood covered Seth's hands, but Nora couldn't see any other wounds as she leaped to help Lydia, who was applying pressure to the gaping neck wound.

"Airway's clear." Inside her mind she was screaming Seth's name, ordering him to *live*, goddamn it! But panic wasn't going to save him, so she pushed all that aside.

"Pulse faint, but it's there." Lydia grabbed a pillowcase to use as a pressure dressing. "Left carotid and jugular lacerated, maybe the trachea as well. The right side looks okay. He needs to get to the OR. Now."

Nora ran from the room. The OR was only two doors down, although it was almost deserted on a weekend afternoon with no scheduled surgeries. She barged through the doors marked AUTHORIZED PERSONNEL ONLY, STERILE ATTIRE REQUIRED and raced into the nearest room that had its lights on. An orthopedic surgeon looked up in annoyance, reluctantly turning his saw off so that she could be heard.

"Someone slit Seth Cochran's throat," she told the scrub nurse as she grabbed supplies from the anesthesia cart. "Down the hall in the call rooms. Get a stretcher. You"—she pulled on an anesthesiologist's arm, the man looking as bewildered as if he'd just woken from a coma himself—"come with me. Now."

Minutes later, she and Lydia, the anesthesiologist, and two surgical nurses were wheeling Seth's body into a vacant OR. It was a scene eerily reminiscent of Karen's failed resuscitation, made worse as a scrub nurse pushed Nora from the room, gesturing at her bloody street clothes.

"We've got him," she said, closing the door.

Her fists pressed against the window, Nora watched as Lydia barked commands, racing to save Seth.

"Hang on," she whispered, her voice choked.

Diana DeFalco, the trauma attending, ran past her, banging through the door as she snatched up clean gloves, not stopping to scrub. Soon more people crowded around the small window in the door, jostling Nora and asking what happened.

She didn't answer, despite several pointed remarks that somehow this was her fault. Lydia glanced up and gave her a quick, reassuring nod before going back to work.

"Hey, Nora! Nora Halloran!" A man's voice called her name. The crowd parted long enough for her to see a civilian at the entrance to the OR. Pete Sandusky. Complete with camera. The flash flared several times in a row, Nora reflexively raising her bloodstained hands to shield her eyes.

"Someone get him out of here." Glen Bakker latched on to Pete's shoulder and propelled him into the arms of one of his security guards. "Anyone see anything?" he asked the assorted surgical staff.

They all shook their heads, looked away. Glen frowned at Nora, appraising her as if she were a victim rather than a witness.

She wasn't a victim. Breathing deep, she blinked away the veils of gray that shadowed her vision, fighting against panic. Glen took her hand and led her away. "Nora, what happened?"

"WHAT HAVE WE GOT?" DIANA DEFALCO ASKED as she rushed into the OR.

Lydia looked up from where she was holding pressure on the left side of Seth's neck. "Zones one and two penetrating neck injury," she told the trauma surgeon. "Carotid nicked at the very least and the external jugular as well. No crepitus and airway seems intact. He was bradycardic, but heart rate is up after a fluid bolus."

"Don't overload him," Diana said. "I don't want that blood pressure above seventy. Get the cell saver hooked up to suction and tell the blood bank to wake up. I need six units O neg up here now."

"He's moving air well," the anesthesiologist said.

"Get him on a pulse ox and monitor; let's make sure we're getting oxygen to his brain," Lydia ordered.

"I've got it, Dr. Fiore," Diana said in a low tone. Not confrontational, just reminding Lydia that there was a reason why there was only ever one command doc in a trauma.

Lydia wanted to snap at the surgeon but swallowed back her adrenaline-fueled retort. "He was unconscious when we found him, barely had a pulse, so who knows how long he was down."

A security guard poked his head in the door, holding a mask to his face. "We're evacuating the operating rooms. You all will need to get out."

"Hell you are," Diana told him, not yelling like most surgeons would, simply stating a fact. "Post a security guard outside all the ORs where there are still cases going and search the others."

"But, lady, Mr. Tillman said—"

Diana looked up from where she was exploring the wound between Lydia's fingers. "I'm no lady, I'm a surgeon. You tell Mr. Tillman if he doesn't post those guards and guarantee my staff's safety I'll make sure JCAHO hears of it and that this hospital loses its trauma certification."

The guard frowned, shook his head, and left. A few minutes later, another took his place but simply stood outside the door, watching.

"Okay," Diana said. "Let's get him prepped. Include his legs in case I need a saphenous graft from there. Lydia, once I scrub, I'm going to come back and relieve you. And we'll get this under control."

AFTER RETURNING TANK TO THE PICU AND Narolie's side, Gina realized that her dress for the gala was at Jerry's. No better time, she thought, walking out to her car. He'd be gone for the day, working; she could clean out all her stuff, make it easier on both of them.

She barely noticed the snow falling; already there was a few inches on the ground, making the roads slick as she drove over to Jerry's East Liberty apartment. She knocked and got no answer, then turned her key in the lock and opened the door. Before she could finish the movement, the door flew from her hand and she was yanked inside.

In a whirlwind of motion, her legs were swept from under her. Her breath whooshed out as she slammed against the floor. Then a man's weight pinned her down, one hand over her mouth.

Stunned, she couldn't even think to fight back. The blitz attack left her helpless, unable to think of more than her next breath.

"Make a sound and you're dead," a man's voice rasped into her ear.

Fear jolted through her. It was the rapist, the man who had killed Karen. He was going to rape her, cut her like he had Karen. A primal instinct for survival propelled her to squirm beneath his weight, fighting to break free.

It was useless. The man knew what he was doing, enough to hold her still with little effort. She relented, stopped struggling, a small whimper escaping her throat.

She was going to die.

The man ground her face into the doormat. "Hold still."

She complied. The sound of tape tearing filled her ears. He wrenched her arms behind her and with cruel efficiency bound her wrists. Then he rolled her over, one hand still over her mouth.

They were face to face. He straddled her, his weight crushing her. The other hand now held a knife.

She couldn't look away from the knife. It filled her vision.

"If you scream, I'll kill you." His tone was casual, as if this were an everyday affair for him. "Do you understand?"

She nodded.

"Where's your boyfriend?" he asked, removing his hand but keeping it near enough to squelch any shouts for help.

"I don't know." Her mouth was dry enough that it took her twice the effort to produce the choked whisper.

The knife hadn't wavered, but her vision finally expanded enough for her to get a good look at him. He wasn't wearing a mask or any attempt at disguise. Her insides chilled as she realized this was a death sentence. If he was going to let her live, he'd hide his face.

He was a white guy, late twenties, with sharp, hawkish features and a cruel twist to his mouth. Or maybe it was the knife and the empty gaze that made her think that. His eyes were dark brown, as was his hair, but his gaze was a barren void. No hope there.

Especially when she realized that she'd seen him before. Just last night.

The delivery man with the flowers. He must have been following her, knew about her and Jerry, just as he'd followed Karen and Nora. Panic ricocheted through her, and she bucked and strained, fighting for her life.

But it was no use. She was helpless.

AMANDA FOLLOWED DR. KOENIG DOWN THE STAIRS from the OB-GYN floor. As they emerged from the stairwell, she was surprised to see several security guards gathered at the elevator banks at the far end of the hallway.

Dr. Koenig didn't notice; he was too busy telling Amanda about his other "largest, unpublished case series" that he'd collected over thirty years in practice. He seemed inordinately proud of collecting case reports from all over the world even though he had never published any of them. His excitement at finding his own—Narolie had already become "his" case—unique medical oddity had added a touch of mania to his speech and gait. He almost knocked over Zachary Miller's parents as he barreled into the PICU.

"Let's get the ball rolling," Dr. Koenig said as he plowed past the ward clerk to grab Narolie's chart. "You go tell Stone, I'll get consent and arrange for an OR."

Like a fast-moving squall, he was gone. Amanda shook her head, feeling dizzy. The atmosphere in the PICU had changed. She looked around. Families were present at every patient's bedside, all looking fearful. In no rush to face Lucas and let him know that Dr. Koenig was commandeering Narolie's case, she joined the Millers at Zachary's bed. His vitals were good—better than this morning, even.

"Everything okay?" she asked.

"They said someone got hurt," Mrs. Miller said, clutching the bed railing. Her husband had his arm around her.

"Stabbed," Mr. Miller put in. "The guards told us all to leave the family room and stay here with our children while they searched the floor."

"Stabbed? Who? Where?" Amanda glanced at the nurses' station. The clerk and two nurses there were all on the phone. The rest of the staff was nervously hovering near the entrance, as if ready to guard their patients against any attack.

"They didn't say. No one here seems to know anything more." Anger undercut Mr. Miller's tone—the most emotion she'd seen from him all week. He'd seemed stunned by Zachary's accident, unable to do more than react to the situation.

"Well, the good thing is that Zachary is doing better. In fact, from the looks of his last blood gas, it looks like his lungs are starting to work again." She stopped herself before giving them too much hope—after all, she was just the medical student, not the attending. But it was remarkable how much better the boy was this afternoon. Maybe the tincture of time was more powerful than all their technology.

"Thanks, Amanda," Mrs. Miller said. "We appreciate what you and everyone here have done for him."

"We're all pulling for him. It's still going to be a long haul," Amanda cautioned. They needed to see how Zachary's brain had fared from the lack of oxygen. That was always the "big if" in any of these cases. Nevertheless, it was nice to finally have something to be cheerful about.

She glanced back at the nurses' station again. Terry was talking with the charge nurse. Maybe she'd know more about what was going on down the hall. Had another nurse been attacked?

"I'd better get back to work," she told the Millers. She left them and approached the nurses' station. "What's all the commotion about?"

"Someone tried to kill Seth Cochran," the charge nurse said.

"Attacked him in his call room," Terry added.

Amanda felt her stomach clutch. "Is he okay? Where's Nora?"

"Nora's the one who found him." Terry shook her head. "He's still alive. In surgery now. Hard to say if he's going to make it."

"I heard he had his throat cut," the nurse said. "Security searched the floor but didn't find anyone. Until the police tell us otherwise, we're keeping all the patients and families right here where we can keep an eye on them."

"But Dr. Koenig wants to take Narolie to surgery."

The nurse frowned. "I'll call security to escort her when you're ready. Glen said he was calling in all his off-duty men to help the police."

"So Koenig agreed with you," Terry said. "Does Lucas know yet?"

"No, I was just getting ready to call him." Amanda hesitated. Lucas had already accused her of putting Narolie at risk by following her hunch. What would he say now that she'd gone behind his back and convinced Dr. Koenig?

NORA RELUCTANTLY ALLOWED GLEN TO LEAD HER away from the OR where Seth was.

"Did you see anyone?" he asked as he escorted her down the hall.

"No. Lydia and I were just stopping—if we hadn't—" Words failed her as she realized how easily they could have gotten there too late.

"From the scene, looks like the attacker was scared off when you knocked on the door. We found a blood trail leading out the other side of the shared bathroom. You were damn lucky you didn't walk in on them." He lay a hand on her shoulder, softening the blow of his words. "Did Seth say anything? Any clue who did this?"

"No, he was unconscious. We barely got a pulse." Her face felt numb; she put her palms to her cheeks, and they were ice cold.

"Nora, stop." Glen gently pulled her wrists down and held them. "You're getting blood all over yourself. How about if you go get cleaned up? Then you can tell us everything." He steered her to the women's locker area.

He stepped inside with her, but simply looked around to make sure no one was concealed—she hadn't even thought of that, that's how out of it she was.

"I'll wait right out here; no one will disturb you."

He shut the door behind him. Nora stood in the empty locker room, uncertain what to do. Her vision was blurry; blinking only made it worse. She couldn't smell anything but blood.

Her stomach rebelled, and she barely made it to the toilet before throwing up. Dry heaves overcame her; all she could think of was Seth's face, his gorgeous face, covered in blood, his eyes staring blankly. . . . She knelt there on the cool tile floor for a moment. Then she pushed herself up, ignoring the smeared red handprints she left behind.

For once she had no urge to clean—no amount of cleaning could restore her equanimity, calm the terror raging through her.

THIRTY-THREE

Saturday, 2:42 P.M.

THE MAN REACHED BEHIND HIM TO THROW THE deadbolt on the door, then stood and lifted Gina to her feet. Shoving his free hand into her pockets, he took her cell phone, keys, and wallet.

He backed her against the wall, and with the gleeful smile of a schoolboy pulling the wings off a fly, he laid the knife against her lips. His smile widened, and he licked his lips.

Then he used the knife to cut another strip of duct tape, smoothing it over her mouth with one hand. It was hard getting enough air as she breathed through her nose, the tape scratching her nostrils with every movement.

"Don't worry," he said, grabbing her arm and pulling her to him. "That's only temporary. We'll be having a long talk later. I want to hear all about your boyfriend. And you'll be telling me everything I want to know." His hand drifted from her throat down to her breast, lingering there.

Then he threw her onto the couch, leaving her there as he ransacked the apartment. Gina fought the urge to vomit, knowing she could choke to death with the duct tape in place.

It wasn't easy; her insides felt as if they were hurtling out of control. She'd never been this scared before—not even during the drive-by shooting.

Why me? Gina wondered. But as the man threw Jerry's notebooks and laptop computer onto the couch beside her, the answer became clear. Of course. Who better for the rapist to target next than the investigating detective's girlfriend? The one who just happened to work in a hospital, like his other victims?

She couldn't help the anger and resentment that flared through her. If it weren't for Jerry—

"You're the one getting the award tonight?" he asked, standing over her, the knife dangling casually from his hand. "Some kind of hero or something."

Gina nodded.

"Yeah, I did my research. I like to know everything about my"—he paused, his gaze zeroing in on her breasts—"subjects. Your boyfriend must think he's hot stuff, dating a good-looking woman like you."

Gina recoiled against the cushions, trying to hide. But there was nowhere for her to go. A stray thought raced through her mind: her parents would say they'd been right all along. After she was gone, they'd blame this on her staying in the ER, working at Angels. Consorting with the "wrong" people.

"So, here's how we're going to play this," he continued, oblivious to the fact that her heart was about to explode from her chest. He knelt beside her so that their faces were close enough for a kiss. She wanted to close her eyes, pretend she was dreaming, but she forced them to stay open. "I can't manage both of you here together—this place isn't private enough, anyway. Walls are too flimsy. You're going to come with me and we'll find a nice spot, quiet and private. Then we'll call Boyle, invite him to join us for the fun."

His lips parted in a freakish grin. A thin scar edged down from the side of his ear toward the corner of his mouth—the injury had been expertly repaired, but there must have been permanent damage to his facial nerve. No wonder he looked so cruel; only half of his face could show any expression.

As the clinician in her analyzed the anatomy of his injury, her fear subsided. Enough that she realized that her best and only chance to stay alive was to follow his orders. Jerry had a gun—she just needed to find a way to warn him, buy him time.

"Come on." The man hauled her to her feet. "We'll take my car." He draped his coat around her shoulders, concealing her bound hands, then ripped the tape from her mouth. "Remember, one wrong move and you're dead."

LYDIA SCRUBBED HER HANDS CLEAN AT THE SINK outside Seth's OR, watching as Diana deftly got the bleeding under control and assessed the damage. As much as she was tempted to stay longer and continue observing, she needed to get cleaned up and wanted to check on Nora.

She started down the hall to the locker rooms when she saw Jerry Boyle arguing with Glen Bakker. The security chief was standing guard outside the women's locker room, arms akimbo, eyes narrowed, obviously not recognizing that Boyle's authority trumped his own.

Boyle mirrored Glen's posture, using his elbows to push his jacket aside, revealing both badge and gun. "I need to talk with her. Now."

"I told you, she'll be out as soon as she's ready," Glen said to Boyle. "She's pretty broken up," he told Lydia. "I called Tommy Z."

Lydia appreciated Glen's thoughtfulness, even if she didn't share his confidence in Tommy Z's abilities. "I was there, Boyle. I can tell you everything you need."

Boyle nodded and pulled her down the hall to where they were out of earshot of Glen but he could keep an eye out for Nora. Lydia quickly went over how they'd found Seth.

"How long do you think he was down before you found him?"

"He still had a pulse, so no more than three to four minutes, given the rate of blood loss. Another minute or so and we would have been too late."

"And you didn't see anyone?"

"No."

"Well, that rules out Lazarov. He was down in security under guard at the time."

"I don't think he killed Karen, either. But he might have stolen the rape kit—he has it in for Nora. Although he was pretty convincing when he said he was being framed. In any case, I'm pretty sure he's the one who's been talking to Pete Sandusky."

"Doubt he will be in the future. Janet really put the fear of God into him."

"Good."

Boyle eyed the still-closed door to the locker room. "She's been in there a while. Maybe you could—"

"I'll go check on her." Lydia nodded to Glen, who stood aside to let her enter the locker room. Inside, the shower was running, steam billowing out into the main changing area. "Nora?"

No answer. Lydia grabbed a towel from the linen cart and pulled the shower door open. Nora was crouched at the bottom, curled up, hugging her knees, ignoring the scalding hot water pummeling her naked body.

"Nora, come on out." She turned the water off, knelt down, and wrapped the towel around Nora. Nora's teeth were chattering even though her skin felt flushed. She didn't look at Lydia, but instead gazed at an invisible point in the distance.

"Seth?"

"He's fine. Diana DeFalco is repairing the damage. I think he'll be okay."

"Really?" Her gaze finally found Lydia's face. "If anything happens to him—"

"He's okay, honest. Come on, let's get you a clean pair of scrubs."

Nora allowed Lydia to pull her from the shower stall. With mechanical motions she dressed in scrubs and towel-dried her hair. Then she pulled her shoes back on.

"Jerry's outside," Lydia told her. "He needs to hear—"

Nora nodded. "I know."

Lydia led her to the door. When she opened it, she found three worried men waiting for them; Tommy Z had joined Glen Bakker and Jerry Boyle.

"Nora," Tommy said. "Are you okay?"

Nora bolted past the others and fell into Tommy's arms. "No. No, I'm not."

DR. KOENIG GRACIOUSLY INVITED AMANDA TO observe Narolie's surgery. She called Tank to update him, as promised. To her surprise, it sounded like a party was going on in the background when he answered.

"I'm downstairs at the gala," he told her. "My mother told me I had to come, to make up for scaring her this morning. Said I'm the man of the family now. But it's not too bad, even if the music's lame. Ken's here; he's going to sneak me up to see Narolie when she's out of surgery."

"I'll call you as soon as she's back in her room." She hung up on Tank and blew her breath out. Time to face the music.

She dialed Lucas and was surprised to hear his phone ring not far away from where she sat at the nurses' station. She glanced around and saw that she was too late. Dr. Koenig had ambushed Lucas at the PICU entrance. He was gesticulating wildly, pointing at her, at Narolie, beaming with delight as if Amanda were responsible for curing cancer. Except, of course, he'd be taking any credit.

Lucas didn't look as excited by the prospect. He nodded and passed Dr. Koenig as the OB-GYN exited the PICU, then headed straight for Amanda, a scowl narrowing his face.

"Lucas, I'm sorry," she said before he could say a word. He came to a halt two feet away from her, standing over her, staring down, saying nothing. Amanda felt compelled to fill the silence. "After the ultrasound revealed the teratoma, I asked Dr. Koenig for advice and things kind of—"

"Is she stable enough for surgery?" he asked, the words clipped.

"Stable? Yes, anesthesia cleared her. We've gotten her blood pressure under control, and she hasn't had any more episodes of bradycardia."

"Okay, then. The OR is waiting for you and your patient." He turned and stalked out of the unit without another word. Or, more hurtful, without a glance back.

Stay calm, stay calm, stay calm. The two words were Gina's hold on reality as the man forced her to drive through the snow and dark. It seemed like she'd never seen the sun at all the last few days. She was going to die, never see the sun again. . . .

Fear surged through her, and she pressed on the accelerator. The man had exchanged his knife for a gun and now poked the pistol into her side, hard.

"Slow down. We don't want to attract any cops." He chuckled. "Not yet."

She did as she was told, and he relaxed the gun, giving her room to breathe.

"Your boyfriend must really love you," he said in a conversational tone. "You know he didn't just rent a tux for tonight's shindig, he actually bought one? On sale, but still. Not many guys would do that. So I'm thinking, with this thing tonight, he'll be expecting you there, right? Be a good place to ambush him. And hospitals have all sorts of private nooks and crannies."

Oh God. He was going to kill her and Jerry right there at Angels. In front of everyone she worked with—in front of her parents . . . again, she forced her thoughts back on track, following the man's directions to drive around the hospital.

"There, pull in there." He pointed to the loading dock at the rear of the research tower. About as dark and private as you could get.

The perfect place for an ambush.

THIRTY-FOUR

Saturday, 5:17 P.M.

"NOW, CALL HIM," THE MAN TOLD GINA, switching her phone to speaker and hitting the speed dial for Jerry. "Get him down here."

Gina stared at the deserted loading dock. The fire exit for the research tower was beside it. On the other side of the building, several hundred people would be gathered to celebrate her heroism. Was she really going to draw Jerry into his death?

"Hey, Gina." Jerry's voice came through the speaker, jolting her back to the present. "I'm kind of busy."

The man jammed the pistol between her ribs so hard that she gasped in pain. "Jerry, I need your help. It's important."

"Are you here at Angels? What do you need? What's wrong?"

The man nodded in encouragement. A light went on in the research tower before her and she thought of Ken Rosen. And his crazy lab, a study in chaos theory.

Gina gathered her strength and threw everything she had into her next rush of words. "I need to see you. It's life or death. Meet me at Ken Rosen's lab."

The slap rocked her head back against the headrest. The man was immediately on top of her, one hand circling her neck to choke her as he raised the gun.

"Gina, what's wrong?" Jerry's voice came from the speaker, sounding tinny and far away. Another voice came in the background—Lydia's? What was Lydia doing with Jerry? Gina wondered through the haze of pain as she struggled to breathe. "Okay. I'm on my way."

The line went dead.

"You bitch," the man said, squeezing her neck so hard that Gina came up out of her seat. "Who's this Ken Rosen? What the hell have you done?"

He released her and she fell back into the seat. She massaged her throat until she found the strength to speak. "Look up. No one's in the tower because of the gala. You said you wanted privacy—it's better than out here where the security patrols could drive by and see something."

A car chose that very minute to drive by. The man forced her head down as the lights sliced through the car windows. He held her there until the coast was clear. Then he dashed from the car and around to her side before she could do anything.

He opened her door and yanked her out.

"If this is a trick," he whispered into her ear, jamming the gun into her spine, "you're going to live a long, long time. And you're going to be screaming in pain every living moment."

"SHE'S NOT GOING TO BE ABLE TO TELL YOU MUCH tonight." Nora heard Lydia's voice as though from a distance. "Can't you take her statement in the morning?"

"I can take her over to my office," Tommy said. "She needs a chance to defuse, to start processing some of these emotions. Otherwise she might not make a good witness for anyone."

"Well . . ." Jerry didn't sound too sure. "I don't want her alone—or without protection. Let me get one of my guys up here."

"I'll stay with her," Glen volunteered. "I'm off duty anyway, and you guys have things covered here."

Jerry's phone rang before he could answer. From the conversation, Nora gathered it was Gina. She and Tommy had already begun heading down the hall to the elevator banks. Lydia and Glen followed.

There was a guard at the elevators, but he nodded to Glen and pressed the call button. Nora turned to Lydia as the doors opened. "Stay here, please. Let me know as soon as Seth is out of the OR."

"You sure you're going to be all right?" Lydia asked, gripping Nora's arm.

Nora had no answer to that.

AMANDA HADN'T REALIZED HOW FAST THE TERA-toma removal would be. It was done laparoscopically, through a small incision. Dr. Koenig might have been a pompous windbag as a teacher, but in the OR he moved with a precise economy of grace that was inspiring to watch.

"There's our baby," he said as the forceps emerged with a glistening blob of tissue, no more than two centimeters in diameter.

"Hard to believe something so small could cause so much trouble," she'd said.

He chuckled. "If you were right. Only time will tell." He deposited the teratoma into the specimen jar the nurse held. "Now we wait."

LYDIA HATED WAITING. SETH WAS STILL IN THE OR, Narolie was in the OR, Gina was probably getting her medal by now, Nora was talking with Tommy—hopefully the counselor was more effective than he had been with Lydia—and she was stuck waiting.

Her phone rang. Oh shit. Trey's mother again.

"Ruby, I'm so sorry—"

"It's me," came Trey's voice. "I wanted to let you know I was at my folks'. In case you were wondering." It might as well have been Ruby. Seemed like Trey had mastered her technique of long-distance guilt induction.

"You have no idea the kind of day I've had."

His sigh resonated through the phone lines. "Look, my family put a lot of effort into planning things for today. They wanted you to feel welcome. I really think you owe them an apology."

An apology? Over a bunch of cookies? She was smart enough not to voice her thoughts out loud. "Okay, I'll apologize. Put Ruby on."

"Not over the phone, Lydia." Irritation crackled through his voice. "Call me when you're headed home."

She started to tell him about Seth, about everything going on—but why? He'd rush over, crowd her, and then it would be two of them waiting with nothing to do. "I will."

She hung up and pocketed her phone. Her clothes were stiff as Seth's blood dried. Thankfully her dark jeans and top masked most of it from casual gaze, but it was uncomfortable. She had running clothes down in her locker, so she headed for the ER.

The sounds of the gala echoed down the narrow corridor that connected the cafeteria to the ER—clinking glasses, laughter, music. Social butterfly Gina would fit right in. No wonder the public had singled her out as the Hero of Angels.

The public as led by Pete Sandusky. The thought of him made her detour to the security office. No way was she going to allow him to shape Nora's life through his slanted reporting and photos.

Tommy, Nora, and Glen rode up to the eighth-floor skyway and crossed it in silence. Tommy's office was on the fourth floor of the research tower, so there was another short elevator ride down. Nora felt dizzy—not from going up and down, but somehow time seemed to be going fast, then slow, whirling her around with it.

They stepped out of the elevator and Glen used his PDA to turn on the hall lights. The three of them walked down to Tommy's office.

"You okay?" Glen asked as she moved to follow Tommy inside.

Nora shrugged in reply. Didn't have energy for more.

She couldn't shake the image of Seth, lying in his own blood. It was frozen in her vision, while everything else swooshed past her.

"Tell me about what happened," Tommy said once the two of them were safely ensconced in his office, Glen standing guard outside. Nora sat on a leatherette love seat and Tommy sat beside her in a similarly upholstered chair. The lights were dim but she could see herself reflected in the window, as if she were looking underwater, into a dark lake with no bottom.

"Seth told you about my attack. Two years ago." Her voice was steady, although her hands weren't. She grabbed hold of her knees as she leaned forward, trying to find her balance.

"Yes. He wanted to know how to help you."

"It was the same man."

Tommy remained silent, letting her go at her own pace. Haltingly, out of sequence, she told him everything—as much as or more than she'd told Jerry yesterday. She wasn't sure—it all seemed such a blur—until finally she collapsed back against the couch, empty. Numb.

"I think that's enough for tonight," Tommy said, his voice strained.

Nora merely nodded, resting her head on the back of the couch, feeling exposed and vulnerable. She drew her knees to her chest and hugged them tight. Silent tears coursed down her face and she made no attempt to stop them or dry them. Tommy stood, sliding the box of tissues close to her hand.

"Take all the time you want." He rested his palm on her shoulder and gave it a squeeze. "I'll be right outside."

The door clicked shut behind him. She sat there, nestled in the corner of the couch. All she wanted was Seth. His arms around her, his grin to cheer her, just to have him near. How could she have been stupid enough to ever send him away?

"You didn't tell him everything, Nora," a man's voice whispered through the air.

Nora jerked her head up. The room was empty. Had she imagined it?

"Tell him how much you liked it," the disembodied, distorted whisper returned. She leaped off the couch. The door was closed tight; the room was empty except for her. She clapped her hands over her ears. God, was she going crazy?

"Tell him how I made you come over and over again, harder, faster than any other man could. Tell him how much you wanted it, how you begged me for more, how I made you scream with pleasure. Tell him, Nora."

"No. No!" Her voice shattered against the walls in a brittle scream. She was surprised when Tommy didn't rush in, but realized that the counseling office was soundproof. Which meant it couldn't be Tommy or someone from the outside. It was all in her head.

Had the session with Tommy opened the floodgates to her unconscious? Revealing the final secret, the one thing she'd kept locked away, refusing to acknowledge even in her own mind . . . that at some point during those two days when the rapist touched her in every way possible, not only had she surrendered to him, but her body had responded to his touch . . . It wasn't something she could help; it was just physiology, hormones, reflexes. Nothing in her control. But the memory filled her with a burning shame. As if she'd been a partner in her own violation.

She spun around in a tight circle, wrapping her arms around her chest, swinging her head back and forth searching for escape like a caged animal.

"You want me, Nora. Just like I want you," the voice returned, insistent.

"No." The syllable emerged shredded and torn.

"We'll be together again, I promise." The voice sounded so certain, confident.

"No. Go away. It's not true!"

Laughter filled the room, washing over her like a tsunami. She crumpled to the floor, trying to block it out. Trying to block out the fear and revulsion and primal urge to scream. Curling up in a ball, making herself smaller and smaller, she fought to disappear entirely. She wasn't really here, it wasn't really happening, oh Lord, not again, she couldn't survive, not again. . . .

An eternity later, she opened her eyes to silence. That one act of defiance gave her the determination she needed to uncurl herself and sit up. She had survived. She would survive.

She remembered the feeling of invincibility that had surged through her last night when she and Seth had made love. Shaking her fist at an unseen assailant, she climbed to her feet, wobbling, but standing on her own.

"I'm not afraid." She tried the lie on for size. It was an awkward fit, made her feel small and childish, like when she was little, checking under her bed for monsters even as panic made her heart race out of control.

She was very afraid—as afraid that her mind had betrayed her as she was that the killer would return for her.

Either way, she wasn't going to do any good standing here in Tommy's office. She needed to get out of here, find a place to hide, to regroup and figure out what was happening to her.

Before it was too late.

THIRTY-FIVE

Saturday, 5:28 P.M.

GINA'S ID GAINED THEM EASY ACCESS THROUGH the fire door. The man hustled her through the dimly lit hallway to the elevator and up to Ken's lab on the seventh floor. He glanced up and down the corridor, nodding at the rows of darkened offices. "You were right. Deserted. Open it."

She held her breath, had to try her ID in the card reader twice, but then was rewarded with a click as the door unlocked. The man shoved her inside, turning the lights on, before he entered with his gun aimed at her.

Except for the two white mice, the lab was empty.

"Wait here," he said as he looked around.

Gina backed up against the incubator holding the tissue cultures. It had taken only a few moments with the door opened wide for the alarm to alert Ken this morning—that was too fast. Last thing she needed was Ken rushing in, getting shot. What she needed was for him to get concerned, bring more people—preferably armed people. Or, best-case scenario, run into Jerry and alert his suspicions.

She settled for pulling the door ajar—just enough to break the magnetic seal holding it shut. The man opened Ken's office door, turned the lights on, and seemed satisfied with the layout. He motioned for Gina to join him in the office. He used the duct tape to bind her hands behind her back and positioned her behind the desk, against the window, where she was visible through the office door.

"Stand there, don't move, don't say a word," he ordered. He tore out the office phone and backed out of the room, his gun never wavering.

He clicked off the lab's lights, leaving Gina in the center of the only light in the two rooms. Then he wedged the lab's door open to the hallway and stood to the side of the door, hidden in shadows. "Now all we need to do is wait."

"NORA, WHAT'S WRONG?" TOMMY WAS ON THE phone in the reception area when she burst through the door and started out of the offices at a headlong pace. "Wait! Where are you going?"

She stopped, gasping for breath. "I heard him, Tommy— inside your office, inside my head, I don't know. But I need to get out of here."

"You heard the killer? In my office?" He stretched the phone cord as long as it would reach and came around the desk, peering through his open office door. "Nora, there's no one there."

"I know." She edged toward the exit, trying to hide the shaking that devoured her body.

"Wait. There has to be a rational explanation. Let me play back the session tape. We'll see what really happened."

She shook her head, the man's voice still crowding her thoughts. The last thing she needed or wanted was confirmation that she had lost her mind. Tommy's attention darted back to the phone.

The phone! He could have set the inner office to speaker-phone, opened a line before he left. The knowledge hit her like a fist striking a mirror, shattering everything she had believed. Her vision fragmented, everything too bright, too focused, as she searched for an escape.

Tommy turned, his mouth opening in surprise, and she realized her expression must have given her away. Before he could say another word, she bolted through the door. And ran for her life.

LYDIA WAS HAPPY TO SEE BOTH PETE SANDUSKY and Jim Lazarov squirming under the watchful eye of the guard left manning the security office.

Well, maybe not exactly squirming. "Lydia!" Pete called out when he saw her. "Care to comment on finding Seth's body?"

"He's not dead," she told him. Pete looked disappointed. She turned to the guard. "Did he have a cell phone with him? I think he swiped mine, and there are some sensitive pictures on there."

The guard pulled out a plastic bin of personal effects, and Pete lunged forward. "She's lying—that phone is mine!"

"Hey!" The guard's hand went to his gun and Pete froze, hands up in surrender. "Back up and sit down."

"You can't do this, Lydia," Pete shouted.

Too late. While the guard had his back turned, she clicked through the photos of Nora, deleting them.

"Sorry," she told the guard, sugaring her performance with a sweet smile. "My mistake."

"Lydia." Jim Lazarov spoke up for the first time, his voice edging on despair. "Tell them I didn't do anything, tell them to let me go, will ya?"

"Sorry, Jim. That's up to the police, and they're a bit tied up right now."

"Hate to put a damper on your party," Sandusky said, "but the kid's right. He's not the guy who talked to me. Much too young. And much too short."

"So you did see him."

"Only in silhouette, he stuck to the shadows. But he was at least six feet, maybe six-one. Walked like a soldier, talked like one, too. Always giving orders." Sandusky smirked. "I might remember more if you give me the inside story on what's really going on around here."

Should've known Sandusky would try to take her for a ride. He probably didn't even see the killer. Lydia started to tell him to go to hell when she noticed the monitors at the desk start to wink out, one by one. "What's going on?"

The guard turned from his prisoners to focus on the monitor display. "That's funny. But those are all from the research tower, and that place is empty tonight. The boss must be shutting them down so we can focus on the folks at the gala."

"How can you be sure it's Glen shutting them off?"

"Easy. 'Cause it wasn't me and the only way to access the research tower security system is from here or from Glen's handheld."

"Really?" Lydia felt her body tense as if preparing to strike out. She touched a hand to the small of her back, reassuring herself that her gun was still there. Suddenly Pete's ramblings made sense. "What else can he control remotely?"

"It's a pretty cool setup—he can control the cameras, even access the room-to-room intercom system, the panic alarms, the lights, door locks. All from the palm of his hand."

Lydia stared at the dark screens. "Can you override his command? Bring up the hallway outside Tommy Z's office?"

"Sure, why?" The guard started punching in a command, then frowned. "That's funny. They're not responding."

Lydia's stomach plunged. "Call the police, get some men over to Tommy Z's office. Now!"

"I'll have to call Glen," the guard hedged.

"You do that and you might get someone killed." She

couldn't trust him not to tip off Glen. But she could trust Jerry Boyle. As Lydia raced from the security office, she dialed Boyle's cell. Damn it, pick up, pick up.

No answer.

THIRTY-SIX

Saturday, 5:34 P.M.

THE WAIT WAS AGONIZING, BUT GINA KNEW IT was only a few minutes. Jerry appeared at the doorway and spotted her immediately. He stepped inside. "Gina, whatever you need, I hope it can—"

The man lowered his gun and placed it at Jerry's temple. Jerry's muttered curse easily carried through the empty lab to Gina.

"You were right, angel-lady, this place will do nicely," the man said as he took Jerry's gun from his belt and then used Jerry's own handcuffs to restrain his wrists in front of him. He closed the lab door and shoved Jerry into the office. "Deserted for the weekend, building to ourselves, no worries about noise or unexpected visitors, especially with the shindig going on downstairs. Perfect."

"What do you want?" Jerry demanded, placing himself between Gina and the gun.

Without warning, the man smacked him across the face with the gun, then brought the butt down so hard on Jerry's clavicle that Gina heard the snap from where she cowered behind Ken's desk. Jerry staggered but didn't fall. He braced himself against the desk, as if he expected more to come.

Of course he did—he was powerless as long as Gina was there for the man to threaten.

Jerry wiped his bloody nose and mouth against his jacket collar. "Look, I can't help you until you tell me what you want," he said in a reasonable tone. "Let Gina go. I'll give you everything you want."

Using her name, smart, it would make her seem like more of a person to the man with the gun. Only the guy wasn't buying it. Instead he smirked at Jerry. "I know all about you, Detective Gerald Boyle. Tough guy. Smart guy. Worked SWAT until you blew out your shoulder."

He brought the gun down hard on Jerry's broken collarbone. This time Jerry dropped to his knees, his jaws clenching as he bit back his pain.

"Stop it!" Gina cried out.

The man aimed the gun at her face. She backed into the corner behind Ken's desk, the farthest away she could get.

"Sure thing. See, I know a tough guy like him will never talk. Will never break." The man stepped around the desk. Too late, Gina realized she was boxed in, nowhere to go. "Not by hurting him. But hurting his woman—well, that's more than most men can take."

"No, don't!" Jerry somehow pushed himself up, putting all his weight on his one good hand, dragging the other along, the handcuffs stretched to their limit. "Tell me what you want."

The man stopped in front of Gina, the muzzle of his pistol below her chin, leveraging her face up until she was choking for air. He ground the muzzle into the soft flesh there, pain searing through her vision.

"Where is she?" he snapped, glancing over his shoulder to keep an eye on Jerry, who was collapsed half across the desk.

"Where is who?"

The man forced Gina's head back even farther. She could no longer even see Jerry. All she could see were red spots dancing before her and the overhead ceiling tiles. The pain was unbearable. Tears escaped her. She tried to stand on tiptoe to relieve it, but the man merely followed her movement.

"Marie Ferraro's little girl. I know you found her."

Gina could barely comprehend their words through the pain. Marie? Who was Marie? Someone who worked at Angels?

"A friend of mine in L.A. was the lead detective on Marie's homicide," Jerry hastened to explain, his words spraying Ken's desk with blood as he spoke. "He's retiring, and the case always bugged him, so he asked me to take a look. A fresh pair of eyes, in case he missed something. That's all. I don't know anything about the kid. Check with L.A. County social services; they took her."

The man released Gina. She dropped to her feet, her bound hands catching her weight on the ledge of the filing cabinet behind her. Before she could drag in a breath, the man sucker-punched her, doubling her over. She fell to her knees, retching, fighting to both vomit and breathe at the same time and unable to do either as pain shot through her belly.

"Don't lie to me again or I'll hurt her for real. I know you're the one who contacted Epson. By the way, his retirement was cut short—I paid him a little visit before I flew out here. How's it feel to know your buddy is the one who gave you up, put you in this spot? Right before I killed him. And that other cop—who knew there'd be two Jerry Boyles in one department?"

The words sliced through the terror and pain clouding Gina's brain. This man wasn't the rapist. This man was the one who had tortured and killed Officer Boyle. And now he was after Jerry.

And she'd led him right to him.

"Epson's dead?"

"Stop stalling. Tell me where she is!"

"I've never met anyone named Marie Ferraro. Or her daughter."

The man reared back, ready to aim a brutal kick at Gina, but Jerry shouted, "I'm telling you the truth!"

Instead of kicking Gina, the man whirled on Jerry and brought his gun down across his head in a slicing motion. Jerry's face bounced against the desk. As Jerry lay there, gasping, the man pulled a copy of a photo from his back pocket, holding it in front of Jerry.

Gina finally caught her breath. She wanted to crawl under the desk, but she couldn't leave Jerry.

It was killing her, watching him suffer. Then she caught a glimpse of the faces in the photo as the gunman dangled it before Jerry.

Her gasp broke the silence. The gunman cocked his head in surprise. He pivoted to her, lowering the photo to her eye level. "You know her, don't you?"

"She doesn't." Jerry was practically on top of the desk, trying to crawl across it to get the man's attention away from Gina. "She doesn't know anything."

But she did. The photo showed a girl, maybe ten or twelve, and a dark-haired woman. The same woman she'd seen in the photos of Lydia Fiore and her mother.

NORA'S FOOTSTEPS RANG AGAINST THE CONCRETE floor of the fire stairs. She stopped, listened. Someone was definitely coming down the stairs behind her.

She grabbed for her cell phone. It was gone—she must have left it behind in the locker room when she changed. She sprinted to the door on the next level.

There was a panic button beside the door.

The bright red button taunted her—should she push it?

She hit it just as she heard the footsteps start again. Now they sounded like they were coming from below her—but that was impossible; Tommy was above her.

"Hello, this is Angels of Mercy Medical Center," a tinny, disembodied voice blasted from a speaker above her head. Nora tried to squash it with her hands, but it was too late. Anyone in the stairwell would know her location now. "Can I help you?"

"I'm in the research tower and there's a man following me," she said, her face lifted up to the grill. "Please send someone."

"Ma'am, I need your location."

"Fourth floor, stairwell."

The footsteps grew louder, faster.

"Hurry, please."

"Don't worry, Nora." A chuckle exited the speaker and clawed its way down her spine. She jerked her hand away. "I'm on my way."

Nora's head buzzed—was she imagining the voice? Or had Tommy somehow taken control of the intercom system? She ran through the door, pressing herself against the wall, hoping that whoever was in the stairwell would keep going past her. The corridor was dark except for a few scattered overhead lights.

As she cowered, gasping for breath, covering her mouth so that she wouldn't be heard, she remembered this feeling. Paralyzed with fear. Exactly like two years ago.

The door from the stairwell slammed open, bouncing against the cement block walls. "Nora, thank God I caught you," Tommy Z said, leaning forward, huffing with each breath. "I figured out how you heard the voice in my office."

"No!" Nora backed away from him, holding her arm straight out, as if that could stop him. "Leave me alone. Please." She hated the way the last word came out, as if she were begging.

He straightened, his forehead creased in concern, and

stepped toward her. "What are you talking about? God, it's all my fault. He told me he was getting help, I never dreamed—" He broke off, his gaze scanning the darkness that surrounded them. "Come with me; we need to go back to my office. We'll be safe there."

She was shaking her head. "No, no, I won't go. I called the police. They're on their way."

He held his hands out, palms up, spread wide as if to show that he was no threat. "Good. I want the police to see this as well. It's okay, Nora. I'm not going to hurt you. I'm here to help you."

"I trusted you. How *could* you?"

"I didn't do anything. Look, we can't stay here. It's too dangerous."

Nora heard the sound she'd been waiting for: footsteps sounded from the stairwell.

"Stay where you are," she told Tommy.

He stopped about five feet from her in the middle of the corridor, hands still wide. Keeping her back to the wall, she warily circled past him so now she was closer to the exit than he was.

"I'm not going anywhere," he said in a calming voice. "I know you're scared; it's all right."

A sharp laugh ripped through her. "You're telling *me* it's all right to be scared? After what you did?"

The sound of footsteps in the stairwell slowed, as if uncertain where to go. "Here! I'm here!" she called out.

"Nora. Honestly, I'm not the guy. I didn't do—"

The door to the stairwell opened. Glen Bakker came through it. Nora felt her lungs collapse in relief as she blew out her breath. Glen took her arm and pulled her behind him, putting his body between her and Tommy.

"Nora," Tommy called out. "Don't—"

A shot blasted through the air, followed by another one. Tommy took a step forward, arms reaching out. Two more shots. He staggered and fell to the ground.

Tommy's lifeless body lay facedown on the carpet, blood slowly puddling from beneath him. Nora sank to her knees, unable to keep on her feet another moment.

It was over, it was over.

"You're safe now," Glen said, holstering his gun.

Nora didn't respond; she was too stunned.

"Nora, everything's going to be okay now. You're with me."

She stared at him, uncomprehending.

"Hurry, we don't have much time."

He grabbed her arm and hauled her to her feet. Then he pivoted her so her back was pressed against his body, one hand curling around her neck. In it, he held a knife. Long, one edge serrated, the other wickedly sharp.

Pressed against her throat.

A sense of déjà vu overtook her. Everything grew hazy as she struggled to breathe. It was just like two years ago, except that this time she wasn't blinded. She could see everything with terrifying clarity. Including Tommy's body.

Glen reached behind them to push open the door to the stairs. He dragged her over the threshold. Awareness slapped back at her, shattering the numbing deep freeze that had gripped her. She spun, clawing at his face but falling short. He laughed and pushed her face forward into the stairwell.

"Don't do anything you'll regret," he whispered. "This is your last chance, Nora."

GINA SAID NOTHING, BUT SHE KNEW HER EXPRESSION betrayed her when the gunman laughed.

"Here I was, all worried about how to break Mr. SWAT-man over here," he said. "He won't talk, no way, nohow." He leaned down, grabbing Gina's bruised jaw in his hand and yanking her gaze to him. "But you will, angel-lady. You will for sure."

"I said, leave her alone!" Jerry was trying to shout, but his words emerged in a thick muffled cough as he spat blood and mucus out with them.

"Guess I don't need you after all," the gunman said, whirling and firing at Jerry.

The shot thundered through the room. Gina shrieked and pushed herself under the desk, colliding with a solid fabric-covered item wedged into the corner. Her bulletproof vest. Ken said he'd kept it.

As she squirmed to put the Kevlar between herself and the gunman, she heard Jerry's body hit the ground with a thump. Blood oozed beneath the desk. She leveraged herself into the corner, pinning the Kevlar against her body, and ducked her head down.

"I'll be with you in a minute, angel-lady. Just let me finish this off." The gunman stepped around to the front of the desk.

Gina's eye level was low enough that she saw Jerry bending his knee up to his chest. At first she thought he was trying to protect himself or aiming a kick—useless against a gun, but she supposed he was desperate.

Then she remembered his backup gun. In his ankle holster. Before she could finish the thought, two shots blasted through the air. Then two more. One of them punched a hole through the side of the desk; the other thudded into the vest that shielded her head and chest.

She lay there dazed, her ears ringing, head throbbing, disoriented. Thudding footsteps, the bang of a door kicked open, broke through her senses.

"What the hell?" came Ken Rosen's voice.

About damn time.

THIRTY-SEVEN

Saturday, 5:44 P.M.

AMANDA RETURNED TO THE PICU WITH NAROLIE. Her vitals were stable, but she still hadn't woken from her coma. She explained to Narolie's aunt that the surgery had been successful, but it would take time. She hoped she was reassuring, but secretly she was disappointed that the results hadn't been more immediate.

As she emerged from Narolie's room, there was a flurry of activity around Zachary's bed. Alarms blared as nurses converged on the little boy.

"What's going on?" she asked. Blood pooled from Zachary's groin area—near the femoral vessels where the large catheters for the bypass machine were inserted.

"Catheter eroded through his artery," the ECMO tech said. "We need to crash him off!"

"Hold pressure," Amanda ordered, surprised at how calm she was. "Get as much volume from the machine into him as possible. Someone call the blood bank, tell them we're going to need four units of packed cells and a unit of FFP." She glanced at the monitor. Zachary's heart rate was bouncing all over the place—no wonder, with a quarter of his blood volume trapped in the ECMO machine and the rest trying hard to escape through his femoral artery.

"Page Terry and surgery. How's he doing on the vent?" she asked the respiratory tech.

"Not bad, holding his own." Thank God for small favors. Zachary's damaged lungs were suddenly being forced to do all the work the ECMO machine had been doing for the past three days. Were they up to the task?

GLEN TWISTED NORA'S ARM BEHIND HER BACK, steering them onto the landing. "What do I want?" he finally said, his tone almost wistful. "The same thing I've wanted ever since I first laid eyes on you. Do you remember when that was?"

"New Year's Eve, two years ago."

He shook his head. "Wrong, Nora. I met you when you first started working here as a nursing assistant. Do you remember? I do. You were so young and gorgeous, bright and eager to learn everything. But you never even knew who I was."

"I—I never knew. Why didn't you say something back then?"

"I did. Tried to ask you out a dozen times at least. Even tried to pick you up at a party the EMS guys had. You never noticed me at all. Then my Guard unit got called up and I knew it was my last chance. But you were with that guy. Matt Zersky. I knew instantly the kind of guy he was, able to worm his way into any girl's pants. No way I was going to let that happen to you. Not to my girl. I decided it was time we got to know each other better."

"So you kidnapped me?" Good God, he was serious. He truly thought kidnap, rape, and attempted murder were acceptable forms of courtship.

"You don't understand. When I left you there, in that

building, after I got so mad—I thought I'd killed you. I thought I'd lost you forever." Glen was silent for a long minute, not moving. "I kinda went a little crazy—"

"You killed Matt!"

"He doesn't matter. *We* matter, Nora. You can't imagine my joy when you showed up at work the next week—like an angel, come back to life! Thinking of you kept me alive the whole time I was in Iraq. I knew we'd be together forever when I got back. Only"—his voice dropped—"only, I didn't deserve you, not after the way I'd fouled things up. I had to earn your love—prove myself as a real man.

"I realized I had to be patient, had to get myself fixed up if I wanted to win you back. Even if it meant watching you hang out with losers like Seth Cochran. But now it's time. Time for us. To be together, forever."

Nora tried to follow his twisted logic. Her mouth went dry as panic flooded her. Could he have gone after Seth again, while she was in Tommy's office, finished what he started?

"Is Seth all right?"

"Why are you asking about him?" Glen snapped, turning to throw her a glare. "We're talking about us. I'm telling you, Nora. This is our last chance. We're going to finish this together. One way or another."

GINA'S RELIEF AT KEN'S ARRIVAL DIDN'T STOP HER panic. Not with Jerry's blood seeping under the desk. She tried to call for help, but only a hoarse scratch emerged.

Her arm ached from where the bullet had impacted the vest, her hands were numb from being trapped behind her, her weight pressed against them, and her throat felt bruised. Other than that, she was physically fine. Mentally, she was . . . exhausted.

Kicking the desk chair aside, she rolled free from her hiding place. Ken reached down to pull her free, taking the vest as well.

"Check on Jerry. Is he okay?" Her voice emerged at top volume, shrill with fear, startling even herself.

Ken said nothing, spinning her around so he could slice through the duct tape restraining her wrists with a pair of scissors from the desk. As he worked, she faced the window, with only her and Ken's reflections visible; Jerry was below the desk. Jerry, oh God, she couldn't even think, imagine—

"Is he"—her voice faltered—"is he . . . dead?"

The tape finally parted. Ken left her to check on Jerry as she clawed her hands free and shook the feeling back into them.

"I've got a radial pulse," Ken said.

Gina rushed to Jerry's side. Acid scratched at her throat as her stomach convulsed with horror.

Blood stained Jerry's shirt, not a lot, but enough. His face was swollen, disfigured from the beating. And there was a small hole just behind his left eye. Going into his skull.

The gunman lay beside Jerry—dead. Very completely, obviously dead with a bullet hole through his right eye. Ken had kicked both guns to the corner of the room.

"I need police and security." Ken's words were clipped as he spoke into his cell phone with one hand while holding pressure on Jerry's wound with his other. "I've got a dead man and a police officer with a gunshot wound who's going to need to get to the OR."

Gina quickly assessed Jerry. *ABC's*, she told herself, trying hard not to think about how much his wounds resembled the other Officer Boyle's. The one who had died.

"No," she interrupted Ken, her brain finally kicking into gear. "Not the OR—it will take two elevator rides to get there from here. We can take him right down to the first floor and straight into OR 13 in the ER. It's faster."

He nodded his agreement. "We need a trauma team waiting for us in the ER. We're on our way."

Ken ducked into the other room, then reappeared, pushing a wheeled stainless steel table before him. Together, they lifted Jerry onto the table. Gina steered from the top of the table, holding Jerry's airway open, as Ken raced alongside, keeping pressure on the belly wound. There was nothing else they could do until they got to the ER.

"Sorry about your tissue cultures," she told Ken during the prolonged agony of the ride down in the elevator. Prattling seemed the only way to keep her sanity. "It was the only thing I could think of—"

"No worries," he said, squeezing her hand. "Glad you thought to call me."

"Good thing you're so obsessed with your research."

Jerry gurgled as blood filled his throat, but there was nothing Gina could do about it without equipment. Tears threatened to overwhelm her, but she shook them off.

"He'll be okay, Gina," Ken said in a low tone, serious and solemn enough to pierce her panic. "Everything will be okay."

WITH THE CROWD OF THE GALA BETWEEN HER and the research tower, the fastest way to reach it and Nora was to go through the basement tunnels. Lydia ran down the nearest set of stairs and sprinted through the deserted corridors, her footsteps accompanied by the din of overhead steam pipes and the clanking of distant machinery.

As she ran, she tried Jerry again, then Nora. No answer from anyone. Finally, she called 911. The operator didn't seem to understand the situation. "Ma'am, I'm showing officers already headed to that location."

"No. They're here, but not at the right place. Tell them to go to the research tower, fourth floor."

"Ma'am, there's already a response called in. Officers en route. There were shots fired, so you need to stay away from the scene, let the officers do their job."

"Shots fired? Was anyone hurt?"

"I'm sorry, ma'am, I don't have that information. Please

stand by, I'll direct an officer to your location. Do not enter the scene of operations." The operator seemed peeved by Lydia's persistence.

Stand by? Hell with that.

She stopped short at the door leading to the research tower's stairwell. Every rule of emergency response told her to make sure the scene was safe—just as the irritatingly calm 911 operator had reminded her.

But it could be Nora, lying there bleeding. Needing her help.

She edged the door open, listening. Voices came from above her. She entered the stairwell, keeping to the shadows, straining to hear who was speaking.

"Glen, let me go. They'll find Tommy's body, know it's you."

Nora. She was still alive. And it sounded like Lydia's instincts about Glen had been right. She drew her gun, debating her next move. Sneak back into the tunnels and tell the police where to find Glen and Nora?

Glen's next words made up her mind for her. "I don't care anymore, Nora. After we were together my life hasn't been the same. I can't even look at a woman; you did something to me—the docs said it was nerve damage, said it was from the drugs I mixed, trying to satisfy you. I've been to all the experts, searching for a cure, but all I found were women who reminded me of you, except they weren't you, they were laughing, making fun of me because I was no longer a real man."

"That's why you raped them, why you killed Karen? Because they knew you were impotent and laughed at you?"

Good girl, Nora. Keep him talking, stall for time. Lydia hugged the shadows, listening carefully.

"Karen, she was the worst of all. Back in October, I had another procedure done here—my last chance, they said. I thought that afterward, we could finally be together. But three days ago I went for my follow-up test. As I woke up, there was Karen laughing at me, making jokes. Saying I'd never be a man again. But I showed her; I watched for my chance, and I took her, made her pay." His voice trailed away as if he were unable to remember everything that had happened.

"It all happened so fast. After—I realized that was no way to win you back. I didn't need any doctors or miracle cures. All I needed was you. With you, I could be a man again. A real man. You'd never laugh at me. You'd know how to love me.

"Somehow I can only be right, feel right when we're together. But you couldn't see that, no matter how hard I tried to show you that there's nothing left for you here. Why, Nora? Why can't you see that this is our last chance?"

Nora gave out a small gasp of pain.

"I figure we either make it out of here alive," Glen continued, "or we die together."

THIRTY-EIGHT

Saturday, 5:54 P.M.

THE ELEVATOR DOORS OPENED ON A CROWD OF elegantly dressed men and women, many holding champagne glasses and sparkling with jewels. Gina had totally forgotten about the gala or that they'd have to go through the atrium to reach OR 13.

"Clear a path!" Ken ordered in a voice that would have made a military drill sergeant proud.

The confused throng obeyed, Gina yanking the makeshift stretcher along, shoving people aside.

"I said move it!" she yelled at two gawking matrons draped in fur.

They sped around the corner into the back of the ER, and then through the doors to OR 13, where the trauma team was gathered.

"Thirty-seven-year-old male"—Gina called out the information, fighting to keep her tone neutral despite the churning anxiety tearing through her insides—"shot at close range through his left upper quadrant and left temporal parietal region. Unresponsive, but pupils equal and reactive. Heart rate one-thirty, good carotid, weak radial pulse. Abdomen distended, airway needs suctioning, respirations around twenty-four."

Ken helped them move Jerry onto the OR bed, then stood to one side. The nurses and the second-year ER resident swarmed over Jerry's body, cutting his clothes off and getting him on the monitor. Gina realized she was the senior physician. The command doc.

The one holding Jerry's life in her hands.

"Someone page surgery, tell them to get their asses down here! Suction his airway and set up for intubation," Gina ordered. "Give me two large-bore IVs, run them open for now with LR until the blood arrives. I want six units of O neg on the rapid infuser, trauma labs, X ray of his chest, abdomen, and head, NG and Foley." The team leaped into action, following her commands.

She pushed the second-year resident out of the way and swiftly intubated Jerry. No way she was trusting a critical procedure to a second-year. She listened intently. It was hard to do with her own pulse thundering through her ears. "Down on the left. We need a chest tube. Where the hell's X ray and surgery?"

The second-year started a central line while she set up for the chest tube. "His pressure's spiking," a nurse called. "Heart rate dropping."

Damn. "Ken, take over here. You remember how to do a chest tube, don't you?" She checked Jerry's pupils. "Blown on the right. Push the mannitol, elevate his head, and someone get me the drill."

She felt like she needed to be everywhere at once. *Breathe,* she reminded herself, *just breathe*. As she prepped Jerry's skull, carefully palpating the landmarks to decide on where to place the burr hole, she talked Ken though the chest tube.

"Wouldn't the bullet hole decompress the brain for him?" the second-year asked as he sutured the central line in place.

"Not if he has a contrecoup injury on the opposite side of his brain." Which meant there was a good chance the brain between the entrance wound and the new area of bleeding was jelly. Gina shoved that thought aside and steadied her hands against the drill. Slowly she cranked the handle until she broke through the skull. "I think I'm in." She pulled the drill out and a gush of blood followed.

"BP dropping back to normal, heart rate improving."

"Nice work," Diana DeFalco said as she flounced into the room. "Sorry to be late. The operator insisted that you all were bringing him up to us. And once I figured out that you were down here, security wouldn't let me through. Something about a shooting in the research tower."

"Yeah, Jerry," Gina said, lowering her hands out of sight before Diana saw their trembling.

Diana's gaze flicked over Jerry, assessing him without asking questions. "That purse-string suture needs to be tighter, Dr. Rosen," she told Ken, who quickly retied the suture. "Hand me the ultrasound."

As Diana scanned Jerry's belly, she continued, "They said there was a second shooting. Lydia Fiore called it in? Anyway, looks like my work's going to be easy. A splenic bleed, nothing too serious. I want to run his bowel, of course."

She handed the ultrasound back to the nurse. "Okay, let's get him packaged. The neurosurgeons cry like babies when they don't have all their toys at hand, and this is obviously going to be their show. Page them stat to OR Four, tell them we'll meet them there. And someone wake up radiology—I want them ready for immediate angiogram and CT when we need it."

The nurses were trying to wheel Jerry away when Gina realized she was still gripping his hand. Ken gently pulled her away. "He's in good hands, Gina."

Diana held the door open as they pushed Jerry out. "You did a good job, Gina. If it weren't for you, he'd never be making it to the OR alive."

Nice words—but meaningless if Jerry died. Gina stared after him, feeling like she was drowning, gasping for air . . . and finding none.

GLEN FORCED NORA TO MARCH DOWN THE STEPS. He was so agitated that the knife shook in his hand and he'd nicked her neck. Blood trickled down her collar.

Two years ago, surrendering had saved her life.

But this time she was in control—despite the knife at her neck. She could choose: fight or flight.

Nora scoured the space before her, searching for an opportunity. She chose her moment as they approached the next landing.

She stepped down onto the flat ground. Glen, midstep above and behind her, lowered the knife as she pivoted to make the turn. But instead of continuing down the next flight of steps, she spun and pushed him as hard as she could, hoping to topple him over the railing.

He was too big for her to push over, but he did stumble, losing his footing, slipping down the final two steps, sprawling backward as he caught himself, the knife dropping beside him.

Nora seized her split second of freedom. She could run—but he'd make up for the lost ground before she got far. So she chose to fight.

He was drawing his gun. She went for that hand, smashing it against the corner of the step. Glen rolled over on top of her, pinning her beneath his weight. She twisted his wrist back, using all her strength to force it past its breaking point.

He grabbed her hair, yanking her head back so hard and fast that her vision darkened to red.

"Let her go!" Lydia's voice came from below.

Nora kept a firm hold on Glen's gun hand and fought to draw in a full breath as her neck was twisted. Glen's grip on her hair only tightened.

"Let her go now, Glen!" Lydia arrived on the landing. Nora saw she had her gun out, was holding it on Glen.

Glen slowly uncurled his fingers, releasing Nora's hair. Nora didn't relax her grip on his gun hand, using both her hands to keep it jammed against the step.

"Drop the gun," Lydia ordered, her voice as steady and calm as it was during a trauma.

Glen relaxed his grip on the gun. Nora hefted it in her hand, feeling its weight, the surprising warmth of its grip. Power coursed through her veins, releasing her fear, unleashing a giddy feeling of lightness. The colors surrounding her were bright, blinding, yet her vision remained clear, refusing to allow any gray to shadow the truth.

She wanted to kill Glen. She would kill him.

Her breath whistled through her bared teeth. He stared up at her, at first blankly, then with a knowing smile. "You and me, Nora. Together. It doesn't have to be this way."

She shoved his weight off her. As she stood and stepped back, she held the gun awkwardly, but it was pointed right at him—that was all that counted.

Glen didn't stop smiling. "Go ahead. You can do it. Pull the trigger. It's the one way you and I will always be together. You'll never forget me. Every breath you take, every moment you're alive, I'll be with you forever."

Nora's index finger caressed the trigger.

"Nora, don't listen to him," Lydia said. "Step back toward me and give me the gun."

Lydia's voice was brittle, sharp-edged. Nora spared a glance in her direction and saw that Lydia looked afraid. Of her?

"Go, get help. I'll deal with him," Nora ordered Lydia.

Lydia glanced at her, ready to argue, then nodded solemnly and took a step back to the edge of the landing. But she didn't leave, instead stood silent, watching.

Now it was only Nora and Glen. Just as it had been two years ago. Except this time she was the one who held life and death in her hands.

"I love you, Nora," Glen crooned, as if he thought he could sway her with words. "Everything I did was because of that. It was all for you. If you had accepted me, looked at me, looked *at me*, we'd be together now and none of this would have happened. I did it all for you."

"For *me*?" Nora said, her voice breaking with nervous laughter.

He sat up, inching closer, grimacing when he moved his injured leg. "It's all your fault. I tried everything I knew. I loved you every way I knew how. I gave you everything." He paused, his hand sliding out along the floor as if he were too weak to support himself.

Nora knew better, saw that he was reaching for the knife lying on the step above him.

"It's not too late," he continued in that same hypnotic singsong. "We can still be together. Forever. Just the way it was always meant to be."

His gaze never left hers as his fingers curled around the knife's handle. "You and me, Nora. Isn't that what you want?"

Nora backed up a step. Her pulse drummed through her in a smooth rhythm as compelling as Glen's words.

All her lies had been laid bare for the world to see. And she no longer felt fear. She was in control here; she had the power. Not Glen, not her terror, not the past.

Glen lashed out with the knife, springing to one foot, aiming for her heart.

Nora pulled the trigger. Again and again and again until she couldn't pull it anymore. The sound was deafening as the bullets flew through the tiny space. Glen crumpled to a kneeling position, the knife still clenched in his hand.

Lydia pulled Nora away, then cautiously took the knife from Glen.

Nora didn't understand why there wasn't more blood. Surely at least one of the bullets had hit him. But the only blood came from his left arm.

"Is he dead?" she asked.

Lydia reached for his pulse.

Glen's eyes popped open as he launched himself at Lydia. She flew over the railing. Her body hit with an ugly thump on the steps below.

He turned on Nora, spit trailing from his mouth. Nora raised the useless gun, realized she had no other defense. "You bitch. Why couldn't you love me?"

His hands closed around her neck, pinning her against the wall. As she pummeled her fists against his chest, they hit something hard. A bulletproof vest.

Her vision constricted. Glen's face was the only thing she could see clearly as he towered over her. Then even that began to twist and blur as a haze of red overtook her and her body slumped.

Another blast sounded. This one close, so close that Nora thought she was the one shot. Warm blood sprayed against her face.

Glen's hands relaxed their grip. His body fell forward onto Nora, then toppled to the floor. A large hole gaped where his left eye used to be.

Lydia stood at the edge of the landing, her right arm dangling limply, her pistol still raised in the left, following Glen's body to the floor. Her chest was heaving, but her arm was steady.

Nora blinked, her vision clearing. A red puddle spread out from the back of Glen's head. Her heart thumped against her chest wall, galloping.

Footsteps pounded down the steps accompanying the calls of "Police, hands, hands, hands!"

Lydia dropped the gun to the floor, grabbing Nora's hand and holding her tight even as armed men swarmed the stairwell, surrounding them.

THIRTY-NINE

Saturday, 10:47 P.M.

IT WAS HOURS BEFORE THE POLICE LET NORA GO. She rushed to the surgical ICU, her thoughts focused only on Seth.

He wasn't there.

A frozen void consumed her. It took her a few moments before she had the courage to walk back to the clerk at the nurses' station. "Seth Cochran?"

Her fingernails dug into her palms as she waited for the clerk's reply.

"We needed the room—they brought in that cop, you know."

She did know. Jerry was at the far end of the unit, surrounded by family. But Seth—a thousand worst-case scenarios blossomed in her mind. He could have thrown a lethal blood clot, stroked out, maybe there was damage to his airway after all . . .

"Let's see. Here he is. Room six-oh-six."

"What?"

The clerk looked at her with exasperation. "I said, room six-oh-six."

Nora fled through the door and took the stairs up to the med-surg floor. They must have extubated him—which meant his airway was okay. And they wouldn't have let him leave the recovery room if he was hemodynamically unstable or showed any brain damage or other complications. . . . She pushed open the door to room six-oh-six. And stopped.

Seth lay sleeping, his IV dripping clear fluid into his arm, bandages peeking up above the left side of the soft cervical collar that protected his neck. But other than that, he looked . . . fine. His color was a little pale, but his face was peaceful. More than peaceful, he was beautiful.

She couldn't hold back her tears any longer. She crept across the floor and sank into the chair beside him, reaching for his hand. That wasn't close enough, so she lowered the bedrail and laid her arm alongside his.

Still not enough. She needed him in a way she'd never needed him before. Slipping her shoes off, she climbed into bed with him, the two of them barely fitting. Taking care not to jostle his monitor leads or injured side, she curled her body against his, fitting just right, sharing her warmth with him. As she nestled into his side, she reached down and intertwined her fingers with his.

At last, she could sleep.

GINA SAT AT JERRY'S BEDSIDE, IGNORING THE stares in her direction. People were saying that she'd saved him, that she shot him, that she killed the gunman . . . How wrong they were. She'd survived—because of him. That was all.

She hadn't been a hero, had barely even been thinking clearly. It was Jerry who had saved her. And she didn't like the anger she felt about that. She wanted to love him, to think of him as a hero, but instead there was only anger.

Anger at him for being a cop, for putting her in a position where she'd been forced to watch him suffer, for being shot, for lying there on the bed oblivious to everything going on with her, for not waking up, damn it!

For making her love him—but also resent him. She didn't want to feel this way, this constant buzz of fury and fear.

"Regina?" Her mother's voice startled her.

"What the hell are you doing here?" Gina snapped. So typical of her mother, barging into the ICU, totally ignoring the rules to do what she damn well pleased.

LaRose didn't censure her for her tone or language. Gina squinted at her—was she okay? Her mother kept a safe distance from Jerry and the medical paraphernalia, holding the skirt of her ballgown as she maneuvered to Gina's side of the bed. Then she laid her palm against Gina's cheek as if feeling for a fever. So not like LaRose.

"You're hurt." LaRose gestured to Gina's split lip. Good thing she couldn't see the other bruises.

"It's nothing." Gina turned her attention back to Jerry. She was too tired to spend energy deciphering LaRose's machinations.

"I'm sorry you didn't get your medal. They announced that they'll hold the ceremony sometime after New Year's. Hopefully Moses will get to see you accept it. It would make him so proud."

Her words finally penetrated. Gina raised her head. "Moses isn't even here? He didn't come?"

LaRose shrugged one shoulder. "Emergency with a client. He called to check on you when he heard."

"To see if I'd embarrassed him, no doubt." Gina didn't bother to disguise her scorn.

"No, baby. To see if you were okay. He was worried. So was I."

Gina stared at her, disbelieving. LaRose didn't meet her gaze, but instead concentrated on smoothing the wrinkles from her dress. A Dior, Gina recognized.

"Tell him I'm fine."

There was a long pause. "I will. I'd better go now."

LaRose stepped back as Janet Kwon entered the ICU and made a beeline for Jerry's bedside, scattering anyone in her way. "Take care, Regina."

"How's he doing?" Janet Kwon asked, ignoring LaRose as the other woman left.

"Stable." Gina hated that word.

"I wanted to ask you a few questions."

Gina looked up at that. She'd already talked with the cops ad nauseam—Janet wouldn't be investigating the case, not when her own partner was the victim.

"What?" She had no energy for pleasantries.

"The gunman. We found an old newspaper clipping in his pocket. You know anything about it?"

Lydia. Gina's anger blazed into fury. This was all Lydia's fault—and Gina had no idea what to do about it. Try to warn Lydia? Tell the cops? Say nothing and let whatever happened, happen?

"Ask Lydia Fiore."

Janet didn't look surprised. "I wondered. Jerry mentioned some cold case she was involved in. Guess it's not so cold after all."

Gina felt her fury settle into a low simmer that warmed her gut. "What did the surgeons tell Jerry's family?"

"A lot of muckety-muck. Not sure if they understood it all, but they didn't paint a pretty picture." Janet surprised Gina by taking Jerry's other hand in hers, stroking it with her thumb. "Why do I get the feeling they might have been optimistic?"

"The bullet didn't exit; it plowed over the top of his frontal cortex, came to rest on the opposite side. It's a miracle he's alive," Gina said, her voice flat. As if she were talking about someone else, anyone else besides Jerry. In a way she was. "Whatever happens, even if he lives, he might never be the Jerry Boyle you and I knew."

Janet's lips thinned, and she brushed her eyes with her hand. "Okay. Thanks for giving it to me straight, Gina." She kissed the back of Jerry's hand and tucked it under the sheets as if she were putting a child to bed. "Oh, one more thing. Diana DeFalco found this in his pocket."

She opened her fist, revealing a woman's diamond ring.

Gina blinked back tears blurring her vision. She turned away to focus on Jerry's face. Swollen with bruises and post-op fluid retention, he looked grotesque, nothing like her Jerry.

But he wasn't hers anymore, was he? She'd acted like a coward, she'd led him into danger, she didn't deserve him. "It's not mine."

"I thought maybe you'd like to hold on to it," Janet said in a quiet tone. She pressed the cold, hard diamond into Gina's palm, wrapping her fingers around it. "Jerry would want it that way."

As Janet walked away, Gina's tears were finally free to fall, splashing onto Jerry's cheek where they glittered in the harsh overhead exam light.

She sat there, head bowed, eyes closed, trying hard not to think, not to remember, not to feel. A man laid his hand on her shoulder. She didn't need to look to know it was Ken Rosen.

"Are you all right?" he asked, standing behind her.

No one had asked that. They asked about Jerry, asked about what happened, asked about the gunman.

Only Ken had wanted to know about her. She bit her lip, desperate to tell him the truth. Her shoulders quivered with the effort it took to hold herself together, but she refused to surrender.

She straightened, tucked in the sheet around Jerry, and folded her hands in her lap, still not looking back at Ken. Jerry's diamond was sharp against her sweaty palm. "Why'd you keep the bulletproof vest, Ken?"

He sucked in his breath, his fingers curling against her shoulder. Holding on tight. As if he needed her strength. Hah. Not Mr. Zen Master.

"That day back in July," he finally said. "I didn't save those kids because I was any kind of hero. Just the opposite. Those guys started shooting and there I was and all I could think was it was my chance to—" He faltered, his fingers slipping from her shoulder. Gina reached back, anchoring his hand beneath her own. "I thought I'd be with my family. At last." He cleared his throat. "Silly, since I don't believe in heaven or anything. But I was . . . ready."

His words hung in the air until the beeping of Jerry's heart rate on the monitor scattered them. Gina sneaked in a breath, afraid to say anything. Behind her, Ken shifted his weight.

"Anyway, that's when you showed up. Saved me."

She shook her head, glad he couldn't see her face. "Wasn't me. It was Jerry—he gave me the vest. Without it, we'd both be dead."

He spun her in the chair so that she faced him, her back to Jerry. He took her hand in both of his and crouched down until they were eye to eye. "Don't you believe that, Gina. Jerry wasn't out there on that street. You were. You were the real hero. You *are* a real hero. Even if you don't want to believe it." He squeezed her fingers so tightly they hurt. "Don't you ever forget that. I won't. You saved my life."

The icy numbness that had encased Gina was slow to crack. Something splintered inside her as his words chiseled into her awareness. Then he surprised her by kissing her forehead, his lips warm against her chilled skin. "Thank you." He walked away.

Gina wanted to say something, wanted to race after him, wanted desperately to believe his words.

But she needed time.

She sat there, watching him leave, her eyes glazed over. He looked back at her once, before the ICU doors closed behind him. A wistful glance that told her everything she needed to know. She let her breath out and curled her fingers around Jerry's ring.

"Everything's going to be all right," she whispered. Jerry's heartbeat beeped steady. She took that as a sign. "I'll make it right. For everyone. I promise."

"NICE JOB," LUCAS TOLD AMANDA WHEN SHE FI-nally turned away from Zachary's bedside. The little boy had surprised them all. His lungs were working, keeping him alive. "You have a talent for this. Have you thought of critical care medicine?"

This discussion wasn't about her choice of specialty, and they both knew it. Amanda motioned him into the break room. He followed her, standing motionless at the door, while she paced the room, finally coming to rest at the window over-looking the snow-covered cemetery. Even the vandalized angel where Karen had been found looked peaceful in the snow.

"I owe you an apology," she started. "I'm sorry. It all just kind of—"

He shook his head at her sternly. "No. That's not the prob-lem. It's not about your overeager need to solve the problems of the world. It's about the fact that if I were any other at-tending in this medical center, hell, in the state, you'd be on your way to being dismissed from medical school right now. It's about your gambling with your career and using me to do it."

His anger propelled her back against the window despite the fact that he hadn't raised his voice or taken a step in her direction. It didn't help matters knowing that he was right.

"I was wrong not to talk to you," she admitted. "I should have called you as soon as I confirmed the teratoma."

"Yes, a phone call before my patient was whisked away to surgery would have been most appreciated." He scowled, crossing his arms over his chest, still not moving toward her.

"You could have trusted me," she protested, her own an-ger beginning to flare.

His eyes grew wide with surprise, and he dropped his arms to his side. "I do trust you. I would believe you if you told me the sky was polka-dot," he said. "But don't ask me to change the way I treat patients, not based on a gut feeling. I need facts. I can't risk their lives on anything less."

"But I had facts—"

"One case study is not a fact. It's one person out of six billion."

"Two. Now it's two. Plus those reports Dr. Koenig has."

"Unpublished reports don't count." He waved Dr. Koenig's cases aside. "I can't practice medicine with my gut instincts, not like Lydia. And you're still learning; you should learn how to interpret things like case studies, how to be a little cynical about what you read, research methodology, conclusions—"

The door burst open and Tank rushed in. He'd somehow conned his mother into agreeing to let him stay at Narolie's bedside.

"She's awake!" he shouted. "She said my name, she's talking and everything!"

He slammed the door again, dancing a little jig as he rushed back to Narolie's room across the hall. Amanda felt her heart rise with joy.

"See?" she said to Lucas, joining him at the door and taking his hand. "There are two cases. You just needed to have a little faith."

"Faith? Faith had nothing to do—" His words stalled as he got a faraway look on his face. "There *are* two, aren't there?"

"Lucas?"

"There are two! You still need to do a research project for your senior thesis, right?"

"I was going to do a chart review—"

"No. You're going to learn how to do real science. Not some piddly chart review where the computer does all the work for you. You're going to learn how to think." He held her around the waist as if they were waltzing. "How to think like a real scientist. So next time you won't need to trust in faith to save your patients."

"You want me to document the antibodies that caused Narolie's symptoms? But how? Would we need her brain tissue?"

"Think it through." He stood at arm's length, his hands on her hips, head cocked as he watched her.

"Wait. We have her blood. Before and after the tumor was removed. And"—her face lit up—"we have the tumor. We can tag the white blood cells, bathe the tumor in them, do an immunofluorescence stain—"

"Right, and we can do follow up titres a month or two out."

"Lucas, it's perfect. We can even get it published, I bet!"

"I'm sure of it." His smile lit his face. "Only one problem."

"What's that?" Amanda asked, her mind still spinning through the science.

"I won't have time to plan a wedding if I'm working on a new research project with you."

She laughed. "Actually, I think that would be the best gift you could ever give your future mother-in-law. She'll love taking it on."

Amanda stopped. Through the glass walls of Narolie's room she saw Narolie sitting up, beaming as she gestured animatedly to Tank. "Look at those two. It's so beautiful. You know what? We need to run a quick errand before we go in." She tugged at his hand, leading him toward the PICU doors.

"Wait, where are we going?"

"Outside, where it's snowing, Lucas. Snow! We're going to get Narolie a wheelchair and take her out to see it. You and Tank can show her how to make a snow angel."

His laughter echoed through the hallway, startling a nurse's aide walking from the elevator. He pulled Amanda tight to him. "You're the only angel I need."

LYDIA LAY ON HER BACK, HER FINGERS TRAPPED in small cages that held them suspended as the ortho resident added more weight to the stack hanging from her right arm. He'd been trying for almost an hour to realign the bones in her forearm. A broken ulna and radius and an assortment of bruises were her only injuries from Glen Bakker's attack.

She still had to deal with the nonphysical fallout. Starting with the police questioning her endlessly, and now Trey, who had rushed over but had been kept waiting until the police were done.

Wincing as the weight settled into place, she turned to face Trey. It seemed like their conversation kept spinning in the same circles: that she somehow should have abandoned Nora to Glen, how she should have called Trey—as if that would have done any good with him across town at his parents' house—and that she needed to stay in the hospital overnight to be on the safe side.

Wrong on all counts.

"She needs more fentanyl," Trey protested when she gritted her teeth and her heart rate spiked on the monitor above her.

"No, I don't." She wanted to keep a clear head. The cops had told her about Jerry—what little they knew, at any rate. "Did you reach Janet Kwon yet?"

"She said she'd be down as soon as she checked on Jerry."

"How's he doing?"

"Bad. They evacuated an epidural hematoma but there's swelling already and no one knows—"

She squeezed her eyes shut at his words. "He'll be okay." He had to. She had to hang on to that. "And Seth?"

"Did fine, no airway damage, so they actually extubated

him in recovery. I don't think they even sent him to the SICU—at least he wasn't there when I called up."

"Good."

The resident finished smoothing the fiberglass cast. "Okay, I think I got it. Let me get an X ray and we'll see. If not—"

"I don't want to go to the OR," Lydia muttered.

"You want to use that wrist again, don't you?" Trey said, sounding a lot like his mother.

She rolled her eyes as the X ray tech wheeled the machine in. The tech laid a lead apron on top of Lydia. "You'll have to step out, sir." Trey obeyed, and Lydia had peace and quiet for a few minutes until Trey and the resident returned, waving the X ray in triumph.

"Perfect alignment," the resident boasted. "Let that dry and you'll be good to go." He waved a hand and left once more.

Before Trey could settle into the chair beside her, Janet Kwon appeared in the doorway, her usual frown lines deepened into furrows.

"Trey, why don't you go home?" Lydia asked.

"But—"

"I mean it, Trey. I'll meet you at home."

He narrowed his eyes, debating. After a long moment he gave her a grudging nod and left.

Janet slid into his place beside Lydia. "He's not a happy camper."

"Not many are tonight. You saw Jerry?"

"Just came from there." Janet's voice cracked the smallest bit. Something she would surely deny. "He's stable."

Neurosurgeon talk for still having vital signs, but nothing else was certain. Jerry might not make it through the night. And even if he did . . .

"We got a hit on the shooter's prints with Live Scan. The guy's a hired thug, got two strikes against him already in California," Janet continued, her voice now holding an edge. "Gina tells me you might know why he decided to visit sunny

Pittsburgh. Said the gunman had an old picture of you and your mother."

Lydia startled so violently that she rocked her cast and the newly positioned bones inside it. Pain screamed along her arm, up her neck, clamping her jaws together with a snap.

"Help me up," she gasped. Her stomach was churning, if she was going to vomit, she didn't want to be lying down. Janet took her good arm and supported her as Lydia swung her legs around and sat up. Her vision went black for a moment, but after she heaved in a few breaths, it cleared.

"I know you had Jerry working a cold case," Janet continued, her fingers still gripping Lydia's arm. "You need to tell me everything."

"I don't know much." Quickly she explained to Janet about her mother's murder by an unknown man wearing a law enforcement uniform eighteen years ago. "Jerry asked a friend of his in LAPD to see what, if anything, they had on the case."

"A friend? You mean Mitchell Epson?"

"Yeah, how'd you know?"

Janet's face clouded, and Lydia knew there was more bad news coming. "He was found dead in his home. Murdered. He'd been there a few days—probably happened three, four days ago. LAPD has no leads. But according to Gina, it was Epson who gave the killer Jerry's name, sent him here to Pittsburgh."

Lydia recoiled as if she'd been sucker-punched. "Why? There wasn't anything new on Maria's case."

"It gets worse. From what Gina said, sounds like the man who shot Jerry found another Jerry Boyle—an Officer Jeremiah Boyle from Zone Two—and tortured and killed him yesterday."

Acid clawed its way up Lydia's throat, and she had to swallow hard to control her nausea. Jerry had been shot because of her—Gina almost killed as well. And two more police officers dead. All because she'd told Jerry her secret, told him the truth about Maria's murder.

"I never asked Jerry to look into Maria's murder. I told him to leave it alone. It was so long ago—" She looked up at Janet, frowning in confusion. "I don't understand. Why is this all happening? Now, eighteen years later?"

"You tell me. What the hell is so important about your mother's murder that two cops were killed and my partner—my friend—is lying upstairs in a coma?"

"Believe me, Janet, I wish I knew."

Before Janet could ask more questions that Lydia had no answers to, a nurse bustled in, carrying a sling and a sheaf of discharge instructions. "Let's get you out of here, Dr. Fiore," she said. "It's been a long night for you."

"We'll talk more tomorrow," Janet promised. "You think of anything, you call me."

"I will."

Janet started out the door, then stopped. "And Lydia, be careful. Jerry will kill me if anything happens to you."

After fleeing the ER and avoiding the press gathered around the hospital, Lydia walked the familiar route past the cemetery, her fingers gripping her keys so tight they bit into her flesh. The police had taken her gun, of course.

She paused at the locked cemetery gates, hauling herself up one-handed to see past them. The movement jarred her broken arm, the pain knocked her teeth together, but in a way it was welcome. Gave her an edge.

The weeping angel was draped in snow, most of the graffiti now hidden, with only a few remnants of crime-scene tape visible to memorialize the horror that had occurred at her feet. In the dim light, with her curling hair chiseled around her shoulders, she looked a little like Maria. The same distant, sad expression Maria used to get. As if she could see the future but was powerless to stop the pain that was coming.

Lydia's good arm shook with exertion. She reluctantly stepped back down to the pavement. Her entire body was trembling as she turned her back on the angel.

Despite the blowing snow she kept her hood down, the

better to see at the extremes of her peripheral vision. After years of running from a faceless, nameless danger—after all that time—the danger had found her. It was out there somewhere in the night, stalking her.

Taking aim at anyone near her.

She stopped at the end of her drive, listening intently. The tall hemlocks blocked all light except the faint pinpoint of her porch light.

She pulled out her keys, fingering them with her left hand until she found her car key. She could leave. Now.

There was nothing at the house she needed except Trey and the cat. They could take care of each other—better than she could.

Wind sighed through the trees, cascading snow all around her as if she were caught in a snow globe. She stood there long enough for her toes to grow numb, her fingers white with cold as they gripped the flimsy piece of steel.

She could run. She should run. But for the first time, she didn't *want* to run.

Arching her neck, she glanced over her shoulder at the street behind her. Then she took a step. In the opposite direction. Toward home.

She wouldn't run. Not this time.

As she approached her house, Trey and Ginger Cat appeared in the front doorway. Both looked worried: Trey by the way he held himself back, giving her the space she needed. And Ginger Cat by the way he rushed past her, darting over the threshold, searching for danger, then slipping back inside before she could close the door.

"You okay?" Trey asked, taking her coat from her, taking care not to jostle her sling or cast. "You're freezing. I was getting worried."

"I'm fine." Damn, wasn't that what Nora had kept saying? She squared her shoulders, her decision made, no regrets.

Before he could say anything more, she rubbed her palm against his cheek, circling to the back of his neck and pulling him down for a kiss. His lips were warm, as were his arms as he wrapped them around her, ever so gently. Even after the kiss was over, he held her there, his chin resting on her hair, her face pressed against his chest.

"Thought you might like your Christmas present early," he said when they finally parted. "Close your eyes."

Too tired to argue, she complied. He took her hand and led her through the archway into the dining room. "Okay, open them."

She gasped. In the corner where her surfboard used to stand was a large Douglas fir, complete with lights and sparkling ornaments.

"Surprise!" Trey's parents, Ruby and Denny, stepped out of the shadows. "I'm sorry the kids had to leave, it was past their bedtime," Ruby said.

"But we old folks could wait up for you," Denny added, brushing Lydia's cheek with a kiss. "So what do you think of your present?"

Lydia turned away from the tree that had captured her attention and saw that the rest of the wide-open space had been filled by a large Shaker-style cherry dining table and chairs. On the top was a large platter of homemade cookies.

"This is why I was so edgy about you coming home unexpectedly today. Dad and I have been working on it for a month," Trey said proudly, skimming a hand over the table's polished surface.

"And don't worry about the tree," Ruby said. "Denny found a place that sells them live. After New Year's you can plant it, let it put down roots."

Her words sent a chill through Lydia. She shoved her hand into her jeans pocket, clutching her car keys again. The urge to run was so overwhelming, she felt breathless.

She pulled her hand free, leaving the keys behind. "It's beautiful," she told Trey, reaching for his hand and holding on tight. "It's all so beautiful. Thank you. I don't know what to say."

"You don't have to say anything," Denny told her. "No need for thanks. This is just what families do."

NORA JOLTED AWAKE WITH A START. BRIGHT sunlight streamed in through the window. She sat up and saw that Seth was already awake, staring at her.

"Morning," he said, his voice raspy but strong.

"Are you—" She faltered, remembering how they'd argued before he was attacked. The last words she'd spoken to him. "You're all right?"

"A little sore." He patted the cervical collar that supported his neck.

Nora gently slid from the bed, taking care not to jostle him. She raised the head up for him. He'd kicked the sheets aside in his sleep, and she couldn't help her smile at the sight of Seth's hairy, muscular legs barely covered by the patient gown and the thigh-high surgical stockings. Pulling the sheets up to cover him, she busied herself by tucking them in around him.

"I'm sorry," she stammered, wondering why he wasn't furious at her, why he was treating her like everything was, well, normal. She'd almost gotten him killed.

"Is he—" His face clouded.

"Dead." She paused, not sure how much to tell him. He'd hear it sooner or later. "So is Tommy Z."

"Are you okay?" Seth grabbed her hand, stilling her movements, scrutinizing her.

"I'm fine." For the first time in two years, she really, truly meant it.

He didn't let go of her hand as he stretched his other one toward the bedside stand and a tray full of materials for dressing changes.

She grabbed the tray with its tape, bandages, scissors, and set it on his lap. "What do you need?"

He just smiled. Not his usual wide-eyed grin. This smile

was tentative, as if he were trying something he'd never dared to try before. "A second chance. Close your eyes."

She frowned at him. "Seth—"

"Just do it."

She closed her eyes. A strange flutter took control of her heart. Not fear, not panic . . . anticipation.

He raised her left hand and she felt something slide down her ring finger. He kissed her hand.

Nora's eyes popped open. He kept hold of her hand—a ring made of surgical tape sat on her finger.

The muscles around his mouth and jaw tightened as he worked to draw in a deep breath. "Nora, I love you. I want to marry you, have babies with you, share my life with you. I'm a selfish, inconsiderate, sometimes downright-stupid bastard. I'll work long hours, forget birthdays and anniversaries, leave the toilet seat up, but if you'll have me, I'm all yours."

His voice broke at the end of the speech—and it had nothing to do with his injuries. He watched her, waiting.

She admired her makeshift ring. Better than any diamond. "What girl could resist a proposal like that?"

He started to smile, a real smile this time, then it faded. "Is that a yes?"

"Yes, yes, yes." Just in case he still didn't get it, she cradled his face in her hands and kissed him.

Not a perfect, Hollywood, fairy-tale kiss—far from it. A sloppy, nose-bumping, hard-to-avoid-his-left-side, clumsy, eager, excited, real-world kiss. An honest kiss that acknowledged past pain, future clashes, and present complications.

A kiss that said she knew him, he knew her.

A kiss that promised they belonged together.

NOTE TO READERS

Thank you for joining me for Nora's story. I understand that her experiences may not be the usual subject matter for entertainment, but I needed to share her story in the most honest way possible. I've cared for too many assault victims to do otherwise while still honoring the trauma they survived.

Although Urgent Care *is fiction, most of the facts surrounding Nora's story are true: according to the U.S. Department of Justice, more than 60 percent of sexual assaults go unreported. Every two minutes someone in the U.S. becomes the victim of a sexual assault.*

If you or someone you know has been the victim of a sexual assault, there are people who can help. Call 1.800.656.HOPE or go to www.RAINN.org for more information.

On a lighter note, if you'd like to learn more about how Gina and Jerry met, I've written a short story titled "Toxicity," which will be available as a free download. See my website, www.cjlyons.net, for more details.

As always, there is a whole team behind the scenes helping me share the stories of the women of Angels of Mercy's ER. I'd like to thank my agent, Anne Hawkins; the team at Berkley/Jove, including my editor, Shannon Jamieson Vazquez; and my ever-patient critique partners: Toni McGee Causey, Kim Howe, Margie Lawson, Caro-

line Males, and Lois Winston. Plus, a special shout-out to Joe Hartlaub for the Swahili translation.

I'd also like to thank all of you, my readers. Without you, these stories would never see the light of day. Thanks so very much for helping to spread the word about my books, for your wonderful fan letters (keep them coming!), for comments on my website, for the fun face-to-face meetings at book signings, and for your continued support. Feel free to send any comments to me at cj@cjlyons.net and visit my website, www.cjlyons.net, for sneak peeks and insider information on upcoming books.

Thanks for reading!
CJ

Penguin Group (USA) Inc.
is proud to present

GREAT READS—GUARANTEED

We are so confident you will love
this book that we are offering a
100% money-back guarantee!

If you are not 100% satisfied with
this publication, Penguin Group (USA) Inc.
will refund your money!
Simply return the book before
January 3, 2010 for a full refund.

M504G0609